Touchy Talents

Day S. Grant

Untangling Words Press

Print ISBN: 978-1-966242-01-7

eISBN: 978-1-966242-00-0

Editor: Kelly Helmick of Dog Star Creative Co

Contents

a maven is an expert in their field

Chapter 1

Rick

2065

45 years post-Crisis

Suspicion sank into Rick's gut as his mother hummed a happy tune at the kitchen window, framed by the early morning light. It was as if she was trying to embody the image of a 1950's housewife. It wasn't that her jeans, shirt, or slippers in their gleaming state-of-the-art metal kitchen fit the image, but her attitude at the moment sure did. His visits home didn't normally inspire such unadulterated contentment. Sure, she was happy when he came home, but not so happy she was humming. With difficulty, he swallowed his first bite of the welcome-home pancakes she had cheerily plunked down on the table the minute he stepped into the room.

A familiar rumble sounded outside, and he knew what she was seeing — Melissa Juniper leaving on her brother's old motorcycle. Rick knew every inch of that bike. He and Bobby had built it together in high school fifteen years ago. The first eleven years after high school had flown by so fast — laughter, grenades, missions, jokes —

then, nothing. Bobby disappeared. At this point, everyone assumed he was dead. Not even their boss Jade Triggs, with all her secret connections, had any indication otherwise — no news, no body, no hope. Rick still wasn't sure Bobby was dead, but he'd stopped voicing his doubts three years ago, much to his team's utter relief.

It wasn't the bike though that made his mother happy. In fact, she hated bikes; she called them "the epitome of a hurtling death trap" on the regular. But she adored Melissa. Always had. Every time Rick came home for a visit, his mother pushed him to ask Melissa out — his best friend's little sister and, literally, the girl next door. She'd doubled her efforts ever since Melissa had started house sitting for her parents. Twice, his mother had gone so far as to tell him she'd rather he knew every inch of Melissa instead of their bikes.

"Rick, darling," his mother's voice sung out with false sweetness, "it seems I forgot to buy coffee. You'll have to go out to get some."

He rolled his eyes. *If*, and that was a big *IF*, his mother didn't have coffee in the house, it wasn't on accident. Most likely, she had tucked it away just to make him go down to Melissa's coffee shop the first morning of his week-long visit. He should have guessed at her plan when he hadn't smelled any coffee brewing when he came into the kitchen.

"I can go a day or two without coffee," he said. "No need to get everyone riled up." People in town got excited when they saw him. They didn't even have to know him to find him intriguing. The tall, scary guy that blazed around on a motorcycle and glared at anyone who dared to speak to him — apparently that never went out of vogue — not with the ladies, not with the guys. It didn't matter how large Granberg had gotten since the Crisis, the city retained a small college town feel.

"I'm sure everyone who matters already knows you're in town." His mom glanced over her shoulder and batted her eyes at him with faux-innocence behind her cat-eye glasses. "Plenty of people have driven by the house on their way to work."

"You didn't actually post a sign out front saying I'm here, did you?" His alarm was genuine. She'd threatened him with that the last time he'd visited for more than a day and hadn't told anyone he was around — especially not Melissa. He had to keep his distance from her no matter how much he liked being around her.

"Of course not." She gave an offended sniff at the mere thought. "But your bike does just as good of a job."

His eyes widened.

"It's much more effective than a sign would have been. People don't always read signs."

She was devious, his mother.

"And how, *exactly*," he growled, "did my bike get out of the garage?" His growl made grown men cower in fear when he was at work, but it only brought a silent, knowing smile to his mother's face.

Rick rubbed his forehead. She must have gotten up before dawn to roll it out. He almost wished he'd seen her do it. She gave his bike a wide berth and the evil eye like it was poison waiting to claim his life every time he straddled it. Now, though, she'd used it against him. She'd somehow figured out how to get his six hundred plus pound bike into neutral and hold it steady while rolling it out of the garage. Rick groaned.

"Finish eating and get yourself ready to head out," his mom ordered. Several minutes later, he let her "haul" him out of his chair and push him toward the bathroom as if he were twelve rather than thirty-two. His long sleeves protected him from making skin contact, but he knew she wasn't worried about him dragging the truth out of her now; she'd completed the day's manipulation. She probably didn't have any further plans in the works — at least for the moment.

Rick did as ordered: he brushed his teeth, and put on his boots, gloves, jacket, and helmet. In all likelihood, Melissa would have his favorite coffee blend hot and waiting when he walked into her shop since she'd have seen his bike outside. She always had his favorite coffee queued up when she knew he was home, unless she'd found something he'd like even better that she *needed* him to try. Climbing onto his bike — which his mother had parked practically on the sidewalk in order to garner even more attention — Rick glanced back at the front window of the kitchen where she was standing, smiling brightly and waving him off like it was the first day of school. He shook his head and eased onto the street. He'd do anything for his mother — anything except ask Melissa out.

Suburbia whipped by in a blur of older, classic homes and sporadic modern ones. A few of the houses were even more inventive than anyone would have thought forty-five years ago. Rick slowed down when he passed Professor Torres's home. It was his favorite and one of the eccentricities that made the older professor so popular at the local university. The entire bottom half was an aquarium — glass walls and filled to the brim with water, fish, and plant life.

Professor Torres often had students come to his home and sit on the stones that made up his front yard. Then, he'd hook himself to a water-proof microphone and jump in to give his lectures. In his hybrid form, he didn't even need an air tank. Depending on the day, Rick had seen him pushing kelp aside while waving his students to the glass to peer deeper into the watery habitat or leading a school of fish around in a merry chase so students could see them in movement as he talked.

This early, all Rick saw was Torres' silver dorsal fin as he swam past a window. Rick would stop by another day and say hi; he'd gotten to know Professor Torres a lot better since the man's nephew Carl had joined the Mavens and been placed on Rick's team, Team Gamma, six years ago.

Rick saw more people out and about as he left his childhood neighborhood behind. A number of people were walking their pet dogs — a few were in human form, but he saw three dog hybrids, two cat hybrids, a monkey hybrid, and a chameleon hybrid with their pets as he got into the denser section of town with apartments on top of store fronts.

The last three decades had seen an explosion of hybrid-centric shops and services that made Granberg even more welcoming to hybrids, particularly the rarer ones. Groomers for shedding season were common enough in other cities, but Granberg took making people feel welcome to a whole new level. There weren't a lot of cities that had scale shiners and gill specialists in Rick's experience.

As soon as the Crisis hit, Granberg had a different feel than other cities. For some reason, Granberg University's animal science department, the local aquarium staff, and the zoo employees had been particularly dedicated to their jobs, and every person at those institutions, except the occasional surviving full-human, had been saved, not by a pet at home, but by one of their charges at work. While being saved by zoo and aquarium charges was not unheard of, the resulting percentage of exotic hybrids in Granberg far exceeded the norm. The city instantly became a hotspot for anyone who was hoping to find their place.

When Granberg hit the news with a huge range of hybrids (including aquatic-hybrids), a significant number of atypical hybrids — ostracized in their own communities — made permanent pilgrimages to the city or came to study without major plans to move on. That was why the city kept expanding with no indication of stopping. To an outsider, the hybrid population felt even higher than normal because no one in Granberg was pressured to stay in their human forms like in other cities Rick had been to. From the outset, everyone in Granberg was encouraged to be in whatever form made *them* most comfortable. Rick had envied the hybrids growing up — there had definitely been times he would have liked to have a second skin. The one he had was problematic, to say the least.

As he got closer to Melissa's coffee shop, Rick couldn't help but marvel at the changes that had taken place in the last few years. A talon and claw salon now stood where a drunkard's liquor store had been. The dark and dirty alleys between buildings now had colorful, artistic murals that invited people in to peruse as if they were art galleries. The trash that had once littered the walkways and the edges of the buildings was nowhere to be seen, and every tree had its own little fence around it. The chipped and faded paint that used to be omnipresent had been replaced with clean colors. There wasn't even a single broken window in sight. It was hard to believe it used to be so run down.

Rick parked his bike a block from Melissa's coffee shop, knowing it would be nearly impossible to find a spot any closer. As he turned the engine off, he could hear laughter and the rustle of leaves above. A man in a yellow polo shirt and a parakeet hybrid with stylish sunglasses eyed him as they walked past. The parakeet was a few inches shorter than the man and his arms were covered in short feathers that wouldn't support flight. When Rick took off his helmet, the two leaned their heads together and started whispering urgently. They weren't even bothering to hide their stares. Rick didn't appreciate the attention. He'd much rather have no one notice him since *that* would stop people from approaching him rather than him having to be menacing to make people keep their distance. Rick glared at them, which caused them to promptly flit away. Rick thought the man's movements were more fluid-like than feather-like; he probably wasn't a bird hybrid like his friend.

A group of boys who should have been in school were gaping at his bike as he hopped off it. One of them had pulled out his phone and was typing away. Rick rolled his eyes; the kid wouldn't find anything about the bike's make and model online. It was custom and had so many top-secret military modifications that it was nearly impossible to identify the base model components at this point. The base had been inspired by the first Harley Pan-Ams from before the Crisis, but Rick and Bobby had changed so much even before the Maven's engineer got his hands on it at Jade's request. His bike was a mixture of matte and shiny blacks that camouflaged it in the dark and was fully equipped for missions.

As Rick walked down the sidewalk toward the coffee shop, a lithe calico cat hybrid gave him a once-over. She purred so loudly that he had no doubt it was an invitation. When he didn't turn his head to look at her, her whiskers drooped and her tail flicked in agitation, making her mini-skirt swish in his periphery.

Just as he reached Melissa's coffee shop, three college girls burst out of the front door, laughing. Rick could easily imagine the scene they would make in a college brochure. Beams of sun sliding through the trees lining the street to bathe them in speckled light. Their heads thrown back. A cow hybrid lounging in a coffee shop chair with a lizard hybrid and a human (or a hybrid in human form) at the table behind them. One of them had brought their pet cat, and it sprawled on a chair wearing a harness and leash. The whimsical violet script that read Juniper's Java above their heads, playful and inviting.

Rick's frown deepened. It was too picturesque. The city should be dumping money in Melissa's bank account. Not that they knew the slummiest part of town had become the safest and most popular area because of her. Still, it irked him. The college girls split apart with gasps as he stepped through their little group — one of them shifted in surprise and revealed herself to be a rare orca hybrid. Rick ignored her shift and yanked open the door like it had personally wronged him.

As he stepped inside, he found himself wrapped in a cocoon of coffee and chocolate. Straight ahead, behind the cash register, Melissa stood, her laughter overpowering the tinkle of the shop door. The black leather jacket she wore when riding Bobby's bike hung on the pale-yellow wall behind her. Her hazel eyes were glued to his glower. To her right, Rick vaguely registered that Melissa's childhood best friend Kate — human for the moment with a pixie cut that resembled her hybrid cat ears — and her middle school or high school friend Danny — a blond-haired russet lizard hybrid in a blue sweater to keep her blood warmer — were frozen behind the counter, their eyes flicking between him and Melissa. All three had seen the leaving college girls scatter, but only Melissa saw nothing in him to fear.

"Looks like you'll need a large cup," Melissa said with a grin that squeezed his heart. She was everything he'd ever wanted.

Rick jerked his head once, already regretting being here. The way she smiled at him gave him flashbacks to growing up next door. She would run up saying she wanted to come with them, even when she didn't know what they were up to. Bobby had always denied her request, but then Melissa would grab Rick's arm and make the same plea — he understood *all* she wanted was to spend time with them. She had no other agenda. Rick rarely came across anyone that genuine. She never changed what she said like most people did after having touched him. She made him want to be a better person, so he'd tell her she could come with them despite Bobby's half-hearted grumbling. Rick hadn't understood what *her* touch did at the time. Now that he did, he kept his distance. He didn't need to be her hero.

Settling in at a table in the back left corner away from the front window and tugging his gloves off, Rick tried to be unobtrusive in the bubbly space while continuing to scowl at anyone who looked at him too long. It only took a minute or two for Melissa to fill a large cup with his favorite blend. He heard her boots click on the tiled floor as she came to his table and slid in across from him. He waited until she'd pulled her hands away before reaching for the steaming cup and letting the warmth seep into his fingers.

"When did you get into town?"

He took a sip of the smoky and nutty coffee she'd exposed him to two years ago. While the flavors of his first sip coated his tongue, he took in the sight of her. The casual tie-up tank she was wearing matched her lipstick perfectly, and soft brown hair escaped her ponytail. He'd stare at her all day if it wouldn't be weird.

"Last night."

"And I assume you didn't park your bike on the sidewalk?" she teased.

He sighed. "It was taken out of the garage while I was sleeping."

Melissa's burst of laughter drew curious attention to their corner. Rick glared at the voyeurs, but Melissa didn't seem to notice his dark demeanor. "Jessy did not!" she said in delighted disbelief. "I didn't think she knew the first thing about motorcycles."

"I know. I can't even be mad about it."

Her ponytail swished behind her as she shook her head. A few more soft strands broke free to hang around her face. Rick's hands tightened around his coffee. He waited a breath to see if she'd push the strands back, but she didn't.

"I know Kate has been working here awhile," Rick said, glancing at Melissa's friends behind the counter.

"Until her jewelry business takes off," Melissa reminded him.

He nodded since she'd been saying that for the last two years and continued, "but I thought I saw Danny bartending at Badminton Boxies in Placerton not far from my place."

Melissa's eyes grew stormy and distaste crossed her face. The combination grabbed all of Rick's attention. He didn't even bother to keep scanning for unwelcome interest as he pinned his eyes to Melissa.

"The hybridist pig that runs it took issue with her being a lizard most days."

"But she's most comfortable like that," Rick stated the obvious.

"Despite hiring her, knowing she's a lizard hybrid, he decided scales weren't in line with the feel of Boxies."

"Did she file a complaint? If anything, she's more alert to guests' needs as a lizard. Everyone knows lizard hybrids are extremely aware of their surroundings."

"Which he should have seen as a huge bonus. But no, she didn't have any hard evidence. She's crashing at her parents' place while she searches for a better gig. I need a new hire, so she's filling in until either I find a long-term barista or she finds a job that doesn't require a smile in the morning."

Rick nodded. Reptiles and amphibians had a hard time proving cases of discrimination, and there weren't laws in place yet to help them. Really, any hybrid that wasn't seen as "cuddly or beautiful" by the general public didn't have it easy. And those who were extra cuddly or beautiful had different harassment issues — unwelcome petting was a common complaint, as was increased sexism for some women who needed "protecting" in their hybrid form. A few coalitions were hoping to pass updated laws before the fiftieth anniversary of the Crisis, but if they succeeded in the next five years, Rick would be more than impressed.

"I have to get back behind the counter," Melissa said. Rick realized he'd been silent for too long, and like always, she didn't want to impose and overstay her welcome. He just nodded and watched her get back to work. He'd subsisted for years on small moments like this one. It was all he had.

Rick tried not to stare at her while she worked, but it was hard to look away. Melissa smiled all the time. She hugged each of her two friends twice. Her hands brushed almost every person that came in as she gave them their change or passed them their insect infused coffees, fruit sangria teas, prey-syruped hot chocolates, and whatever else they ordered. That much touching made his gut twist. He did everything he could to make his coffee last so he'd have an excuse to stay longer and watch Melissa, but when it was finally empty, he needed to leave. If he stayed longer, her friends behind the counter would start getting more ideas than their smirks said they already had. He didn't want them to push Melissa into more than just having his favorite coffee waiting for him.

As Rick stood to leave, movement at the door caught his eye and caused him to freeze. A man in a leather jacket had come in without taking off his dark shades. The man paused at the door, and his lip curled back in a snarl. His weathered jacket had a clawed rip in the upper arm. It could have been torn in a fight since the tear was where you'd grab someone when grappling. The man's gait did not reassure Rick in the least — he didn't make a sound on the tiles. He was stalking. Eyes glued behind the counter, the man went straight by the line and to the register. Then he grabbed Kate's wrist.

Kate's eyes turned to slits and her fur instantly poofed out, turning her into a five-foot-something fluffy gray cat in a purple summer dress. Her fangs were out in a terrified hiss as she tried to pull her fur-slick wrist free. The man was saying something to her, but Rick couldn't hear him. At Kate's pained yowl, Rick moved toward them, his chair banging against the wall as he forced it out of the way, but he was too slow.

Melissa was already there.

She placed a hand over the man's. Rick saw the man's brow furrow in confusion behind his sunglasses as his head bounced between the two women. He let go of Kate's wrist like he had been electrocuted by Melissa's touch. His shoulders crowded his ears in a sheepish or mildly apologetic gesture. He mumbled something before shoving his hands into his pockets and turning to leave without another word. Everyone in-between him and the door parted to let him through.

Rick leaned back cautiously to survey the room, feeling like time had slowed down. He didn't want anyone to pick up on why the man had turned tail so quickly, least of all Melissa herself.

Chapter 2

Melissa

M elissa only caught the scowling man in sunglasses' "Tell me" and Kate's frightened "I don't know," but that was more than enough for her. Setting down the half-made mushroom espresso she was preparing, she reached out and placed her hand over the scowling man's. It had been a long time since such an aggressive individual had made its way into her coffee shop; back when she'd first opened, angry people like him had been a weekly occurrence. But, like always, this would turn out to be a misunderstanding and nothing more.

When she touched his hand, he looked at her and his brow furrowed for a second before his eyebrows rose up over the edges of his sunglasses in surprise. He glanced back at Kate and at his grasp on her wrist. He gave himself a little shake that Melissa felt as he snatched his hand away from them. Melissa barely heard his mumbled "Sorry" before he turned and hurried out the door. Which was just what she expected to happen.

Melissa had no doubt she'd see him again in a week or three. The more upset and intimidating a person was the first time they came to her coffee shop, the more likely they'd become a regular. At least, that had been her experience in the four years she'd been in business. Those same angry customers were also the most dedicated to helping the community. They were just misunderstood. She saw evidence of it all the time.

"Nothing to worry about," Melissa said loudly into the shocked silence, before giving a big, reassuring smile to the two dozen customers who had witnessed everything.

At least three customers had shifted from the commotion the man had caused. The six-foot iguana and the barely five-foot tall ostrich hybrid clutching their drinks at the table by the door definitely hadn't put in orders with her. She didn't see the otter or bat hybrids who'd been chatting with two humans or hybrids-in-human-form at one of her bar tables either, but one might have slipped out without her noticing since that table had three people who looked like humans now. A handful of other customers, shifted or not, cast watchful eyes around to see if anything else out of the ordinary would happen.

Being grabbed had startled her best friend, but Melissa wasn't worried about the guy in sunglasses being a real threat. "Just a misunderstanding," she called out. Kate's furry arm brushed against her own as her friend fled to the back of the shop, every eye zeroing in on her hasty retreat. "Kate's a little shaken, but she'll be right as rain before you know it."

When it was clear she wasn't going to say anything further, a more animated than usual hum filled the coffee shop. The typically relaxed atmosphere was now filled with tension that defied the calming pastels she'd decorated with. Everyone was discussing what had happened and making it into much more than it was. One set of eyes stayed on her, but she couldn't deal with Rick at the moment. She didn't want to leave Kate alone or, worse, have her slip out the back. Kate had always been easily frightened. Melissa reached out and pulled Danny front and center.

"I'll be back out in five minutes," she whispered to Danny.

Danny nodded.

Melissa slipped into the back, leaving the lemony walls behind for the faint pink ones of the staff area. The buzz of conversation from the main room dimmed, but didn't disappear, much like the smell of coffee and frothy drinks. A sigh of relief slipped past her lips as she spotted Kate. She was sitting in a pool of sunlight on the crate of coffee beans between the staff room's two plush mismatched armchairs — one red, one grandmotherly floral. Crouching down in front of her friend, Melissa reached up and gave her comforting arm pets, smoothing down her friend's silky medium-length gray tabby fur. It was still standing on end and hid the turquoise pendant on her neck that Kate had designed a month or two earlier. Her friend's eyes screamed fear.

"Do you know him?" Melissa asked after a minute of silence. That would be the most logical explanation for the man to have gone directly to Kate.

"No, but he's looking for Tommy!" Kate hissed. Her ears were pinned back until even the earrings along the edge of her ears disappeared into the remnants of her pixie haircut. Shifting did odd things to Kate's hair, so she kept it short.

Melissa frowned. Kate's brother Tommy was two years younger than them. At twenty-seven, he had yet to find his "passion" — his words, according to Kate. He always stayed out late, wearing baggy clothes that were distinctly not something that would help him get lucky despite his claims to be "prowling for pussycats." He had absolutely no spine. Kate might fit the definition of a scaredy-cat when confronted with menace, but Tommy was the jumpy furball that the cat dragged in.

"If he wants to find Tommy, why'd he grab you?"

"He said they can't locate him!"

"'They?'" Melissa took Kate's furred fingers in her own and gave them a squeeze. The more she could get out of Kate before she blew the whole thing out of proportion, the better. Melissa had yet to figure out why her friends would freak out about events like this; they never amounted to anything in the end. Still, she knew Kate was actually panicked, and she wouldn't disregard her friend's emotions.

Kate shook her head in bewildered confusion as she continued: "He wanted me to tell him where Tommy is. I don't *know* where Tommy is. He isn't picking up his phone either." Melissa's eye caught on the phone clutched in Kate' shaking hand. "I sent him a message, but you know him. I'm his big sister. He probably won't even read it."

She had a point. Tommy was known for ignoring family calls, messages, and even emails. Melissa doubted he would read Kate's message and solve the problem himself, no matter how insignificant the problem likely was. For now, Kate needed to calm down. Maybe getting her to listen to some of the Akdwenian music she loved so much would help. Melissa tried to remember if the hybrid cat god their parents' generation had popularized was about more than flexibility and ferocity. Kate listened to their meditation music to relax, so there had to be more to it. The music was too disjointed for Melissa's tastes, but—

Near silence from the front of the coffee shop reached Melissa's ears a second before Danny's voice.

"Don't mind him. He grew up with Miss Ju-uniper." The rising lilt of "grew up" and "Ju-uniper" had Melissa and Kate exchanging a glance. It was hard not to giggle or snort at the ambiguous implications of Danny's comment. Danny was not helping Rick frighten anyone off by broadcasting that.

As if on cue, Rick's shoes and jeans appeared beside them. Melissa's eyes slid up his legs, past his clenched fists, one of which squeezed his black motorcycle gloves, past his green-gray shirt — most likely long sleeved, he always wore long sleeves — past his leather jacket, to his very unhappy face.

"What did that guy want with Kate?" Rick snapped. Kate flinched at Rick's tone. He was just as angry at the occurrence as Bobby would be if he were still around.

None of her friends had spent much time with Rick, so they didn't understand that his gruff demeanor was all an act. If they were old friends like Kate and Danny, they'd seen him from a distance at school and when he hung out with Bobby, but he'd stayed away from people even back then. Melissa's other friends had only seen Rick on the rare occasions when he swung by for coffee and they were at the shop.

"Tone it down," Melissa said, narrowing her eyes at him and subtly flicking them at Kate. Given how much Kate was shaking, Melissa decided no amount of meditation music would relax her. "He's apparently friends with her little brother."

"He didn't seem friendly," Rick said.

"If he were dangerous, he wouldn't have just turned and left," Melissa reasoned, emphasizing the last part specifically to Kate who took a deep breath and tried to nod at the logic.

Rick was being overprotective, like Bobby had been. Many people were labeled as much more dangerous than they really were — Rick himself being a prime example. He'd served in the military with Bobby before they both joined whatever the Mavens really was when their contracts were up. Melissa didn't believe for one second that the Mavens was your everyday bike mechanic shop slash motorcycle club. It didn't matter how intimidating Rick tried to be; she knew he wouldn't hurt anyone. His *mother* rolled his bike out front for goodness sakes, and all he did was shake his head. He'd always been like that — trying to scare people off but never doing anything to back up his tough guy act.

Melissa had many other examples of misleading impressions beyond Rick. The strongest came from the first year her coffee shop opened. She'd been warned off the location by more people than she could count, but it was the only place in town she could afford, so she'd ignored them. A few scary types had come by, but she talked with them and gave them coffee. Now they were some of her regulars and had done most of the work tidying up the neighborhood. People just had prejudices against anyone who had "scary" vibes. Melissa thought Rick would understand.

The look in his eye said he didn't agree with her — he believed the man was dangerous — but he didn't say anything to refute her claim. Melissa rolled her eyes and turned back to Kate.

"Tommy is going to be just fine. You'll see," Melissa assured her.

Kate didn't seem convinced, but her focus had moved more onto Rick's presence than on her brother for the moment. She darted her eyes to Rick before looking back down at Melissa, then widening them with either a *I'm-not-going-to-talk-in-front-of-him* or a *what-do-we-do-about-him?* look. Melissa wasn't sure which Kate was trying to convey.

"Rick?" Melissa fought a grin, and Kate narrowed her eyes, suspicious of Melissa's change in tone. Her friend knew her so well. Since Akdwenian music wasn't going to cut it, Melissa decided to see if a distraction was exactly what Kate needed. "Do you want to sit back here and keep Kate company until she's feeling a bit more relaxed?"

"I'm sure Danny needs help out front," Kate said as she shot to her feet, knocking Melissa down. As if fleeing from a demon, Kate quickly edged around Rick's large frame, the end of her tail swishing agitatedly beneath the edge of her asymmetric purple skirt. That wasn't exactly the reaction Melissa had expected, but she'd go with it and keep an eye on how Kate held up. If she had to, she'd close the shop and get Kate home herself.

Rick shook his head at Melissa and didn't offer his hand to help her up. "It's not nice to threaten people with me, Mel," he said. Melissa's gut clenched at the nickname like always. Bobby had called her that, and his friends had followed suit. But they were the only ones. A few people had tried since Bobby died, but she hadn't let it stick. She didn't correct Rick though; she never did. And she hadn't meant to use him as a threat anyway. She had been thinking along the lines of lighthearted flirting. Surely Rick could have provided that kind of distraction for her friend.

"You're not threatening," she scoffed. "Unless you think riding a motorcycle and having a leather jacket makes you threatening. If that were the case, I wouldn't have customers. Anyway, hopefully, working will be enough of a distraction. Otherwise, she'll worry herself silly about the imagined danger."

Melissa rocked forward on the balls of her feet, and even though she didn't *need* help standing up, a little devil in her made her reach out and tug on Rick's hand to finish her upward motion. She could have sworn he tensed at the contact, but he could have just been bracing for her tug.

"I hope you're staying in town for a few days," she said. "You don't have to run back to Placerton, do you?"

"I promised my mom more than a weekend's visit."

"So, I'll be seeing you around a little more?" Melissa smiled at him. Maybe she could convince him to hang out like they used to do before Bobby died. She missed getting to see Rick be himself rather than the intimidating person he pretended to be around other people.

"Here and there, I'm sure. I need to head out."

"Feel free to slip out the back door if you don't want all the women out front drooling over whatever soft image Danny is spinning for you. She's quite imaginative. The scarier a person seems, the nicer her stories make them out to be. She's probably making you sound like a giant teddy bear right now." She didn't mention that Danny was more inclined to believe the scary image than her own stories.

Something like fear passed through Rick's eyes, but that couldn't be right. There was no reason he'd be afraid of a bunch of admirers. Besides, she'd been half-joking. She wasn't sure Danny was still talking about him.

Regardless, Rick took her at her word. His entire body abruptly turned, and his footsteps sounded his retreat into the alley where Melissa had parked her motorcycle not that long before Rick had shown up. She shook her head. Somehow, he could tell when her jokes weren't really jokes like most people thought.

Walking back into the main area of the coffee shop, she was greeted by a slight pause in the chatter as her customers' attention slid to her and then to the empty hallway behind her. A near-collective sigh sounded from the room when Rick didn't reemerge. Despite their disappointment at his absence, many were throwing curious looks Melissa's way. She could only imagine everyone was wondering how she grew up so friendly with a guy who could scare ghosts off with little effort.

"What exactly," she asked as she passed Danny, "did you tell everyone about Rick?"

"Oh, you know. The typical knight in shining armor stuff. That he can sweep three damsels out of danger at a time without breaking a sweat. That he rescues forgotten children in war-torn countries. The usual."

"The usual," Melissa muttered dryly. That was oddly tame for one of Danny's embellishments. Normally, at least one aspect was physically impossible or out of character — Melissa wasn't sure Rick couldn't do those things if he wanted to.

"The guy that grabbed me," Kate said as she slid by to grab a tree leaf pastry, "is loitering at the end of the block. One of the regulars came back to warn me." Her movements were jerky as she put the pastry into a bag. She was still in her hybrid cat form, so Melissa knew Kate was even more rattled than she let on in the back. Kate was grasping at calm with her mental claws and not doing the best job of it.

If she were calm, she'd have shifted back by now. Kate's purple sun dress was a little too tight with her fur, so she only wore it on days she planned to be in her human form. As it was, her fur spilled over the top edges of the neckline like her chest was being squeezed, and the snug bodice crushed her fur. Luckily for Kate, Danny's tales about Rick being Melissa's old friend took her out of the hotseat by putting more eyes on Melissa than Kate.

"You don't think he'll try to grab me when my shift ends, do you?" Kate's fur vibrated with her tremors.

"If he wanted to grab you, he would have just done it earlier when he had your wrist," Melissa said — the voice of reason as usual. "He would have had to drag you out of the shop, which wasn't the best plan." Kate took a step closer as she listened. Melissa reached out and squeezed her hand in comfort. "He made no move to physically remove you, Kate. He just wants to find Tommy. He's probably hoping your little brother will swing by for a free cup of java."

"You know Tommy never comes here," Kate said. Her canines nibbled at her lower lip, making her whiskers twitch like they did before a sneeze.

"We know that," Danny said, nodding along. "But *he* doesn't." Melissa wondered if Danny was playing along or actually agreed with her that Kate was blowing things out of proportion. Danny didn't normally side with her in these situations.

"Just to be safe, Danny or I will leave with you when your shift ends to make sure that doesn't happen." Melissa soothed. "We can even sneak you out the back."

Kate relaxed a bit as the day went on, but she checked her phone every few minutes. And Melissa couldn't blame her.

"Anything from Tommy?" Melissa asked when Nick came in for the afternoon and evening shift.

"Nothing. I messaged my dad since I didn't trust my voice to call. I said I was trying to meet up with Tommy, but he was MIA. He said Tommy grabbed something from his old room two days ago. That's the last time one of us saw him."

"You're really worried," Melissa said, pulling Kate in for a hug. She wished Kate could see that she didn't need to stress about this.

"I would swing by his place, but with that guy watching...."

"How about this," Melissa began. "You go home with Danny. Either crash at her parents' with her or have her take you to your parents' for the night. I'll swing by Tommy's after closing, and if his light is on, I'll give him an earful about at least reading his messages."

"Are you sure?" Kate asked.

"Of course. If that guy is still looking for Tommy and sees me riding past his place, he won't even realize it's me."

"Okay," Kate said. Her eyes didn't leave her phone as she agreed.

Danny left her shift early to head out with Kate. Ilona would be coming in before the afternoon rush got too bad, so they'd only be down a person for an hour. Or that would have been the case if Ilona hadn't been late. When the afternoon rush hit, Melissa had to forgo her break, and she had made a point, ever since she'd managed to make enough money to hire a full staff, to never do that.

When Ilona finally arrived, she burst in the door, leaving a few brown feathers floating in her wake. "Sorry I'm late!" she squawked in the nasally voice she had when she spoke with her beak shut. Her unisex, floor-length skirt was stretched to its limit by her tail feathers. A rat hybrid half-dove out of her way as she swept past the line. Ilona all but hip-bumped Nick off the register so he could make drinks while she stood still long enough to calm her breathing.

When Melissa finally had a few moments to think through what she was actually going to do that night, it was already getting dark. Although she'd told Kate she'd swing by Tommy's, that wasn't the full story. Kate was truly scared of the guy with the sunglasses. Much more scared than necessary, but, just in case there was a reason for Kate to be worried about her brother, Melissa wasn't going to stop at just knocking at Tommy's door if he didn't answer.

Chapter 3

Rick

Swinging off his bike behind Tommy's apartment building, Rick scowled at how easy it had been to get the address. A few clicks through social media and he had enough of a profile on Tommy Nolan to know the guy was most likely doing something with illegal drugs, but nothing he saw raised a flag that would send someone after Kate. Then, he dropped a casual question to his mom that led her to believe, though he didn't confirm it to be true, that Melissa and Kate were going to a party at Tommy's place that evening. In as little time as it would have taken his team to find the information, his mom mentioned Tommy's address while obviously searching for any indication that he was finally going to make a move on Melissa. When he'd said he was going for a ride, his mother had tried to hide her delighted grin as she told him to enjoy the evening rather than sniffing at the mere mention of his bike.

Rick tugged his gloves off and crouched in front of Tommy's ground-floor apartment door. A quick touch of the dull copper lock told Rick that all he'd need were the two pre-bent bobby-pins in his pocket. Given the ease he had with picking locks and the fact that the locks practically told him how to pick them, his team never questioned where he had gotten the bobby pins. Not even Bobby knew the story behind them, which was for the best.

Rick slid the bobby pins into the lock, jiggling them just so. As he always did when he used them, Rick remembered following Bobby and Melissa into their house after a high school dance. Bobby had been ticked off that he had to bring his little sister home instead of going to a party. Melissa hadn't known about the party, which suited Bobby just fine since he was on edge about how much attention his freshman sister got at the dance, especially from his fellow seniors.

Melissa had started plucking bobby pins out of her hair in the car and kept on going as she walked into the living room. Rick had been baffled at how many pins were magically appearing in her hand and her hair was barely half down. She dropped two bobby pins as she crossed the room and headed to the bathroom. Rick had picked them up and was about to go after her when Bobby stopped him, saying he could give them to her later. The bobby pins ended up in his pocket as they plotted how to sneak out to the party without Melissa any the wiser.

Every time Rick used the bobby pins, he viscerally remembered how Melissa had made him feel even back then — like he had so much potential and was going to do good in the world. The sensation had his chest close to bursting.

While teasing Tommy's lock open probably wasn't the good in the world Melissa would have imagined, it was in her best interest that he had a look around. He just didn't know if that was his idea or something caused by her grabbing his hand that morning.

Click.

The lock turned. It had only taken a few seconds. Rick slid the bobby pins back in his pocket and opened the door.

Stale air that smelled like it'd been trapped in a full garbage can for days hit him first. His eyes watered a little at the stench as he closed the door, shutting himself in. He paused to adjust to the semidarkness. Enough light trickled in from outside that he wouldn't have to use his flashlight. A few flies buzzed around old takeout containers on the counter under the kitchen window, telling him Tommy hadn't been home for several days. Laundry that Rick hoped was clean, but doubted was, spotted the floor and couch. A few books were strewn about, but none appeared read.

Tidiness obviously wasn't Tommy's first concern given the smells and mess. Rick took a few steps to the window and cracked it an inch in an effort to make the air tolerable. He didn't know how Tommy could stand to be inside the apartment unless his nose was next to useless. Tilting his head to the side, Rick considered the thought. Certain drugs damaged a person's sense of smell. Maybe Tommy was snorting one of those.

Bracing himself for possibly worse olfactory carnage, Rick cracked the fridge open. Nothing massively offensive assailed him on his first tentative sniff, and it was soon clear why. Tommy wasn't big on using the fridge for food. Assorted drinks lined the shelves — water, sodas, energy drinks, beers, and a jar of pickles. The freezer was packed solid with ice cream, including the revolting fish flavors. Rick's tongue scraped along the roof of his mouth as he involuntarily recalled his first taste of the stuff — it was decidedly more to hybrid tastes.

He made quick work of the kitchen drawers because, at a touch, he could feel they didn't contain anything malicious. There was a chance they had information about where Tommy had gone, which is why he'd even looked inside. But he already knew they wouldn't contain evidence of what had caused Tommy to disappear — which was likely related to the drugs he was doing. Rick just needed more information to point him in the right direction. He eyed the bedroom door. It would make more sense to hide something in the bedroom where a guest wouldn't find it, but he liked to be thorough. Luckily, there weren't many places to hide things in the kitchen and living area, and after a quick search, he was walking toward the dark bedroom.

Rick had barely begun to search Tommy's bedroom when the squeak of the kitchen window sliding open wider stopped him in his tracks. Tommy wouldn't sneak back in his own window — not when he'd left it shut. Hidden just inside the bedroom door, Rick waited to see what his next move should be.

Immediate gagging noises almost made Rick laugh as he imagined the new intruder had accidentally put their head directly over the old takeout containers when hoisting themselves into the apartment. The scrape of jeans against the windowsill came next. The clunk of a shoe on the counter. A disgusted puff of air from the intruder's nose. Possibly from a woman given the pitch. But women could be just as dangerous, if not more so, than men. Whoever she was, it was unlikely she was a cat or bird hybrid; they'd have more grace than he was hearing. Two clunks as her shoes — heels from the click of them — hit the ground.

"Blegh."

Rick's whole body clenched. The exclamation painted a solid picture in his mind. The same black boots from that morning. Jeans that clung to all the right places. A red tie-up top. Hair probably braided for her helmet. Probably bobby-pin-less. Given the night's weather, he added her black leather jacket to the image.

Melissa.

Stifling a groan, he knew exactly what she was doing. Trying to help her friend. She hadn't followed him there or something like that; he'd checked for a tail and kept an eye out for anyone watching Tommy's place. She was just looking out for Kate.

To his knowledge, Melissa had never been in any situation that turned out badly for her. Even when she got pulled over for speeding, she got a warning rather than a ticket because somehow she always made physical contact with everyone she met.

He'd watched her more than he should have over the years and could tell she didn't do it on purpose. She had no idea what her touch did to those around her. And, because she hadn't ever had a situation turn out *not* in her favor, she thought nothing bad would happen from breaking into Kate's little brother's place despite Ripped Jacket's blatant threatening demeanor in her coffee shop that morning.

Rick leaned the back of his head against the wall as Melissa took tentative steps in the dark, likely trying not to step on the clothes or one of the books. When he heard the slide of skin along the wall, he jerked back to attention.

What was she thinking going for a light switch? You can't break into someone's place *and* turn the lights on.

Before he'd thought it through, he was across the living space with an arm around her waist. His hand covered her mouth as he yanked her away from the wall where she had almost brushed the switch. The instant he touched her, she fought back, but she wasn't fast enough or skilled enough to break his hold. As he pulled her body against his, he realized what he'd done.

The skin on his left palm was flush with her lips. Her cheeks were silky soft under his fingertips and the heel of his hand. She squirmed against him, causing her shirt to bunch up around her waist and exposing her skin to the fingertips of his right hand. The compulsion to do the right thing thrummed through him. His awareness of her effect on him only made the feeling stronger.

"Mel, it's me," he said as soon as he could manage a word. Ending her panic was the right thing to do in that moment.

She stilled in his arms. The little jerk of her head against the pressure of his hand told him she was tilting her head, or at least trying to. Her exhale warmed his knuckles. Carefully, he lessened the pressure of his hand over her mouth and pulled it away, his fingertips loath to lose contact with her skin.

"Rick?" she whispered.

"You can't break in and turn on the light," he whispered back right in her ear.

"I hadn't thought of that."

That much was more than obvious.

Melissa's body relaxed against his after her admission. Her head tipped back, and her hair pressed against his cheek, forcing him to realize that the heels of her boots put her ear right next to his lips. So close, her coffee infused scent broke through the stench of Tommy's apartment.

She let out a frustrated noise. "I was so pleased with myself for getting through the window too."

Rick chuckled. "Pleased with almost throwing up all over the old takeout containers?"

"It is rancid in here."

"True," he said. If he hadn't been touching her, he would have expected her to make a joke or a verbal jab, but all she could tell him were truths at the moment. Shaking his head, he realized he needed to let go of her — it was in both of their best interests.

"Hmm?" Melissa asked, rolling her head toward him, and bringing her skin closer to his. She'd felt his head shake.

"We need to get you out of here," he whispered. He didn't know how much more he could take of her pressed up against him like this. He was becoming too invested in the idea of burying his nose in her hair to see if he could smell more than coffee. Maybe even planting a small kiss by her ear.

"But I need to find out what Tommy has gotten himself into. Kate's worrying herself sick. She's at Danny's parents' because she's too scared to be alone and can't hide her feelings enough to face her own parents to crash at their place."

"I'll look into Tommy," Rick murmured, sliding his arm back across her stomach to disentangle himself from her shirt and jacket. He imagined that her breath caught as his fingertips slid along her skin just under the hem of her shirt, a touch longer than was truly necessary.

"Why?" she asked.

"Because I have more experience with things that could be dangerous."

Melissa seemed about to argue with him, but she took the comment as intended. She assumed it was a reference to his time in the military rather than a fact about his current occupation as the co-leader of Team Gamma for the Mavens. She didn't know the Mavens weren't mechanics and a motorcycle club. She didn't know the government contracted the Mavens to do jobs so far off the radar that every Maven's file had been scrubbed from existence.

With her decision not to argue with him, Melissa's eyes went to the window, and she frowned at it, probably thinking about climbing back out it. Rick walked over to the offending window and slid it shut, latching it closed.

"We'll go out the front door," he told her, carefully placing his hand on the back of her jacket to avoid further noble impulses or affecting her too much in exchange.

"Don't you think Tommy will notice the window has been shut?"

"Considering that I opened it, he won't notice a thing."

"You came in the door?" she whispered.

Reaching out and turning the handle, Rick let it swing open in front of her rather than answering. He hadn't bothered to lock it behind him, which was an oversight on his part. He was used to working with a partner or two from his team, and they would have taken care of that. Once outside, he turned around, slipped Melissa's bobby pins out of his pocket, and quickly relocked the door.

"How—?" Melissa was staring at him.

He shook his head at her, walking her to her bike, which was parked out in the open. He used the fresh air to ground himself. Pushing away the need to wrap his arms around her again and hold her close. He couldn't keep touching her. Eventually that would cause a problem, and she'd say something he couldn't unhear. Crossing his arms, he tilted his head at her and ordered, "Home."

She narrowed her eyes at him.

"I'll wait for you," she said. "We can ride together."

Rick had intended to go back inside Tommy's, but he felt compelled to see her all the way home. What if Ripped Jacket or someone else hunting for Tommy was watching? They could follow her home. It would be better if he went with her so he could check for tails. He'd just have to come back tomorrow night to finish his search.

He nodded and went around back to his bike, which was hidden, unlike hers. When he joined her out front, they both put their helmets on and straddled their bikes. He could have sworn Melissa's eyes glittered in challenge a second before she revved her engine and zoomed off, forcing him to chase after her. It wasn't difficult to catch up since his bike was not fifteen years old and built by a pair of teenagers. How her bike was holding up between his visits when he broke into her garage and tuned it up without her knowing should have been a miracle. Even the damn motorcycle wanted to do its best for her.

Chapter 4

Melissa

Melissa frowned at the pale pink tinge of her childhood bedroom's ceiling as the first rays of light streamed through; she had never bothered to change the paper-thin curtains after she outgrew her "frilly" stage. It didn't matter that it was her day off, she woke up before dawn. Despite her contemplative stare for the last ten minutes, her ceiling didn't give her any answers about the past twenty hours. It didn't tell her what Tommy had gotten into. Regardless of the fact that she was sure the guy in sunglasses was harmless, Melissa was certain Tommy wasn't on the up and up, no matter how much Kate would reject the idea. Anyone doing decent things at minimum took their trash out before disappearing. At least, that was Melissa's philosophy.

Her head tipped to the hot pink wall she'd painted back in middle school and toward the house beyond it. She frowned. Maybe Rick could tell her what Tommy had gotten into. She replayed the events of the night before in her head. What had Rick been doing in Tommy's apartment? She hadn't even asked him. It was as if her mind had short-circuited the minute he grabbed her. Remembering his fingers dragging along her skin under the edge of her shirt, Melissa threw her dark blue comforter off. The memory was too hot to contemplate while being smothered in down.

Not once in all of her twenty-nine years had Rick ever grabbed her. But she was not remotely opposed to being pressed up against his body. Last night, she'd felt his heat seep through every point of contact, except for where her leather jacket covered her. She found herself wishing she hadn't been wearing it so she could have gotten the full impact. She hadn't even gotten close enough to him to feel his body heat the times they'd gone dancing with Bobby when she was in college. He'd kept his distance.

Shaking her head at the memories, Melissa forced herself to get up, and by the time she'd finished her shower and gotten dressed, she had a plan. After indulging in a few extra minutes on her makeup — a woman had to have a little vanity in such situations — she moved to the front of the house to keep an eye out for the right moment. She didn't have to wait long.

The kitchen light next door flicked on, casting a faint glow onto the front lawn, and Melissa stepped out into the frigid morning air. Jessy's house looked like it always had. Creamy white walls. Red door and shutters. Blooming window boxes that made said shutters impossible to use. On the inside, the floor plan mirrored Melissa's parents' house. As she walked up toward the door, she was saved from having to decide how loudly she should knock because Jessy saw her through the front window. The smile on Jessy's face was so contagious Melissa couldn't help but smile back. The front door opened before she even reached the porch.

"Come in," Jessy said, waving Melissa in out of the cold. Jessy's short hair was already coiffed, but she was wearing a light blue robe and slippers. "I'm making a breakfast frittata. You still like that, right?"

"Definitely," Melissa said, as she gave Jessy a hug. "What are you putting in it?"

"Normally, I'd just do veggies, but I'm adding sausage chunks for Rick and whipping up bacon, too."

Melissa's mouth watered. "That sounds amazing. How can I help?"

Jessy didn't hesitate to put Melissa to work chopping up asparagus, artichoke hearts, and cherry tomatoes. While Melissa and Jessy talked regularly, it was usually outside on the curb as they were coming and going. Melissa hadn't been in her kitchen since before Bobby died, but everything appeared the same as before. Jessy had her preparing ingredients at the metal, chef-style counter to the left of the kitchen sink, where Melissa had seen her cutting board every previous visit. Jessy cooked up the sausage in a skillet on the gleaming stove along the right wall. She finished that just as Melissa cut into the last tomato, and Jessy passed the sausage to her to slice as well.

As Melissa started on the sausage, out of the corner of her eye, she saw Jessy climb up onto the counter, balance on her knees just past the stove, and reach deep into the high cabinet that held fancy china and crystal for parties. When Jessy pulled out a bag of Rick's favorite coffee blend, Melissa barely contained her riotous laughter.

"Don't you dare tell him," Jessy said with a mock glare, having caught Melissa's shoulders silently shaking.

"I wouldn't dream of it." Melissa grinned. Jessy had bought the coffee grounds just the week before, giving Melissa a nonchalant heads-up Rick would be visiting soon. "Do you really think he thought you didn't have any?"

"It doesn't matter if he knows if I have any or not. What matters is that he doesn't know where to look." Jessy paused and stared at Melissa for a moment, making it clear it was the latter part she didn't want Melissa to tell Rick.

Melissa tipped her head in acknowledgment before slicing up the last of the sausage. She had wondered why Rick had shown up in her coffee shop so early when his mother had gotten coffee especially for his visit. A few minutes later, the frittata was in the oven and the kitchen started to smell more like coffee than apple sausage.

"Let's sit," Jessy said, sweeping her arm to the kitchen table that was, as it always had been, near the far wall between the hall to the bedrooms and the garage door. As they sat, Jessy passed Melissa a red mug that had one partially flat side; it might have been pushed against a rippling wall before the clay had dried or experienced some other creative intervention. "Any news from your parents?"

Melissa nodded and dove into what most people wanted to know about — their academic endeavors. It had been forty-five years since the Crisis, and nobody had answers yet for the changes it wrought. Jessy stayed particularly informed on the subject because she was her mother's colleague at the university and close friend, so Melissa didn't beat around the bush.

"They're knee deep in research. Last week, they were trying to map the differences in a mixed bird hybrid family. The grandparents are a parrot and a canary hybrid who were saved during the Crisis. Their son married a full human, and they have three kids: one is a classic yellow canary, another is a parrot-red canary, and a third is a parrot-redhead human with no apparent shifting abilities. The team hasn't found any predictability in hybrids as genes are passed down."

"The original canary and parrot hybrid couple must have had kids right after the Crisis."

"Yeah. The grandparents had just started dating when the Crisis hit; they were in their late twenties and both working in a pet store. Their son was born two years later. He and his human partner had their first kid in 2050. The next in 2054. The last in 2056."

"The family ranges between their seventies and single digits?"

Melissa made an affirmative noise. She could see the wheels turning in Jessy's head. After an update like this, Jessy often had insights that helped Melissa's parents with their research once she'd mulled over the facts for a few days.

"Any special tendencies?"

"Nothing clear. The parrot-redhead human has an uncanny ability to mimic voices like his grandfather, but there isn't enough data to know if the ability skips a generation, is only in men, or was complete chance." Melissa was interested in, but not obsessed with the progress toward understanding how the human-hybrid races would interact in the future. She listened to her parents closely and made notes after their conversations just so she could talk to Jessy, who had been obsessed since the Crisis hit, and a few others her parents worked with and who wanted the nitty-gritty updates any time they saw Melissa. Melissa shrugged and added, "Regardless of lack of correlation, my parents talk as if they're on the verge of a breakthrough."

"I imagine they would. *New knowledge is just around the bend.*" Jessy laughed as she parroted Melissa's parents' favorite saying. "Will they be coming to visit you any time soon?"

Melissa paused at the false, off-handed tone Jessy used. She had said it as if Melissa didn't live in her parents' house, but rather in her *own* house, which was categorically not the case.

"Have they ever said anything to you about how long they plan to be on the research project?" Melissa asked. Her parents had specifically asked her to move out of her apartment and back into the house to take care of it while they were gone for a *one*-year research sabbatical with a groundbreaking team of scientists. That was over three years ago. During that time, they had visited twice and canceled visits five times because of "research emergencies" that revolved around "narrow windows of opportunity."

"Rick," Jessy said, looking over Melissa's head with a smile and ignoring her question, which made Melissa more suspicious that Jessy knew something she didn't. "It's great you could join us for breakfast."

Melissa twisted in her chair and saw Rick in the opening to the hallway, leaning against the wall. He was dressed in jeans and a green long sleeve shirt that hugged muscles Melissa had only been able to speculate about the feel of before last night. He was barefoot and his hair stuck up in all directions.

"You got coffee," Rick commented. His chin tipped down as his brows rose in expectation.

"Yup," Jessy answered brightly.

Clearly unsatisfied with her response to his non-question, Rick continued, "When did that happen?"

Melissa almost laughed at the confirmation that Rick knew his mother had hidden the coffee the day before, but she managed to keep a straight face — barely.

"I'm allowed to go to Melissa's shop too, you know." Jessy stood up, effectively brushing off the conversation. "Why don't you keep Melissa company while I go get dressed?"

Jessy swept out of the room, giving Rick a less than discreet shove in the back, pushing him toward the kitchen. Half asleep, he walked to the freshly brewed coffee and filled the mug his mother had set out for him. It wasn't until he sat at the table that Melissa realized what Jessy had done. They both stared at the other's mug for a minute before making eye contact. Melissa instantly wondered if Jessy was like her own mom, always dropping hints that she and Rick would make a great couple. Before last night, Melissa had never truly entertained the idea.

Rick cleared his throat, and asked, "When exactly did she buy the coffee?" before pinning her with a stony stare and taking his first sip.

Taking her cue from Rick, Melissa ignored that their mugs were designed to mold together as part of a matching set — their rippling fourth sides meant to fit together in harmony. "Customer-supplier privilege," she said, taking a sip of her own coffee.

"That's what I thought." Rick rubbed his forehead, and Melissa wondered if he had gotten enough sleep or if his mother's antics were giving him a headache.

The buzz of the timer made Rick glare at the oven and clench his jaw. Melissa shook her head and grabbed the mitts off the counter. Opening the oven door released a steamy puff of the frittata's savory aroma into the room to tangle with the coffee. Melissa's mouth watered.

"So, about last night," Melissa said as she set the frittata on the stove to cool.

Before she could turn back to Rick, Jessy's voice erupted from the hallway, aborting any thought of movement. "Last night? Did you and Rick have fun at Tommy's?" Jessy asked.

"I—" Melissa paused and spun toward Rick, slack-jawed and unable to believe he had tattled to his mom about her breaking into Tommy's apartment. His eyes betrayed nothing as he watched her. "I hadn't expected to see him there," she finally said.

"Were there a lot of people?"

Melissa narrowed her eyes at Rick. "More than I expected." Rick's smirk laughed at her dry tone.

Jessy came back into the kitchen dressed in her typical blue jeans and a plain tee-shirt. She paused to slip shoes on. "Rick," she said, "why don't you fry up the bacon. I completely forgot I'm supposed to have breakfast with Maria today."

Rick and Melissa blinked at Jessy's announcement. Melissa looked at the frittata in confusion as Rick asked, "Maria?"

"Yup," she said, grabbing her purse from the back of a chair. She was gone before either Rick or Melissa could say another word.

Melissa stared after her.

"I don't remember your mother being forgetful."

"She isn't." Rick's frustrated tone brought her attention back to him. He stood up and walked past her, careful to swing wide as if he didn't want to chance brushing up against her — which was in line with Rick's actions with everyone, including her before last night. "Sit down. I'll start the bacon. How many strips do you want?"

"Two."

Rick had the pan heating and six slices sizzling in no time. "When did she invite you to breakfast?"

"She didn't. I just popped in. I had my fingers crossed for pancakes, but the frittata will be fantastic." There was something about Rick standing barefoot with messy hair at the stove that she couldn't look away from.

"Pancakes are the first morning of my visits." He paused. "She *didn't* invite you?" he repeated as he shook his head, like the notion was unfathomable.

"No," Melissa said, wondering why he sounded so surprised. She and Bobby had often popped in for breakfast over the years; granted, she hadn't done so since Bobby died. Maybe Jessy *was* as enamored as her mom with setting the two of them up. "The first day of all your visits?"

"Yeah. It's pancakes, then frittata, then coffee cake. If I'm here longer, breakfast has a little less fanfare."

"You'll have to let me know when your next first day will be. I don't know what your mom does, but her pancakes are amazing. Granted, I've never had her coffee cake," Melissa muttered that last thought more to herself than to Rick.

Rick divvied out the bacon, ending the sizzling of fat that had been the background of their conversation, and cut slices of the frittata. An odd silence stretched as Melissa watched him carry their plates to the table. Without a word, he sat down across from her. He took a bite of the frittata and then gazed off into space for a minute while he chewed.

Melissa stared at his jaw as he ate, remembering how it had tickled a few strands of her hair as he whispered in her ear. Giving herself a mental shake, she took a bite. Her eyes rolled up as the flavors melted together on her tongue. She tried to contain her happy little sound at the deliciousness. Shaking her head at the goodness, she grabbed another forkful. She was about to put the second bite in her mouth when she looked at Rick and froze with her mouth open and her fork poised right in front of her lips. He was staring at her as if *she* were on the breakfast menu. When he noticed her watching, he quickly looked down at his plate and studiously took another bite without raising his eyes. Melissa put her second bite in her mouth and watched him *not look at her*.

The image of Rick's eyes devouring her was wreaking havoc on her body, and Melissa was caught in a moment of active despair that she had no covers to throw off now. The combination of the memory of him grabbing her, his heat enveloping her, his fingers on her skin, and now his stare was almost enough for her to buy into her friends' speculation that there was something between the two of them despite the lack of previous evidence. And if Jessy had been pushing Rick toward her for years now, he'd at least thought about it.

Frowning at the direction of her thoughts, Melissa picked up a piece of crispy bacon and took a bite.

"Mmmm!" she said, wide eyes glued to the remaining piece between her fingers. "What type of bacon is this?" Dragging her eyes from the deliciousness, she looked at Rick for an answer.

His gaze pinned her in place as he said, "Apple-smoked." His voice was lower than when he'd been cooking.

"Apple sausage. Apple-smoked bacon. I'm sensing a theme."

He nodded and picked up one of his four pieces of bacon and slid it onto her plate without a word. She smiled her thanks.

"So, about last night," she prompted.

"About last night," he repeated flatly.

"You said you would look into Tommy," she trailed off for him to continue.

"And I will."

"You didn't find anything last night?"

"I was interrupted." He raised his eyebrows in accusation.

"Is there something I can tell Kate besides the fact that her brother has become a worse slob than before? A bunch of us are getting lunch later," Melissa shared.

"Nothing that's going to put her at ease."

She narrowed her eyes. "That means you did find something."

Rick didn't answer. He crunched on a piece of bacon like he was pleased with stonewalling her. It was as if he didn't remember that she had never bought into his tough guy facade.

"If you don't want to share...." She shrugged as if it were all the same to her. "I guess I'll just have to go back to Tommy's tonight and find out for myself."

"That's not a good idea."

She shrugged again. Taking another bite of frittata, she smiled with exaggerated sweetness at him.

"I won't crack the window this time," he warned.

"How hard can it be to pick the lock? You relocked it in the blink of an eye. I'm sure with a little reading this afternoon, I can figure it out." Melissa watched as something akin to panic crossed his face. Maybe it really was that easy to pick a lock. "Or," she offered, "you could take me with you tonight."

She watched Rick as he opened his mouth to argue with her, then thought better of it, came up with a new argument, opened his mouth to speak again, closed it, and finally stared at his plate. Picking up her last piece of bacon, the one Rick had slipped her, she hummed happily as she devoured it. She licked the bacon grease from her fingers with a triumphant flourish.

"What time should I be ready?" she asked.

Rick chewed on the inside of his cheek. "Nine," he grumbled.

Chapter 5

Rick

Hours later, Rick was still scrambling to find a way out of taking Melissa with him that night. No matter how much he thought about it, he couldn't think of a strategy to talk her out of it. Rick started up his bike, knowing that if Bobby was alive and knew about this, he would punch Rick or worse. Much worse. And while helping Melissa break and enter didn't seem like a *good* thing to do, he also knew she would do it one way or another. She'd be safer if she was with him. His reasoning sounded flawed, but he didn't see an effective counter argument.

Rick barely noticed any of the houses as they whipped by. He didn't even slow for Professor Torres' house and the gaggle of students peering at him while he stroked a real hammerhead shark. Rick had sat in on the hammerhead shark lecture when he was a kid and learned a lot about the differences between hybrids and their animal counterparts. The hammerhead shark presentation was a classic for Professor Torres since he was a hammerhead shark hybrid; he'd been working at the local aquarium when the Crisis hit. Any other day,

Rick would have asked himself what Professor Torres had learned in the last twenty years to update his lecture. Today though, all of Rick's attention was on replaying the morning — mostly the same series of images that were muddling his mind.

Melissa in the kitchen with his mom as if it were the most natural thing. Melissa bending over in front of the oven, which was apparently a view he liked a lot better not in the kitchen. Melissa moaning at the taste of the frittata in pure sensory pleasure. Melissa purring at the bacon in surprised delight as if she savored every new experience. Melissa knowing she'd backed him into a corner and that he had to give in, which wasn't something he'd let anyone do to him in a decade. Then, her moaning with her eyes rolled back again. And bending over again. And smiling like a cheshire cat. The more the images repeated, the less the kitchen and food appeared. By the time he parked his bike near the town pond his friend Neil ran, Rick was physically uncomfortable straddling his bike and could barely remember what he and Neil were supposed to talk about.

Strolling around the perimeter of the pond, Rick focused on his immediate surroundings and forcibly pushed Melissa from his mind. He had to hand it to Neil. He'd done a great job with the pond, though it bordered on what most people considered a lake. His old-fashioned red barn-like restaurant was incredibly popular with aquatic hybrids and therefore all their friends. Most aquatic hybrids had to get their skin wet at certain intervals which made the pond a near necessity after the Crisis. For a quarter, anyone could jump in and out of the water or use the rinse stations for a quick douse. For a few dollars, they could swim in a supervised section of the pond. That aspect was practically a community service.

Neil's restaurant model used the majority of the pond itself. The restaurant's leading characterization was "catch and cook." Neil kept the pond well stocked with a variety of delicious fish — non-hybrid, of course. Hybrids could pay to go fishing in their animal forms, and anything they caught, within reasonable eating limits, was theirs. They could take it home with them or rent a grill at his restaurant and eat pond-side. There was also just the cook option for the grills if fishing didn't tickle a customer's fancy and tables inside the barn that could be reserved if customers weren't cooking. Grill stations and small docks lined a third of the pond's perimeter. Another layer of grills with cheaper rental rates sat farther away from the water's edge.

It was just after eleven in the morning, and there were kids getting their gills wet while a lifeguard watched for funny business. Rick thought he saw a handful of large shadows moving under the water, indicating a few people were fishing. When he reached the weathered red restaurant and its white wooden sign which hung askew and read Pond Side Grill, he peered through the entrance. Two families were setting up for lunch time grilling, but there was no sign of Neil.

A teenage frog with bulging eyes and slimy green skin greeted Rick with an eager lopsided grin: "You must be Rick," he said. One of his webbed hands hung onto the edge of his jean pocket like he'd hooked a thumb inside it. He was striving for calm, but the grin and the jerky hops of his body as he tried to stand still betrayed his awe. Rick didn't remember seeing him before; Neil must have hired the kid in the last few months.

"Boss said to keep an eye out for the tough guy in a leather jacket. You're at Grill #1." He pointed down the side of the pond. That particular grill put them far away from most people who would reserve a lunch-hour grill.

Rick glanced at the kid's name tag. "Thanks Conner. I'll just wait for him over there."

"Grab the box sitting on Grill #17 on your way."

Nodding, Rick grabbed the box and then walked past six empty pond-side grills to the last one. Or the first, since it was labeled #1 — an old joke between them from high school about them being "#1". This spot was the farthest from the street and backed up to trees filled with chirping birds. Grill was a highly inadequate term to describe each cooking set up. There was technically a grill for any fish caught, but it sat in the middle of an elite kitchen setup. Nearly smooth stone countertops appeared to balance on fake boulders that functioned as cabinets, which were filled with pots, pans, utensils, and anything else you might need to cook up a meal.

Rick set the box on the end of the counter and opened it up. On top was a towel. Rick chucked it onto the dock overhanging the edge of the pond so Neil could grab it when he climbed out. Next in the box were shorts and a tee-shirt. He set Neil's dry clothes on the farthest left edge of the counter so they'd be easy for him to grab too. Then there was the food: tortillas, salsas, chips, guacamole, beans, rice, limes, electrolyte drinks, and a bulging folder that looked like it had been yanked hastily out of a filing cabinet with edges and corners of papers sticking out here and there.

The creak of the dock pulled Rick's eyes away from the folder. A fish lay twitching on the planks while a shiny, deep brown Neil hauled his body out of the water in a fashion that had gotten him teased endlessly in high school — like he was trying to beach himself and failing. Once he got his shell up and flopped down with a thud, he looked slightly less ridiculous when he reached forward, slipped his fingers into the slats of the dock, and dragged himself forward enough to get a knee up beside him. The murky brown swim trunks he wore were almost the same color as patches of his *less-than-lustrous-when-dry* hybrid turtle skin. When wet, the trunks just mimicked dried mud on sleek, slippery sludge. Neil often had to explain to new fishers that wearing a swimsuit the closest color to their hybrid skin helped camouflage them when fishing. Watching Neil clamber onto his knees without any bend in his torso was still, after all these years, flinch inducing. The man was not graceful. The second silvery fish clenched in his teeth that flopped about in contrast to his brown tones didn't make the picture any better.

Grabbing the fish he'd thrown out of the pond in one hand and the towel in the other, Neil stood. He toweled off what he could reach — his fish-holding arm, a touch of his thighs, his neck, his face (around the fish in his mouth), and his currently brown hair — as he walked up off the dock. Partially dry, he tossed the towel over his shoulder and pulled the second fish out of his mouth.

"Have you started the grill up yet?"

"No, I just got here. I'm still unpacking the box."

Neil set the two fish down on the stone, and Rick heard two sparks click to life as Neil started the grill from his side. Rick turned back to emptying the box. A frustrated grunt from Neil made Rick look up. Neil's towel had gotten caught on spikes that protruded five inches from the rounded back of his shell. Rick frowned, but before he could offer to unhook the pierced material, Neil grabbed the edge of his trunks and shifted into his human form, frustration still engraved on his face. His now oversized trunks had room for two more people.

"Since when did the surface of your shell get *so* spiky? Last time I saw you swimming—" Rick paused and reflected, he couldn't remember the last time he'd seen Neil in his hybrid form. Unless he was in the water, Neil spent all his time in human form. He was one of the few unfortunate hybrids whose two forms differed vastly from one another. "—didn't you only have spikes along the edges?"

"Yeah, but the small bumps I got during puberty — you remember the *shell acne,* as we called it — have continued to grow and have gotten pointy over the last five years."

"Any idea how long they'll grow to be?"

"No." Neil sounded tired.

Rick tipped his head in sympathy as Neil swung the freed towel around his body. He let go of his trunks as he reached for his dry clothes, which didn't have holes along his side and butt for his shell spikes to stick out of, but were stretchy enough not to rip to shreds if he had an unanticipated shift. They would get punctured and holey, but they wouldn't leave him naked. While Neil finished changing, Rick busied himself with getting the fish on the grill.

When Neil finally ambled around the counter to take over the cooking and survey his pond, the fish were sizzling and half-cooked. Ambling was the fastest Neil ever moved. Most hybrids had no noticeable effects from their animal forms when they were human, but Neil, again, wasn't lucky. He could not move quickly. He couldn't even get a driver's license because he couldn't react fast enough in an emergency.

"What's in the folder?"

"You asked if I knew about drugs in town." Neil tipped his head toward the folder on the counter. "It's all in there."

Neil didn't ask Rick why he wanted to know. He had never asked many questions, even when they were kids. He was one of the few people who knew what Rick's touch did. Because of that knowledge, he knew without being told that Rick wasn't a mechanic in a motorcycle club. And that if Rick asked about something sketchy, like drugs in this case, he planned to do something to improve the situation. Neil would be right there with him, and Bobby when he was still around, if he could, but his slow movements prevented him from joining the army after high school and from being a Maven now.

"Why do you have so much information about the local drug situation?" Rick asked as he flipped through the inch thick folder.

"This is the local watering hole, for better or for worse." Neil slid the fish off the grill. "A lot of the teens in the city feel like they've known me forever, so when they don't want to go to their parents about a friend experimenting, they come to me. They know I'm chill for the most part, but I don't like drugs. I've gotten a bit of a rep about handling it well. Educating them. Helping them find resources on the down-low. Never cracking down on them in a way that encourages further rebellion."

"Helps that you can't catch them if they run," Rick muttered. He was impressed though. Neil was making a serious impact in his own way.

"I'm quintessentially non-threatening, yes," Neil deadpanned. Rick watched as Neil methodically made two plates of fish tacos. "Once I get them talking, I keep records on who's dealing and which dealers are dangerous. A few kids have passed on photos of their friends cutting deals, so I have headshots of the dealers, too. Some kids think I need proof before I'll help. It's all in there."

They sat down at the stone table and ate in silence while Rick went through the folder page by page. There was a list of different drugs with check marks tallying up how many times Neil had had to deal with each one. The sheer number of checkmarks made Rick do a double take. Clearly, Neil had been at this for a while and hadn't exaggerated about kids coming to him for help.

The dealers were assigned colors ranging from yellow to red to indicate how dangerous they were. There were even notes on their suspected level in the dealing structure. Rick would have suggested Neil go to the police with all the information he had if it weren't for the commentary on the orange and red marked dealers about who was currently incarcerated, their released dates, and their previous arrests. Obviously, Neil was already talking to someone at the police station.

Halfway through the folder was a familiar face with one of the few official mug shots. Rick stopped skimming and stared.

Theo Barre.

"What do you know about him?" Rick tapped Ripped Jacket's face. All the page said was that Theo Barre had been released from jail a few years ago. He'd ended up behind bars for roughing up a buyer while dealing Nip — a low-level cocaine product that was more catnip than coke and highly addictive when snorted but extremely difficult to overdose on.

"Mid-range dealer when he was put away. Rumor has it he's a dog hybrid, but no one I know has confirmed that. He's new to our area as far as I've been able to find out. I haven't seen him or had any kids deal with him. I heard he was mostly in Lunser, but he hasn't been seen dealing recently. However, he's surrounded by people who do deal, so my guess is that he's moved up in the chain of command. Did you see him here?"

"He accosted Kate Nolan at her place of work yesterday morning, trying to track down her little brother."

"Nolan? As in Tommy Nolan?" Neil frowned.

"Yeah, you know him?"

"Of him."

Neil reached for the folder and flipped deeper into the pages. Having found what he was searching for, he spun the folder back around and pushed it to Rick. The page was marked with the lightest shade of yellow to indicate not dangerous. There was a blurry photo of a ragged looking gray cat hybrid in a patchwork sweatshirt and baggy jeans exchanging something with a kid who was fourteen at the most.

"I wouldn't even call him a dealer, but he does sell occasionally. The kid he's selling to in that photo told me Tommy had the shakes both times he bought something from him. The few whispers I've heard tell me he's sloppy."

Frowning and stuffing the last bite of his taco into his mouth, Rick wondered how anyone missed the signs that Tommy was shady. Tommy clearly hadn't spent much time around Melissa, otherwise she would have had skin contact with him and none of them would be in this mess.

"You think Tommy got himself into something bigger than he can handle, and his sister is getting dragged into it?"

Rick nodded as he swallowed.

"Where does his sister work?"

"Juniper's Java." Rick's voice was grim. He did not like the idea of drug dealers — neither the non-dangerous ones like Tommy nor the dangerous ones like Theo Barre — anywhere near Melissa.

"Shit," Neil whispered.

"Kate is Mel's best friend."

"Crap. I didn't make that connection. Kate comes here with Melissa and another of their friends a few times a year... Bobby would be flipping out."

"It's worse. Mel is determined to help Kate. And with her touch, she'll be able to get into more trouble than otherwise."

Too busy staring at the photos of Tommy and Theo, Rick missed the telling quirk of lips that would have tipped him off that Neil had snagged hold of an old topic.

"And how," he dragged the *how* out, "would you know that?"

Rick glared at Neil's teasing tone and the fact that, once again, Neil refused to even consider that Melissa had a *touch talent* like Rick did. Neil wasn't sold on Rick's theory that all humans who survived the Crisis did so because they had some sort of magic *talent* either pre-Crisis or that developed from the Crisis. He also didn't agree with Rick that Bobby was alive and out there, just impossible to find because of his *talent.*

Neil was focusing on the other age-old topic instead; while Bobby had always given Rick's mother a weird look when she'd hinted she'd like to see Melissa and Rick together, Neil had known for a long time what Bobby couldn't see — Melissa was pretty, sweet, and, after growing up around the three of them, rather fearless.

"When, exactly, did you last see little miss Juniper?" Neil continued when Rick didn't deign to respond to his last comment.

There was no way out of this last question so Rick said nonchalantly, "She cooked me breakfast this morning."

Neil's mouth hung open long enough that a passing fly could have flown in.

Chapter 6

Melissa

Melissa squeezed her eyes shut and sucked a fortifying lungful of air in through her nose. Pushing away the thought that Rick knew *something* about Tommy that would worry Kate, she rapped her knuckles against the navy-blue door in front of her.

Danny's dad opened it. Melissa blinked for a minute at the bulging jaundice stomach that dipped out of his polo shirt and over the top edge of his khaki pants. Bright yellow spikes replaced his gray beard along his chin. She didn't think she'd ever seen him in his hybrid form — overweight bearded dragon was not a good look on him. He scanned the street over Melissa's shoulder as if on watch for a threat. Then, his chilled, scaly fingers clamped around her upper arm and pulled her inside. Startled, Melissa barely realized she was inside before the door clicked shut behind her.

"Mr. Stone?" Confusion colored her voice.

"Kate's a mess," he informed her. "Danny muttered some fake excuse about a raving dog who came in for coffee and chased her up a tree, and that you took care of it. But whatever *it* actually *is*, it's clearly not taken care of."

"It's getting taken care of," Melissa clarified.

"By you?" Mr. Stone squeezed his bloodless lips together in a line that went from ear to ear in scrutinizing doubt while he paced in front of the terrarium that took up a fair portion of their front room. The four lizards and turtle inside watched him with interest.

"I have help."

Mr. Stone stopped pacing and glowered at her. "What qualifications does your help have? And your answer better include the words *a police badge*."

"Will a sterling military service record count?"

His lips shifted to a slant, making his face incredibly lopsided. It was like one ear dropped to his throat and the other raised up to his eyebrows. Danny was lucky to not have inherited her father's mouth.

"For now," he said ominously.

He let Melissa pass and collect Kate from Danny's bedroom. Danny wasn't home since she had an opening shift at the coffee shop. Kate was wearing Danny's clothes — the yellow sweater had a high neck for warmth rather than framing cleavage, and the skinny jeans were tighter than anything Kate would choose to wear over fur if she shifted. The jewelry she wore was the same as the day before — a rare occurrence for her. Because Mr. Stone had trailed Melissa to Danny's room and then back to the front door, neither Kate nor Melissa said a word about Tommy until they were outside.

"Well?" Kate whispered when they reached Melissa's bike.

Melissa handed her the spare helmet she'd brought along. "He wasn't home," she told her. She didn't tell Kate that she had climbed through Tommy's window, that Tommy hadn't been home in a few days, or that Rick had grabbed her in the dark. Melissa did smile and confide that Rick was going to help her find out what was going on though.

"Seriously?" Kate's eyes searched Melissa's for a sign of a joke.

Melissa nodded and hopped on the bike. Kate climbed on behind her and they headed off to Micky's, the bistro where they were having lunch with the rest of their friend group — minus Danny, of course.

Micky's was a post-Crisis restaurant that catered to hybrids and humans alike. It was in a long, skinny building in Eucalyptus Park. The walls were made of glass, and the ceiling mimicked the tree canopy much farther over their heads outside. The entire restaurant was only a single row of tables deep. Most were typical table and chair combos, but there were two pool booths for aquatic groups that wanted to soak while they ate. It also had rather eclectic items on the menu — catering to vegetarians, the broadened spectrum of omnivores, and the near carnivores since some hybrids couldn't fight their animal's diet tendencies.

When Melissa and Kate walked up, Greg was already sitting at their table cleaning his glasses and staring off into the park. He wore a button-up shirt that screamed, I'm working today; when not working, he preferred tank tops that showed off his arms now that he had "the guns." Having been particularly scrawny in a middle and high school that favored football players had left a mark on him.

"Getting lost in the park's Dewey rating?" Melissa joked.

"Har har," he said, rolling his eyes and standing up for hello hugs. One drunken night soon after Greg and Melissa had met, he professed he "saw the world in Dewey" and waxed prosaic on the Dewey Decimal System for a good hour; now, they always teased him about it.

Before they could all sit down, Bethany swept in the door in what she coined as *bat-chic*. Most people would have called it elegantly gothic. Her naturally white hair tumbled in waves down her back, regardless of which form her willowy frame took. Her black top hung mostly open on the sides in case she broke out her wings. She wasn't one for destroying clothes in a shift or looking anything less than stunning. The fact that she spent most of her time reading books in the university library for her dissertation didn't mean she couldn't flaunt what she had.

Ted showed up next. He'd joined their friend group after Greg answered his ad for a roommate. His skirt was plastered to his hairy legs as he hurried to their table. Ted's hybrid form didn't completely match his human one, and he dressed accordingly. When his legs ripped into four tentacles each, he did not want to be trapped in pant legs. His face and bald head were redder from exertion than his normal pink complexion, making his face resemble his red octopus hybrid form more than was typical.

"Sorry I'm late," he said. "I got sucked into the code I was working on."

"Breathe," Bethany said, much like one of her yoga instructors. "We just sat down."

They had barely glanced at their menus before their waitress showed up, but they knew their orders. "What can I get everyone?"

"The muscles over kelp, please," Ted ordered.

"Muscles like these?" Greg asked, going to flex his arm only to be flummoxed by his shirt sleeves.

"No one here wants to take a bite out of you," Bethany scolded Greg, before turning to the waitress whose snorting oinks endeared her to the group immediately. "I'll have a caterpillar leaf salad with a double serving of fruit."

"The spicy jambalaya for me," Greg said, a little deflated from Bethany's cutting quip.

"I'll have a burger with shoestring fries," Melissa said.

"You don't even wear shoes with laces," Greg muttered.

"It's not like they'd even fit through the shoelace holes," Ted pointed out.

Bethany rolled her eyes, saying, "As if any of us would wear potato laces."

"I'll have the tuna." Kate ordered as if no one was debating the merits of shoestring fries as functional footwear accessories. "Can I get it deep fried with cucumbers on the side? I'm going to need a sardine martini, too."

Silence fell over the table.

"Is everything alright?" Ted asked, giving voice to the universal concern. Any type of fish deep fried and a sardine martini was Kate's classic life-sucks order.

Kate shook her head.

"I'll leave you guys to talk," the waitress said gently. She placed a sympathetic hand on Kate's shoulder and gave a gentle squeeze. She likely thought Kate was going through a bad break-up.

With the waitress gone, Melissa helped Kate share the events of the last twenty-four hours. She was very circumspect in what she added, since she didn't want to give Kate any extra worries. And no way, no how, was she going to cop to climbing through Tommy's window last night.

"What are you going to do?" Bethany asked Kate. "You can't just move in with Danny and her parents. Especially if Mr. Stone is as freaked out as Melissa said."

Kate took a large gulp of the martini the waitress had just brought over and slumped under the weight of her worries. Melissa reached over and rubbed her sweater-covered arm. She searched for something to either alleviate the worries around the table or change the topic smoothly to take the pressure off Kate for a moment.

"The real question is," Kate said, her eyes narrowing to slits, clearly with the same idea, "is how quickly do you think Melissa and Rick will figure out what my brother has unwittingly gotten himself into? They're working *together* on the problem."

Ted, Bethany, and Greg all spoke at the same time.

"It's about time you wrapped that biker around your finger." Ted smiled. He was convinced Melissa's relationships would last longer if she'd just pick more interesting men.

"How did you get that hunk of a man to help you?" Bethany asked. She'd seen Rick twice when he'd passed through the coffee shop. She'd said more than once that she'd be down to hang off any of his appendages.

"Are you sure that's safe?" Greg asked. He'd never taken it as a given that Rick was harmless given his membership in a motorcycle club.

Melissa almost groaned. It had taken her years to realize how much she talked about Rick. It was hard not to say anything when he was in town since she would see him and flashback to all the fun she'd had with Bobby and his friends. Rick and Bobby had been constants in her life. Now it was just Rick, and he was around much less than he used to be. Then, to top it off, when he wasn't in town, Jessy was right next door reminding her of Rick, even if she didn't say anything. And after breakfast, it wasn't lost on Melissa that both Jessy and her own mom were attached to the idea of being one big family. Even if the family they were imagining wasn't quite as big as it used to be.

"He was there when the guy grabbed Kate," Melissa said. They didn't know he'd broken into Tommy's place last night or that he was taking her to break in again that night. A smile threatened to take over her face at the idea, but she managed to hold it back and focus on the conversation at hand.

"And he did nothing?" Bethany's voice was a mix of disappointment and disbelief. For whatever reason, she'd placed Rick in the role of superman intent on saving the day — or at least, she acted that way to irritate Greg. Their waitress returned with their food then, which gave Melissa a moment before she had to respond.

"He didn't need to do anything," she said firmly. "The man was harmless. I got his attention, and he was aghast at his own actions and left straight away."

"Rick did follow Melissa and me into the back of the shop." Kate's brow furrowed. "You never said what you two talked about after I—"

"Ran away like he's more frightening than the guy that grabbed you?" Melissa finished for her.

Kate sniffed indignantly while Greg frowned at her assessment of Rick.

"Nothing happened," Melissa said. "He helped me off the ground where you'd left me when you *knocked me over*. He mentioned he'd be in town for a bit. That was all."

"Wait," Ted said, picking up a second bite of kelp. "If that was all that was said, how did you secure his assistance in this sticky endeavor?" The way Ted twisted the word sticky had hopeful innuendo written all over it.

"Oooh, good point," Bethany said.

"He's staying at his mother's," Melissa said. She hoped that would suffice as an explanation. She wanted to keep the memory of breakfast with Rick that morning for herself. The way he looked at her while still a little befuddled with sleep? That was just for her. When no one said anything, she added, "so he's staying next door...."

"And?" Bethany prompted.

"It's easy to bump into him," Melissa said vaguely.

"I don't like it," Greg said, startling everyone. "How do we know he isn't working with the guy that approached Kate?"

No one said a word. They all stared at Greg like he'd lost his mind. This was *Rick* they were talking about. After several seconds, Greg grimaced.

"Fine, so it's unlikely. But for the record, I'm not a fan. He clearly puts Kate on edge."

Bethany lightened the moment by ribbing Greg about his suspicion, and the lunch drifted to other topics with a keen eye kept on Kate and her second sardine martini. She was listening to everyone, but mostly staring at her message-less phone on the table.

Melissa promised herself she'd find out what was going on with Tommy that night. Or at least as much as Rick knew.

Chapter 7

Rick

"Melissa! Come in!" His mother's delighted voice slipped under the door to his room.

Rick looked at his watch and groaned. It was five after nine. He grabbed his jacket and hurried to the front of the house. Melissa was standing next to his expectant mother in the same clothes as that morning — a tight blue tee-shirt, black skinny jeans, black boots, and now her black leather jacket. His mother, on the other hand, was wearing a grin so large it was close to a painful rictus.

"What are your plans?" his mother asked. Her eyes bounced between the two of them as Rick stepped beside Melissa.

"Like last night—"

Almost of its own accord, Rick's arm whipped behind Melissa and around her head, his hand clamping over her mouth. He squeezed his eyes shut in a grimace at the contact and at what his mother would think. That morning, he had never corrected the assumption Melissa had that his mother knew what they were doing at Tommy's. When he cracked his eyes open, his mother's jaw hung open, and her eyes were about to fall out of their sockets.

"I'll just..." her voice trailed off. Glancing at Melissa for a moment, his mother took a step back. She'd never seen him purposely touch anyone without a protective barrier — herself included — once they knew what he could do. Even with his skin covered, he eschewed her hugs most of the time for fear of an accidental touch forcing her to say something she didn't mean to. "I'll just leave then." His mom walked away, but glanced back over her shoulder, no doubt seeing Melissa's confused eyes over his hand.

"Let's discuss the plans outside," he said quietly, removing his hand from her skin.

Melissa followed him out of the house without a word.

"I don't understand why you did that," she said after he shut the door.

Hand at the small of her back, he walked them toward the street where their bikes stood side by side.

"She's under the impression Tommy threw a party last night. I don't exactly tell my mother I'm heading out to commit a misdemeanor."

"I wasn't going to say that."

"What were you going to say?"

"That we're going for a ride."

"Oh." Rick stretched his neck to the side. He hadn't needed to touch her in front of his mother. Did touching his best friend's little sister fall in the "good" category? Logic told him no, but for some reason, he didn't feel like he'd done something wrong in touching her. In fact, his fingers itched to slide back across her skin. He pulled on his gloves to try to suffocate the urge to reach out to her and see if touching her was a good thing to do.

"What was up with your mom? I couldn't tell if she thought you were being rude, if she was startled, or something altogether different."

"She's used to me telling her where I'm going during my visits," Rick said. Which was true, but not the answer to Melissa's question.

Melissa crossed her arms as if she was waiting for a better answer, but Rick was determined not to give her one. Instead, he focused on his plan for the evening. He was careful to avoid asking Melissa any further questions since she literally couldn't choose what she said in response for another minute or two. Rick felt even more ethically torn than normal because he hadn't touched just anyone; he'd touched *her,* and she didn't know what his touch did or what her touch did to him.

"We'll ride to Tommy's but take a different route than we did last night. It's not smart to go directly there and back. When we get there, we will not park directly in front of the apartment and announce our presence." He gave her a meaningful look. "I will give you one minute to pick the lock. If you don't finish in that time, I'll take over. We can't linger out front. Understood, Mel?"

"Yes, sir." She smirked at him. Rick rolled his eyes. If she didn't want to be ordered around, she shouldn't have asked him to help her break and enter. Plans and precision kept his team alive — especially now that their missions didn't have Bobby there to help people overlook them.

"Get on your bike," he said as he shook his head and reached for his helmet.

"Shouldn't we just take one bike? It'll be easier to hide."

Rick stood perfectly still. He immediately imagined Melissa's legs pushing up behind his as her torso curved against his back and her arms wrapped around his middle. Maybe her hand would slip down, dangerously close to the edge of his jeans, keeping more of his attention on what she was doing than on the road.

"We can take two," his voice was barely a rasp. He needed his head clear, and having Melissa against him would make that impossible.

"Come on," she coaxed. "I've never ridden a bike like yours."

She might have just as well suggested she give him a lobotomy, but she was gazing at his bike with longing and missed the petrified expression on his face entirely.

"I saw how much more speed it has than mine. I want to feel it."

"Okay."

Melissa's elated smile shook him.

Rick glanced around, not only to check if someone had mimicked his voice and agreed for him, but also to make sure no one was around to see Melissa's smile — he didn't want to share it with anyone else. Part of him couldn't believe he'd agreed given the way images of them together had hijacked his mind. The other part of him, the part that knew she was still influenced by his earlier touch, couldn't deny her honest desire. She wanted to ride his bike and nothing else. She didn't have ulterior motives to her request; she would have told him — if she intended to or not.

They both put their helmets on, and Rick glanced at her hands. She didn't have gloves. It would be easy for her to slide her hands under the hem of his shirt and press her palms to his stomach. His whole body tensed at the thought. Not that he thought she'd try to get a piece of him — Melissa wasn't like the women he'd been around when he was younger and less dedicated to being intimidating. Even now, when he actively tried to make people keep their distances, she didn't fear him in the least. It didn't matter what he did; she thought he was a good person.

Stifling a groan and trying to focus on their mini-mission rather than the fact that he liked the idea of her hands on him, Rick swung his leg over his bike, kicking up the kickstand. Melissa was there an instant later, her hands on his shoulders as she straddled the bike behind him. She settled into place, her legs pressed along the backs of his, her chest crushed against his leather jacket. When her arms slid around his waist, he started the engine. She squeezed him in excitement, a full body hug.

Not sure what had gotten into him, Rick sped away from the curb inordinately fast. He heard a muffled shriek from Melissa as she clung to him. Feeling just a bit like a bastard, he took the *extra* long way to Tommy's apartment and sped through all the turns a little faster than he needed to just to feel Melissa laugh against him.

Rick pulled over two blocks from Tommy's apartment near a streetlight that was blocked by an overgrown tree. Before Melissa got off the bike, she gave him another delighted squeeze that left him smiling as he pulled off his helmet and joined her on the sidewalk.

"That was fantastic," Melissa whisper-squealed. She clasped her hands together in front of her like she was stopping herself from hugging him.

Rick thought, *Why the hell not?* Taking a step toward her, he wrapped an arm around her waist and pulled her flush against his side. She made a small, startled sound and caught herself with a hand on his chest, but she continued smiling as she gazed up at him. She was on an adrenaline high.

"Let's go," he whispered into her ear, breathing in the smell of coffee on her and feeling her shiver at his voice. As they moved toward Tommy's building, Rick continued whispering close to her ear. If she could taunt him with moans and complete trust, the least he could do was tell her how to pick a lock. "Did you do any of the research you mentioned about lock picking?"

"A little." Her voice was breathy and brought his attention down her body to her chest, which he realized he had a rather spectacular view of from his position.

"What did you find out?" His voice felt tight in his throat. He dragged his eyes up and scanned their surroundings, looking for anyone watching Tommy's place but didn't see anyone.

"It's a bit more complicated than I thought."

"It can be tricky," he said. A few strands of her hair had escaped and tickled his lips. "You just need to know what tools are needed for which type of lock. Take Tommy's lock, it's simpler than it should be for an apartment. You only need two small tools."

"Oh?"

"Mmmhmm," he hummed in her ear. His mind, drunk on the smell of coffee in her hair, supplied different ways and situations in which Melissa might say "Oh?" and none of them helped Rick clear his head.

They walked in silence, pasted together. A small hoot and a rustle of leaves in the trees were the only noises on the street. After two minutes, Rick finally came up with a justification for continuing to hold her: on the off chance anyone saw them, they'd look like a couple on a stroll. The excuse assuaged his conscience, but that he needed one at all didn't sit well with him.

Before they strolled up to Tommy's door, Rick regained enough presence of mind to scope the area out again, but nothing had changed. At the door, Melissa knocked, clearly hoping Tommy had turned up. He hadn't. Rick loosened his arm at her waist and turned to her.

"One minute," he said, holding up her old bobby pins between them.

"Right," she said, analyzing the bobby pins for a second before sliding her eyes past them and focusing on his mouth. Her tongue flicked out over her lips. Rick took a step back and held the bobby pins out to her as if they would protect him. She took them and knelt in front of the lock.

Rick wasn't getting any saintly medals. He'd stayed as far away from Melissa as he reasonably could over the years until he'd grabbed her last night. Now, he was touching her without any reason to and currently noting how high her head was while she kneeled next to him and peered at the lock. Namely that it was at the *perfect* height. To give himself something to do, he tugged his gloves off. He'd need his hands unencumbered to finish picking the lock if Melissa couldn't do it.

Melissa slipped the bobby pins into the lock and twisted them with a wiggling motion. Rick felt the small *click* of the lock reverberate through the air as if the catch had been to his belt, not the door. The lock hadn't hidden its secrets from Rick, but with Melissa, it wanted to be *good* for her. It wanted to open for her.

"Wow." Melissa looked up at him with complete surprise. "That was much easier than I expected."

"Like I said, it's a simple lock." Rick's voice was a rough growl. He was not happy his suspicion was right; she could have easily broken in without him and found herself in real trouble. There was no way he was going to tell her it wasn't as simple of a lock as he'd made it sound. There was no way he was going to give her ideas to try something like this without him there to watch her back. He was doubly upset because Melissa's upturned face was undoubtedly going to haunt him in his sleep.

Not hesitating to touch him, Melissa grabbed his forearm and pulled herself to her feet. She held the bobby pins out to him and smiled. Rick plucked her bobby pins from her fingertips, careful not to make skin contact, before reaching past her and opening the door. The stench that hit them was just as revolting as the day before. It was the perfect distraction to pull his mind from the illogical sentiment that she was asking him to hold her bobby pins safe for her — just like he'd been doing for over a decade.

"Where do we start?" Melissa asked as Rick made sure to lock the door behind them this time. They stood just inside the door for a few moments, letting their eyes adjust to the darkness.

"I already checked this room, so we just need to check the bedroom and bathroom."

"Wait." Melissa's fingers closed around his forearm. "How long were you here before I arrived last night?"

"Long enough."

Rick could easily make out that nothing had changed since the night before. The clothes were in the same spots; the books were still carelessly underfoot; and not one of the takeout containers was disposed of. He started forward across the room and sensed more than saw that Melissa was close at his heels.

The night before, Rick hadn't had time to do more than get the general layout of the bedroom — a large bed centered on the opposing wall, a single nightstand to the right, a closet and bathroom on the left. The generic furnishing probably came with the apartment — very college-town like. Tonight, he noted the discarded clothes, the trash sticking out from underneath the bed, and the stale stench of something he didn't want to consider. He did not envy the person who rented after Tommy. Cleaning could only do so much.

"What should I be looking for?" Melissa cut into his thoughts.

Rick glanced at her, realizing he was going to have to tell her what Tommy was doing. It was better if she knew what they were dealing with.

He grimaced but shared on a resigned sigh, "Drugs."

"You found drugs in the kitchen?" The squeak in Melissa's voice made him inordinately mad at Tommy for being such an idiot.

"No, I haven't found any yet. If we find any here, it should be in powder form, but I can't rule out the possibility of injectables, so don't stick your hands in anything without doing a visual check first."

"Back it up," Melissa said. Her voice was a touch defensive. "Why do you think he'll have any?"

Rick dragged his hand down his face as he laid it out for her. "On social media, he has photos in a number of local locations known to be popular with druggies. He was high in several of his photos."

"You pulled up his social media? His account isn't public—"

"It isn't, but his security settings are pathetic." Rick looked at Melissa. "For that matter, you should get better security on yours. So should Kate. Perhaps all your close friends if they're as lax as yours."

Melissa blinked at him in the darkness. He couldn't quite make out her face, but her eyelashes were moving up and down as if working something out of her eye. As he watched for a more discernible reaction, his words echoed in his head. He might have overstepped, but without Bobby around to tweak her security settings, it was in her best interest that he made her aware of the issue. Rick frowned. That sounded a little convoluted.

"Rick." Melissa's voice was cautious, almost timid. "*You* don't have social media." He heard the question she didn't ask: How did you get into all of our social media accounts? He ignored it. His hacking skills were trivial at best, but enough to get into a social media account. Anything more and he'd have to get his team involved, but he wasn't going to admit that to Melissa.

"Beyond my assumptions from his own photos," he continued as if he hadn't just divulged something that might have to do with his job, "he's been caught on camera selling drugs with reports that he was going through some rough withdrawals."

"And where did you find *those* photos?" Melissa's voice was slow, as if the words were a struggle to push out. Rick didn't know if it was disbelief making her hesitate or her realization he was sharing things he shouldn't be.

"I'm not at liberty to say," he finished. Neil hadn't said his *hobby* was a secret, but he also didn't say it wasn't. Moreover, Rick did not want Melissa going to Neil for help. It made him feel a little bad, but Neil couldn't protect her like he could. Neil didn't have the training or the speed to deal with a rough situation.

Melissa and Rick both just stood there, saying nothing.

Inside Tommy's bedroom.

In the dark.

Rick wished he had a clue what Melissa was thinking. He figured she was stunned, but he didn't know if it was because of what he had access to, his dubious sounding methods, or the information about Tommy itself. That he had revealed as much as he had also felt like a bad sign. If his team knew how wrapped around Melissa's finger he was, he'd never hear the end of it. At the back of his mind, Rick vaguely wondered if he'd violated his non-disclosure agreement with the Mavens again. He'd done so once before, but that had been to make sure Bobby knew to make himself appear useful and get himself invited to join.

"I'll start in the nightstand," Melissa finally said. She walked directly over to it. Whatever she thought about everything he'd shared, she was keeping it to herself. Rick saw her pull her phone out and turn on its flashlight before he got down on all fours to check under the bed.

Tommy was officially a slob. Old food wrappers from chips and other snacks that luckily didn't smell were under the bed in an alarming number. A partially torn-up pair of sneakers stuck out in all the trash. Rick reached out and grabbed one, turning it over to make sure it was empty. It was, if you didn't count the cockroach that crawled out and scuttled over trash wrappers, making unsettling crinkling noises. The other sneaker was both empty and uninhabited. With care, Rick searched under the edges of the mattress as Melissa said she didn't find anything in the nightstand or under the pillows.

Rick moved to the bathroom, and Melissa started searching the closet while carefully checking all the pockets she came across. The bathroom wasn't as bad as the kitchen since it didn't smell, but even with the small light from his phone, Rick could see mold on the walls and that the toilet bowl, whose seat had been left up, hadn't been cleaned in several months if that year.

The bathroom drawers and cabinets held nothing suspicious. Even the medicine cabinet behind the mirror was benign. Frustrated, Rick searched for fractures in the caulking between tiles to see if one was loose, but such a hiding spot was likely beyond Tommy if he was as addicted as Neil had made it sound.

"Make sure to look inside any shoes or between any stacked clothes," Rick said to Melissa as he stalked back into the bedroom. She made a sound of acknowledgment from inside the closet.

There had to be something at the apartment to corroborate Tommy's drug usage and or hint at what he'd gotten into. Rick made his way over to the nightstand, not because he thought Melissa's work needed to be checked, but because he needed to find something. He opened the drawer and saw it — a straw that split into two tubes that ended in two comma shapes pointing in opposite directions. Melissa obviously hadn't known what it was. Carefully, Rick picked it up and put it in a plastic baggy he pulled from his pocket.

"What's that?"

Rick turned and saw Melissa watching him from the other side of the bed.

"It's for snorting drugs. This one is specifically designed for a cat hybrid's nose. If we're lucky, there'll be Nip inside that will help me track it back to which dealers sell the same strand." Rick made a mental note to message Jeremy to meet him the next day to process it. Knowing who the different players were and how Theo Barre tied into Tommy's mess would help Rick get a lead or two to follow. He had hoped whatever Tommy was doing would be an easy fix, but if what Neil had mentioned about Theo Barre was true, Tommy was in it over his ears. Rick's team would help, even if this wasn't on the books.

"Nip?" The worry in Melissa's voice made Rick want to comfort her despite the fact he usually left comforting to other people. Nip was first advertised as a social drug and considered as harmless as catnip, but the addictive qualities of cocaine were deeply embedded and once someone was hooked, rehab was not an easy path. It had taken public officials a year to prove it was almost as bad as straight cocaine because of the debilitating levels of addiction; it took even longer for the recreational users to take the findings at face value. Tommy might have started using when it was thought to be less dangerous than alcohol.

"You find anything in the closet?" Rick asked, still crouched next to the nightstand.

"Nothing I recognized as drug related."

"He probably took any drugs he had left with him if he thought he was in trouble."

"The backpack he carries isn't here," Melissa volunteered. "Could be he kept what he needed in it."

Rick couldn't remember if there was a backpack on Tommy in the photo Neil had, but it had been rather grainy.

"What's the backpack look like?"

"Just a black backpack. Nothing special. It's rather old. He should have replaced it ages ago."

Rick nodded before he realized Melissa couldn't see much of him.

"Rick?" Melissa's voice held a slight tremor. "Why do you have access to drug analytics and dealer tracking?"

Again, he ignored her question. The only answer that came to mind was the truth, and he couldn't tell her the Mavens were contracted to solve a wide range of problems. Any example he could think of — taking down out-of-control crime syndicates that normal channels couldn't get anything on, off-the-book rescues around the world, and a number of missions that weren't quite ethical without the full backstory — were *not* things that would put her at ease. "We should head out," was all he said.

Standing up, Rick walked back into the main room and motioned for Melissa to follow. Without a word, he took them outside and quietly relocked Tommy's door behind them. Melissa's brow was wrinkled, and she'd shrunk into herself in a way Rick didn't care for. In an effort to distract her, he wrapped his arm around her waist, pulling her against him again and letting her coffee scent push away the stench of Tommy's apartment. When his fingertips brushed along the soft fabric of her jeans, he realized his gloves were in his jacket pockets. Careful not to make direct skin contact, he walked them back toward his bike.

Halfway there, an idea occurred to him, not that he'd tell anyone. Ever. He leaned in close and asked, "You want to drive on the way home, Mel?" Melissa's surprised half-smile was a reward in and of itself. He already knew wrapping himself around her on the bike would be an exercise in pure torture that would keep him up for the rest of the night.

Chapter 8

Theo

Theo Barre frowned as he watched the couple break into Tommy-the-dipshit's apartment. When they had walked by the alley where he was loitering, he had barely taken any note of the two lovers beyond smirking at the woman's obviously flustered breathing that was clearly caused by the guy whispering in her ear. Neither of them had seen him, but generally, no one peered in dark alleys between buildings while exchanging dirty fantasies. But then, *then*, they had the temerity to walk straight to Tommy-the-dipshit's door.

The always-on porch light was dim, so it was hard to make out too many details from where Theo stood, wrapped in shadows, but he saw the guy pull something out of his pocket and hand it to the woman. She seemed vaguely familiar, but Theo couldn't place her. She might have one of those faces, or he might have seen her before. He couldn't be sure from this distance. When the woman dropped to her knees and picked the lock in less than thirty seconds flat, it was obvious she was a pro. When Theo had picked that lock, it had taken him over a minute, maybe more than two. Worse, the woman had the gall to be delighted and tease the guy about it from what Theo could see.

Once inside, they didn't turn on any lights. Eventually, a bit of a glow in the bedroom appeared, meaning they had flashlights. Theo knew there wasn't anything to find, but he scratched at the stupid bracelet on his wrist anyway; the bracelet always bothered him more when he was agitated. Tommy-the-dipshit had nothing worth stealing in his pigsty. Theo had forced his nose through the horror of sniffing through the entire place for any scent of drugs. Tommy-the-dipshit had taken the product with him.

When the couple finally came back out, they were empty-handed, so Theo knew they hadn't found something he missed, but the woman looked lost, like something was deeply wrong. Theo wracked his brain for what could have caused her distress. He loved that expression on his playthings' faces, but that was when he put it there. Making something go horribly wrong for those he got to toy with was just so gratifying. But he hadn't gotten to cause this.

He'd had someone watching the building since he searched the place early that morning. Had Tommy-the-dipshit snuck in somehow and overdosed? Theo had given little thought to who he'd assigned as lookout since it was just Tommy-the-dipshit, but a dead body when you didn't expect one could account for shaking a professional thief or whatever the fuck these two were. Theo growled. He'd have to recheck the apartment again after they left.

To Theo's immense disappointment and dismay, the guy relocked the door even faster than the woman had unlocked it. The woman was probably the guy's prodigy-in-training — advanced training, from what he'd seen.

The two backtracked toward him. The guy had pasted the woman to his side like before, and whatever he whispered this time took away the stress lines on the woman's face. He was hyper-alert now and looking around constantly as they walked. As they drew closer to the alley, from deep in the shadows, Theo took a few snaps of them to use to find out who they were. He hoped the photos would be clear enough to make out their features.

Theo's senses tingled, telling him he'd seen the woman before; she was too pretty to be a generic face. Despite her leather jacket, she appeared oddly innocent for her line of work, which she likely used to her advantage. Her partner, on the other hand, looked like a professional who could do some damage if the whim struck. He would be more likely to punch a guy for speaking to him than to listen.

When they backtracked past his alley, Theo tucked himself behind a trashcan close to the street in case they said something above a whisper. But no luck in that regard. Some weird date they were on, but who was he to judge what got them off?

He dialed his little sister's main line then put his phone to his ear. Theo couldn't follow the couple without being seen coming out of the alley, so the picture would have to do for now.

"Better be good news," Allison snapped into the phone as the couple sped past on a tricked-out bike without license plates. Surprisingly, the woman was driving; he'd have guessed it was the man's bike.

"Two people with record-breaking lock picking skills just went in and searched Tommy-the-dipshit's place," Theo said, ignoring his sister's tone and the rustling of sheets that confirmed he'd woken her up. She was always in a mood, in Theo's opinion, which made her devious and underhanded.

Theo had learned early in life not to get in her way unless going against her for a split second immediately turned things to her benefit. He didn't know why other people didn't see it. Others only noticed that Allison was ambitious and business savvy. They didn't pick up on the fact that she was never nice — not unless she could benefit from it. Theo had known from the start the family's candy company was never going to be enough for her. After she'd taken the reins from their dad, she'd branched *way* out of sweets and pulled Theo *way* in and that suited him just fine.

"I got photos of them, but I couldn't follow," he told her.

"Send the photos to Troy. If he can't ID them, I'll call in a favor. Did they find anything in the apartment?"

"Shouldn't have, but one of them was off when they left, so I'm going to go check it again."

"Don't call me back unless you find something worthwhile," his sister grumbled.

Theo tucked his phone into his back pocket, rubbed his wrist under the stupid bracelet, and padded up to Tommy-the-dipshit's door. If dealing with this mess took much longer, he was going to have to find a shorter name for Tommy-the-dipshit.

Chapter 9

Melissa

After a few hours of Rick-riddled dreams that were not remotely of the restful sort, Melissa dragged herself to her coffee shop. She didn't have an opening shift, but she justified showing up three hours early by reminding herself that: first of all, she owned the place; and secondly, Nick had a history exam later that afternoon and he could use part of his shift to study.

She let herself in the backdoor while it was still dark out and long before Nick and Danny would arrive. With only the faint glow from streetlights slipping in the windows, Melissa was hit with a memory from when she'd last seen her brother.

It had been at about the same time of morning. She had wanted him to see her coffee shop before he went out of town to do some mechanic work the Mavens had been hired for. Melissa remembered rolling her eyes at him because she didn't believe he was a mechanic, but he just smiled back. That morning, he'd dragged Rick with him so they could head straight out after seeing all the work she'd done for the opening the following week. While originally Bobby had been dead set against the location she'd picked — the only one she could afford that was anywhere near downtown — her brother had conceded that she'd done a good job fixing it up and it looked nice, if out of place in the neighborhood. Rick had wished her luck with her grand opening and assured her that her shop would be a success regardless of her brother's grumbling. Rick had said the same thing when she'd first picked the location which had ticked Bobby off to no end.

Given the last thirty-six hours, it wasn't too surprising that, rather than the memory focusing on the coffee shop or her brother, this particular morning, it focused on Rick. Her memory of the way he stood and the expression on his face were much clearer than Bobby's. Still, she wasn't sure she had the details about him quite right. She didn't know if she truly remembered Rick wearing a black shirt under his leather biker jacket or if she just picked to dress him all in black so that he'd be able to sneak through shadows like the enigma he now presented.

Melissa knew Rick was still with the Mavens, and *mechanics* didn't die without any details or body when off fixing bikes out of town like her brother "had." Then there was Rick's ease at picking locks and hacking into online accounts which lined up much better with something that would interest her brother. And furthermore, it was clear Rick had resources or a network of some sort — which she had an inkling was just the Mavens themselves. Rick had ignored her questions last night, but she didn't hold that against him. He and Bobby had to have had strong reasons for not sharing what the Mavens actually did.

Shaking Rick out of her thoughts, Melissa grabbed the coffee shop account books and sat at the front counter to work. In the early morning silence, she lost herself in the task. A bit later, knocking on the front door pulled her from the orders she was reviewing. Nick was standing there, clutching a textbook to his chest like a sacred pillow. Melissa let him in and sent him into the back to study with a cup of coffee. Five minutes after that, Danny lethargically came inside.

"You could have switched shifts with me," Danny grumbled. Her blood was sluggish in the morning, or so she claimed. It was her go-to excuse for not being a morning lizard. Her winter jacket, red sweater, and full-length cream leg-warmers that came up under her short skirt to let her tail have unimpeded movement didn't compensate enough for the morning chill, or so she always claimed.

Over the next two hours, customers trickled in as per usual. Melissa busied herself with making coffee, unloading the pastry delivery, and chatting with customers. She barely shared any of the work with a slow-moving Danny, which earned her several grumpy *why-did-I-need-to-come-in?* glares, which Melissa ignored. When the sun peeked in the window of the staff lounge, Danny slipped back to curl up in the sun-soaked floral chair and made Nick stop studying and get to work up front. A little after eight, business picked up.

At nine, Bethany swooped in with Kate in tow. She'd crashed at Bethany's since she continued to fret about Tommy — and with what she knew now, Melissa couldn't blame her. Tommy doing drugs was not something Kate would want to hear; it meant Tommy was actively making bad decisions rather than just having a bit of bad luck. Given the small duffel Kate held and that she was in her own asymmetric, cleavage baring clothes with a different set of jewelry, Bethany had accompanied Kate to her apartment for necessities.

The two of them sat at a table, drinking coffee and eating muffins — a candied fruit muffin for Bethany and a sardine muffin for Kate, who was still in a comfort-food mood. Greg showed up soon after them and joined their table; he generally had a 10 a.m. shift at the library and stopped by on his way in. Danny brought his coffee to the table and stood there to chat for a few minutes, but Melissa kept working, not sure what to say to Kate about her brother's drug habit. Maybe she should have called and filled her in last night, but she hadn't. Kate was going to be incredibly upset when she learned her brother was making such poor decisions. Melissa wanted to be certain Rick was right before they crossed that bridge.

Thirty minutes after her friends arrived, Nick stopped dropping hints that she take a break and insisted — in an exasperated little-brother way — and she finally gave in. She handed off the half-made straw tea that went with the chinchilla hybrid's salt lick caramel sucker. Melissa was certain the customer wouldn't be in her hybrid form in most other cities unless she enjoyed being stroked by strangers. Chinchillas were just so soft and looked so snuggly that some people forgot the hybrid they saw was also a person. How people forgot was beyond Melissa, but she'd heard a lot about it over the years from the fluffier hybrids who had spent time in other cities.

Melissa glanced over at her friends and saw Bethany looking at the door with a half grin and Greg frowning at it like it confounded him. When Melissa looked over, she saw Rick, wearing a red shirt under his jacket, had just walked in carrying a brown paper bag in his gloved hand. He appeared extremely self-conscious and had no doubt noticed how many eyes had fallen on him. Since he regularly drew people's attention, Melissa didn't think that was why he was uncomfortable. Granted, her friends' eyes were snapping between the two of them in such a way it was a wonder they didn't experience whiplash, so maybe he *was* uncomfortable. Melissa herself was experiencing an elevated heart rate that had more to do with his whispering in her ear, holding her close, and the things he'd said to her in her heat slick dreams that night.

Rick walked up to the counter and placed the brown bag in front of her as Danny set his preferred coffee next to the register and nudged Melissa. Rick slid the bag across the counter.

"Coffee cake," he muttered. Glancing up, he met her eyes and gave her a good rendition of a helpless shrug. A choked sound came from Danny behind her that left Melissa fighting a smile and Rick frowning deeply. Helpless was not part of his normal tough-guy act.

Melissa slid the coffee to him. "I have to take a break. Let's join my friends." She tipped her head toward her friends' table and, from the corner of her eye, saw them all look away immediately.

Before Rick could decline, Melissa came around the counter, grabbed the brown bag, and hooked her arm through his. Ignoring the fact that he tensed — very different from the night before, she noted — she pulled him toward the table, only slowing to let him reach back and snag his coffee. Her friends were moving to make room at the table, leaving one side of the booth open for her and Rick.

Rick paused, so Melissa slid in first, which put him between her and Greg who had grabbed a chair from another table to sit at the end. When Rick sat, Melissa did not miss the frown he shot Greg's arm before he squeezed a little closer to her than was necessary. She got the faintest whiff of steel and motor oil from his jacket when his shoulder gently bumped hers. His squeezing in close wasn't missed by any of her friends at the table.

"Thanks for bringing me a piece of coffee cake," Melissa said to break the tension. She opened the bag to find a large tinfoil-wrapped slice whose sugary goodness drifted into the coffee-filled air.

"You made coffee cake?" Bethany leaned forward as if drawn in by Rick's mere presence and a desire to take a sniff of the treat he'd brought Melissa.

"No," Rick said, picking up his coffee and taking a slow sip while he dropped his right hand under the table. Melissa felt his gloved fingers brush back and forth along the side of her thigh as if he was nervously rubbing his own or trying to comfort her. She didn't know which reason caused the action. In either case, it made it extremely hard to swallow the bite of coffee cake she'd just put in her mouth.

"Did you find my brother?" Kate asked, her voice shaky.

Rick narrowed his eyes at Kate, making her sit back in her seat. Melissa met his gaze when he turned it to her, and she could see he hadn't liked the question.

"I had to tell her something, and otherwise, they'd worry — unnecessarily, mind you — about me hunting Tommy down alone." She gave a stern look to each of her friends in turn.

He took a long sip from his drink as he let that sink in. Melissa imagined he was wondering how much she shared. Guys had weird ideas about what women shared with friends sometimes.

"Not that we think you're good enough protection," Greg said in a tone that might have been teasing, but Melissa wasn't completely sure.

Rick choked on his swallow of coffee.

Melissa chuckled and patted his back. She knew the comment surprised him. After his time in the army and whatever he did with the Mavens now, he was more than qualified to protect her — not that she needed protecting. Her laughter and smile earned her another glare from Rick.

"Tell me Kate," Rick finally said. "Did you notice any changes in your brother's behavior before... all of this?"

Kate rubbed her arm, and Melissa reached across the table to squeeze her hand. Rick's fingers tensed against her thigh, and Melissa slipped her left hand under the table to discretely touched the back of his hand and calm him. She didn't know why he hadn't taken off his gloves.

"He might have been a little jumpier than normal," Kate said. "He's always been easily scared, but it might have been more than before." Melissa wondered how easy it was to conflate jumpiness with withdrawals if you didn't know drugs were involved. "Two or so weeks ago, he had an argument with our dad."

"What about?" Melissa prompted.

"I didn't stick around to hear it. Two male cat hybrids yowling at each other can be rather unpleasant. I assume it was something related to his aimlessness. I heard my dad yowl, 'no more!' with finality." Kate paused. "But it was at least two weeks ago, maybe even three or four."

Melissa watched Rick out of the corner of her eye. He sat nearly motionless. His fingers were tapping against his thigh and hence tapping against hers as he thought. He took a pensive sip while Melissa took another bite of Jessy's mouthwatering coffee cake as they all waited out his silence.

"Could your parents have cut him off?" Rick finally asked.

"Because he was freeloading off them," Greg mused, forgetting to be wary of Rick for a moment.

"Have they been paying for his rent?" Bethany asked in surprise.

"I have no idea," Kate admitted. Her eyebrows drew down as she considered the idea. Kate had been paying her own rent since graduation, but she'd also had jobs, unlike Tommy.

If Tommy had been supporting his Nip habit with money from his parents, he'd have had to step up his income stream to compensate. That would mean getting into something bigger than just snorting.

"But why would that lead to a guy trying to grab Kate?" Greg frowned. "And why would Tommy disappear?"

"I should get going," Rick said suddenly. Everyone looked at him. He cleared his throat and leaned toward Melissa. "I need to go..." his eyes flicked around the table, "take care of that thing."

"Right." Melissa nodded in wide-eyed understanding. He had to go test the snorting straw and do whatever came along with that.

He glanced at everyone else again before pinning her in place with his gaze, "Don't do *anything* until I get back?"

"When are you coming back?" she countered. Melissa remembered Bobby trapping her into such promises and then being gone for several months. It had been doubly infuriating because Bobby had always known he was going to be gone for a while but hadn't shared that information.

"Hopefully tomorrow."

"Okay then." It was no hardship to agree. Kate was spending the night at her place next, so it wasn't like she'd be investigating with Kate in tow.

Rick nodded and slid out of the booth, careful not to bump into Greg. Once standing, he paused, nodded to the table, and left. They all watched him leave. Melissa didn't know if Bethany and Kate were paying more attention to his butt or his shoulders; personally, she was having a hard time picking between the two.

"You two were rather cozy," Bethany said, turning back toward Melissa.

Greg slid into Rick's vacant spot. "I don't know," he huffed. "They weren't even touching each other."

"But they *were* sitting rather close together," she countered.

Melissa didn't point out that they were, in fact, touching each other under the table — particularly since that sounded way more salacious than it had been. Instead of saying anything, she ate the last bite of Jessy's coffee cake as Bethany and Greg continued to bicker about her and Rick.

"Why did he bring you coffee cake?" Kate interrupted Bethany and Greg's argument.

"I hadn't tried it before," Melissa said. She was infinitely curious about where Rick was going to do the testing — was it near the garage where all the Mavens supposedly worked? If he hadn't been purposefully cryptic in front of her friends, she would have pushed him a bit to see if he'd say.

"You've never had coffee cake?" Bethany asked, aghast. "You run a coffee shop. You literally have coffee cake for sale next to your banana bread."

"I've had coffee cake before," Melissa said. "I've never had *his mom's* coffee cake." After she said it, she realized she had just admitted something new to her friends.

"And what other of his mom's breakfast foods *have* you had?" Bethany asked. She had leaned forward as if Melissa were about to drop a juicy piece of gossip.

Melissa sighed before admitting, "I think her pancakes are my favorite, but it's been years since I had them, so I can't be sure."

"But why did he bring you the coffee cake today?" Greg was baffled.

"I may have mentioned I hadn't had it before."

"When?" Bethany pushed.

"Yesterday?"

"When?" she repeated.

"At breakfast." Melissa's cheeks were heating.

Danny arrived just as Bethany began to chirp in uncontainable laughter.

"Melissa. Nick is leaving and we're getting close to the pre-lunch rush."

"Of course," Melissa said. She half shoved Greg out of the booth so she could get back to work. Kate came with her. A few minutes later, Bethany and Greg headed out to the university library together.

It was several hours later when Kate caught Melissa's arm and asked, "What weren't you two telling us about Tommy?"

Melissa sighed. "Nothing is definite yet, but it's likely your brother hasn't been making the best choices. I don't want to worry you with theories until they're confirmed."

Kate's frown indicated she wasn't sure if she believed her, but she didn't push for more. There was no way Melissa wanted to accuse Tommy of doing Nip unless they were certain. Rick had made it sound like a done deal, but Melissa would wait until the tests came back before sharing. Kate knew her brother was aimless and maybe living off handouts from her parents, but as per usual, she was convinced he'd never do something wrong on *purpose*.

Chapter 10

Rick

Rick pulled his bike into the garage the Mavens "ran." It was tucked behind Triggs' Triad — the pub the Mavens were known to hang out in.

At a glance, the garage wasn't anything that would knock someone's socks off. The left wall was equipped with all the tools they might need to do motorcycle repairs — some of which were mounted above the steel work tables that ran the length of the room and others were organized in drawers underneath. The main area of the garage was open and could fit six cars with the majority of their parts spewed out around them, not that they worked on cars often. The whole place smelled like oil, metal, fuel, and sweat despite the large, open garage doors.

Rick pulled his bike up next to the others on the right side of the garage — a few feet away from the secret trapdoor that led to the garage below. A few of the supposed motorcycle club members, who were in truth security guys and extra muscle for Maven ops, or Team Pi Rho as they called them, were working on a bike in back. Its parts littered the ground, and the guys tipped their chins up in greeting. Rick returned the gesture and took the stairs tucked in the back right corner of the garage two at a time.

Jade had named the retro yet state-of-art pub in the front Triggs' Triad as a secret nod to the three businesses she ran in the building — the pub faced the street, the Mavens' garage was around back, and the actual Mavens business hid above the pub and garage. To enter the second and third floors of the building, you had to pass significant security measures — fingerprint scanners, voice identification, weight matching, heat signatures, saliva analysis — anything that was picked for that day to accompany the cameras trained on the entry. Some of the measures were inside jokes they had built over the years, but it guaranteed no one could con their way in.

At the top of the stairs, Rick took in the start of today's security measures. The symbol-based panel was out, so he started with that entry code: ₹ɒΩẓℲ. A black touch screen opened directly above the symbol panel with the directions: "Write your Latin identifier backwards." Rick rolled his eyes at the new prompt; it was a handwriting prompt that changed regularly. When he didn't see a stylus, he tugged off his glove and used his finger to write "s a t i r e v." The screen blinked red, and he knew Jeremy was inside messing with him because the screen's question changed to "What did S threaten D with last week?" Rick glared up at the camera and could easily imagine Jeremy laughing at his expense. Shaking his head, Rick wrote "appendage trampling" in reference to Susan's impatience with Dave during a training session when he wouldn't tone down his innuendos while they sparred. The door unlocked.

Rick stepped into the small freezing cold foyer made of metal panels and waited for it to do its thing. He didn't know if the floor was measuring his general weight today or his mass index, or if sensors were cataloging his body heat or recording his breathing rhythm...

Impatient, his mouth pulled to the side. A minute later, the inner door across from the entrance opened, and he was fully inside their headquarters.

He strode down the dark gray hallway to the fourth door on the left and stepped inside Team Gamma's primary tech and meeting room. Team Delta, their team of dog hybrids, and Team Kappa, their team of cat hybrids, each had their own primary rooms. Other doors on the second floor led to their two in-house medical rooms, a shared kitchen and lounge, and an even more secure access staircase to the third floor where their boss Jade's office was. The Maven's fourth team was Team Pi Rho; they were a mix of various hybrids with honorable discharges from different military branches and only had a down room off the garage on the ground floor; they were the public faces of the Mavens and the only team that exceeded seven members.

In his team's room, Jeremy was sitting halfway down the long right wall, smirking. Well, he was smirking as much as a six-foot black cockatoo hybrid in jeans and a polo could smirk; his beak didn't allow for the most mobile of expressions. Which was why he spent so much time in his hybrid form — he could easily hide his reactions. In human form, Jeremy had trouble stopping whatever he was thinking from playing out across his face. His feet were propped up on the edge of the main computer desk in front of several screens he'd claimed, which was to the left of the five or so surveillance feeds they had running at any given time. The room as a whole felt empty with just the two of them; most of the time they worked in teams of three. Generally, at least one more of their team members would be around, sitting at the large conference table or checking something out on the other, smaller computer setup past Jeremy. Or all six of them would be there.

"What gives?" grumbled Rick. He stalked to one of the chairs between Jeremy and the large conference table and straddled the seat, crossing his arms across the chair back. He didn't bother taking in the view out the wall of floor-to-ceiling windows directly across from the door, past the conference table. He'd seen the view a hundred times before and the treetops of the park weren't as important as stopping Melissa from getting herself into more trouble than she could handle.

"You're the one who called me in on the first official day of our vacation. I'm entitled to make you jump through at least one extra hoop. I, unlike you, was actually on vacation. What does Jade have you working on?"

"She doesn't have me working on anything. I need a favor."

The sound of Jeremy's feet dropping to the ground as he swiveled his chair to fully face Rick echoed in the tech room.

"Of course," Jeremy answered.

At Jeremy's earnest response, it occurred to Rick that he'd never asked anyone on his team for a favor despite working together in life and death situations for close to a decade. Rick rubbed the back of his neck to try to smooth away the awkward chill he'd gotten at the realization. He pulled the snorting tube from Tommy's nightstand out of his pocket and held it out to Jeremy.

"I need you to confirm it's Nip, and if possible, narrow down the dealer."

Jeremy took the proffered baggy from him and went straight over to their testing station along the wall opposite of his computer station. Jeremy was their team tech wizard, with Shawn being a close second, and while the Mavens sent stuff out to a few trusted labs for analysis, they had a handful of machines at hand for quick identification tasks.

"I also have photos that might help with your search for dealers," Rick said over the whir of the machine Jeremy had started up.

"Email them to me," Jeremy said without turning around.

Rick sent the snap of Theo Barre's headshot Neil had and a few of Tommy from his social media to Jeremy. While Jeremy worked with the snorting tube, Rick fired up the computer to the left of Jeremy's station and checked the records in their system for Theo Barre just in case one of their teams had dealt with him before. Their system came up empty.

He would have to leave digging for information in various databases they may or may not have been granted access to to Jeremy. After his stint in the NSA, Jeremy had his feathers plugged into too many cyber crannies to count, and none of them — not even their boss Jade — asked for specifics. Rick's team joked that the cockatoo half of Jeremy mainlined computer bytes. He looked positively wired with how his eyes constantly twitched between his multiple screens. Both Jeremy's eyes and his feet were common physical changes for bird hybrids that differed from basic human anatomy: his eyes shifted out to the sides of his head a fair amount, and his feet split into talons, necessitating specifically designed glasses and boots that accommodated his body in both forms.

"It's just your run-of-the-mill Nip," Jeremy said, not turning away from the task at hand. "Barely any crystals, but enough to say there aren't any particular markers to point to a certain supplier. There're two types present: a low-grade that's mostly catnip and a high-grade that's much closer to pure cocaine. The latter is a little fresher."

"What does that tell us?" Rick asked. He didn't think Tommy had come into a windfall if it was true his parents cut him off. He shouldn't have been able to afford higher grade Nip.

"That whoever you swiped this off of needed his next fix faster than he was used to." Jeremy walked over and sat down at his computer station — all three screens of it. He typed Theo Barre into a search engine Rick wouldn't mess with himself; he didn't know how to navigate the hacking software like Jeremy did.

"I know you said this was a favor, but this seems a lot like work."

"Was there a question in there?" Rick looked at Jeremy out of the corner of his eye, waiting. They'd taken down a drug lord or five for the government over the years, but only when they got so out of hand that it needed to be done off the record. So, while this wasn't their first time dealing with drugs, it was way below their pay grade.

"Why are we doing this?"

"A friend of mine needs help."

"No offense, but you never mention friends outside of the team. I think most of us assumed you didn't have any."

Rick tipped his head back in hopes the ceiling might collapse on him and save him from such conversations, but it did no such thing. Between the revelation that he'd never asked his team for a favor and that his team also thought they were his only social life — true or not — Rick missed having Bobby around more than he typically did. Bobby had kept him grounded, but that might have just been because Rick spent most of his time at Bobby's side making sure his best friend didn't finally cross the line of no return and do something truly awful. Bobby kept him so busy Rick didn't have time to meet other people, and he hadn't bothered to remedy that since Bobby's disappearance. That realization didn't feel particularly great.

When Rick didn't say anything, Jeremy continued: "Does this friend have a Nip problem?"

"No. My friend's friend got physically accosted at work because their idiot brother has a Nip problem."

"This guy showed up?" Jeremy pointed at Theo Barre's photo on his computer screen.

Rick grunted the affirmative.

"The brother must be into something bad," Jeremy muttered.

"I figured."

"Theo Barre has supposedly graduated from being a tracker and muscle for various drug rings. He isn't known for his finesse, and the court files from the time he got nailed show he was a slice away from killing the guy. He's apparently the new face of the Wrappers."

"Rappers? Like the type of musicians?" Rick's brow furrowed. He'd never heard of a musician drug ring.

"No, like candy wrappers. They sell their hits in different colored candy-looking wrappers that appeal to kids and to the already high. They're a big problem twenty minutes east in Lunser. Their drugs have trickled over here in Placerton, but they don't have a foothold here as far as anyone knows. Is the friend's brother local or over in Lunser?"

"Granberg." Rick said his hometown like it was a curse.

It wasn't lost on Rick that Jeremy had stuck to protocol and asked rather than just pulling up the GPS hits from Rick's watch and bike the last few days to make an educated guess. They weren't supposed to look at the tracking unless it was needed for a job, and Rick appreciated that everyone followed policy as far as he knew.

Jeremy looked at Rick askance.

"Is this friend the turtle you and—" Jeremy stopped speaking. No one ever mentioned Bobby to Rick. He hadn't taken his best friend's disappearance well, to say the least, and no one on the team forgot that. Even though he exclusively interacted with people who knew Bobby, Melissa and Neil were the only ones who ever said Bobby's name around him.

"No, it's not, but he's hooked into the local law enforcement somehow and is more or less the local teenager rehab support guru, getting kids off drugs. He's how we have Theo Barre's name at all."

"When did this all go down? And where? I'll pull up security footage in the area and see if I can pick out his movements or car or something."

"Saturday morning at Juniper's Java. The camera inside is so ancient it likely only has local backup."

Rick watched as Jeremy's fingers froze for an instant before they started flying over the keyboard to pull up street cameras around Melissa's coffee shop.

"I thought his parents were professors. I didn't know they had a coffee shop."

"They are professors, and they don't."

"Then who—"

"Melissa opened it just before he disappeared."

Jeremy's head cocked to the side, and he swiveled one eye at Rick, resembling a bird more than a human for a second. He'd stopped typing and the silence between them pressed down on Rick.

"You know how protective he was of her," Jeremy said, eyeing Rick. "He had that family photo he carried around. You know the one." Rick nodded. The photo had changed over the years. The Junipers had a family joke of taking a nearly identical photo every year. They even tried to wear the same clothes as the year before, but as Bobby and Melissa grew up, their clothes had to be swapped out. "When Dave said that Melissa was pretty, he made it clear if any of us touched her, he'd make sure it was the last thing we did." Rick hadn't missed that, although this was the first time someone on his team had talked about Bobby in three years, Jeremy still didn't say his name.

"Imagine how poorly he handled her dating," Rick grumbled while his conscience berated him. He'd definitely been touching Melissa of late, even if it wasn't skin to skin for the most part. He could still feel her body pressed against his side if he closed his eyes. Bobby would not approve.

"How friendly are the two of you?" Jeremy finally asked.

Rick just glared at him.

Jeremy gave him a somewhat pitying smile that didn't make Rick feel any better. It was common knowledge on the team that Rick didn't date. He'd tried. He had. At some point, they had to touch each other, and the things his dates said were things you never wanted to know. They were hung up on their ex. Their friends had a challenge to see how many members of the Mavens Motorcycle Club they could sleep with that month; he would make five. They thought it weird that he hadn't kiss them by the third date and was just trying to hold their hand then, did he have a *problem*? They thought he'd be more aggressive in making moves on them. They didn't think he was relationship material but wanted to take a spin on his *engine*. Nothing was ever said that made him want to pursue the dates further.

Luckily for Rick's morose thoughts, Jeremy had gone back to searching and hadn't come up empty. Rick found himself looking at the reported hierarchy of the Wrappers. There weren't a lot of facts, but rather a lot of supposition. The Wrappers were particularly good at not getting caught. They carried actual candy in their drug wrappers and none of the dealers ever had drugs on their person. Only the users who bought from them had drugs in the candy wrappers. Enforcement was stumped. They didn't know how the dealers were hiding the drugs when they got searched.

All clues pointed to Allison Barre and her brother, Theo, as the top dogs — literally, as they were both husky hybrids, very wolf-like huskies. Allison ran the family candy factory, Barres™, and was reported to have the smarts to be in charge of a dual candy and drug operation, even if no connection had ever been proven. Theo, at a glance, seemed more likely to be the main boss, but he wasn't known to be cunning. He was known for his sadistic tendencies.

The only other person listed as significantly involved with the ringleaders was Matt Helms. Everyone wrote him off because he was a full-human rather than a hybrid and was just Allison's boyfriend, but that was not a mistake Rick was going to make. Rick knew it was complete bull that humans had remained normal after the Crisis while their hybrid compatriots had changed. Humans were even more diverse and unpredictable than hybrids. With hybrids, you could deduce some of their specialized skill sets from their hybrid type, but humans, you never knew what they could do. Each one had their own special *talent*. Rick himself was just one of the more outwardly disruptive examples. Most flew under the radar.

"I'm going to go check out the factory," Rick said.

"I thought you might. Shawn will be here soon to go with you. I'm going to keep digging."

Rick didn't argue. It'd be nice to have the only dog hybrid on their team with him. Shawn had originally been an emergency addition to their team for a single job where they knew they'd need a trained medic on hand. He'd meshed so well with Team Gamma that they'd kept him. It helped that his computer skills weren't too shabby either. He wasn't Jeremy, but he could get the job done. And what really counted for Rick right then was that Shawn was laid-back; unlike Jeremy, he wouldn't hint at something more between him and Melissa.

Chapter 11

Melissa

"Eight!" Tiffany shouted. Her blond hair swished over her shoulder as she gave Melissa and Kate a triumphant look. She had started up the ASS game, or the "accidental shift spotting" game, when she'd arrived for her shift, and she was relentless. Melissa looked around the coffee shop, and over by the tables near the bathroom, she saw the spotted puppy hybrid in the stroller that had been in its human form a minute ago.

Tiffany's nose twitched, drawing Kate's eyes back to her automatically. Melissa found it quite humorous to watch predator and prey hybrids interact. Both Kate and Tiffany were in their human forms, but there was just enough cat in Kate for her to eye the mouse in Tiffany. The fact that, in their case, the mouse hybrid was taller than the cat hybrid didn't matter. At the instinctual level, predator and prey hybrids had just a touch more awareness of the other, even if it was reduced to awareness and not any type of aggression or fear. What type of hybrid you were had nothing to do with your actual aggression levels. It was why so many people misunderstood the scarier or larger hybrids. They just assumed that the more predatory the animal that saved you — or technically saved your parents or your grandparents at this point — translated to your personality, but that had never been the case.

"Nine," Kate said, more automatically than with her heart in the game.

Tiffany and Melissa looked around. Melissa frothed a customer's hot chocolate as she searched, but both she and Tiffany came up empty-handed.

"Can't find it," Tiffany finally admitted.

"The frog outside sneezed," Kate said. Melissa and Tiffany looked out the front window. There was indeed a teenage-looking frog hybrid with bulging eyes and green, wet-looking skin.

"I always forget to watch outside," Tiffany muttered to herself as a reprimand.

Melissa couldn't help but smile. As hybrids grew up, they gained more and more control over their shifts, but as kids and teenagers, life could be unpredictable. Allergies? Better make sure your clothes are comfortable for constant body changes. Embarrassed? Don't worry, everyone already knows because you shifted unintentionally. Even as adults, a shift could be triggered unexpectedly, like when Kate's wrist was grabbed and she shifted into her cat form.

The secondary facet to the game, which was why Melissa actively encouraged it when someone suggested playing, was that if they were constantly looking for any change in their customers, they were all *aware* of their customers' needs. That made them extra responsive to empty tables that needed to be wiped down and wrong orders that were sipped by disappointed customers. On game days, there were rarely dissatisfied customers.

Even if they hadn't been playing the ASS game, Melissa would have spotted the two newcomers the moment they came in. The bell above the door tinkled and more than half of the coffee shop held their breath in admiration. Melissa nearly laughed. It was worse than when Rick came in, but then again, he came in alone. The two newcomers' black leather jackets didn't match since one looked more GQ and the other more broken in, but Melissa was sure they had ridden there, even if she didn't see their bikes out front.

One of them was a lean, athletic-looking Bengal cat hybrid with slightly rounded ears who sauntered in like he knew he was hot — it wasn't quite flat-out arrogance, but it bordered on excessive confidence. He was in the GQ style jacket. The other guy had his black hair shaved close to control what likely became an afro as it grew. He had long stubble that might need a shave or was just how he wore it. He also wore glasses with an adjustable bridge, which gave away that he was a hybrid whose eyes moved significantly when he shifted.

The cat hybrid got in line, ignoring all the eyes glued to him. He was sizing up Kate, who was behind the espresso machine. Melissa frowned at that. Attractive or not, anyone who was interested in Kate at the moment was bad news. Period. She was too nervous from everything going on with her brother to deal with someone approaching her.

Suspicious, Melissa watched the other hybrid as he walked over to a vacant table and shrugged his leather jacket off to hang over the back of a chair. He had a light blue polo shirt on, which did not fit the biker look he had with the jacket. Reaching behind him, he untucked the back of the polo, revealing a long flap. Whatever he was, he had a tail. Long backs of shirts were favored by tailed hybrids who wanted to cover how their pants fit around their backside. Then, he put his boot up on the chair and unzipped the center of the shoe from the front of his ankle, over the center tip, and all the way down the sole. He repeated the action with his other foot. So Melissa knew he had larger feet too. When he straightened, he looked her in the eye and winked.

Just like that, his hair sprung up into long exotic feathers and she was looking at the face of a black cockatoo. His arms had just enough feathers he might be able to sustain flight, but Melissa wasn't sure; most bird hybrids couldn't fly, but there were a fair amount who could. No one called out a number; his shift had clearly been an intentional one. One that every eye in the shop had been watching, and he knew it.

Melissa fought an eyeroll at the cockatoo hybrid's confidence and finished taking an order from a woman who she thought looked a lot like a hedgehog hybrid who had been in the previous month. It was hard to tell if a customer was the same person or not between shifts unless they were a regular.

Next in line was the cat hybrid, who had stopped sizing up Kate and switched his full attention to Melissa. Up close, the small rosette markings on his face were startling in their distinct patterns. His fur looked like sand covered with deep brown pebbles. His nose was slightly flattened compared to a normal human nose, and his lips and chin had the slightest muzzle shape. The cockatoo hybrid joined him at the counter, but his eyes analyzed the coffee shop with more than a casual interest, which had Melissa's guard up. The way they held their bodies at the ready wasn't normal.

"What can I get for you?" she asked, berating herself for making assumptions based on appearances. It just wasn't like her. Rick was not a good influence on her in that regard. She needed to ignore his paranoia.

The cockatoo hybrid's attention focused in on her. His nose to chin had merged into a small flat gray beak, and his eyes had moved several inches farther apart and taken on the swivel look that hinted he might be able to look in different directions at once. His iconic cockatoo head feathers still stood on end, which made Melissa wonder who he was trying to impress with his alertness or if he was on edge about something.

"I'll have the pineapple iced tea," he said. Melissa thought his eyes might have smiled at her, but it was hard to tell.

"And I'll have," the cat hybrid said low and throaty like a purr, "whatever her favorite is." He tipped an ear to Kate.

Melissa narrowed her eyes at him, but, before she could say anything, the cockatoo hybrid's arm snapped out to the side and socked his friend in the stomach.

"What was that for?" he hissed.

"Don't be an ass," the cockatoo hybrid replied. "He'll have a coffee with one of your herd animal syrups. He won't care which."

He pulled his wallet out of his back pocket and that was when Melissa saw it — a swooping M with a little motorcycle in the middle. Her eyes flicked to his watch. It was the same as Rick and Bobby's old watch. Now their alertness made sense; they were Mavens, too. She smiled and reached out, putting her hand over the cockatoo hybrid's lightly feathered one on his wallet. Leaning forward just that little bit brought a hint of a motor oil smell from their bikes to her nose, reminding her of Bobby and Rick when they'd been working on their bikes.

"It's on the house," she laughed.

The cat hybrid blinked at her suspiciously, and the cockatoo hybrid tipped his head to the side.

"What—" the cat hybrid started.

"Tiffany, drag Ilona out from the back," Melissa said. "I'm going to sit with these two and chat."

"How—" the cat hybrid started again. He turned to the cockatoo hybrid and hissed, "No photos, that's a rule."

Turning to whip up their order, Melissa heard the cockatoo hybrid mutter, "That's a legitimate question." She didn't know what either of them were talking about, but she didn't worry about it; neither comment was directed to her.

Melissa turned back with their drinks and walked over to their table with them following. She hoped she would get some answers about their mysterious motorcycle club that was anything but that.

"I'm Melissa," she said, sitting down and smiling at them as they slowly lowered themselves into the other chairs.

"We know." The cat hybrid was looking over his shoulder for Kate as he responded.

The cockatoo hybrid just watched her.

"You're Rick's friends, right?" she asked, just to confirm.

"How did you know?" the cockatoo hybrid asked. The cat hybrid turned back to focus on her, too.

"Your wallet." Melissa said. "It has the Mavens logo on it. Like Rick's gloves and Bobby's vest. You both have the same watch, too." Melissa had always found the watches odd, but only because she'd held Bobby's; it was weirdly heavy compared to her own watches or even their dad's. She'd found Bobby's in his sock drawer when she'd moved back into her parents' house, which was odd since he had never seemed to go anywhere without it before he died.

The men glanced at each other when she said Bobby's name; they had known him, or at least knew of him. Her gut clenched at the thought. Maybe they could tell her more about her brother.

"It's a very discrete logo," the cat hybrid said. Melissa looked him over to see if she could spot where he had his logo, but it didn't pop out to her, and shrugged because she didn't care if it was discrete or not. The logo and wearing the same watch as Bobby and Rick was enough for her to make a connection.

"We're being rude," the cockatoo hybrid said, his crest still standing on end. "I'm Jeremy, and this is Dave."

"What brings you to Granberg?" Melissa asked.

"Eleven," Ilona chirped from behind the counter.

"Twelve!" Tiffany called.

Melissa vaguely wondered if someone had the hiccups as Jeremy and Dave glanced at the three women — or two women and bird hybrid — behind the counter.

"Who's the brunette behind the counter?" Dave asked instead of answering Melissa's question or addressing the random numbers being yelled out.

"My best friend Kate."

"Who has the brother?" Jeremy said cryptically.

Melissa nodded; Rick must have mentioned Tommy to them.

Dave's cheeks fell. "She probably isn't in the mood for a distraction then."

"Not a Dave-flavored one," Jeremy said dryly. "So, Melissa. How would you feel about having modern security cameras installed?"

"That it seems unnecessary?" Melissa searched their faces for a clue as to why this was coming up. She'd never considered getting new cameras. "I've never had any serious issues. Even when that guy came in the other day, the one that has Rick so worried, nothing happened. Rick saw the whole thing. The guy just walked out."

"Rick was here for that?" Dave asked sharply, turning away from his surveillance of Kate. "And he didn't do something?"

"He didn't *need* to. The guy was harmless."

Dave and Jeremy exchanged a glance. Obviously, they didn't agree with her assessment either. Melissa wondered how much of their over-protectiveness came from being around Bobby.

"We've voted and decided it is necessary," Jeremy said.

"We?"

"Yes. Dave, Susan, Shawn, Carl, and I voted yes. Jade even approved the expense."

Melissa blinked at the sudden list of names she'd never heard and that someone named Jade had approved the expense. None of that sounded like a motorcycle club. It sounded more like a protection agency, which seemed a little more like something Bobby and Rick would be involved with, but not something they'd pretend was anything but what it was.

Regardless of the slew of unknown people, Melissa noticed one person was unaccounted for on the list. "Rick didn't vote yes?"

"He wasn't consulted," Dave tossed out. "You're Bobby's little sister, so of course we want to help."

Melissa was momentarily struck silent. She blinked fiercely to contain the tears that wanted to spill out. It had been years since she'd cried about Bobby. In all honesty, no one ever brought him up to her. No one said his name. Not even her parents. Sometimes it felt like he hadn't existed for anyone but her.

"We'd do the same for my little sister," Jeremy assured her in a quiet voice that told Melissa he'd noticed she was fighting off tears.

Melissa latched onto the new fact and focused on Jeremy rather than how great Bobby's friends were. She pushed away the emotion that constricted her throat and asked, "You have a sister? Is she a cockatoo too?" Melissa wrinkled her nose at the "tutu" she'd just said.

"Naw, she's a poodle. My dad, much to his embarrassment in his younger years, is a poodle hybrid. My mom's a cockatoo but peach."

"My parents would love to peek at your genetics. That's their research focus at the moment. They're trying to map out how genes and abilities are passed down so we're equipped to create better medicines in the future." Granted her parents might feel awkward working with one of Bobby's friends; they were so weird about anything that had to do with Bobby since he died.

"I can tell you my sister's fur is a little feathery for a poodle and my feathers will NOT lie flat, which we think comes from the poodle's tendency to puff out. My black coloring comes from my dad; he's a black poodle." Melissa glanced up at his raised crest while she assimilated the information that it wasn't an indicator of anything.

A slight shadow fell over their table, and Melissa looked up to see a familiar face with an unfamiliar scowl.

"Neil!" She jumped up and hugged him tight. He distinctly smelled like soap and pond water. His clothes gave off the impression he was a relaxed surfer dude, but the tension in his body as she hugged him sent a different message. She was clearly more emotional from Jeremy and Dave's offer to look out for her than she'd realized. She couldn't recall hugging Neil with such enthusiasm before. Or ever hugging him, for that matter. Bobby, Rick, and Neil hadn't been big on touch starting around middle school. They didn't touch each other, and they didn't touch other people. Reining herself in, Melissa released Neil.

"Are these guys bothering you, Mel?" he asked.

Shocked back to reality by Neil's harsh tone, not one she'd ever heard him use before, Melissa looked at Jeremy and Dave. They both looked like they wanted to tear Neil apart, too.

"Neil, this is Dave and Jeremy. They're Rick's friends."

"He tell you that?" Neil's suspicion shocked her.

"You the turtle?" Jeremy asked.

Neil's nod was slow, like all his movements.

"The name you gave us was a big help."

Melissa could feel the mysterious and unwarranted tension leave the group, and Neil slowly lowered himself into Melissa's empty seat.

"Are you sure she wouldn't like a distraction?" Dave asked, glancing over at Kate again.

"I'm sure," Jeremy said in the same dry tone as before.

"I'll do a lap and look for suspicious people." Dave disappeared before anyone could respond.

"What name?" Melissa asked.

"What's the plan?" Neil ignored her question. Melissa felt like a little kid again — excluded from her big brother's antics. It punched home the fact that these guys all knew her brother, likely well, and treated her much like he did. It was both weirdly soothing and intensely irritating. Oddly, that feeling was accompanied by a certainty that if Rick were here, he wouldn't ignore her. He never had, even when they were kids.

"I'm going to be installing cameras." Jeremy twirled a finger around to indicate the perimeter of the room.

"Good." Neil nodded.

"I haven't agreed to that," Melissa pushed out, trying to insert herself into the decisions about her coffee shop. Whatever was decided, she had the final say. It was *her* coffee shop.

"Melissa," Kate called from the counter.

"I have to go take care of something." Melissa frowned at the timing. "Neil, I'll have Kate bring over your usual." She didn't want Neil to have to get up and slowly amble through the line and then walk over to get his drink. Twice, she'd seen him do that and frown at his first sip because it wasn't piping hot by the time he sat down at an open table.

When Melissa turned to the counter, her eyes widened. There was a long line. She'd been so caught up in her emotions about Bobby and in what Jeremy and Dave said that she hadn't even noticed. She hurried up front and helped handle the rush of people. After fifteen minutes, they had it under control. Melissa almost forgot to send

Kate over with Neil's drink, but when Kate took it over, she sat down and chatted with Neil and Jeremy. Melissa could have sworn Kate smiled a few times.

Chapter 12

Rick

Rick looked around the bare, windowless room he'd woken in. It was one of the recovery rooms at headquarters — clinically clean and smelling like antiseptic. A faint glow slipped under the door to the hall. He was on a cot, and there weren't any medical supplies out at the moment. It took him a minute to realize he wasn't injured like he normally was when he woke up there; he had just crashed there after he and Shawn had finished planting surveillance cameras around the Barres™ candy factory. He had been bone tired and half-asleep by the time they got back to the garage. Rick hadn't wanted to ride his bike the hour to his apartment, both because he was exhausted and because that would have put him an hour farther from Granberg and Melissa.

Besides putting up cameras outside the factory, the rest of the stakeout had been a bust. He and Shawn had managed to see some faces, but that was it. Allison Barre had been present and dressed in CEO-chic: gray slacks, blood-red top, black blazer, and tall black stiletto heels that looked like they could serve as knives in a fight.

She was either born naturally gray-haired or she dyed it that way. In either case, she didn't look older than twenty, even with the gray hair. Her brother Theo made a brief appearance with Matt Helms, the person Rick was most interested in learning about. Unlike his sister, Theo was obviously not there to do officially sanctioned business with the factory in a tight-fitting tee, jeans, and the same ripped jacket from when he'd grabbed Kate's wrist. Matt seemed like an average guy. He wore a gray dress shirt with the sleeves rolled up. The two men were inside the factory for less than an hour around sunset. The fact that Matt had arrived and left with Theo confirmed to Rick that Matt had something to do with the drug side of their business and not Barres™. They'd have to dig deeper into Matt's history.

The only other noteworthy thing Rick and Shawn observed was Allison looking rather cozy with Matt in her office before she pulled the blinds shut, which confirmed the intel that the two were doing things they didn't want observed. Neither Shawn nor Rick knew what kind of *business* they were conducting, but they both doubted it was about Barres™. At no point throughout the night had the factory completely emptied of workers, so Rick and Shawn couldn't go in to look around or install cameras and listening devices. When the morning shift started to trickle in, Rick and Shawn left.

Checking his watch, Rick saw it was close to four in the afternoon. He had to get back to Granberg. He had no doubt that, should he not return like he had promised, Melissa would do her own investigating and wind up in a heap of trouble. Before leaving, he popped his head into the computer room to see what Jeremy had dug up after he and Shawn had left the day before. Rick hadn't expected to find Susan in her typical overalls and her platinum blonde mane in Heidi-braids sitting in front of the wall of security screens they used when monitoring locations during jobs.

"Did Jeremy call *everyone* in?" he asked her, going straight to Jeremy's empty chair on her left.

"*You* should have. It's the little Juniper." Her accusing look said more than it didn't. There was nothing that irked Susan more than not being given the full picture. She'd gotten more than enough of that in the two years she worked for the CIA. "But no, he didn't. Jade did."

Rick froze.

"What do you mean Jade did?" He had asked Jeremy for a favor. Even having Shawn there was an encroachment on their vacations. Rick hadn't wanted to make this into a big thing. Eventually, he might have called the rest of the team in if he thought it was necessary; it was his prerogative as one of the team leads, but he definitely hadn't planned on looping their boss in. "What did Jeremy say to her? Where is he now?" His voice had gotten louder with each question, but luckily no one else was around. He didn't know how this had spiraled out of control.

"He just finished installing cameras."

"Where?"

"At Melissa's coffee shop." Susan turned her chair so she could look Rick in the eye. Her head tilted to the side, and she narrowed her eyes at him; she clearly hadn't missed him raising his voice. "For now, they're just the slap on ones. Jeremy and Jade are considering more permanent ones since the area had such a bad reputation not all that long ago. As it is, there are almost no street cameras to piggy-back either." She frowned. "Do you have any idea what happened to turn the area around? Jeremy scoured all the city documents he could get his hands on and didn't see any mention of city-planning in that area. Until three years ago, the only documents that mentioned it at all were police reports. Of the nasty variety."

Rick didn't want to lie to Susan, but he also felt conflicted about sharing Melissa's *talent* with anyone who might drop it in a tactical report. For goodness sakes, he'd never even told Bobby, and Melissa was his sister. The only person who knew Rick's suspicion that all humans who had survived the Crisis and been born since had some sort of special *talent* was Neil, and Neil wasn't convinced. Instead of saying any of that, Rick prevaricated with the truth, just not the full truth.

"There weren't any city efforts made," he confirmed. "The neighborhood community appeared to have a sudden uptick in good residents."

Susan's disbelieving snort made him flinch. "An uptick without any resident turnover?"

"That sounds correct." Rick held Susan's gaze and had intended to wait her out, but then what she said sunk in. "What do you mean Jeremy is installing cameras at Melissa's coffee shop? You mean he went there? How'd he introduce himself? How'd he play off being there to install security cameras? What did Melissa do? She can't just be letting anyone install cameras in her shop."

She narrowed her eyes at him. "Protective much?"

Rick glared at her accusation. He didn't care that it was accurate. Furthermore, when he got back to Granberg, he was going to sit down and go through Melissa's social media accounts with her to work on her settings. He'd considered just going back in and changing them, but that would be overstepping.

"Anyway." Susan rolled her eyes. "They didn't have to tell her anything. Melissa made them. She's either very observant, or Bobby told her something." Rick flinched at Susan's blunt use of Bobby's name, but she didn't let that stop her. "Jeremy tried to pay for his and Dave's drinks—"

"Dave went too?" Rick growled, focusing on that important detail instead of Susan talking about Bobby. He didn't want Dave near Melissa. The hybrid was the definition of a player. He liked the ladies, and sadly, the ladies didn't shove his ego down his throat and reject him.

"—and Melissa recognized our logo on his wallet. When they asked how she knew it, she said it was on Bobby's vest and your gloves. The way Dave tells it, she didn't even flinch at us having the resources to install security cameras. And she didn't show any recognition or lack of recognition, which is more noteworthy, when all our names were dropped. Honestly, it'd be worth finding out what Bobby told her about us. Just her knowledge about us could make her a target. I didn't think we'd told anyone beyond maybe our parents the truth. It puts them at too much of a risk."

He slumped in his chair. Taking a deep breath, he forced Bobby's name out: "Bobby didn't *tell* her anything." Rick was sure Bobby hadn't shared, but he wouldn't have needed to if he wanted his sister to think something else. His *talent* would have taken care of that.

"Meaning... you did?" Susan's voice was hesitant but determined.

"Nothing like you're thinking. Melissa is—" Rick searched for a good word, but went with the banal. "She's trusting. She doesn't think anyone is out to do harm."

"Dave said something along those lines. Something about her thinking this Theo character was harmless after he almost dragged her best friend from the shop. But what did you tell her?" When Rick didn't answer, Susan said, "You can either tell me, or I'll go get Jade and you can tell her."

Rick looked at the ceiling, replaying the past few days. "I told her I'd help her find out what's going on with Tommy Nolan, which I was already doing when she broke into Tommy's place while I was searching it."

Susan's snorted neigh made Rick's frown deepen. It had been a long time since anyone had snuck up on him while he was snooping around somewhere he shouldn't have been.

"While I had intended to look into the matter alone, she offhandedly threatened to continue on her own since picking locks couldn't be that hard given how quickly I'd relocked Tommy's when I made her leave his apartment."

"Worst case," Susan mused, "she would have gotten picked up by the cops for attempted B&E."

"You don't know Mel," Rick groaned aloud, hoping he sounded distressed rather than turned on by the memory. "I couldn't let her get herself into trouble. I *had* to agree to take her with me. We went back the next night, and I let her pick the lock. It took her less than thirty seconds."

"That's remarkable," Susan said, sitting up straighter. Her mind was clearly running with an idea that Rick wasn't sure he was going to like.

"Based on our search, she now knows I have some level of hacking abilities, talked to someone who has photos of people dealing drugs, and can get drugs tested somewhere."

"Rick..." Susan's voice trailed off.

"I know." And he did. This was not good. None of them shared what they were really doing with anyone. Even Neil didn't know *what* the Mavens did. He just knew it wasn't what it seemed. Melissa already knew more than that. "She was a little taken aback by those facts but didn't question me much at all. She truly believes people are good."

Rick wasn't even sure what impression Bobby wanted her to have of his job as a mechanic in a motorcycle club. Following protocol to the letter wasn't exactly Bobby's style, so it was unlikely he wanted her to think he actually was a mechanic. He would have wanted her to know they were something else, even if he never told her *what*.

"If she's trying to dig stuff up on Tommy herself and believes that, we aren't going to be able to stop her unless—" Susan paused and got a sneaky smile on her face that had Rick narrowing his eyes with distrust.

"Unless what?"

"Unless *you* keep her out of trouble."

"I had kind of figured that out myself," he muttered.

Susan looked delighted by the idea. She hid it well, but Rick knew she was a romantic at heart. Now that she'd heard he was comfortable enough with Melissa to talk to her about some of the stuff the Mavens did, there was no going back. Susan knew exactly how pitiful his dating life had been, and he could see it in her eyes — she was dreaming big dreams for him and Bobby's little sister. And if it wasn't romance on her mind, she was, at the very least, concocting an excuse to befriend Melissa; she had complained more than once about the acute dearth of feminine energy in the Mavens.

Rick, on the other hand, worked hard to remind himself of all the different things Bobby had done to Melissa's boyfriends, planned to do to the next one, and threatened any and all of his friends with should they even look at her in a way he didn't like. Rick needed to remember why he needed to keep a little distance between himself and Melissa.

After several minutes of silence, something stood out to Rick from their conversation. "Why was all your information from Dave? What did Jeremy report?"

"He hasn't reported in," Susan said with a shrug. "Dave tailed Melissa home, discreetly, but given how aware she is of things, maybe he wasn't discrete enough. He was surprised to learn that she lived next door to your mother, by the way. He joked about stopping by and introducing himself."

Rick was not amused. Bobby and Carl had met his mother, but only because they knew her from before joining the Mavens. "And why hasn't Jeremy reported in?"

"From what I can see on the security cameras, he's having a great time chatting with a dark blond surfer guy and a brunette with a pixie cut that looks like ears. Someone came and joined them recently that I haven't IDed yet."

Rick sat up at the mention of Neil. Scanning the screens in front of Susan, he saw one that had several angles of Melissa's coffee shop. One view was from a vantage near the door, showing the front counter. Jeremy had also gotten two side views that showed most of the shop and a little of the front windows. Sure enough, in all three shots, there was Jeremy, Neil, Kate, and the news anchor from Granberg's local news station. Rick couldn't remember her name. He thought his mother might have told him that the rabbit hybrid was one of Melissa's friends; if his mother had told him, she'd only said it once or he'd be certain.

"We'll need a good view of the front sidewalk," Rick pointed out. "And the staff area in back. There's a door into an alley there." He paused. "Maybe a camera in the back alley, too."

"I'll note that down, but I don't know if Jeremy can reasonably get into the staff area without Melissa there."

"I can do it if we need."

After staring at the collision of his two worlds for a moment, Rick pulled out his phone and sent a group message to Neil and Jeremy telling them to make sure Kate got home safely. He didn't want something to happen to her; one because he didn't want something to happen to her, and two because Melissa would feel horrible about it. On the computer screen, Jeremy and Neil both glanced at their phones; technically, Jeremy glanced at his before Neil even got his out of his pocket.

"Since Melissa has been home for an hour now, you should get going to make sure she doesn't get into anything all by her lonesome. I'm sure whatever she has planned, she could use an extra hand for." Susan's teasing comment hit Rick hard in the gut with an unprompted image of what Melissa could get up to at home alone or how he might be able to assist her with it. The horse hybrid's smirk told him that she'd been spending way too much time working with Dave and had indeed meant to imply the dirty images that Rick's mind had supplied.

Rick just growled and left while Susan chuckled at his sour mood. He had to admit that maybe *he* was the one spending too much time with Dave, or maybe Shawn if he was just growling at people to show his displeasure. Regardless, by the time he pulled up in front of his mother's house, he was nervous about what Melissa would say after meeting his friends. Rather than go into his house, he walked over to Melissa's and knocked.

Chapter 13

Melissa

A bang against her back wrenched Melissa from her memories of Bobby — him helping her up when she'd fallen on her first two-wheeler; him glaring at guys back in high school; him bashing every ex of hers that decided she was too good for them (which was nearly every ex of hers). Another bang. It reverberated through her body. Melissa looked around, just then realizing she had sunk to the floor against the front door when she had gotten home, unable to fight the emotions she'd bottled up.

Coats hung above her to the left, hidden when the front door was open, but currently poofed out because she'd never put away any of the jackets there — not even Bobby's from his last visit home four years ago. A side table stood a bit to her right, littered with old family photos. The cool tiled floor hurt her butt from sitting there too long.

Bang.

Another bone jarring knock at the door.

With a deep breath, Melissa dragged herself off the floor and yanked the door open.

Rick.

All the feelings she'd suppressed at the coffee shop when Dave and Jeremy said that they were looking out for her slammed into her again. They had almost made her feel like Bobby was still around, that she hadn't lost him completely. She'd barely made it home before losing Bobby hit her all over again.

Overwhelmed, she launched herself at Rick. When both of his arms instantly closed around her, pulling her close, she buried her face in his neck.

She let him gently shuffle her backward until they were both inside the front door, hidden from the world that had moved on without Bobby. In all honesty, she'd rather not be crying on her parents' front porch for all the neighbors to see. She gave Rick a squeeze in thanks as she continued to take in his comfort and the faint scent of steel and motor oil that clung to him. It took several minutes for her to notice that one of Rick's hands was making soothing circles on her back and now and then, he'd murmur that everything was okay.

Finally, she choked out, "I miss Bobby."

"We all do, Mel," he murmured low in her ear.

"Nobody talks about him. Not even my parents. If anything is said that even reminds them of Bobby, they just get quiet and change the subject. Most of my friends didn't even know him and the rest didn't know him well. It's like he didn't exist. I hate that."

Rick's arms tightened around her, but he didn't say anything. She didn't expect him to. She let his warmth sink into her as she held onto him, and she didn't feel quite as alone.

He swallowed against her cheek before he spoke: "How about I make you tea, and then we can talk about Bobby?"

She nodded into his neck, which was wet with her tears. After another minute, he slid his hands down to her hips and turned her to face away from him before guiding her to the couch and giving her a little push to sit down. Melissa kicked her boots off and pulled her feet up on the cushions. She twisted so she could look over the back of the couch and see Rick.

He pulled his gloves off as he walked back to the front door and shrugged off his jacket. His movement stuttered when he went to hang it, pausing over the only hook with a single jacket — Bobby's hook. He carefully placed his jacket on top then went into the kitchen.

Rick paused for a second before opening the cabinet with mugs and the drawer with pots. She was a little surprised he knew where the tea was, but it was in the same place it had been when they were kids. As he stood in front of the stove, watching the water heat up, Melissa frowned, really looking at him. His jaw was scruffier than she was used to seeing, and what she noticed in particular was his red shirt. It was the exact same shade as the day before.

"Those are the same clothes as yesterday," she said.

Rick jerked and looked down at himself as if he hadn't realized he hadn't changed. "That seems to be the case," he replied. When he didn't say anything else, she wondered what he'd been doing that he didn't even realize he hadn't changed clothes in a day.

As she watched Rick over at the stove, Melissa noticed how natural it felt to have him there. Even as the silence dragged on, there was an easiness to it that bound them together. After several minutes, he walked back to the couch with two steaming mugs.

"Do you want chamomile or peppermint?"

"Peppermint."

Rick handed her the light green mug and kept the lavender one for himself. He sat down on the couch, partially facing her with his left knee up on the cushion between them.

"So, Bobby," he said. His voice was so controlled that Melissa just blinked at him until he shifted uncomfortably and cleared his throat.

"You said you wanted to talk about Bobby and not act like he never existed."

Melissa felt her head bob up and down of its own accord. It had always been so easy to tell Rick things. Things she'd normally keep inside, hide, or brush off with her friends. Melissa looked down at the tea cupped in her hands.

"Do you guys all talk about him?" She looked up at Rick. "You and the Mavens? Jeremy and Dave seemed to know him, or at least of him."

"I don't know if they talk about him or not. Yesterday was the first time in years anyone spoke to me about him. Jeremy hesitated to mention him and never actually said his name."

Melissa frowned. Dave hadn't danced around Bobby's name. She couldn't remember if Jeremy had said it or not, but he hadn't seemed uncomfortable talking about Bobby either.

"I didn't take his disappearance well," Rick admitted, not meeting her eyes.

"I don't know what my parents were told, but all anyone told me was that he was dead." Melissa took a deep, but shaky, breath. "Do you know anything about what happened?"

"Not much." Rick's voice was quiet. Maybe even haunted. "He just didn't come back when the job was over. He should have come back. He should have made contact. We waited, you know," Rick looked at her. "We waited two months. Searched everywhere in the meantime. Nothing. He was just... gone."

The way Rick spoke about it, Melissa could tell this was still tearing him up inside, but she had so many questions from just the little he'd said. She put her hand on his knee and gave it a squeeze, letting the feel of the denim and his solid leg ground her while telling him she was there with him too.

"What do mean 'job'?" she asked.

Rick's eyes widened a fraction. He looked like she'd caught him with his hand in the cookie jar. After a second, his expression morphed to apologetic. "I can't answer that," he finally whispered. Melissa just nodded acceptance — acceptance for now. She was not going to forget.

"What do you mean when you said you didn't handle his disappearance well? I don't remember seeing you at the funeral." She searched her memory. "I don't recall seeing you for a while after that, actually." And she couldn't. She had no memory of him coming home to visit for the entire year following the funeral.

If that was right, it would mean it had been more than a year between his visits home, which was out of character. He came for lunch or dinner with his mother every month since he only lived two hours away; even if Melissa didn't see him, she heard about his visits from Jessy. The last time she'd seen Rick in Granberg around that time had been when he and Bobby came and saw her coffee shop the week before her grand opening. That was a full four months before they found out Bobby was dead — two months after Bobby had actually died, which was news to her. She didn't know why no one had shared that detail with her.

"I couldn't believe he was gone," Rick said quietly. "Everyone was worried. It was a year before I thought it might be true. During that year, I talked about him like he'd walk in the door the next day. Then, one day, I just stopped, and no one said his name or even alluded to him around me. Excluding my mother, but she doesn't do it often."

Melissa knew they'd cremated an empty casket. Her parents had been unable to function, and planning the funeral had fallen on her shoulders. It had never occurred to her not to believe Bobby was dead. It would have messed with her head if Rick had been around talking like Bobby was alive. Even now, the idea was more than jarring. She didn't know what to do with it. So, she redirected the conversation.

"Tell me a story. A story about Bobby and the Mavens. I never met any of the others until today. It seems odd that he never shared anything. From today, I can tell you were all close."

"We are," Rick said. "We have to be."

He didn't explain, and Melissa didn't push. Between Bobby disappearing on *the job*, their access to databases, their ability to install cameras instantly, and that Bobby and Rick were some of the best people she knew — Melissa had no doubt that they weren't at all what they seemed to most people. Instead of pushing, she sipped her peppermint tea, noticing that Rick had added a splash of honey to it, and waited.

Several times, Rick looked like he was about to start talking and then he would stop himself, rethinking his story selection. Apparently, there were a lot of good memories, but none he wanted to tell her. Or maybe none he *could* tell her. She was halfway done with her tea before Rick started sharing.

"I don't know whose idea it was, but Bobby and Susan decided to play a prank on Dave. He'd been bragging about his talent with women; he wasn't as humble as he is now."

"That was him being humble this afternoon?" Melissa snorted, making Rick smile.

"Yeah. So, you can imagine how bad he was before. Anyway, Bobby, Susan, and I snuck into Dave's place while he was out *demonstrating* his pick up skills for Shawn and Carl, who were new back then." Melissa wanted to know more about who Susan, Shawn, and Carl were, but she didn't interrupt. "No one noticed us heading in, and I picked the lock. We beat his security system; granted, Jeremy had installed it and gave us a rundown since he couldn't be there to take care of it himself. Once we were inside, Susan presented us with so much cotton candy pink pony paraphernalia that it looked like a three-year-old with a rash had vomited everywhere."

"The pony from the TV show?" Melissa asked, remembering her own toys that used to be lined up along the hot-pink wall in her childhood bedroom.

"Yeah. Susan was a *big* fan." Rick smiled at the memory. "We changed his sheets, pillows, covered his couch. There were even doctored pictures of Dave in a pony costume that we put up to replace his other photos. Little figurines were everywhere. We barely finished redecorating before Carl messaged us and said Dave had picked some girl up. We slapped up a few cameras for the show and disappeared. Susan has a blackmail recording now of Dave showing up, being stunned, and the girl running for her life because the macho-motorcycle-club guy she'd met took her back to a pink pony apartment."

Melissa laughed. Pink ponies were *not* Dave's style.

"The entire time we were there decorating," Rick continued, "Bobby cracked jokes and snapped posed pictures of shocked horror at Dave's pony-centric interior design."

Without being asked, Rick pulled out his phone and started thumbing through it while Melissa brushed tears out of her eyes. He set down his tea and scooted closer to show her. Melissa leaned against him as he flipped through a dozen or so photos of Bobby surrounded by an off-putting amount of pink. With each photo, Rick made a quip that had to have been something Bobby had said that night.

They were both laughing so hard that it wasn't until Rick finished showing her Bobby's staged photos that she realized she had fallen against him and he'd put his arm around her, holding her close. It felt good to talk to someone who had loved Bobby — to remember the good times. She didn't want to remember them alone anymore, and with Rick, she didn't have to.

Chapter 14

Rick

Rick had been losing it since the moment Melissa had fallen into his arms sobbing. Her face and tears against his neck had been a searing heat that went straight to his bones. That she only faintly smelled of coffee told him she'd been home for a while and possibly upset the whole time. Nothing could have stopped him from pushing her inside the house and protecting her from prying eyes.

Then her admission about missing Bobby had made him hold her even closer, regardless of the skin contact. He'd been so concerned about her it had taken him several minutes to realize she made the admission *because* he was touching her. He couldn't remember ever forgetting what his touch did to others, not since he'd learned the truth. At least, he thought she shared because he'd touched her, but then again, Melissa had always been honest around him. She never changed what she said after touching him. In either case, once Rick managed to separate the two of them, he had been careful not to ask her any questions beyond her tea preferences as he gave into her request to talk about Bobby. Something he never wanted to do, even if it was the right thing. Talking about her brother hurt.

Now, feeling her laugh against his side as he showed her pictures of Bobby in Dave's apartment (though he was careful not to show any photos of the team members she hadn't met), he was torn between his need to move away to ensure their skin didn't touch again and his desire to hold her closer and run his bare hand along her exposed arm.

When he finished sharing the photos and she didn't move away but rather relaxed into him, he felt his throat go dry and remembered Susan's teasing smirk. This felt like something — something he couldn't ever have — which made him want it even more. After a minute or two, he cleared his throat and asked, "Have you eaten yet?"

Melissa shook her head and made a quiet negative sound without pulling away from him.

"Maybe we can go to Bobby's favorite restaurant," he heard himself say. He wished he could take the words back the instant they left his mouth. Mortification sank into his bones at the idea of going to Velini's Tacos. He had too many memories of Bobby there for it to be a remotely pleasant experience.

"Oh!" Melissa jumped up.

Dread settled in; she was thrilled with the idea.

But then, she went straight to her purse, which was against the wall under the jackets. She came back with a piece of paper and sat back down right next to him. He hadn't even moved his arm away for safety's sake because he couldn't take his eyes off her. He squeezed his eyes shut, unable to believe that he hadn't thought of changing position and creating some distance, but then snapped them open when Melissa's hands landed on his leg. She smoothed the paper out on his leg, brushing from his mid-thigh to his knee twice in a firm motion. The crinkle of the paper sounded like an echo of each muscle in his abdomen tensing more and more.

"This is a list of all of Tommy's favorite places," she said.

Rick looked through the list of a dozen places Melissa had mysteriously procured. None of them were particularly nice, but neither were they as sketchy as the places Rick had identified as most popular in Tommy's photos online.

"Why don't we go to one of these restaurants?" Melissa suggested, pointing at four eateries — only one of which Rick would deign to call a restaurant. "We can keep an eye out for Tommy, ask if anyone has seen him, and then go check out some of the others."

"Okay. We can grab something to eat at," Rick skimmed the list, "Joe's Diner, then go past the Riverside Park and hit up the Lickety Split Creamery." None of those places were dangerous, and none of them had memories filled with her brother. Plus, going out would make her feel like she had done something to find Tommy, while also keeping her out of trouble. He needed to make sure she felt like she was part of the search; he had a bad feeling about what she'd get up to if she struck out alone.

"That sounds good." Melissa nodded. "On the way back, we can ride past a few of the other locations to see if Tommy's loitering there if we don't find him at the first few."

"Right," Rick said as he stood up to put some needed space between them. "I'll meet you out front in fifteen?"

Melissa blinked up at him for a moment before her eyes dropped to his shirt, and she agreed. He swung through his mother's house, let her know he was going out, took the world's shortest shower, put on clean clothes, lost the battle about taking separate bikes, and was seated in a surprisingly cozy booth with Melissa before an hour had passed.

The curved red vinyl booth was one of five along the side wall and raised up at a small round bar table. When Rick had slid into the booth section and sat on the ripped cushion, instead of taking a stool that put his back to the door, he hadn't counted on Melissa sliding in next to him. The bench was made to sit two, but it was tight. Rick worked on ignoring the feeling of Melissa's thigh pressed against his and the occasional brush of her arm. His arm was thankfully encased in its typical long-sleeve shirt, protecting him from influencing her and vice versa, but he still felt each movement she made.

There were a few other diners at the tables between them and the bar kitchen. One set of diners was studying while eating pancakes. Another set was animatedly discussing something and laughing a lot over what looked like soups. The third set was staring at the waiter and three hybrid diners like they were aliens, which meant they were probably from out of town; a bulldog, a calico cat, a mixed breed dog, and a parakeet hybrid were nothing out of the ordinary, but if the third set of diners lived in a town where people didn't feel comfortable being in their hybrid forms, it would seem odd. Rick dismissed the different diners before the waiter even took his and Melissa's order. There was nothing to see as far as finding Tommy was concerned.

While Melissa took the first few crunching bites of her salad and he took a bite of his burger before the grease soaked into the bun and made it soggy, they fell into silence. Rick found himself reliving Melissa's disturbingly reasonable — and successful — argument about taking one bike. This time she'd had a whole new approach. She'd pointed out that if Tommy was trying to be scarce, he might recognize her on her bike alone, but he'd never think she'd be the second rider on another bike.

"Why not?" Rick had asked.

"Never dated a guy with a bike," she'd shrugged. "No one with a motorcycle even gives me a second glance. Probably because my bike is so old."

Rick had just stared at her while she twisted her lips into a pouty grimace at her helmet. He knew exactly why none of the guys with bikes in Granberg considered approaching her. Bobby had warned them off long before he disappeared. Rick had generally been with Bobby when he had done the warning. Because Rick was still around, apparently the local guys with motorcycles had assumed he'd carry out Bobby's threats, even if Bobby was presumed dead. They must have passed the word on to any new bikers.

It was beyond not okay for Bobby to have threatened every guy that gave his sister a once-over or who he thought might in the future, but Rick had to pick his battles. He'd chosen instead to make sure Bobby didn't carry out the threats. There'd been several times he'd had to step in and stop Bobby from terrorizing a guy that appreciated Melissa a little too openly for Bobby's tastes. Twice he'd literally had to pull Bobby off some poor guy who had had the temerity to go out with Melissa. Nothing good could come from telling her about Bobby's behavior, especially with him gone; it'd taint her memories of him, so he'd stayed quiet.

It wasn't until they were walking up to the diner that Rick realized there was no reason for Tommy to avoid Melissa and the entire argument about her not being recognizable on his bike didn't hold water. He hadn't been touching her skin right before that, so he didn't know if she truly believed that, wanted to ride his bike, or needed to wrap herself around him.

"So, does Jeremy's sister live nearby?" Melissa asked out of the blue, jarring Rick back into the moment. Her slight movement against him reminded him they were touching, even if it was through their clothes.

"His sister?" Rick stopped absently scanning the diner and looked at Melissa. Her messy braid hung over the shoulder of her pink shirt, which clashed terribly with the cheap, red vinyl they sat on. He wanted to flip the braid back over her shoulder so it didn't get into her salad dressing.

"Yeah, he mentioned he had a little sister."

"Vicki is halfway around the world in Gli Aeries studying fashion design." Rick's mind scrambled to figure out why Jeremy had talked about Vicki. He mentioned her from time to time; perhaps more often since she'd moved to the fashion capital of the world and he'd started taking her phone calls when they were on jobs; the time difference was tricky to juggle if they had a mission that took several weeks. "Is there anything I should know from Jeremy and Dave's visit?"

"What do you already know?" Her expression was expectant but not angry. Her tone cut right to the point; she knew the Mavens weren't what they seemed.

"Mostly that cameras were installed," Rick said, choosing the information carefully.

Melissa raised her eyebrows at him, implying he should say more. He tipped his head toward her in response to tell her he wouldn't say anything else. She rolled her eyes and ate a bite of salad.

"Both Dave and Jeremy were overly protective, much like Bobby. It's not like my old camera needs replacing. If anyone robs us, the one I have will catch the action. It's sweet that they want to make sure my shop is safe, but it's overkill. I didn't even have problems back when the neighborhood was bad."

Rick chose not to comment on her misinformed camera stance, at least for the moment. And this definitely wasn't the time to explain to her why her shop had never had any problems she would define as serious. That nothing had happened over the years when she was off-shift was a miracle.

She continued when he didn't argue: "Also, Neil was oddly confrontational and mistrusting when he showed up before he and Jeremy started talking in code about a name Neil had given them. That made no sense to me." Melissa paused and looked at him to see if he'd fill in the blanks; he didn't, and she frowned at him. "In any case, Jeremy and Neil were chatting with Kate and Erika when I left. I have no idea what Dave got up to, but Jeremy stopped him from messing with Kate; so I don't think he would have come back and tried to seduce her out of staying at Erika's tonight."

"Erika Craggs," Rick muttered, having remembered the rest of the news anchor's name when Melissa supplied the first half. He knew little about her other than that she grew up in Granberg. He was still processing Melissa's summary of the afternoon when she confirmed the name.

"How do you know her?" he asked.

"Erika? I'd seen her here and there growing up, but didn't know her; she's a year younger than me and was homeschooled until college. We were in the same group for a business class project and became friends."

"And Kate's staying at her place tonight?"

"Yeah." Melissa slumped against the seat, abandoning her salad. "Kate's freaked out, and we both know she shouldn't be so worked up about this. Tommy doing drugs, which she doesn't even know yet, isn't something that's going to put her in danger. Now that the guy who grabbed her knows she hasn't seen her brother, there's no reason for him to come around again asking after him."

Again, Rick refrained from trying to correct her.

"First," Melissa continued, "she stayed at Danny's, then Bethany's, last night she was with me — we drank until she was too drunk to remember giving me the list of Tommy's favorite places — and tonight she's staying at Erika's. If she doesn't feel comfortable staying at her own place soon or at least stop worrying about overstaying her welcome at one of our places, we're going to have to loop Greg and Ted into the slumber party rotation. And let me tell you, I've seen their places. Greg's screams nerdy bachelor pad, and Ted's is like being inside a freaky computer aquarium. Not a welcoming vibe for Kate. Granted, Bethany's place isn't her style either, but at least it's cozy."

Rick stared at Melissa; he was at a complete loss for words. Finally, his brain started functioning and little alarms sounded. "I don't know any of those people." He couldn't pinpoint why that was a problem, but he knew it wasn't *good* that he didn't know them.

"You know Danny and Kate. I've been friends with them forever," Melissa pointed out. "You also met Greg and Bethany when you brought me your mom's coffee cake."

"I don't know them well," he amended. Rick wasn't even a hundred percent sure he remembered what the last two looked like — he remembered Greg's bare forearm too close to him on the table and Bethany's shocking white hair, but nothing else about them had stood out. Melissa's delighted sounds as she tasted the coffee cake though... those he remembered very clearly. "And I only know who Erika is because of her job. I think you mentioned someone with an aquarium house who I don't know at all."

"And?"

Melissa crossed her arms and pursed her lips at him like he was acting unreasonably. And maybe he was. On the one hand, if she interacted with all her friends the same, then she touched them often. That would mean she constantly pushed them to be good people. So, in theory, they weren't dangerous. At least not directly dangerous to Melissa. On the other hand, he wanted to know — no, he needed to know — who she spent time around and who she trusted.

"Maybe I should meet them," Rick said.

"You want to meet my friends?" she said slowly. Her eyelids fluttered a few times in surprise and her arms uncrossed as she leaned minutely toward him.

It dawned on Rick that he was entering uncharted territory. He'd met a few of the Mavens' friends, but never asked to. What he just said held significance. Melissa tilted her head and bit the left side of her lower lip.

"Do I get to meet your friends too?" she asked.

"It looks like you will," he said. In all honesty, it was inevitable. There was nothing he could do about it. She'd met Dave and Jeremy earlier. Susan wouldn't be far behind after the talk they'd had. She was already more invested than Rick wanted her to be in the idea of Melissa. Shawn and Carl might or might not seek her out on their own. Time would tell.

"Okay then." Melissa's hand settled on his thigh and squeezed. Rick forced himself to breathe normally as her hand stayed in place. He could have sworn she had moved her whole body a little closer, but he might have imagined it. In either case, he was overheating, and his thoughts short-circuiting.

They ate the rest of the meal without talking. Rick had no idea what Melissa was thinking as his thoughts centered on her fork sliding past her lips and the heat of her body where it pressed against his, even though the table wasn't *so* cozy that it required it. There was also the fact that she'd left her hand on his leg for several bites before removing it.

"Who do you think we should ask?" Melissa said after he paid the bill.

"Ask?"

"About Tommy. We have to find him and get him help, so Kate can relax."

Rick had forgotten that they were "checking" places for Tommy. The diner, while nothing fancy, wasn't a place someone on the run from drug dealers would frequent. It was at minimum one step up from that, if not two or three. Part of him wanted to explain that, but he also didn't want her to realize that what they were doing wouldn't get her closer to her target.

"I'll check with the hostess on the way out," he said instead of explaining. It didn't hurt to ask, and it would assuage Melissa's worry and maybe help Kate relax. He doubted Theo Barre was interested in Kate at all now since Melissa had touched him. Kate was easy enough to find and hadn't been approached again, even though Theo could have easily sent someone else to grab her. He'd know it wouldn't be a *good* move. Honestly, Melissa was more at risk than her friend because she insisted on looking into the problem personally.

In the end, the hostess hadn't recognized Tommy from his photo but said she'd keep an eye out with a flirty smile. That smile resulted in Melissa sliding her arm through his and leaning against him in a way that made it difficult to swallow. She was getting ideas Bobby really wouldn't like.

Outside, Melissa didn't let go of Rick as they walked toward his bike. He didn't try to disengage himself either. He felt like reality was slipping, but he didn't want to fight it anymore. When they reached his bike, Melissa slid between him and it, her hands coasting up the front of his shirt, partially beneath the open sides of his jacket. His fingers automatically hooked through the belt loops at the sides of her jeans, simultaneously pulling her against him and tempting him with her skin a hair away from his exposed hands.

"Can I drive again?" Her voice was breathy, like when he'd walked with her to pick the lock at Tommy's apartment.

"And why would I let you do that, Mel?" he rumbled. His voice was a tad deeper than he'd intended as he flirted back. He had practiced flirting in case he needed to do so on a mission, it just wasn't normally accompanied with anything of real meaning — like meeting the other person's friends — and he'd always been bad at it.

"You let me before." Her wide eyes looked up at him. He almost growled when they flicked to his lips and then back to his eyes as his hands tightened on her hips.

"I think I'll drive," he said. There was no way he could sit behind her without her realizing what she was doing to him. To his surprise, his mouth kept moving: "but you can hold on as tight as you'd like."

Melissa rolled her eyes and shook her head, but he saw her smile. She turned out of his grasp, and he released her. He pulled on his gloves before he gave into the desire to yank her back against him. She had her helmet on before he picked his up off the bike. When she climbed on behind him, she slid her hands into the pockets of his jacket to protect them from the wind, making him think about buying her a pair of gloves; she should be wearing them — on her bike and off. He shot off the curb just to feel her grab onto him. He didn't bother worrying about how much he liked it. He could worry about that later.

After he watched her lick up an ice cream cone and was paralyzed by tantalizing flicks of her tongue.

After he'd driven her by the other places where they wouldn't find Tommy.

After he'd slipped back out of his mother's house to go look at places Tommy might actually be.

Yeah, he'd worry about it then.

Chapter 15

Melissa

Red tinged rocks rose to the sky in the early morning light, making the bland mountainous boulders look soft and unreal. There was a quiet flutter of wings as Melissa rounded a puddle and passed near a bush. If she weren't so distracted, she'd have soaked in the majestic sight and the peaceful weight of the morning on her approach.

"Someone looks pensive," Greg said instead of good morning. His dark hair was flattened on one side from sleeping. He hadn't attempted to fix it. He wore black gym shorts and a sleeveless tank despite the morning chill, as well as grippy shoes.

Melissa tipped her head in acknowledgment. Pensive was better than any other words she might have used. Flustered? Confused? Hopeful? Comforted? Distracted? Flushed? Pensive definitely sounded less emotionally charged than she was.

"Gear up." Greg threw her a climbing harness. He already had his on. "I have to get to the library by nine today, and ideally, I'd like to shower first."

Melissa caught the harness and strapped it on over her beige cargo pants while she followed Greg to the middle section of the cliff face to the advanced human climbs, which overlapped with easy to mid-range hybrid climbs (depending on the hybrid type). While Greg hooked his carabiner to the safety rope that was ready and waiting, Melissa picked up her half of the headset next to his backpack. They'd been climbing together long enough that Greg didn't bother for her to be fully set up as the belay; he knew she'd be ready to catch him by the time he got as high up as her head. The headsets had originally been so Greg could have Melissa, who was a much less experienced climber, be his belay as he taught her the process. They'd never stopped using them — not for safety reasons, but because they could talk the entire time he climbed. When Melissa climbed, she needed to focus on what she was doing and Greg coached her some through the headset.

"Belay on," Melissa said as she tightened up the slack in the line.

"So, what has you pensive? Something new with Kate?"

"No. Tommy hasn't been seen at any of the places Rick and I hit last night. No one recognized him from the photo we showed them, either."

"So, if it's not something to do with Kate, can I assume it has to do with Rick?" Greg dipped his free hand into the pouch on his harness to get a little extra chalk on his fingers.

Melissa didn't respond.

Everything had to do with Rick.

First, he'd talked with her about Bobby, and then they might have gone on a date. She wasn't quite sure. She had no idea why she'd warned the hostess off at the diner when the woman had flirted with Rick. Actually, that wasn't true. Rick had asked to meet her friends, and none of her boyfriends had *asked* to do that. She had wanted the hostess to know that he was with her, even if he wasn't really. She liked him. He was a great guy.

Before he and Bobby had joined the Mavens and become "extra intimidating," Kate had suggested multiple times that Melissa go out with him. Melissa had never let herself entertain the idea, not until the other night when he'd caught her — literally — in Tommy's apartment and let his fingers trail along her skin. A shiver ran up her spine, and she wasn't sure if it was from the cool temperature or the memory of Rick's fingers. Before that, she wouldn't have said he was aware she was the opposite sex.

"I'll take that as a yes," Greg huffed as he hauled himself farther up the cliff. "Are you sure he's safe? Motorcycle clubs aren't known for their safety factor."

Melissa nodded hello to another set of climbers that came out in the mornings — a goat hybrid and a raccoon hybrid — as they passed her on their way to the most advanced climbs; then, she rolled her eyes at Greg's backside as he kept climbing. He was already twice her height up from the ground. "I've known him my whole life. He's safe. Don't forget, my brother was right there beside him."

She frowned. Right there beside Rick, until Bobby didn't return from a *job*. The Mavens had covert security cameras that could be set up at a moment's notice. They had resources. She knew they weren't a motorcycle club or mechanics like Bobby and Rick said they were. Not that she'd tell anyone that. They clearly didn't want people to know. That made finding out information about what Rick did and what Bobby had done before he died a lot harder.

"Sorry Melissa," Greg said. He paused to take a leap at an outcropping just beyond his reach. Once he had reestablished his grips, he mumbled, "I forgot about your brother."

"Most people do," she said without judgment. With Greg, it hurt less than with others. He'd joined their group of friends after Bobby had died. Melissa had been close to functioning normally by that time, though she'd been taking too many shifts at her coffee shop to distract herself rather than hire more baristas. They'd actually met *because* she was always at Juniper's Java; he was a regular even before they became friends. One day when Greg had been making chitchat while she made his drink, he'd mentioned that he climbed. The next thing she knew, she'd had a climbing invite. It had been a great way to push Bobby out of her thoughts and just focus on moving. It was understandable that Bobby wasn't at the forefront of Greg's mind.

"Still, not cool of me."

"Forgiven."

"So, what about Rick has you so pensive?" A grunt sounded through the headset as Greg's foot slipped and his body slammed into the rock face.

"You good?" Melissa asked while she leaned back a little to prepare for Greg to need her weight on the rope.

"Yeah," he huffed. A few seconds later, he had firm hand- and footholds. "So, you, Rick, pensive?"

Screwing up her face, she admitted, "I'm not sure, but I think we might have gone on a date last night."

"You're not sure?" Greg sounded like he was choking. "He doesn't look like someone who accidentally goes on a date."

Melissa made a non-committal noise into the headset.

"Tell me what happened."

Greg was, by far, the most experienced of her friends when it came to first dates. When Melissa first met him, he had a new girlfriend every few weeks. After they'd started climbing together, he'd admitted that he'd had a hard time in high school and even most of college — both with bullies and with girls — and he was catching up on what he missed out on earlier. Their group of friends accepted that he dated *a lot*, even though he didn't talk about his dates anymore and none of them had seen him on one in a while. At some point, he had to find new people to date, so it made sense his dates would happen farther from their group's general hangouts.

Melissa needed the advice, so she told him about the evening. She started with the comforting. Then told him about dinner and the request to meet her friends. She didn't tell him about how Rick hadn't been able to string a sentence together while she ate her ice cream cone or that the way he was looking at her had made her think her skintight shirt was overkill under her jacket. She did tell Greg that anytime they walked rather than rode, Rick looped his arm around her waist and held her against him.

"But he didn't kiss you?" Greg asked as Melissa lowered him down from the top edge of the cliff. When his feet hit the ground, he said, "Off belay."

"Belay off," Melissa said, shaking her arms after Greg's descent, before answering his question. "If he'd kissed me, I would have either mentioned it or not been confused in the first place." Her frustration cut into her voice.

"I can tell you he wasn't acting brotherly, but I also don't know what he's like on dates to know if that's his normal behavior or not," Greg said, walking them over to an easier climbing section for Melissa to have a go at.

She started to climb as Greg advised her on handholds and possible paths to the top. While her muscles started burning, Melissa tried to remember if Rick had dated in high school, in the army, or after. She could remember Bobby mentioning dates back when she was in college and Neil having a girlfriend or two in town over the years, but nothing about Rick.

Once she reached the higher levels of her climb, she had to stop ruminating over Rick's dating habits and focus. Her forearms ached from the tricky handholds she was clinging to. Greg kept more tension on the rope than she did for him, so she knew if her fingers failed, she wouldn't fall more than a foot or two. Despite that, she clung to the oversized boulders of her climbing section like her life depended on it.

Greg coaxed her to jump for a ledge that was about a foot beyond her reach. The cold air stung her lungs as she gulped it in and pushed past her survival instincts. After a deep breath, she crouched the best she could against the vertical rocks and did her best frog imitation. She fell short of the ledge, but Greg caught her on the rope and confirmed that she was ready to be lowered down. With her extremities protesting any and all movements, Melissa didn't hesitate to call it a day.

"Great work. That was a much harder route than you usually take," Greg commented when Melissa was about halfway down. "Staying to the right at the start would have led you to an easier climb."

"I wasn't focused on the climb at the start," she admitted as her feet touched the ground. "Off belay."

"You were focused on Rick?" Greg smirked. "Belay off."

"I don't know about any of his past relationships," Melissa said. They were both used to picking conversations back up after climbing interruptions.

"Then he's either made a point not to talk about them around you over the years, or he's exceedingly discreet, which doesn't mesh with him walking with his arm around you."

"So," Melissa took a long drink of water and worked to slow her breathing to a normal rate while the implication worked through her brain. Rick didn't seem to mind touching her in public, despite the fact that she never saw him touching people. Also, he'd never shrugged off her touch over the years, and she was very tactile. "You think he's purposely hidden his past relationships from me?"

"If he's liked you for a long time, it's a possibility. Are you sure you would have known about his past relationships?"

"Maybe not, but his mom would have said something at some point, right?"

"It's anyone's guess." Greg didn't look satisfied with the situation. "Maybe Ted and I will gang up on him when we meet him." A grin lit up his face. "We can ask him his intentions."

"Don't you dare!" Melissa laughed.

"Come on!" Greg teased. "Someone has to. Maybe I'll ask around, make sure he's safe."

"Do you investigate all the guys we talk with?" Melissa scoffed.

"Whenever they look dangerous," Greg said without hesitation. Melissa froze and looked at Greg over her shoulder. He was serious and unapologetic. "Granted, none of your boyfriends have been worth looking into," he admitted. "I just don't like that Kate thinks he's more intimidating than the guy that approached her in your coffee shop."

Ignoring his lingering worry from Kate's skittishness, Melissa frowned. Whose past boyfriends was Greg talking about? Before she could ask, Greg glanced at his watch and said he had to run as he jogged away to his car.

Greg had landed somewhere between a friend and a replacement brother for Bobby. A *way* more laid-back brother. She looked at her cell and saw it was a little later than they usually ended because of their conversation. He'd be lucky if he made it to work on time with his earlier than normal shift.

She changed her shoes and slipped her motorcycle jacket on over the thin workout jacket she'd climbed in. Another set of climbers drove up and parked next to her, crunching the small rocks that made up the road. They exchanged hellos, and Melissa successfully fired up her bike after it stuttered twice.

During the forty-five-minute ride into town, she rolled her eyes several times at the idea that Rick had had a crush on her for years. If pushed, she might have an example or two that showed his interest, but they were stretches. Any example she had also had Bobby in it, and Rick could have just been backing Bobby up in the overprotective brother olympics. But Greg had said Rick was not acting brotherly, so where did that leave things?

Dissatisfied with her lack of conclusions, Melissa walked into the back of Juniper's Java. At the sound of the alley door closing, Nick peered into the staff room like he always did when she arrived on Wednesdays. She waved at him, and he gave her a nod. Plopping down in the flowered armchair because the sun poured through the window and onto the red chair, she pulled the coffee shop calendar off the wall and grabbed her pen. The dim hum of the coffee shop out front trickled back to her as she got to work creating the upcoming schedule. Nick brought her favorite tea and a granola bar back a few minutes later.

"Thanks," she said. The warmth of the tea was a soothing sensation against her tired fingers. "Anything I need to know about your availability the next few weeks?" She switched from nibbling on her pen to nibbling on the granola bar.

"Nothing new, but remember two weekends from now I'll be out of town. I'm visiting my parents during the lull in my school assignments before midterms."

"Right," Melissa said, noting his comment down on the edge of the calendar next to her reminder that Kate wanted to switch her days off in four weeks to go to an expo as research for starting up her jewelry making business in earnest. Hopefully, Kate's nerves and things with Tommy would calm down by the expo. Melissa really didn't want to go to it with her. She'd gone once before and been bored out of her mind. She'd also spent too much money on jewelry she never wore.

As things stood now, with Kate's freak out and Tommy off sniffing himself into the gutter, Melissa only had the schedule for next week ready. She always had the next week scheduled, but tried to be two or three weeks ahead. Having never invested in scheduling software, she spent the next few hours fitting her employees together like puzzle pieces to cover all the shifts. Even with Danny helping, Melissa had to schedule herself out front for forty hours, which meant all the stuff she did because she owned and ran the shop would be on top of those hours.

Grumbling at her good fortune of running a popular coffee shop, she started drafting up a job announcement to hire two new employees, maybe even three to compensate for when Danny eventually left. The hiring process was not her favorite. Many people thought working at a coffee shop was all fun and games. It didn't matter how great the customers were, many new employees did not appreciate the hours they spent on their feet or constantly being friendly with people they'd never met. Satisfied with her initial draft of the job posting, Melissa headed home to take a shower and stretch out her tired muscles.

Despite having noted the time when she got home, Melissa had to scramble for her phone when it rang. Wrapped in her towel and only partially dry, she ran across the hall and into her bedroom. She snatched her phone off her bed, and on the fourth ring, she answered it.

"Hello sweetie!" her mom sung out happily. Her parents must have found some good data for her mother's tone to be *that* bright.

"Hi Mom. How are you and Dad doing?" She smiled. Her weekly phone dates with her parents were always informative in one way or another.

"We're fantastic! We've stumbled across a flying squirrel hybrid whose family's interested in participating in our study! Despite marrying a dog hybrid of indeterminate breed, all their children are flying squirrel hybrids."

"That follows your theory that the rarer a hybrid species, the more dominate the genes." Melissa adjusted her grip on her towel so she could pinch the phone between her shoulder and ear while she pulled out a change of clothes.

Her dad cut in to assert, "But if they balance out in ratio to other hybrids, I think their genes will decrease in dominance."

Melissa rolled her eyes. She had heard her parents discuss this issue at length more times than she could count. So she grabbed onto the odder fact they'd brushed past: "It isn't common for a dog hybrid to be of an indeterminate breed, right? Don't they favor one or two breeds regardless of the original pet that helped its owner survive the Crisis?"

"Yes," her mom said. Melissa tossed a red bra onto the jeans she'd put on the bed and dug into her underwear drawer to find the matching panties. "Though, as we are traveling around to volunteers, we are seeing more and more dog hybrids that can't be categorized beyond their dog's function. Jessy theorizes the dog hybrids might lean toward the majority of cat 'breeds' in the future — categorized more on color or fur length or size than actual breeds."

"What I want to know," her dad said, his tone stern, "is if Jessy's right, and you're going out with Rick now, or if she's off her rocker."

"Erm," Melissa glanced out her bedroom window toward Rick's house and saw him frozen in the window opposite hers. His eyes were wide, and he looked panic stricken. Her head tilted to the side in worry, and his head jerked up. He hadn't been looking at her face. Suddenly, she was very aware that she was wrapped in a blue towel, had wet hair dripping on the floor, and had a pair of red panties dangling from her hand. Not to mention the fact that her head was angled awkwardly to hold her phone in place. She watched Rick spin around and leave the room that mirrored hers. She thought it was an office in their house.

"Melissa?" She could hear the smile in her mother's voice.

"What?"

"Are you and Rick dating?"

"Rick's helping me with a problem," Melissa said, figuring it was better to skirt the issue.

"What kind of problem?" her dad demanded. He had never liked the part of town where she'd opened Juniper's Java. He'd been more vocal about it than Bobby by a long shot.

Melissa squeezed her eyes shut before walking around her bed to close her curtains. Her father's disapproval came from having witnessed several upset patrons during Melissa's first seven months of being open. It wasn't completely uncalled for, even if his impression was severely outdated.

"There was a tough guy that scared one of my employees. You know how rough the neighborhood used to be." She added extra emphasis on *used to be* to remind them the area was nothing like it was in the past, even if they hadn't seen the drastic changes in person; they so rarely came home. "I'm sure it's nothing, but Rick wants to make sure."

"Oh." Her mom's voice fell in disappointment.

"Good," her dad said at the same time. Melissa wasn't sure if that was about her not dating Rick or approval of Rick helping her.

Chapter 16

Rick

In the dark hallway, Rick leaned against the door to the study. Hands in his hair. Wide eyes glued to the bathroom door in front of him, unseeing. His entire body felt like it had been shot out of a volcano — rock solid, but burning up. He cursed the instincts that made him pay attention to sudden movements. Sudden movements next door in this case.

He didn't know who Melissa was talking to on the phone, but it had to be important for her to run to the phone dripping wet. From across the short fence between their two houses, he had seen her brown hair plastered to her shoulders, trailing downward, with an occasional rivulet of water glistening down her skin until it hit the top edge of the blue towel she held precariously around her body in a single fist at her chest. The towel drooped until he could see most of her bare back when she had turned away from him.

Rick had no idea what had her flicking her eyes over to the study, but the way her body stilled drew his eyes from the scrap of red fabric in her hand and back up to her face where a few clumps of hair stuck to her upturned cheek in wet squiggles. The next thing he knew, he was in the hallway.

Releasing his grasp on his hair, Rick rubbed his neck and hung his head. What was he going to say to her? Did he address the fact that he'd been staring? Did he comment about leaving abruptly? If he were Dave, he would have done something stupid like wink at her or give her a come-hither finger crook. Thankfully, he was not Dave, so he didn't need to worry about Bobby, specter or not, appearing suddenly and justifiably gutting him. The idea of Bobby gutting him, literally, was a sobering image.

"Everything okay?" his mother asked.

Rick turned his head and saw her standing at the opening of the hallway. She was wearing a buttoned-up dark red cardigan with the collar of her polka dot shirt poking out, reminding Rick that she'd been at work all morning. In his mini-freakout, he hadn't heard her come in through the garage.

"Yeah, I just realized I was going to make us late to lunch," Rick lied.

"Hurry up then."

He got his shoes on and grabbed his jacket and gloves from his room. A few minutes later, he was in his mom's car, and they were off to lunch. She picked Priscilla's Eatery downtown.

Rick normally avoided downtown; it was even more popular than Melissa's coffee shop's neighborhood and the likelihood of accidentally touching someone increased in crowded areas. He vividly remembered a few times in crowds when he'd bumped someone and been witness to a secret being spilled. It didn't matter that he no longer left skin exposed for such accidental touches, his experiences had left a permanent mark.

The worst had been when he was out with a new friend's parents just after he'd learned what he did to people. He'd caught himself on the mother's hand to stop himself from falling while playing tag with his friend. The friend's father had then asked, "What did your friends and you do last night? I don't remember hearing the details." The fight that ensued when his friend's mother truthfully answered that one of her male friends had pleasured her several times over had been ugly. Rick hadn't seen that new friend again; the kid's parents split and moved soon after. The conversation about adult relationships with his mother later that week had been much more in-depth than any eleven-year-old wanted, but it was also what he needed to know given what had happened.

Rick's mother parked in a parking structure and led them down a bench-lined pedestrian street that was disorientingly void of trees. Most areas of town, even the most rundown, had what would have been excessive amounts of foliage fifty years ago. This particular patch of their very hybrid-inclusive downtown was so lifeless that it sent a tingle down Rick's spine. For work, he'd been to cities that tried to suppress hybrids, ignoring the reality that there were four hybrids to every one human. Those cities looked a lot like this street.

"What's the history of this area?" Rick asked, wondering why he'd never been on the street before.

"About five years ago, it opened back up. All the apartments on this street, above the shops, had no pet policies when the Crisis hit."

Rick looked up at the few apartments above the brightly colored restaurant awnings and artisanal boutiques. From the outside, the apartments looked like any others — clean but from seventy years ago. The implication of a no pets rule meant fifty percent of the inhabitants likely died when the Crisis came and none of the original inhabitants turned into hybrids. Those who survived, Rick was positive, had special *talents* like all the full humans he'd encountered.

His mother leaned toward him and continued in a hushed voice to impart the shameful history of the area: "Those who survived did not handle the new world dynamics well. For the last forty years, the majority of inhabitants who didn't flee our diverse city spent most of their time shouting obscenities at any hybrid they saw. The shops did their best to evict them, but it took time. Eventually the shouting stopped, but the residents still gave the evil eye to anyone they didn't know was a full human. Even humans wearing hybrid-friendly clothes were targeted." His mother shook her head at the memory. "The shops that were here failed, and it's been nearly empty or full of struggling businesses until the last of the adults moved out or on to nursing homes. The stores here now are trying to revitalize the area and bring it back into good repute."

"I hadn't realized we had any sections of town like that," Rick muttered. He slipped his gloves off since the street wasn't packed.

"It's the reason we're eating here. To show support for the new businesses. My friend Maria's daughter is a chef at Priscilla's."

"From breakfast," Rick said, remembering that his mom had run off to eat with Maria and left him alone with Melissa who made his jeans too tight when she made sounds of delight and licked bacon grease off her fingers or nibbled on coffee cake.

"Breakfast?"

"I knew it!" he said. "You didn't have breakfast plans with Maria the other day, did you?"

His mother raised an eyebrow at him, neither confirming his suspicion nor denying it. He raised an accusing finger at her to say more, but she cut him off.

"Do *not* interrogate me, Richard Henry Thompson!"

He blinked at her, then realized he'd raised a bare hand up.

"You know I wouldn't do that," he whispered, shoving his hands into his pockets. His mother was the only person he'd ever sat down with and explained how he used his touch at work; he was the person who got answers from people and, if needed, interrogated them without them any the wiser about why they were spilling their secrets. Luckily, those interrogations were rarely messy unless the person refuse to say a single word, and Rick let Bobby make the messes when he was around; Carl had stepped in to fill that gap on their team if it was called for now. Rick even assisted Teams Gamma and Kappa with their interrogations because it made things easier for everyone.

"Of course not," she murmured, giving him a little smile as if that softened her response. Still, her strong reaction gave him her answer. He was positive she didn't have breakfast with Maria the other day. She just didn't want to admit to trying to push him and Melissa together through *active* manipulation. He dropped the issue since they couldn't change the past. His mother just wouldn't accept that he couldn't be with anyone, not once his touch was factored into the equation.

Priscilla's Eatery had a two-tone yellow awning hanging over a front patio with metal tables and chairs. The outdoor tables were notably empty, but so were all the other outdoor dining areas they'd passed — either because the weather was starting to turn chilly or due to the history of the street. The restaurant facade was painted a bright white and had Grecian columns on each side of the windows.

A waitress met them at the door and showed them to an unadorned brown table inside. The classic columns from outside continued in the interior decor, but now they also had bright yellow stucco flowers with red centers near the ceiling. The smell of fresh bread hung in the air, which was much more appetizing than whatever scent the fake flowers might have suggested.

Rick noticed that the people eating were a majority human or in human form. The wait-staff, on the other hand, were all in hybrid form, wearing black floor-length unisex skirts and black tees with wide arms to allow for a variety of arm shapes. So far, he had seen an orange cat, a spotted gecko, and a black dog hybrid. Rick skimmed the menu and quickly picked the tuna melt on focaccia bread with a side of mixed vegetable soup. When he set the menu down, his mother had a small, smug smile on her lips. Rick frowned at her.

"You know," she said, "next time Lindsay and Jonathan swing through for a visit, we should all go out to eat. With Melissa, of course. It's silly for us all to have separate Wednesday lunch dates."

"Wednesday lunch dates?" Rick echoed.

"Yes, Melissa has lunch every Wednesday with her parents." Jessy tacked on a look that suggested that he was falling down on visiting since he only made it home about once a month and sometimes missed a month if he was working a job.

Rick could only stare at his mother after hearing this odd piece of news. Melissa had been on the phone with her parents. Dripping wet. Barely covered by a towel and trying to get dressed. He wasn't the only person who was late for lunch today.

The clink of a neighboring table's silverware on their dishes brought Rick back to the moment.

"When did you last talk with Lindsay?"

"This morning. She called to see if I had anything about flying squirrel hybrid representation across the globe. I think they're trying to get every type of hybrid represented in their study."

His mother's smile stayed in place as she put in her order with the waitress. Rick knew she wasn't telling him everything. After the waitress promised to return with their food, Rick chose not to push his mother about why she was so happy. There was, however, another matter about Melissa's parents he was curious about.

"You never answered Melissa the other morning about how long her parents told you they'd be gone. You avoided answering by pointing out my arrival as if I hadn't been standing there the entire time she was telling you the latest on their research."

His mother's shoulders fell, and she carefully smoothed the wrinkle-free cloth napkin in front of her. Rick's stomach clenched. Whatever she knew, it wasn't good.

"What did they tell you?" he asked, bracing himself.

His mother pinched the bridge of her nose and squeezed her eyes shut. "You have to promise not to tell Melissa," she said as if the burden of the secret were too great to keep all to herself any longer.

He tilted his head to the side and narrowed his eyes at her. He would not promise without knowing what it was. His mother screwed her mouth to the side at his expression but must have decided it was too late to back out now; she continued without his assurances.

"First off, I want you to know I have been clear from the start that I don't agree with their decision." Rick gave her level stare a nod of acknowledgment. "You recall they left less than six months after Bobby's funeral? Any earlier and they wouldn't have been able to get the funding or secure the positions. They couldn't stand being reminded of Bobby every day, living in the house where he grew up and seeing all the places they had taken him over the years." The feeling of dread in Rick's stomach grew each time his mother said Bobby's name. "They aren't on an extended research sabbatical," she whispered.

"What do you mean?" His heart felt like a delayed drum, slow and twice as powerful as normal.

"They were hired to *lead* the research team," she continued whispering. "They aren't on a team or in temporary positions; they are in charge of the entire endeavor. It's a decades long project. They resigned at the university in all capacities except advising. They aren't coming back — at least not permanently."

"They abandoned her?" he hissed.

"Well... I mean... that isn't how they see it," his mother replied weakly.

The waitress chose that moment to keep her promise of bringing them food. How truly cutoff Melissa had been since Bobby disappeared hit him hard. Not only was her brother gone, but her parents were too, in a way she didn't even know. Rick seriously considered throwing up as he put himself in her shoes, but through sheer willpower, he suppressed his roiling stomach. The smell of warm bread and tuna no longer appealed to him. After Melissa had hugged him last night and cried that no one would talk to her about Bobby, not even her parents, this news was devastating. Sure, no one talked to him about Bobby, but that was all because of his own behavior. Melissa hadn't had a say in the matter; and then, her last bit of family just up and left for good without even telling her they were doing it.

His mother didn't push him for a response and eventually he found the will to eat his lunch, dredging up his military training about not rejecting nutritional meals regardless of what was happening in the present vicinity. It had been a long time since he'd had to use that skill. The taste didn't even register as he ate.

"Was the food alright?" the waitress asked when she brought the bill. Unease coated her voice. Rick knew it was his unhappy demeanor that had the waitress's fur standing on end.

"It was delicious," his mother said. "Just a tough discussion."

Rick paid for their lunch. On the walk back to his mother's car, he noted more than one person gave him an even wider berth than normal. His mother drove him back to the house trying to make small talk, but he wasn't in the mood to cooperate, so she dropped him off at the house with an apologetic look and squeeze on his arm before heading back to work. He was alone on the sidewalk before he could decide which house to approach.

His phone buzzed in his pocket. The screen showed a photo of Jeremy in bird form trying to mimic a flamingo doing yoga on his bike. Rick answered the call.

"We got a bead on Matt Helms," Jeremy said. "Lock onto Shawn's location and meet up with him for surveillance."

"Okay," Rick said automatically and hung up.

Instead of going into the house to grab his keys and take off on his bike, Rick walked up to Melissa's front door. As he knocked, he remembered how the entire house was still set up like it was her parents' house. It had been exactly the same as when Bobby was alive, down to Bobby's damn jacket behind the door. She had not taken over the house in any way. She thought they were coming back. Melissa opened the door, and Rick felt like he'd been punched in the gut.

"What's wrong?" she asked. She reached out toward him as if to put her hand on his cheek and paused. Against all of his instincts and training, he tipped his head just enough to the side that her palm caressed his cheek. He welcomed the feeling of goodness that flowed from her and that reinforced what he needed to do.

"I have to go check out a lead tangentially related to the people looking for Tommy," he told her.

"I can be ready to go in five minutes." She pulled her hand away from his cheek and glanced over her shoulder back into the house as if running through what she needed to do to get ready.

"No," he said quickly. "One of the guys is coming with me. It's *tangentially* related."

Melissa nibbled on her lip, drawing Rick's attention to her mouth. He stood there transfixed until she spoke, agreeing to stay behind. He had no idea what she thought about the fact one of the Mavens was going with him instead of her, but he didn't want to press his luck and ask.

"I won't be back till late. Don't do anything tonight, okay?" he tacked on.

"Fine," she muttered, looking none too happy about it.

"And I want to talk when I get back," he added. It was the right thing to do. She'd trusted him with how she felt about Bobby, even if his touch had influenced her. At that thought, he took a step away, reminding himself that it wasn't okay to force her to tell him the truth when she didn't know he was doing it.

"O-okay."

She looked a little nervous, and when he met her eyes, she blushed. Instantly, he remembered her in her towel earlier. He'd forgotten after hearing the news about her parents. His eyes flicked involuntarily down her body and back up. An image of her wearing nothing but the red panties thrust itself into his head.

"I have to go." Rick jerked his thumb over his shoulder, nodded once, and walked across both their lawns. He didn't pause until he was inside the house, kicking himself about what she might be thinking.

Chapter 17

Theo

Theo was not pleased to find himself sulking on a shadowy door stoop down the street from Juniper's Java. It had been three days since he'd watched Melissa Juniper and that guy break into Tommy-the-dipshit's apartment. And still, he had no idea what had freaked her out when she and her boyfriend had been inside. Nothing had changed in the hours between *his* trips inside.

It had taken their computer tech Troy two entire days to find her name and another to find that the only connection to him was this coffee shop, which was where Theo had seen her before, apparently. He'd been so focused on Tommy-the-dipshit's sister that he hadn't paid attention to the owner of the shop.

Normally, he wouldn't loiter on a door stoop waiting, but he knew deep down that going into the coffee shop and dragging the girl out for questioning wasn't a good idea. The only data he had to support this feeling was that when he'd gone in and set his sights on Tommy-the-dipshit's big sister, he'd suddenly realized she couldn't help him find her brother and definitely not *in there*.

As it was, Theo was too far away to even smell the coffee that beckoned people in off the street, but there was no way he was going to fight the instinct that made him stay so far away. His instincts had served him well in the past and let him indulge in what his prison therapist had called his "less than savory pursuits."

Troy's research had been next to useless, which was out of the ordinary for the kid. He found out the girl grew up in Granberg, studied at the local university, and opened up her coffee shop all on her own. Her parents were researchers and hadn't visited in a long time. Troy's theory was that they were estranged, as if that mattered. Only two things in her profile matched what Theo knew to be true about her: she rode a motorcycle and looked disarmingly innocent.

Her cover was excellent.

The real question was, who had established her cover? Was it a crime boss? A drug lord? Or a government agency? She was a thorn in his paw. He didn't believe for a minute that anything Troy found was based in fact. He wanted to be off dealing with Tommy-the-dipshit. That promised to be more *interactive*, but his sister had deemed this girl and her boyfriend's interference more problematic to their plans to expand the Wrappers' territory to include Granberg than Tommy-the-dipshit making off with several bricks of product and taking his skills with him.

In the seven hours he'd been on the street, Theo had almost scratched his wrist raw as he itched around the annoying bracelet Allison and Matt insisted they all wear. He understood why it was necessary, and he appreciated that he couldn't be connected to any of their drugs because of it, but damn, was it annoying.

And for all his scratching, he'd only seen the girl when she arrived in back at seven thirty-five in the morning, where she hadn't remotely checked her surroundings, and then he'd seen her moving around inside through the front window. Once, she'd come out and cleared empty cups from the sidewalk tables, chatting with a pair of customers, an older man and rabbit hybrid, who'd brought their pet border collie with them; normally her employees cleared the tables from what he had seen. In truth, there wasn't much of anything to see at all.

There weren't even sketchy looking characters going into the coffee shop. Maybe he could send a low-level dealer in to scope out if there was action happening inside that he was missing. If she was selling in her store, they could learn a thing or two about staying off the radar from her. The Barres™ candy factory's profile was as clean as a whistle with Allison running it and Matt's itchy jewelry, but they'd still been searched three times since they expanded to drugs.

Theo considered putting the tracker that was in his pocket on her bike while it sat out back, but he didn't want to go near the coffee shop, even in the alley. His instincts said that would be a bad move. He was going to have to follow her the old-fashioned way and plant the tracker when she was somewhere else.

Hopefully that would lead them to the identity of her boyfriend and mentor. He was a complete mystery. His photo brought up no hits in the databases Troy could hack into. Troy couldn't even find a cover identity for him. It was likely he wasn't a local. He had no name, no back story, no connections.

Wanting something to happen, Theo pulled his phone out again to see if Allison had heard anything yet. She had stepped in when Troy came up empty and had sent the photos to a contact from her MBA who had deeper pockets in hopes that they could identify the mystery man. Theo remembered meeting the contact around the time Allison decided to expand Barres™ and form the Wrappers.

At the time, Hughie Minfried was just a businessman who even Theo didn't want to mess with. There was something about him that made Theo feel like an amateur. It didn't help that Allison acted all coy and besotted around him, which set off all sorts of alarm bells. Neither of his nor his sister's reactions made sense when he considered that Hughie was an overly large hamster hybrid.

It wasn't until Hughie took over for his brother and started running the Minfried crime family over in Rafity City that things started making sense. Theo hadn't been familiar with Rafity City's crime scene, but apparently all the Minfrieds made Theo look benign in comparison. Each and every member of the family, except for Hughie, was in prison and convicted of being sick fucks. Theo didn't know enough to figure out if Hughie was just as bad or worse than the rest of his family. But since the hamster wasn't local, he ignored whatever contact his sister might be having with the rodent.

While Theo chafed at being assigned basic lookout work like the low man on the totem pole, at least he wasn't watching Tommy-the-dipshit's empty place anymore. It was slightly better to be watching a person than a place, but watching was boring. He preferred making his point with much more *impact*. He was much more useful *doing* something, but Allison wanted him here and there was no way he'd ignore a direct order. He liked who he was just fine and didn't want her to dig her nails deeper into him.

His phone didn't have any new messages. There still wasn't news from Hughie. Or at least news that Allison wanted to share yet.

To pass the time, Theo cracked his knuckles and fantasized about what he'd do to Tommy-the-dipshit first when they found him. Would he start with the basics? Bone breaking? Fingernail removal? They only needed him to be able to snort Nip and rhapsody about the experience. There were so many possibilities Theo could explore with him.... Maybe he'd even get the chance to pull out his knives.

Finally, after another hour and a half, the girl left the coffee shop and hopped on her bike. Theo followed in his car.

He had been prepared for circuitous routes and her checking for a tail, but he saw no evidence of either. Keeping track of her as she rode her bike was ridiculously easy — alarmingly so. Not only did she do nothing to lose him, her bike was so old and rickety it sounded like it might combust at any second. She was either clueless that she'd been made the other night, or she was doing something to check her surroundings that he wasn't aware of. Theo even started looking around to see if someone was following her behind him, acting as her lookout, but no one was there.

When she stopped at a grocery store and went inside, Theo lurked at the edge of the parking lot for several minutes before finally slinking up to her bike and planting the tracking device. He would have slipped it inside the frame near the engine, but given the state of the bike, she might take it in for work any day. Since the newest part of the bike were the wheels — they'd been changed somewhat recently — he settled for an easier to locate position in the wheel well.

After she came out with her groceries, Theo tracked her, at a much greater distance, through suburbia and to a house that looked like a family home. Frowning, he decided to come back and search the place after dark. If she had kids crawling around, it'd be better to look when they were all in bed. Particularly because, if she had kids, they couldn't be very old and little kids were the worst. Theo never knew where they'd be or how loud they'd scream when an unknown person waltzed through. Subduing kids who couldn't even buy their product was where he drew the line. Once they were old enough to start buying, they were fair game.

However, the last thing Theo expected when he showed up after eleven that night was to see the girl wheeling a different bike than before down the street like she was a teenager trying to sneak out without alerting anyone.

Chapter 18

Melissa

After waiting in suspense since yesterday afternoon for Rick to come by for his *talk*, Melissa was more than a little frustrated. And, unlike most nights, she had plans. It was Flight Night, and no way she was bailing on Bethany.

Melissa grabbed her jacket and a warm scarf before heading to the garage. Carefully, she started rolling her bike down the dark street. One of her neighbors, a pair of dog hybrids, had a newborn who only slept the first half of the night. Melissa had no intention of stealing that respite from the young couple. She hadn't thought her bike was overly loud, but it wasn't nearly as quiet as others, which she was much more aware of after riding with Rick. Though his bike was bigger, it was significantly quieter than hers. As she rounded the corner at the end of the block, she hopped on her bike and started up the motor. It took her a half-hour to get to the university fields.

Parking with the other vehicles in the mostly empty parking lot, she walked to the middle of the field where twenty or thirty people had gathered. Bethany waved Melissa over to what was command central for the night — a handful of folding chairs that lay in a haphazard pile and a set of folding tables set up in the middle of the field. On the tables were basic first aid supplies for in-flight injuries and refreshments for after the event.

Flight Night was the only time Melissa ever saw Bethany in something less than chic; granted, on her, leggings and a highly reflective tank top were only a step below formal attire. Even her rare ponytail and bare feet didn't detract from her style. Around Bethany stood a few other grad students who regularly helped her organize the event. Then, there were the participants — some of whom looked confident (the veterans of the event) and many who were nervous.

"Okay, everyone," Bethany shouted over the general conversation. "We've gone over the rules and safety procedures. If you haven't already, please take your hybrid form." Bethany paused and snapped her arms out from her body with her webbed bat-wings prominent. Her skin had darkened a few degrees to being nearly black. Her long white hair was a stark contrast to the night sky she would soar through in a moment.

The gathered students were all winged hybrids — there were two other bats and a handful of owls, but the majority were daytime birds who wanted to try their hand at night flying. Most of the daytime birds had goggles to help them see better in the dark.

"Now, line up with your flying buddy," Bethany continued. "If you're nervous, remember your partner has had at least one former night flight experience. Those of us in reflective neon yellow are all experts. You can flag any of us down in the air. If you want to stop at any time for any reason, return to this field and land. Melissa and Tony," she pointed at Melissa and the man next to her, "are non-hybrids and will be here to help you or summon an expert if needed. They have been here for many Flight Nights, and while they don't have personal experience of the night, they are well-versed and a good resource should you have questions on the ground. And now, may the wind fill your wings!"

In pairs, students took to the night sky. Some of the pairs had a synchronized take off with a smooth rustling of their feathers. Others, had a partner flapping excessively as their wings made frantic and ungainly swipes at the air. She always winced at this last type of take-off. Tonight, there were three students who clearly didn't grow up in hybrid-friendly areas because it looked like they hadn't had a lot of experience taking off. That or none of the bird hybrids they knew growing up could fly.

Melissa imagined flying was like riding her motorcycle, but more. More freedom. More exhilaration. More terror of making a mistake and hitting the ground. The first timers impressed her with their courage, even if they were awkward to witness. They were taking a chance and doing something new and unsettling.

"Don't worry," Tony said beside Melissa when she cringed at one bird's ungainly takeoff. "Enrique is noting who to watch."

Tony wore a university sweatshirt with Kelly the Mosquito on it holding up a sign that read, "You can't smack me down!" The mosquito was a rather new mascot, but reasonable because there weren't any known mosquito hybrids. No one wanted to give the appearance of favoring a certain hybrid just by the nature of their historical mascot. Granberg University's former mascot was a bear, but bear hybrids weren't well regarded because at the time of the Crisis, half of them had been illegally raising bears as pets. No university wanted to inadvertently sponsor that.

"Enrique works at the local flight school Winging On, doesn't he?" Melissa remembered Bethany saying his name before.

"Manages it, yeah."

Melissa nodded and pulled one of the folding chairs out of the pile to sit down in. She could hear various calls above her — tips, warnings, general encouragement, or even just a love of the night air. As she watched for glimpses of the reflective fabrics of the flyers and Bethany's moonlit hair, Melissa imagined flying with them. The faint breeze that brushed her face would be a torrent of air that rippled her clothes against her body. The roar of air in her ears would make her wish she had earmuffs. Her arms would be taut and straining as she let an air current fling her higher and higher.

Flying had to be intoxicating.

It wasn't long before the first pair of flyers landed, and Melissa stopped daydreaming. The lovebird hybrid in the pair was shaking badly and had numerous leaves wedged between his feathers. He was only wearing silver running shorts to make the most of his feathers in the air, which had bitten him in the butt tonight. Tony immediately went to him and started carefully pulling leaves out and reassuring him that this was a common occurrence on first night flights. It would take a while to get all the debris out of his feathers, even with the two of them working at it. Melissa brought a hot cup of tea to the lime green budgie hybrid that had been flying with him.

"Here," Melissa passed her the tea. "How are you doing?"

"I thought he was ready," she said. "I let him take the lead on the second pass. I should have had him do a few more laps." Melissa knew they had particular flight paths to discourage collisions and certain sections were for doing tricks instead of just mastering not running into the trees that grew along the edge of the field.

"Don't beat yourself up. At least one flyer gets a little roughed up each Flight Night, often more when there are a lot of flyers who aren't nocturnal."

"I know," the budgie sighed. Following the budgie's lead, Melissa sat back down in her chair to give the lovebird and Tony some breathing room to remove the leaves. From previous nights, Melissa knew more than two people were a crowd when pulling out twigs.

A second set landed soon after — an experienced bat hybrid and a zebra finch hybrid with little flight experience. The zebra finch looked both exhausted and elated. He was one of the flyers she had winced at earlier. The budgie and bat conferred with their flying partners before leaving them behind to take to the air again.

When the zebra finch hybrid plopped down next to Melissa, he was already talking a mile a minute about the experience. He didn't even pause when he shifted to his human form. Melissa smiled and listened to him as she watched the sky. A few minutes later, he went over to Tony and the lovebird hybrid to help pick the remaining twigs and leaves out of the lovebird's feathers. If the lovebird hybrid switched back to human form with those still embedded, they ended up being nasty splinters. Melissa had been told that even that explanation fell short of the actual experience.

Feeling a little chilled, Melissa got up to move. She did some squats and jumped up and down to keep her legs warm and get her blood pumping. Then, she started to set up for when everyone landed by pulling the refreshments out of their boxes and setting up the chairs.

She also looked at the field for anything that might disrupt landing and saw a lone figure standing in the parking lot. She told Tony she was going to go tell whoever it was that they were welcome to come learn about the event, and he assured her he had things covered. Many a Flight Night, someone too nervous to attend watched from afar. They came and participated in the next Flight Night if Melissa or someone else on the ground got the chance to talk to them.

As she got closer, the person's silhouette became clearer, and Melissa could tell it was a man, but not much else. She had just reached the edge of the grass and raised her hand to say hello when she heard a rough exhale and a blur collided with her, knocking the air out of her body. Her vision went black for a moment, and she worked on gulping air into her lungs to remedy that issue. As her vision cleared, the first thing she did was squeeze her eyes back shut to hide the sight of the ground speeding past. She was tucked under someone's arms like a ball while they ran, jostling her violently with every step. Even with her eyes closed, she fought the urge to vomit. A bounce pushed her jacket and shirt up her midriff, and she felt two bands of soft silky fur wrapped across her middle and the cold pads of the person's hands on either side of her body.

The entire experience only lasted a minute or two, but when the person set her down, she had to brace herself on her hands and knees while she tried to get her bearings. She wasn't in the field anymore, but in the wooded area past the parking lot. On her own it would have taken her fifteen minutes to reach the spot. She hadn't even known it was possible to move that fast on foot. Whoever had grabbed her took two steps away from her; they moved so quietly that she was certain they were a cat hybrid. It was rare for other hybrids to be *that* stealthy. She wracked her brain for a fast cat hybrid that she knew and came up blank, but it didn't make sense for someone she'd never met before to grab her.

"Who—"

"Quiet, Melissa," a vaguely familiar voice whispered.

Pressing her lips into a thin line, she held in her questions for the moment and spent her time trying to identify the man. He was wearing long athletic shorts and possibly no shirt, but under the trees, the light was even worse than out in the field. His ears were more rounded at the tip than was typical for a cat hybrid and reminded her more of a bear's than a cat's. Nothing about him telegraphed his identity.

"Shit, Melissa," the man said in irritation after a moment. "I know you didn't think he was dangerous, but you didn't really invite him out here in the middle of the night, did you?"

"Invite who?" she snapped, not liking this person's tone or the stabby twigs she was kneeling on.

"Theo."

"I don't know *anyone* named Theo."

A growl emanated from the man.

"*Who* are you?" Melissa said in response.

"Rick's going to be pissed," he said instead of responding.

Melissa blinked at the mention of Rick and thought of the only cat hybrid she knew in connection.

"Dave?"

"Yeah?"

It was Dave. So, not one of her friends, but rather one of Rick's. That made more sense.

"Who was in the parking lot?" she tried again.

"Theo Barre, the guy trying to find Kate's brother."

"Why'd he come to Flight Night?" Melissa had no idea what would bring him there. But given Dave's frustration, she doubted he would give her answers, so she kept explaining: "Tommy never comes to these events. Even Kate doesn't come. Any predator/prey connections are avoided in case someone triggers the participants' fight-or-flight responses. Anything and anyone that could cause panic or key up new flyers is avoided, which begs the question as to why *you're* here."

"What's Flight Night?" Dave asked, walking over and offering her a hand up. Melissa grabbed his hand, feeling the cool pads of his fingers and the super short, silky fur along the back of his hands. Her midsection twinged but didn't hurt too badly as he helped her up.

Pulled to her feet, she explained the premise of Flight Night as Dave tapped a message out on his phone. When he finished his message, she reiterated her first question to see if he'd answer or, at minimum, acknowledge the question this time: "What is the Theo-guy doing here?"

"Not a clue," Dave said. "Rick will be here in an hour to take you home unless you have another reliable ride to call." Before Melissa could answer, he added, "And by reliable, I mean someone who could beat Theo in a fight if needed."

"Can't I go get my bike and ride home?"

"No. He could be watching. He might have tampered with your bike. It's in the lot where he was standing, right?"

Melissa tamped down the unfamiliar feeling of panic that rose in her chest. Maybe this guy *was* up to no good. Anyone who messed with her bike — her daily connection to her brother — had issues.

"You should have Rick do his bi-annual bike maintenance on your ride to check it for anything suspicious," Dave continued, oblivious to Melissa's world tipping sideways. "He'll be able to tell if there's something wrong faster than the rest of us. Shawn said Rick muttered something about it being a month overdue."

"A month overdue?" She latched onto his weird comment to avoid freaking out about the Theo-guy messing with her bike.

"The maintenance Rick does on your bike twice a year. He said something about being a month overdue. Rick didn't like the way it rumbled or something."

Melissa reached out and grabbed Dave's forearm. She waited for him to look up at her instead of at his phone and made a conscious effort not to stroke his fur to soothe herself.

"Rick services my bike twice a year?" Melissa could feel her eyebrows stay in their raised position when she finished speaking and had to force her forehead to relax lest Dave think they were stuck like that.

Dave blinked at her like a deer in headlights. "Umm, it sounded like that to Jeremy and Susan over Shawn's comm."

"The mechanic has always been floored that my bike runs as well as it does. I mean, Bobby and Rick built it when they were seventeen. I just thought they did a good job."

Dave's tongue flicked out in a nervous tell Melissa had seen people do when they misspoke.

So apparently, Rick had been breaking into her parents' garage and taking care of her bike twice a year during his visits to his mom. She didn't know what to make of that, but Greg's theory that Rick had secretly liked her for years was seeming *much* more plausible. And had he been doing that when she'd had her own apartment, too?

"Um, other faster rides than Rick getting here with a car?" Dave asked.

Melissa shook her head and let the topic of Rick secretly maintaining her bike slide.

"You're fast," she pointed out after a minute or two of silence.

Dave shrugged, looking around them as if he thought Theo might burst through the trees. As if anyone could keep up with Dave.

"Like really fast. You—" Melissa's eyes nearly popped out of her head. "You aren't a Bengal cat!"

He looked at her then, with his head tilted to the side and his eyes narrowing like he found her unpredictable.

"You— Are you a cheetah hybrid?"

"Mostly," he said hesitantly.

"Mostly?"

"It's kind of personal," he muttered.

"Sorry." Melissa rubbed a hand across her eyes. That was horribly rude. You never asked what type of hybrid someone was or even if they were a hybrid. "My parents always ask. They're mapping the hybrid genome and always share details about rare hybrids. I didn't mean to pry."

"If you could, you know, not mention it to people, I'd appreciate that."

"Of course," Melissa said.

They sat in awkward silence for a while until Melissa found herself smiling about the other night with Rick.

"You giggled," Dave said. "What's funny about this?" He was trying to figure her out.

Her smile grew, and another giggle escaped her. "I was just remembering your obsession."

"My obsession?" He narrowed his eyes at her.

"With pink ponies."

His eyes flew open in shock. "How do you know about that?"

"That makes it sound like you *do* have an obsession." When he just glared at her in response, she relented. "After you and Jeremy came to the coffee shop, I asked Rick to tell me a story about Bobby and you guys. Bobby never shared much of anything with me about the Mavens. It sounds like a great memory to have." She gave Dave a small smile.

He draped his arm over her shoulders just like Bobby had done a few times when he'd broken his and Rick's no-touch rules and shook his head, tickling her with his whiskers. "If you tell anyone, I'll deny it." He let out a little snort. "But it *was* hilarious. More so in retrospect. Some time, I'll have to tell you about what I did to Susan to retaliate. Bobby helped then, too. He was in favor of all pranks."

"That sounds like Bobby." Melissa smiled into the night and relaxed against Dave. He smelled like warm fur and made Melissa think about soaking in the sun with Kate. "What other pranks did he help you pull?" She couldn't hide her anticipation about hearing more of her brother's antics.

Dave chuckled and told her about a prank they pulled on Jeremy while they waited for Rick to show up.

Chapter 19

Rick

Rick slowly drove his mother's SUV with the headlights dimmed along the service road that went into the woods behind Granberg University. Dave had sent him GPS coordinates for a rendezvous point and little other information. As he drove, Rick reminded himself that Dave knew what he was doing, even if he hadn't said anything about the locked gate that Rick had to pick to access the service road. Before joining the Mavens, Dave had been a Marine. He could be ready to act on a threat in seconds. Melissa was safe. Still, worry ate at Rick while he searched for any sign of them.

The trees on either side of the road looked dense in the dark, but he knew he could easily look through them for quite a distance during the day. It was frustrating to be able to see so little at the moment. He rolled his windows down in case Dave and Melissa saw him and called out, but the night was eerily silent. He wasn't sure if it was him driving down the road or something else that had sent the wildlife into hiding. Normally, even at this hour, insects would chirp and leaves would rustle as nocturnal animals crept along branches for their nightly hunts. Having reached the GPS coordinates, he stopped and waited.

A few minutes later, Rick narrowed his eyes at Dave's grip on Melissa's elbow as they came out of the trees. Dave was shirtless as he helped her up a three-foot slope on the side of the road. Rick knew Melissa didn't need assistance for that... unless Dave wasn't telling him something.

Rick's grip on the steering wheel didn't ease up until Dave removed his hand and, despite being shirtless, didn't do anything that looked like he was coming on to Melissa. The cherry on top was that Melissa didn't even seem to notice Dave's furry chest. Rick had seen way too many ladies petting any exposed part of Dave's fur to not be aware that it was remarkably soft. Furthermore, thanks to Dave himself, Rick knew the cheetah hybrid used conditioner on his entire coat, not just the longer bit on his head that resembled his human form's haircut. Putting the car in park, Rick jumped out to make sure he got as much information as possible.

"Sweet ride," Dave said. His smirk was directed at the front bumper sticker that said, "Beware, I'll biology all over you." It was a gag gift Rick's mother had gotten from students after refusing to speak to them about anything but biology, even if she ran into them at the grocery store.

"What happened?" Rick asked, ignoring Dave's commentary all together. As he asked the question, he ran his hands over Melissa's shoulders and down her arms, checking for injuries and reasons why Dave would need to help her up that small slope. She looked to be in one piece, but more tired than he'd seen her since the days when she was working twelve-plus hours fixing up her coffee shop.

"Basically, what I told you. Theo was here; I got Melissa away; and she needed a ride." Dave tilted his head questioningly at Rick. Rick ignored the unspoken question about him and Melissa. He didn't want to have to define his comfort levels or lack thereof around Melissa and touching her.

"I asked you not to go out looking for Tommy on your own. You agreed not to," Rick said to Melissa.

"First off, you asked me not to do that *last night*. You said nothing about tonight." She staunchly pointed out. Rick did not appreciate the technicality and made sure to look at her with sarcastic disbelief. "Second, I wasn't looking for Tommy. It's Bethany's Flight Night. Either Greg or I help out each month. This month was my turn."

"Bethany was at the coffee shop the other day, right? Next to Kate? She flies?" Rick took a step away, having determined that Melissa was unhurt.

"She's a bat hybrid," Melissa supplied helpfully.

"So, Dave was running by, doing reconnaissance, happened to see you in the vicinity of Theo Barre, and pulled you away before he saw you?"

"Not exactly," Dave said. "I noticed an atypical grouping in the field with a lot of air traffic for the late hour and decided it was worth investigating. Theo was standing in the parking lot among the cars, watching her. Then Melissa started walking over to him without a care in the world." Dave said the last part with an accusing tone at Melissa.

"I thought he was a reluctant flyer," Melissa said with a touch of defensiveness. Her accompanying shrug told Rick she really had thought that, but there was enough hesitation she might be questioning how "harmless" she considered Theo, which was about damn time. "As part of ground detail, it's my job to have a word with anyone I find and let them know they're welcome."

"Before she got to him, in plain view, I ran through and grabbed her."

"Please tell me you slowed down." Rick held his breath.

"Of course I did!" Dave paused until Rick exhaled. "At least... as much as truly necessary." Rick's curse was cut off by Dave's defense: "It's important not to get identified. We can't have them connecting anything to us."

Rick immediately reached back to Melissa and stripped her jacket off, ignoring her shocked inhale. Underneath, she had a skin-tight yellow tee and an orange scarf at her neck. There were faint bruises on her left arm which he did *not* like. He brushed his fingertips over them as he kept searching.

"And, I couldn't have hurt her much." Dave gestured at Melissa in a sort of lost way. "She barely squeaked when I grabbed her."

"I squeaked?" Melissa asked. "I only remember my vision blacking out."

Shooting Dave a threatening glare at Melissa's addition, Rick slipped his hands under the thin fabric of her shirt along her skin and pushed it up. Multi-hued bruises had already appeared around her middle and would soon hurt badly if they didn't already.

"Rick?" Dave asked.

Rick angrily turned his head toward Dave and saw his teammate's eyes glued to his bare hands on Melissa's exposed and colorful mid-section.

"It doesn't hurt a lot," Melissa whispered to reassure him. Rick looked back at her and took in the tension in her brow. He didn't believe her, but he'd deal with that later. His mind finally registered where his hands were — namely *in* her shirt and against her incredibly soft skin. It took conscious effort, but Rick managed to pull his hands away.

"So, Theo saw a flash of you as you blew by and grabbed her," he reasoned, trying to focus on the facts like this was a mission rather than Melissa. "What about other people at this," he glanced at her, "Flight Night?"

"I hadn't even thought about that! I need to call Bethany." Melissa's voice rose as she tugged her shirt back into place. She grabbed Rick's forearm and gave it a meaningful squeeze. "She's going to worry. I've never disappeared during a Flight Night. And even if no one's worried about me, my bag's there and everything. I need a phone."

Dave shook his head before responding to Rick's question: "The people flying would only have noticed if they were watching Melissa, and the people on the ground were focused on one of them. Like fixing an injury or something."

"One of the flyers got leaves and twigs stuck in his feathers, but they knew I was going to talk to someone by the parking lot. Bethany is going to freak. Phone," Melissa prompted, looking between the two of them as if she didn't care which one helped her. Not liking that, Rick pulled his phone out.

"Do you know her number?" he asked her, barely holding himself back from Dave. When she shook her head and bit her lip, Rick stared at her and dialed Jeremy. "I need Melissa's friend Bethany's phone number." A minute later, he passed his phone to a wide-eyed Melissa who squeezed her lips together, not asking him how he got her friend's number.

She put his phone to her ear and bent over to grab her jacket from the ground, but a small, pained sound slipped from her lips. Rick rounded on Dave, who had the presence of mind to look like he felt bad about hurting her.

"I didn't break anything, I swear," Dave said, his hands up between them, but with his claws extended to make his point.

Between the look on his friend's face and his claws, Rick realized that he did not have it together. Considering he was thinking of pounding Dave into a pulp, that seemed accurate. Shoving his hands into his pockets, Rick took a breath and reined himself in even more. Melissa was oblivious to their entire exchange; she was too busy talking fast on the phone and assuring Bethany that everything was fine.

"Did—" Dave hesitated. "Did Bobby know?"

Yanking his attention back to Dave, Rick just stared at him.

Dave didn't back down.

"Did he know how you feel?"

Rick pressed his lips together and turned back to the car. Instead of answering Dave, Rick held the front passenger door open for Melissa. He didn't need Dave on his case about her. His mother *and* Susan were more than enough to worry about. And that was when they didn't have a clue how he felt about her. The worst part, though, was that he couldn't tell if Bobby would approve or if he was just caring a lot less about Bobby's opinion on the matter.

"Thanks," Melissa said to Rick, setting the phone in the cup holder between them when he climbed back into the driver's seat. "We got lucky; Flight Night ran a full half hour late in the sky, so Bethany hadn't known that I was gone until about ten minutes ago. That and that I didn't scream. She's adamant I'd be a screamer if someone tried to kidnap me or something."

"How much time has she spent considering how you'd react to being kidnapped?" Dave murmured incredulously from the back seat.

Melissa didn't hear him and continued, "I barely talked her down. She was on the cusp of phoning the police because she didn't believe Tony when he said I had ditched him and left him to do everything by himself."

"What excuse did you give her?" Rick asked. He ignored the name Tony since Melissa sounded as annoyed as he was that someone would think that about her.

"I was going to tell her I found someone with a twisted ankle and helped them to their car, only to have to drive them to the emergency room because it was their right ankle and they couldn't drive. But, for some reason, I told her what happened."

Rick resolutely stared straight ahead, ignoring the wary look Dave was giving him in the rearview mirror. He should have thought about the fact that Melissa would answer any and all of Bethany's questions with the truth after he'd had his hands on her, but he hadn't. Earlier, he'd actively thought she was lying to him about being okay after Dave grabbed her, but that was impossible. He'd been touching her. She, at the very least, believed she wasn't too hurt and told the truth. As it was, she still couldn't control what she said. His touch hadn't worn off yet. He truly hadn't remembered he was forcing her to tell the truth. They'd just have to deal with the fallout from whatever she told her friend, and he'd need to be more aware in the future.

"What did you say?" Dave asked when Rick didn't. Melissa didn't know Dave well enough to hear the apprehension in his voice, but Rick could feel it in the air.

"I can't believe I told her. I told her the guy that tried to grab Kate had been loitering in the parking lot, and one of Rick's friends was around and hauled me off in case he had nefarious intentions like you all think. She was both relieved I had people looking out for me and alarmed the guy had been at her Flight Night."

"So, nothing about me—"

"Being a cheetah hybrid? No, that didn't seem relevant."

Dave sunk back against the seat in relief, but when he caught Rick's eye in the rearview mirror, Rick watched him mouth the question he had been dreading: "Why haven't you told her?" Rick couldn't remember a time before this past week when it might have been something Melissa might have needed to know. He had kept his distance, so she hadn't been on the short list. Outside of the Mavens, only Neil and his mother knew. His father didn't even know; granted, he hadn't been around long. Rick and his mother had only ever talked about him once back when Rick was seventeen and thinking he might want to know his father; apparently, the cheating bastard had been seeing three other women and suddenly had difficulty lying to his mother about it after Rick was born — imagine that. With that knowledge, Rick had lost interest in getting to know the man.

Back at their houses, Rick drove straight into his mother's garage, closing it before Melissa could even suggest going directly to her house. Inside the kitchen, Rick didn't hesitate before speaking over the echo of their shoes on the tile.

"We have to assume Theo has somehow decided Melissa is a person of interest in Tommy's disappearance or he remembers her from the coffee shop. We will assume he knows her name."

"And hence her place of residence and her bike," Dave nodded along.

Melissa stared at the two of them like they had lost their minds. "You think that, not only might he have tampered with my bike, but that he's going to come..." she trailed off and looked toward her house.

"It's a possibility. I'll pick up your bike tomorrow and check it out," Rick assured her as he flicked the kitchen light on. He focused back on Dave. "That said, I haven't slept in thirty-six hours."

"You want me to watch her house," Dave said, following his train of thought.

Melissa was starting to pull in breaths like there was a slight oxygen shortage. Rick reached out to her and placed a hand on the small of her back so she wasn't alone, but kept talking to Dave.

"I'll set you up in the study; it's directly across from Melissa's room." A fact that Rick wouldn't be forgetting any time soon, and even less so while touching her, even if it was through her clothes. "If he breaks in tonight, he'll be most interested in that room; it's the only bedroom that clearly has a someone living it."

"What's the picture situation?" Dave continued. He was studiously not looking at Rick stroking a calming hand down the back of Melissa's jacket.

"Lots of Bobby."

"I'll go in and remove all those before he gets a chance to see them."

"Why?" Melissa's voice was an octave higher than normal, which Rick had never heard before. Granted, he'd never broken through her enchanted view that everyone was, deep down, a good person.

Dave stared at his feet, leaving the decision of how much to say up to Rick. Rick sighed.

"There are no pictures of the Mavens," Rick said carefully. He turned fully toward her so she'd know she had his full attention. "None, Mel. No online photos, no shared photos, no photos in any database. The only photos of us are the ones we have of ourselves or our family has, and we never share those with someone who doesn't know us."

"So," Melissa swallowed, "there's no way to identify you."

"Right," Rick said.

He watched Melissa carefully and decided she did *not* look okay. Pretending Dave wasn't there, Rick pulled Melissa to him and wrapped her in a hug. She pressed her face into his neck like the other night, and all he could do was hold her a little tighter. The skin of her cheek was cold, and he hoped his body heat would bring a little color back to her face. Without meaning to, he got a lungful of her coffee infused scent and let his eyes drift shut for a second. Hugging her was the right thing to do. Protecting her, keeping her safe, was the right thing to do.

"You're going to stay here tonight," he said, guiding her toward the hallway and away from Dave.

Melissa pulled free from him and went back to give Dave a hug. Rick heard her whisper, "Thanks for looking out for me," to him and distinctly noticed that, though she touched him, she didn't pet him. Not that Rick doubted Dave would do a good job watching over Melissa's house, but after being touched by her, he would do an even better job, regardless of the dampening effect of his fur.

Rick ushered Melissa down the hall, pausing to grab some pain meds from the bathroom and then continuing on to his bedroom. The lights were off, and Melissa went directly to his bed and sat down. He didn't know what to think of her knowing her way around his room in the dark even though it'd been years since she'd hung out in there with him and Bobby. Rick set the medicine on the nightstand. Then, he rifled through the dresser on the left wall and gave her one of his old tee-shirts and a pair of his sweats from high school. She started taking her jacket and boots off; her stilted movements proved she was starting to hurt from Dave grabbing her.

Rick didn't know how he managed to get out of the room with her in it. In all honesty, they'd been alone in his bedroom for barely a minute, but his body was having all sorts of thoughts about her in his clothes and in his bed, even if it was his old bed at his mother's house. He was not proud to admit how much time he spent in that bed trying not to think about Melissa over the years.

The door behind him creaked open. Rick turned and looked at his mother, who was not even attempting to be subtle in the flicks between her eyes and his bedroom. He put a finger to his lips and shook his head, telling her to be quiet. He wasn't surprised when she followed him back out to the kitchen. In her robe and pajamas, she smiled grandly at Dave, who looked torn between freezing up and acting like it was perfectly normal to meet Rick's mother after midnight while shirtless.

"This is Dave. He's a friend." Rick flipped his hand at Dave in a dismissive gesture.

"It's wonderful to meet you," his mother said. She surged forward like she wasn't in her pajamas and shook Dave's hand. "You can call me Jessy."

"Dave will be in the study helping me with something," Rick continued before Dave could respond. Walking over to the key dish, Rick pulled out Melissa's key. It was easy to find with the red lanyard Bobby had made at camp when they were seven years old. Rick tossed the key to Dave, who nodded and slipped out without another word. Maybe Dave wasn't keen on "meeting the parents," even if it wasn't a girl's parents.

"Why is he going to Melissa's if she's in your bedroom?" his mother asked.

"I'm helping Melissa with a problem," he answered.

His mother took her time deciding if she approved of the response, but in the end, she did. Her smile spoke volumes. In her opinion, anything, even a problem, was good if it pushed him and Melissa together. And Rick was too tired to set her straight.

Chapter 20

Melissa

The impact of Dave's arms colliding with her middle jarred Melissa awake.

She jack-knifed up in bed and her shoulder brushed curtains that let in the morning light. They weren't hers. Melissa froze at both the excruciating ache of her midsection and the surroundings she hadn't seen in almost a decade. She looked around as she wrenched her breathing down to slow pants that didn't hurt quite as much.

Rick's bed was much smaller than hers and sat against the wall under the window. The room looked the same as it had when he and Bobby had first left fourteen years ago. Their decision to join the army should have been more obvious to her given the single-themed posters around the room, but the choice had surprised her at the time.

Directly in front of her, above Rick's dresser, was a poster of the G.I. Hybrid Force that had been recognized for freeing hybrids and humans alike from a collapsed building during a natural disaster. Without the team's hybrid abilities, not everyone inside would have been freed, and none as quickly as they had been. It had been all over the news when Melissa was ten, not that she'd paid much attention to it at that age. Rick had two of the action figures sitting on his dresser, and Bobby had the other three on his desk to complete the set. Over Rick's desk, next to the door was another poster. This one had a variety of military grade vehicles with detailed specs of their hybrid modifications. The small bookcase in the corner of the room had school books that should have been gotten rid of long ago. On the top shelf of the bookcase stood Rick's half of the model motorcycles he and Bobby had painstakingly put together in middle school.

Once Melissa had her breathing under control, she swung her legs over the side of the bed. Her eyes fell on the bottle of pain medicine Rick had left her with, and she took another two pills. Carefully, she stood up and walked to the door to look in the full-length mirror there. She was swamped in Rick's plain black tee-shirt and his bumblebee yellow Granberg High P.E. sweats. She slid the tee-shirt up her stomach to reveal blacks, blues, and purples in two loops from her hips to her rib cage as if she'd been hooked by two steel bands and crushed rather than carried by Dave while he sprinted. She squeezed her eyes shut and let the shirt fall back down, ignoring the faint smell of motor oil and detergent from the shirt. Bracing herself against the movement, she raised her arms and pulled her hair up into a messy bun on top of her head. Faint bruises on her left bicep caught her eye, but at least they didn't hurt.

Feeling like she'd been hit by a truck, she carefully opened the bedroom door. Quiet kitchen sounds trailed down the hall, and the smell of pancakes pulled her out of Rick's room. She walked to the bathroom with measured steps, testing how moving felt. Everything felt worse than last night, that was for sure.

After she finished in the bathroom, she stuck her head into the study and found it empty — at least of people. The desk, on the other hand, was littered with picture frames she recognized from her parents' house. Wanting to find out what was happening, she continued down the hall and into the kitchen.

"Morning," Jessy said from the stove. She was bustling about and had a stack of pancakes beside her that looked fit to feed a squadron of soldiers. She was already fully dressed despite not being done cooking, which wasn't her norm. Melissa took in the table set for five and a fresh set of clothes and her basic toiletries sitting on the couch in the living room to the left. "I went over with Dave, Carl, and a black cockatoo, who was too busy to introduce himself, and grabbed you a few things. I thought it best if I went rather than have the lot of them digging around unnecessarily."

The image of Rick and three of his friends — one she hadn't even met yet — digging through her underwear drawer flashed through her head. "Thanks," Melissa said, relieved to know that wasn't what had happened. "The cockatoo is Jeremy. I'll just go get dressed."

"Feel free to jump in a shower. The boys won't be back from your place for at least ten more minutes."

"What are they doing over there?" Melissa asked, staring toward her house as if she could see through the wall.

"I don't know, but there were mutters about security. I don't know what trouble you're in, but Rick and his friends seem to have a handle on it. Though I do *not* like that they all showed up on motorcycles. You'd think one of their mothers might have gotten through to them that it isn't safe to be whipping around at high speeds without thousands of pounds of steel protecting them from the other drivers out there."

"If you thought that was possible," Melissa shook her head, "then Rick wouldn't be riding one anymore."

Jessy's response was a discontented noise that came out her nose. Melissa left her in the kitchen and took a quick shower, noting Jessy had even grabbed her conditioner. The hot water relieved some of the tension in her body, but not all of it. Melissa took comfort in the fact that Jessy felt that Rick and his friends had things under control. She might not know all the details, but her assurances helped soothe Melissa. Feeling more like herself after getting dressed, she went back out to the kitchen and found it empty.

Melissa made herself a plate of mouth-watering pancakes and almost dropped it when she turned around. Standing between the kitchen and the living room was a bald man two and a half times her own size. He was not only tall, but his shoulders and muscles intimated that he could probably pick up her motorcycle and throw it across the room without a care in the world. The muscles in his arms pushed his tee-shirt sleeves to the limit. Melissa's first instinct was to move away, but she fought it, suppressed the twinge from her bruises when she tensed, and continued to the table to set down her plate. Turning back to the hulk of a man, she extended her hand toward him.

"Hi, I'm Melissa."

He cracked a half smile and shook his head at her.

"They were absolutely right. No self-preservation instincts."

Melissa frowned and was about to withdraw her hand when he reached out and shook it. His large, darker hand enveloped hers with ease and instilled her with a distinct chill. His cold skin might mean he was a reptile hybrid.

"I'm Carl."

"What do you mean, no self-preservation instincts?" Melissa cocked her head to the side as she looked at the third friend of Rick's that she'd met in as many days.

"Most people take one look at me and turn tail." He shrugged.

"I've never met anyone who was as mean as they looked. Most people are just too quick to judge," she pointed out. She couldn't understand why no one else got that. She had met so many people who, from a glance, appeared dangerous but, in truth, wouldn't hurt a fly. "Anyway, Jessy made double the number of pancakes she usually does. Help yourself."

She watched Carl as he walked over to the pancakes. He had a slit down the center back of his shirt, leading her to modify her guess to something that had large spikes down its back or a fin in their hybrid form; Professor Torres, a few blocks down, wore shirts like Carl had on, and they looked a lot alike.

"Are you, by any chance, related to Professor Torres?" she asked.

"Yeah, he's my uncle."

Melissa blinked at that news.

"And you're aquatic too?" That Professor Torres was a shark spoke to his working in the aquarium when the Crisis hit and not to any familial genetics, but between the chill of Carl's skin and the slit in his shirt, she couldn't help but ask.

"Yeah, he had helped my mom get an internship at the aquarium. She was working there during the Crisis."

After piling seven pancakes on his plate, he turned around and walked to the table. Maybe Jessy hadn't overestimated their appetites.

"I can't wait to try these," Carl admitted as he sat down. "Bobby raved about them and bragged about how Jessy made them special just for him."

"She makes them the first morning of all Rick's visits."

"You're kidding." Carl's eyes glinted dangerously.

Melissa shook her head. He was probably a predator — a dolphin or whale hybrid perhaps, unless he was a shark hybrid like his uncle. It wasn't surprising that people found him intimidating.

Dave and Rick walked into the kitchen when Melissa was halfway through her pancakes, which were, in fact, better than she remembered. Dave looked dead on his feet, and Rick didn't look much better.

"How are you feeling today?" Dave asked, pointing at his midsection.

Melissa started to shrug in response but stopped herself before she could complete the painful action. "Could be worse," she said.

Dave had the sense to look guilty when Rick muttered something to him while they both filled their plates. After they sat down, neither of them said anything.

"So, my parents' house?" Melissa prompted them.

"We got lucky," Dave said. "I got all the photos and was slipping out the back when he entered the front."

"Who entered the front?"

"Theo Barre," Carl said off-handedly before taking another huge bite of the pancakes he'd steadily been demolishing.

"He was in my house?" Melissa's hand flashed out and closed around Rick's forearm, hoping he'd tell her they were having a laugh. Her voice rose so high both Dave and Carl stopped eating. They stared at her hand on Rick's exposed forearm. The fact that Rick's sleeve was pushed up in a rare display of skin only partially registered.

"That's why we had Dave getting Bobby's photos and watching the house, yeah?" Rick said, covering her hand with his. Dave drew Carl into a separate conversation while Rick stroked his thumb along her skin, and she tried to focus on the soothing warmth and the rough ridge of a callous that dragged back and forth.

"Jeremy has removed the two cameras and the tracking device on your parents' car in the garage that Theo left behind." Melissa's hand clenched tighter to Rick's arm at that news, but he didn't stop there. "We have photos of him leaving and might have his prints on the electronics. Once we know why he's interested in you, we'll charge him with breaking and entering and leaving behind surveillance cameras. It was sloppy. It was illegal. But without knowing why we don't want to show our hand. Jeremy is putting in a security system and cameras at the front and back doors, the garage, and at the windows to make sure it doesn't happen again."

Melissa just stared at Rick. This couldn't be real.

"Do you understand?" Rick asked when she didn't respond.

She nodded slowly, feeling like she'd forgotten how to blink.

"I'm going to need to you say it aloud, Mel." Rick gave her an apologetic smile. Dave and Carl went silent again when Rick asked her to speak.

"The literal words you just said? Yes, but I don't understand *how* this could happen." Melissa's mind unfroze and flew in all directions at once. "Have you checked Kate's place? She and Danny stayed there last night. This Theo-guy didn't seem any more dangerous than any of the other people that have come into my shop before. What is going on?" What Rick was saying went against everything she knew.

"Tommy got in way over his head," Rick said. "These people are serious about finding him. We don't know why *you* are on their radar, but I checked Kate's place myself after we got ice cream. There's a street camera near her place that can see her door. No one has gone there without Kate with them."

Melissa nodded.

"Hey," Jeremy's voice came from behind her. "Have you caught Melissa up on the security situation?" He stopped next to the table, and when Melissa looked up at him, he was staring at her hand under Rick's.

Melissa tried not to read too much into it, but they clearly thought it was a rather big deal since they all kept staring at Rick and her hands. She knew Rick didn't touch a lot of people, but this was getting ridiculous.

"He was in the process of it," Carl said under his breath.

"Right," Jeremy replied in the same *I'm-not-here* tone of voice. He walked across the kitchen, made a plate of pancakes, and sat down at the table. Dave instantly pulled him into whatever he and Carl had been discussing.

"Are you okay?" Rick asked Melissa.

"No. This is ridiculous." She threw her free hand up in the air and winced. "My entire abdomen twinges at the slightest movement, and this Theo-guy was watching me last night and then broke into my parents' house, leaving behind cameras and tracking devices! Before that, he was clearly harmless. Somehow, that is not the case anymore. Then, to top things off, Bobby's friends are suddenly falling out of the sky to help me out, and *you know* how people handle Bobby."

Melissa pulled her hand away from Rick so she could drop her head into her hands. None of this made sense. It vaguely registered that she was hanging her head over half-eaten pancakes.

"*And beyond* all that, there is the entire photo thing you threw at me last night. I'm certain, for some reason, that I'm not supposed to tell anyone that you aren't in a motorcycle club or anything resembling it. Oh! and Jessy told my parents that we're dating, and I didn't know how to answer them when they asked me yesterday," Melissa huffed at her plate.

"That's why you looked over yesterday when you were on the phone," Rick muttered.

"Yes. I had no idea you'd be standing there staring at me in nothing but a towel." She couldn't stop herself from saying as she looked up at Rick.

"Maybe we should go," Jeremy suggested.

Melissa turned red. She had forgotten the others.

"But I want to know which one of them was in a towel," Dave said. Jeremy's elbow jabbed into Dave's side, making him grunt. Dave didn't look remotely guilty about increasing her blush.

"How do people handle—" Carl paused to glance at Rick, "—Bobby around here?" Rick tensed slightly beside her when Carl said her brother's name.

"They don't," Rick answered for her. "No one talks about him, not with me, not with her, not with Neil."

At Carl's questioning head tilt, Jeremy quietly supplied, "The turtle."

"I find it hard to believe," Dave said, "with all the photos in the house and his untouched room, that your parents don't talk about him. With the reminders everywhere, how can they not?"

Melissa's heart contracted, and she saw Rick squeeze his eyes shut at Dave's comment. She knew Rick was thinking Dave was just rubbing salt in the wound she'd exposed to him the other night.

"They left on a year-long research sabbatical just a few months after the funeral. Somehow, it keeps getting extended," Melissa whispered. Admitting to all of them that she'd been alone made it worse.

"I asked my mother what she wasn't telling you about that," Rick said, meeting her eyes. He pushed his pancakes away like they were making him nauseous. "It's why I told you I wanted to talk." He took a deep breath. "Your parents aren't on sabbatical, Mel. They quit their positions at the university and are in charge of the entire research endeavor. That's why everyone treats their visits as just that, 'visits.' Your mom convinced my mother and whoever else knows not to tell you."

Melissa couldn't tear her eyes from Rick as he waited for that news to sink in. She'd never questioned why her parents sounded like they were in charge. Whenever they had talked about their research before Bobby died, they'd been in complete control over every aspect. They'd acted exactly the same the last few years, even though they'd made it sound like they were just part of a team. Hundreds of little hints from their phone calls snapped into place in Melissa's mind.

What Rick said made complete sense.

Her heart hollowed more, which she didn't know was possible. She was even more alone than she'd felt before.

After what had to be at least a minute, Carl's fork scraped along his plate and Melissa swung her eyes around the table to him. Everyone was watching her, except Carl. He was finishing his pancakes and eyeing Rick's plate in the middle of the table like he was considering eating Rick's portion too.

"My mom is nothing if not persuasive," Melissa said flatly, watching Carl. Rarely had she ever seen someone turn her mom down once she made a well-reasoned and impassioned argument. That was how Melissa had ended up house-sitting for her parents in the first place. Looking at her own plate, she took another bite, but it didn't taste nearly as good as before. She saw Jeremy and Dave cautiously start eating again. It was a toss-up which upset her more, that the Theo-guy had been in her house and was dangerous or that her parents had literally abandoned her.

The rest of the morning passed in a haze. Carl and Dave did the dishes while Rick and Jeremy showed her the new security system that they had installed in her parents' house. Whenever she got overwhelmed, they paused. Rick would wrap her in a gentle hug, and Jeremy would change the topic to talk about her friends until she was ready to continue. They both stressed to her that Theo Barre was very dangerous, and she heard them, but she wasn't able to process the information very well. There were too many things coming at her at once.

When Melissa and Rick left to go get her bike, she didn't enjoy the ride or the rumble of his bike. She barely pulled through the fog when Rick cupped her cheek and told her to take his bike to the coffee shop for her shift and that he'd bring hers over when he finished looking it over.

When she walked through the back door to the coffee shop, the sight of Bethany and Greg sitting in the staff area with her purse from the night before should have surprised her, but she was so far past surprise at that point that she just sat down with them and spilled everything that had happened since her maybe-date with Rick. The only things she left out were anything that hinted the Mavens weren't a run-of-the-mill motorcycle club, which meant she left out a lot.

Chapter 21

Rick

Rick pulled Melissa's fully serviced and now tracking-device-free bike next to his in the alley behind Juniper's Java. It was the first time he'd ridden the bike since the year he and Bobby built it. If anyone but Melissa had been riding it all these years, he had no doubt it would have stopped running ages ago. Granted, Rick had to admit that if he wasn't the one servicing it and having all its parts tell him the truth about how they were doing, it might not have held up as long, even if it did want to do its best for Melissa.

Technically, her bike wasn't exactly tracking device free since he'd installed a Maven one for extra safety, but he wasn't going to think too much about that. Half of him knew it was a good move because he needed her safe, but the other half vaguely felt like he was making a mistake because he had no intention of telling her. Pushing away his unease, Rick got off her bike. He tried the handle of the coffee shop's back door to reassure himself that it was secure, but it swung open without any resistance.

"This should be locked," he groused to no one as he glared at the offending handle as if it was its fault.

"I agree," a man's voice said.

Rick looked up and saw the staff room was inordinately full. Melissa was squeezed in the flower chair with Danny, who looked like she was trying to steal Melissa's warmth. Rick suspected Melissa was uncomfortable, but didn't want to alarm her friends about her bruised midsection. Only one bruise on her arm stuck out past her shirt sleeve and it looked like it could have come from bumping into something rather than Dave turning her at a full run in order to grab her around the middle. The idea of Melissa experiencing any pain made him frown.

Bethany, in a bright red flowy top that contrasted with her dark skin and white hair, sat in the faded red chair closest to the door and to Rick. She smiled grandly at him and ignored his frown completely. Kate was sitting on the crate between the chairs like he remembered her doing after Theo had grabbed her, but this time in loose pants rather than a sundress that didn't fit great. She seemed to be better than the last time Rick had seen her — her shoulders weren't crowding her ears at least. Finally, there were two men leaning against the wall to the right of the hallway to the front. The closer one was skinny in the way Jeremy was and wore a blue unisex skirt. The other had been here when Rick had brought Melissa coffee cake. Rick thought it was the latter who had spoken.

"We're taking Melissa and Kate out for a Friday night dinner," Bethany said, smiling up at him.

"You should come," the same guy as before said. His tone was more inviting than when he'd given his agreement about the door, but it didn't sound quite right to Rick.

"Greg," Melissa's tone held a warning that set off alarm bells in Rick's head.

"I insist," the skinnier guy in the skirt said.

"Ted!" Melissa sounded exasperated, but everyone else smiled. Even Kate had a small smile on her face.

"Sure." Rick said. He'd wanted to meet her friends, and maybe they could distract her from everything going on. He hadn't liked how distressed she'd been when they'd parted earlier. He didn't even care that her friends were likely going to give him the third degree. They were looking out for Melissa, and anyone who did that earned a place in Rick's good books.

"Great," Bethany said. She bounced to her feet in a motion that would have made most people look childish, but somehow made her float with elegance. "We're going to Little Rock. You know the way?"

Rick nodded, watching Melissa as everyone started streaming out of the staff area. He hadn't been to Little Rock since Bobby's disappearance. Before then, he'd gone once a year. It was Melissa's favorite restaurant, and the one she picked every year for her birthday.

When they were alone, he took a step toward Melissa and held out his hand. "Come on, we can ride together." As her fingers wrapped around his, he regretted that his gloves were on. He wanted to feel her skin against his fingertips. He wanted to thread his fingers through her hair and find out if the strands were just as soft as they'd felt against his face the other night. Pushing down the wave of nerves that accompanied not wanting a barrier between them, he pulled lightly on her hand.

"Will it be safe for me to go to the house tonight?" she whispered as she let him pull her up to her feet.

"Yeah. Theo just put up cameras for monitoring, and we removed those. Based on the kind of hardware he used, he won't know that it's been disconnected until he tries to access the feed, so we have some time. Also, I'll be right next door and will come right over if we see something on the security cameras Jeremy put in this morning."

Melissa nodded.

Rick had planned to let go of her hand once she was up, but his body countermanded that decision when he saw the small wince cross her face as she straightened. He pulled her the extra step toward him until she was standing in his space looking up at him. He'd meant to ask her how much pain she was in, but his eyes flicked to her lips as they pushed together. He yanked his gaze back up to her eyes by sheer force of will, only to see she was looking at his lips. The notion that she was thinking of kissing him shut down all thought. He found his free hand had slid to the back of her neck, and her eyes met his. When her lips parted, just slightly, Rick almost groaned.

"Don't mind me," Kate squeaked as she slipped past the two of them and grabbed the purse she'd left behind.

Rick closed his eyes, sucking in a steadying breath as quietly as he could. Melissa's head tipped forward till her forehead touched his lips.

"Feel free to be late," Kate teased on her way back out.

Melissa shook her head with a chuckle.

"Do I get to drive?" she asked, drawing back to look up at him. Her head was cocked to the side, and she gave him a crooked smile, daring him to say yes.

"I'll drive," Rick responded, turning and pulling her out the back door before he gave into temptation and kissed her. He climbed on his bike while he watched her lock the back door. No way would he be able to hold it together through dinner with her friends if he had her pressed in front of him on the bike. His attraction to her would be blatantly obvious and impossible to hide.

Melissa climbed on behind him with an amused shake of her head — probably at his insistence that he drive. Because her movement was slower than the last few times she'd climbed up behind him, Rick eased the clutch and pulled out onto the road, careful not to make her tense up as he drove.

Little Rock was a humorous misnomer. The restaurant design gave the impression that the interior was carved into the giant boulder you could see from the street. It only looked like stone; it was actually made of sculpted concrete with dyes to make it look like real rock. The Stone Age theme carried through the entire place. The chairs were all "rocks" that even a child could move with one hand. The plates and bowls looked like giant leaves. The silverware resembled whittled wood. Even the lights were crafted to replicate glowing mineral formations.

The restaurant was owned by a pair of adventurous reptile twins who had been toddlers when the Crisis hit. They'd designed the place just as hybridization was hitting towns around the globe in full force. Rick had eaten at innumerable restaurants that had tried to create similar spaces, but none had done it quite as well.

Rick focused on Melissa as they walked up to the entrance that looked like a minor rockslide had opened a dark cave to explore. She wasn't walking like she was hurt, but he reminded himself to keep an eye on her, just in case. He gently wrapped his arm around her and pulled her against him.

"So, there's Kate and Danny," he whispered, savoring the way a few loose strands of her hair brushed his face. Her hair held the faintest hints of coffee, which told Rick she hadn't spent much time in the front half of her coffee shop while he fixed her bike. "You said Ted and Greg? And the white hair was Bethany, right?"

Melissa confirmed who was at dinner and added in a few details as they walked up to the table everyone else was already seated around. As he lowered himself into the seat next to Melissa, Rick silently repeated in his head: Kate, cat, barista and jewelry maker; Danny, lizard, barista for now, bartender normally; Bethany, bat, grad student; Greg, human with an unknown *talent*, librarian; Ted, octopus with all eight legs, computer something. He tried to repeat the list a second time, but thought he mixed up the jobs. The two open seats were between Ted and Kate, across from Greg, Bethany, and Danny.

When they sat down and Rick didn't pick up the menu, Ted asked, "Do you come here often, Rick?"

"No."

"But you know your order?"

Rick didn't need to look around the table to know everyone was looking at him.

"More or less." He took a line from his mother and focused on unrolling his silverware and placing his napkin on his lap.

"What are you getting?" Danny asked. Her eyes were full of curiosity. Rick remembered she'd come to the last two of Melissa's family birthday dinners he had attended before joining the army.

"I assume the same thing I used to get."

"Which is?" Bethany prompted. She was reading the menu and sounded more like she was hoping for a tempting suggestion to consider for herself than baiting a trap like Danny might be doing.

Rick purposely focused on his silverware and not at Melissa beside him. "Either the chicken parmesan or the veggie-sausage risotto."

"I wonder how you are ever going to pick between the two." Kate's voice was so full of mock wonder everyone except Melissa looked at her as she grinned like a cat with a bowl full of cream. Growing up, Melissa had gone back and forth between the two in such obvious distress that Rick had just ordered the one she didn't, and had purposefully not finished it so she could have both on her birthday. Kate, having been at those family birthday dinners, had clearly caught on.

Beside him, Melissa swallowed audibly. "I'm having the chicken parmesan tonight," she said in such a forced, casual manner that everyone's eyes came to her.

"Veggie-sausage risotto it is then," Rick said quietly, staring at his water glass.

Melissa's hand slipped under the table and squeezed his where it rested on his thigh. Part of him wanted to keep holding her hand, but he'd taken his gloves off when they entered. Instead of doing what he wanted, he pulled away and draped his arm over the back of her mock stone chair, grateful she was in a tee-shirt rather than a tank top; when his fingers brushed her shoulder, he wouldn't make skin contact and force her to answer her friends truthfully if that wasn't what she wanted. Bethany, Kate, and Danny were all looking at him with their hearts in their eyes, which was making Melissa blush beside him. Greg and Ted seemed to have given him the benefit of the doubt for now. He'd risen significantly in their estimation.

By the time orders were in, Kate's delight about his meal choice had faded. She glanced at him and Melissa often enough that he was sure she wanted to ask about her brother, but she didn't bring him up. Rick doubted that Melissa had told her anything about the previous night; Kate was too calm for that. He could tell that Danny moving in with her until things blew over was soothing her nerves as well. For once, Rick might agree with Melissa that ignorance was bliss, at least in Kate's case.

Halfway through the meal, Melissa had nudged him and nodded at his plate. A slide later, they had switched meals and continued eating. Around this point, Rick knew that there was next to nothing he could do other than expose the Mavens that would put Ted at ease. Ted's conversation veered from casual to probing and frustrated and took all of Rick's focus.

The problem wasn't that Rick looked dangerous or wasn't nice, but rather that Ted was more than good with computers. He didn't just work at Full Byte Solutions; he was the head of his division. And in his late twenties or early thirties, that was an impressive feat. Full

Byte Solutions provided cyber services to some of the best-known companies around the world. Ted's line of questioning made it clear he hadn't been able to find anything about Rick in whatever searches, legal or not, he had done.

Given the Mavens' carefully crafted troublesome exterior, Ted was convinced there would be some mention of him or his photo *somewhere*. The Mavens were mentioned online and in news snippets as much as any motorcycle club would be, but Rick was never identifiable in any of the photos or stories. Ted had only come across Phi Rho team members, or the "cover" members. Their job was to visibly be in a motorcycle club for the public eye.

Rick could tell that Ted didn't buy a word out of his mouth as he gave answers and deflected, but Rick got the feeling that Melissa's friend was more frustrated about his lack of digital existence than worried about Melissa. Beside Ted, Greg listened to the inquisition with a quirked eyebrow, but didn't seem to be for or against him. Rick felt like Greg was waiting to decide if he liked him or not. What the deciding factor would be eluded Rick. Melissa wasn't any help as she talked with the other half of the table about a show they all watched.

Despite Ted's insistent line of questioning, by the time dinner wrapped up, Rick had confirmed that all of Melissa's friends were incredibly good people — no doubt thanks to her helping touch. None of them completely agreed with her view that most people were not as mean as they seemed. They all, in fact, were wary of and a bit baffled by Melissa's charmed outlook. So, at least they'd notice if something dangerous was afoot.

During the meal, Rick hadn't found out anything about Greg that would tell him what *talent* he had. If pressed, he'd guess it was something minor that maybe even Greg hadn't picked up on himself.

When it was time to say farewells, Rick disentangled his fingers from the ends of Melissa's hair and stood up. Casually, he slipped his gloves on. None of them knew he avoided touch as a lifestyle choice, and there was no way they would have picked that up from seeing him around Melissa. To say goodbye, both Bethany and Danny gave him hugs, Ted and Greg gave him a fist bump each, and though Kate missed him in the chain of hugs and fist bumps, she did wave at him from Danny's car as they drove off. Even with a barrier, he'd just had more physical contact with people than he normally did in a week, not including how much he was touching Melissa.

While he had mostly avoided skin contact with her, that didn't mean they hadn't been touching. After nearly kissing her in her staff room, he was having trouble keeping his hands to himself.

Outside Little Rock, Rick swung his leg over his bike and slid to the front before Melissa could ask to drive. She gave him a half smile and shook her head, calling him on the move.

"We'll swing by the coffee shop and grab my bike?"

"No, it'll be fine there for the night. The weather's fair, and the alley camera will have it covered." He was so tired. He'd only gotten a handful of hours of sleep the night before and was running on near empty. Being social and feeling out Melissa's friends had not helped.

"There's a camera in the alley?" Melissa blinked at him.

"There's a camera in every room of the coffee shop, except the bathrooms, and three external angles, one of which is in the alley."

"Isn't that overkill?"

"Let's talk about it later, Mel." Rick tipped his head toward the back of the bike, telling her to get on.

"I have the morning shift tomorrow," she said, not getting on the bike.

"I'll take you," he replied automatically.

Melissa accepted that and climbed on behind him. The drive back should have been easy, and to a bystander, it would have looked completely normal. The fact that Melissa hadn't chosen his coat pockets this time but had instead slid her hands up under the edge of his jacket so they pressed against the thin fabric of his shirt alone would have made the drive a little hard to focus on. Her hands, however, were not still. Every other minute or so, they slid a little. Sometimes it was her own doing, but often it was his fault. Each time Rick accelerated after a light or after slowing for an unprotected intersection, Melissa's fingers clutched him tighter. Previously, the sensation had been muffled by his jacket. Now, it wasn't.

At first, Rick had worried his driving was hurting her and she was flinching, but at one light she'd asked him why he was driving so slowly, and he knew her sliding hands weren't jerks of pain. By the time he pulled up to the edge of Melissa's driveway, he could swear she'd caressed every inch of his abs. His entire body felt hard as a rock and straddling the bike had gotten significantly uncomfortable. Rick fervently hoped his body wasn't going to get Pavlovian training that the rumble of his bike should turn him on.

Once Melissa had gotten off, he started to roll back and over to his own driveway to tuck his bike away in the garage and out of sight. The slight thud of Melissa's helmet hitting the grass made him look at her. She had one hand on her hip. Her brow was furrowed, and her lips pursed just a little. He could tell she was making up her mind about something. Rick planted both feet on the ground and took his helmet off as well; it was basic etiquette — if not moving and the bike was off, it was common courtesy to take helmets off to talk to non-riders when not in danger of being photographed. But she didn't say anything, so Rick broke the silence.

"When do we need to leave to get you to work on time?"

"By 5:30 at the latest. I normally leave by 5:15."

"That's early." It was barely 9 p.m., but Rick would be nowhere near caught up on sleep.

Melissa reached forward and pushed gently on his shoulder. Rick wondered what she was doing but leaned back just a little at her touch anyway. The next thing he knew, her hands were on his shoulders and her left leg was swinging over his handlebars and hooking around the back of his right leg. When she made a suppressed murmur of pain at the position, Rick dropped his helmet, and his hands immediately went to steady her. Without hesitation, she bent the leg still on the ground and jumped. He felt a pulse of worry push through him and half-lifted her, letting her momentum guide his support.

In less time than it took to swallow, she had straddled him with her back to the handlebars and her thighs over his. She looked inordinately pleased by her maneuver. Rick's breathing hitched at the glint in her eye, and his heart seemed to beat inside his throat. Before he could say anything, Melissa moved, bringing her crotch flush with his erection. She froze.

Having never been in such a predicament, Rick did not know what to do. He just looked up into her wide, startled eyes as they stared down at him. When Melissa's lips crooked slightly in a small smile and her head came toward him, Rick's fingers convulsed and gripped her hips harder, inadvertently holding her tighter against him. One of her hands slid from his shoulder, up his bare neck, and into his hair. He was simultaneously terrified of saying something to stop her and desperately wanting to ask her what they were doing.

He didn't get the chance to pick between the two options.

Her lips brushed against his once. Twice. Then, they caressed his top lip and then his bottom lip. His arm slid from her hip to around her waist, pulling her closer as he kissed her back, mimicking her attentions. Her body shuddered, and he groaned at the feel of it. Her tongue darted out and touched the tip of his as his lips parted. He sucked in a breath and swiped his tongue back in return. The kiss was so much better than he'd imagined over the years. He had never thought past her lips on his. The reality of her body pressed against his was more intimate than anything he'd ever experienced. The only sounds he heard were the sweet little moans that slipped out of Melissa when they tipped their heads differently. Each small movement she made atop him ratcheted his already racing heart up a notch as he chased her lips into kiss after kiss. When they broke apart, gasping, Melissa squirmed in his hold, rubbing against him in such a way that he knew he was a goner.

Rick rested his head on her collarbone and Melissa released a breathless laugh by his ear that sent a shiver down his spine. Her fingers at his nape made soothing caresses that rendered him simultaneously relaxed and taut in anticipation. He couldn't believe she was really in his arms. This was really happening.

She pulled back, and Rick lifted his head to look up at her again. Her smile was naughtier than before, and he failed to get control of his breathing. She dipped her head toward him, and he was completely helpless. He didn't have the will to tell her no. Not when he wanted the same thing more than his next breath. Her kiss was soft and felt like a thank you that threatened to suck his heart straight out of him.

"This is fun," she whispered against his lips. "I want to keep doing it." The truth of her words hit him like a train, and he whole-heartedly agreed. "But we have to be up early, and you have to be exhausted." She kissed him again, pulling back up, just out of reach.

Rick's eyes stayed closed as he tried to find some measure of reason, but he wasn't having much luck. Kissing Melissa had felt right. He couldn't argue with that.

"I'm not sure how to get down." Melissa's voice held a tinge of laughter. "Though, I do know you'll have to loosen your grip."

His eyes popped open to see her smiling down at him. With conscious thought, he loosened his hold on her body, sliding his left hand off her ass where it had apparently been holding on for dear life. When both his hands were on her hips, he looked down at their bodies, still pressed together. Forcing himself to move, Rick scooted backward bit by bit until Melissa could sit on the seat instead of on him, but she was facing the wrong way.

Sucked in by how right it felt, Rick leaned into her. He smiled as his chest touched hers and his lips found hers again. This time, when she grabbed onto his shoulders, he slid both his hands down the outside of her thighs to her knees and urged her to wrap her legs all the way around his body. He continued to lean into her, slowly bending her back toward the handlebars until he could shift his hands to them without forcing Melissa to engage her bruised abs. Still kissing her, he kept the bike steady, and swung both of them off it while putting the kickstand down. When his hands returned to her ass to take her weight, Melissa slowly ended the kiss, pulling back to look him in the eye. Her eyes were almost black with desire, and her chest rose and fell against his like she'd run a race. A minute passed before Melissa loosened the hold of her legs around his hips, and he slid her body down his until her feet reached to the ground.

"5:15?" she asked, still pressed against him, his hands glued to her hips. Her voice was low, and his body felt the invitation of it.

He nodded, not trusting his voice, and let her slide away from him and out of reach. He was bewildered that Melissa's touch didn't remind him that kissing his best friend's little sister wasn't a *good* thing to do. The feeling from her touch actually told him the complete opposite. It was a good thing. A very good thing. A good thing that shouldn't stop. He just didn't know if his own need was overriding her touch. Was that even possible?

Rick watched Melissa unlock her front door and go inside before rolling his bike backward into the street and then back up his own driveway and into the garage. He doubted he'd get a wink of sleep.

Chapter 22

Melissa

Melissa smiled at a bleary-eyed Rick at 5:15 the next morning. He was leaning against his bike at the curb. One leg of his jeans was caught on the top edge of his boot like he'd stumbled into it. His hair was sticking up in different directions like the other morning when Melissa had come over for breakfast. It looked like 5 a.m. didn't agree with him.

"Good morning," she said with a grin. The energy that had made it hard for Melissa to fall asleep the night before made it easy to get up in the morning and had her bouncing to a stop with her feet on either side of his. She was relieved the bounce hadn't made her wince. Her abdomen was tender, but not wincing was an improvement.

Rick looked at her with suspicion. "How are you so awake this early?"

In response, she leaned forward just enough to give him a whisper of a kiss. When she met his eyes, they were wide with surprise.

"You already look more awake," she countered.

His lips curved up at the corners as he gave a little huff and tipped his head like she'd made a good point. Rick slipped his helmet on and got on his bike. Melissa decided to play nice and not suggest she drive. Given how riled up he had been after having her ride behind him, she thought it prudent not to push it this morning by sitting in front of him. She hopped on and slipped her hands into the pockets of his jacket for warmth.

Sleeping houses swept by in a blur as the bike cruised down the empty road and the sky lightened a touch. Curled up behind Rick, Melissa didn't feel the biting edge of the morning chill as it whipped by. The power of his bike didn't strike her as quite as excessive as before. Thanks to last night, she had a new appreciation for his bike.

Rick pulled up right in front of Juniper's Java under one of the trees as Melissa relived kissing him the night before. She climbed off and set her helmet on the sidewalk. Pointing at her own head, she nodded at Rick to tell him to take his off. Once she had it, she set it next to hers on the ground. She had five, maybe ten minutes before she *had* to get inside and set up. Melissa was of the mind to make sure those minutes were not wasted.

Placing her hand flat on Rick's chest, she gave him two nudges back and a smile that promised she was up to no good. Rick's response told her he was at her mercy, and he scooted back to make room in front of him on the bike. After making sure he had the bike steady, Melissa squeezed in to sit sideways on the seat with Rick's arm across her back on the street side, making sure she didn't topple over. His free hand settled on her upper thigh. She hooked a finger into the neck of his dark blue shirt and pulled it ever so slightly off his skin; he followed it down to her until his lips met hers.

His kiss was soft like a feather and made her feel like she was floating. With the utmost care, he consumed her lips like she'd break from too firm of a kiss. The sensation was both sweetly intoxicating and maddeningly slow. Unable to resist, she leaned into him, tilting her head back a little further. Her whole body pulsed with each brush of his lips, leaving her wanting more. His tongue teased the corner of her mouth in temptation, and she parted her lips for his exploration. Bit by bit, he intensified the kiss and Melissa melted against him as her head spun, drunk on him.

A delicate throat clearing caused Rick to pull his lips from hers, but Melissa couldn't bring herself to open her eyes and muffle the sensations that pulsed from her lips to her toes.

"Morning," Rick said cautiously from above her. His tone struck Melissa as more gruff than usual, but not necessarily in a good way. Opening her eyes, she saw Rick looking off to the right toward her coffee shop. She dropped her eyes to the front door and saw her employee Tiffany in a green trench coat, grinning like she'd found a treasure chest full of cheese.

"Hi Tiff," Melissa said belatedly. Rick's hand tightened on her thigh, and she looked back up at him. His eyes bore into her with such an intensity her breath caught in her throat.

He leaned in until his lips brushed her ear and whispered, "Maybe don't talk quite so breathlessly to everyone today, huh?" She imagined him smiling against her cheek as he planted a quick kiss under her ear.

Melissa slid off Rick's bike and, with an unprompted assurance of a message about when he'd be back, unlocked the door to let herself and Tiffany inside to set up. A glance at the clock on the wall told Melissa her five- to ten-minute estimate had either been too lenient because Rick had driven slowly, or, more likely, she had lost her entire grasp on time as Rick tasted her with a thoroughness she'd never experienced before.

Tiffany, oblivious to Melissa's lightheaded state, scampered around, setting up the shop and asking numerous questions about her new beau. As Tiffany wasn't one of her close friends, Melissa surprised herself by sharing enough details about Rick at dinner and their driveway make-out session that Tiffany's eyes were dreamily glazed over when she greeted their first customer of the day. She was dazzled by Melissa's theory that the rough and tumble guy-next-door had liked her for a long time and they were finally getting together; Tiffany made it sound like a fairy tale come true.

A few hours after opening, Jeremy walked in wearing another polo shirt and cockatoo-ed himself, much as he had done before. Melissa suspected he preferred to ride his motorcycle in his human form. She made him his pineapple iced tea and let Tiffany take it to him at his table against the wall.

Tiffany was more than willing to take the mysterious dark bird his drink, commenting that this was his second visit and maybe he'd become a regular. Fluffing her blond hair around her shoulders, Tiffany shifted into her mouse hybrid form for reasons only known to her and delivered Jeremy's drink. Melissa had no idea if Jeremy would be coming by the coffee shop often or not, but she had a feeling she'd be seeing a number of the Mavens moving forward.

Watching Tiffany pause and flirt with Jeremy, Melissa realized he was sitting at one of the three tables Rick normally picked. That Rick chose tables against the wall whenever he had come in the past few years hadn't struck Melissa as noteworthy until now.

He had probably picked those three in order to better survey the room and keep tabs on what was happening. When she looked back at a lot of Rick's actions through the lens of... someone in security? still in the military? what she'd seen in movies about undercover agents?... She didn't know, but it made Rick look much less shy and quiet and much more watchful and ready for danger. Maybe Danny's story about him running off and saving children in war-torn countries was more accurate than they knew, he just might do such good deeds more locally. She should just ask him rather than spin fanciful stories.

When Kate showed up for her shift, Melissa took a break and sat down with Jeremy. The coffee shop had a different hum on this side of the counter. The light music she played in the background was a little more prominent without the vibrations of the espresso machine whirring away. Customer conversations were easier to hear, too.

Behind the counter, the sounds of the coffee shop were a constant she barely noticed, especially when there was a lot on her mind. That morning, she'd had more than enough time with her thoughts to have come down off her kissing high. There were a lot of unknowns where Rick was concerned, and her mind was churning with them.

"How are you doing today?" Jeremy asked. His tone of genuine concern reminded her that the last time he'd seen her, she'd been completely overwhelmed that a creep not only *existed*, but had been inside her parents' house and inside her bedroom.

"A lot better," she answered honestly, thinking of dinner with her friends and Rick and that Greg was right that Rick had liked her for a while and not shared. Not that she'd shared her suppressed attraction over the years either, but he had been keeping his distance.

"Yeah?" Jeremy sounded suspicious.

"Can I ask you a question?" Melissa asked, figuring Jeremy was the most approachable of the Mavens she'd met.

He turned and looked out at the rest of the coffee shop as he said, "As long as you know I might not answer it."

"Why has Rick avoided me for so long?"

Jeremy stilled at her question. The one eye on her side swiveled to her and the lens of his glasses moved with it.

"I'm going to need more context to decide if I'll answer."

Melissa sucked in her bottom lip and thought about how much to share. Jeremy was Rick's friend, not hers.

"Rick clearly likes me," she finally said. "And not in the let's be friends in memory of your brother way," she added. "I'm under the impression it's not sudden." She waited, but Jeremy said nothing. He just took a sip of his iced tea. Melissa wondered if he preferred his hybrid form because he could hide his reactions better. His expression hadn't shifted one iota.

She pushed a little more: "I know Rick isn't very tactile and comes off as standoffish. I also know you've noticed he isn't like that with me. You've all noticed. You all stare."

"You're basing this all on him touching your hand yesterday?"

"No."

"How do you know, without a doubt, that he likes you?" Not a single flicker of emotion or any hint at what he was thinking passed over his face. He was completely unreadable.

Melissa knew that without saying it outright, Jeremy wouldn't even consider answering her question. Feeling her face heat, she blurted it out before she could think about it too much.

"I kissed him last night."

Jeremy turned his entire body toward her. If she'd told him she'd wired the entire place to explode in the next five minutes, she didn't think he'd have reacted any differently. He seemed unalarmed, but also like the world depended on her next few words.

"And he... responded?"

"That'd be one way to put it," Melissa muttered, feeling her face heat further. Jeremy looked at her for what must have been a few seconds, but could have been a full minute such was her agony at his silence.

"How much did you date when Bobby was around?" Jeremy asked. Melissa's eyes darted around in confusion. Jeremy's tone and body position had relaxed a little, but he'd also leaned minutely toward her as if intrigued by what she would say.

"As much as any of my friends did," she said despite of the odd line of questioning.

"Can you expand on that?"

"Not much in high school. A bit more in college, but nothing particularly long-term. Since college, I've had a few relationships that have lasted a handful of months." She shrugged. "Danny and Kate's relationships may have lasted a little longer, and they dated more than me in high school, but their boyfriends also never stick around long."

Jeremy's head tilted to the side, and Melissa suddenly wondered if that wasn't normal. It had always frustrated her how guys weren't interested in longer relationships, but she had just assumed they were gun shy or jerks.

"And how did Bobby take you dating?"

"Poorly." She rolled her eyes at the memories. "It was almost funny watching him grill any guy I was with." She stopped laughing as a thought hit her. "Rick was generally there too, just as unamused as Bobby was. Maybe more so if his frown was any indication. Granted, I could have sworn he was frowning at Bobby, not at my dates. Most of those guys broke it off with me soon after meeting the two of them."

"So, Bobby made it clear he wasn't a fan of anyone you dated," Jeremy half asked, half stated.

"Do you think Bobby told Rick to stay away from me?" That seemed extreme to Melissa. If Bobby had warned Rick off, she imagined there would have been a change in Rick's behavior at some point when her brother was alive. She couldn't pick out any major shift in how Rick treated her before the past week.

"I don't know, but I remember when Bobby shared a picture of the two of you with the team and Dave made a comment about you being attractive. When Bobby finished talking to him, Dave's *fur* looked pale."

"Dave barely seems to register I'm the opposite sex."

"Which I do not find surprising given Bobby's talk with him," Jeremy said with great meaning.

Melissa's gut clenched as what Jeremy said sank in. Why would Bobby have thought he needed to do more than tell one of his friends he didn't want him to date his little sister? Why would her brother even warn off one of his friends? She knew Dave was a lady's man, but it was uncalled for.

Then, there was Rick. He'd almost kissed her in the staff room, but, despite wanting her when he'd dropped her off last night, *he* didn't make a move. Sure, in the past week, he'd wrapped an arm around her, whispered in her ear, comforted her, and even played with her hair while they were at dinner, but he'd also created distance between them at times. He was likely never going to make a move if she hadn't made one first. Even now that she had kissed him, he might be cautious without her pushing for more.

Was he wary of her because of Bobby? He'd been dead for four years... Melissa felt nauseous at the idea, and her world tipped on its axis even more than it had with Theo following her around and everything.

"Kate is handling the news of Theo breaking into your house well," Jeremy observed when Melissa just sat there thinking about the implications of Rick and Bobby's friendship on their relationship.

"Hmm?" Melissa had to drag herself out of her building horror to focus on what Jeremy was saying. She looked over at Kate, who was chatting with a customer at the counter. Her friend was outwardly at ease. "We didn't tell her about that. She's still worried about Tommy; he hasn't surfaced yet. She has accepted that the Theo-guy isn't interested in her and just wants to find her brother. Today's the first day she came into work by herself."

"Is that wise?" Jeremy asked. Melissa thought his beak might have turned into a frown at the corners, but maybe his tone had just dropped in disapproval. "He has an interest in you, so why wouldn't he have an interest in Kate that she should watch out for?"

Melissa weighed Jeremy's words.

"I'll let her know he's been seen in town and to keep an eye out." Melissa watched Kate move around behind the counter. "With you guys monitoring the street camera that has a shot of her apartment, I don't know if it's necessary to mention the guy was inside my parents' house. She doesn't need to live in fear."

"How much, exactly, do you know about us?" Jeremy whispered, leaning over the table toward her.

"Hmm?" Melissa shifted her attention back to the cockatoo at his alarmed whisper.

"What do you know about us?" he repeated.

What did she know about the Mavens? She snorted, thinking about all the things she didn't know about Rick or about her own brother's death.

"Enough to know I don't know anything," she said in open frustration. She didn't know what Rick and the Mavens did, and she sure as hell didn't know what Bobby was thinking when he was alive if he was trying to keep the entire male sex away from her.

Jeremy's laughter at her response turned every head in their direction. Melissa just frowned at him.

Chapter 23

Rick

"Did you ride straight here?" Toby asked when Rick poked his head into Team Gamma's room. Rick wondered where everyone on his own team was to have someone from Team Delta monitoring their surveillance cameras.

Toby, a fully brown German Shorthaired Pointer hybrid, was a newer addition to the Delta Team. He always reminded Rick of Dave — he was good looking and knew it, always showing off his tattoo sleeves and letting ladies pet them when they were out in a bar.

"Straight here?"

"From Juniper's Java," Toby clarified, pointing at the surveillance screens in front of him. "That must have been one *uncomfortable* ride." He smirked.

Rick realized not only that Toby had seen him drop Melissa off, but he had seen him drinking in Melissa like a life-saving elixir in the desert that was his touch-deprived life. Surprised embarrassment must have shown on his face because Toby's knowing smirk grew.

"When someone from my team shows up, let them know I'm catching a few hours' sleep," he said instead of acknowledging Toby's teasing.

"I'm sure you need it if you ended your night with a morning kiss like that!" Toby barked out in laughter.

Feeling incredibly uncomfortable, having never been on the receiving end of such teasing, Rick left Toby without a parting comment. He hadn't given any thought to someone watching the cameras outside the coffee shop. In all honesty, he had only thought about how Melissa was just as hungry to kiss him as he was her.

He needed advice and didn't feel comfortable asking any of the dogs on Team Delta or the cats on Team Kappa. He wasn't sure he even felt comfortable asking his own team members. Normally, he'd have asked Bobby, but he wasn't around anymore *and* Melissa was his sister, so that also would have posed an issue, even if he were around.

Groaning, Rick threw himself down on the recovery cot and tried to fall asleep.

A coded tap on the wall above Rick's head pulled him from a Melissa-filled dream. Tap. Tap tap. Click click click click. Tap. Rick bolted upright. His throat smacked straight into Dave's arm as Rick clotheslined himself on the unexpected obstruction. He fell back on the cot, coughing and glaring so hard Dave started apologizing immediately.

"Sorry, man. I just had Bobby on the brain from the snickering Toby was doing about some rev-your-engine action happening in front of Juniper's Java. I was feeling good, and you know that's a quirky memory we all have of him."

Rick grabbed a fresh water bottle from the stash beneath the cot and sat up. He drank it all before daring to speak. Rick had genuinely thought Bobby was back. Bobby had woken team members up that way if the waking fell to him. No one had used the wake-up tap since the first month after Bobby's disappearance as far as Rick knew. Granted, they might have just made sure not to use it on or around him. Bobby had done it as a friendly way to wake up people in the squad who slept with weapons when on a job.

"I'm okay," Rick forced out as he worked through unlocking every muscle in his body that had gone rigid. He could feel Dave watching him carefully, like the entire team had that first year. Forcing himself past the memories of Bobby, he focused on the other thing Dave said. "What was Toby saying about Melissa?"

"He didn't say anything about Melissa. He just said Jeremy will have to save a twenty-minute clip from this morning's surveillance before it gets moved into the archives. Something about two people really getting their engines running." Dave rolled his eyes. "Toby's like me five years ago. He'll calm down a bit, eventually."

"*Do not* let Jeremy save a copy of that recording," Rick blurted out.

Dave's self-comparison didn't put Rick at ease. He remembered Dave's raunchy antics from back then in great detail. If Dave got hold of a recording of a Maven in a compromising position, he played it in a staff meeting, or as background music if there was sound, or have a still made into a poster, or anything else he could think of. Dave hadn't even gone easy on Susan. It was a wonder she had let him live so long.

"Shit," Dave breathed out. "It's of you and—" He didn't finish his sentence. It was like he was incapable of it.

Rick remembered in graphic detail how Bobby had threatened Dave at the mere mention of Melissa being "something he could take a bite of." It had been overkill, but Melissa was in college then and

Dave was screwing every woman who gave him a once-over, which was just about every woman he came across. Rick hadn't minded that Bobby had overdone it to the point Dave avoided being alone with Bobby for several months. He never would have let Bobby carry out the threat, but no one knew how often Rick had stopped Bobby from crossing the line — on and off duty.

Rick just hoped the threat didn't apply to him, too.

"Toby didn't know Bobby," Dave said with a shake of his head. "His team doesn't even know why we're watching the shop. He probably thinks she's a mark or a way in. As soon as Jeremy gets here, we'll get you into the recordings so you can personally delete it without anyone else seeing it," Dave assured him. Rick wondered if it was out of a newfound respect for Melissa and him, or just fear Bobby would haunt his soul if he did anything that sexualized Melissa.

"Good," was all Rick said in response.

Dave flopped on the cot next to Rick and leaned against the wall. He looked like he'd just done a flat-out sprint rather than accidentally been near someone who had talked about Melissa like an object instead of a person.

"Was that why you wanted one of us to come wake you when we got in? To erase the recording?" Dave asked.

"Actually, no." Rick figured Dave had the most experience with women, so he might as well ask him instead of someone else. Tentatively, he said, "I have a question."

Dave's head turned slowly toward him at Rick's cautious tone. Rick was known for making decisions for the team and making them fast. He was decisive. He didn't do tentative. He didn't hesitate.

"Okaaay." Dave drew the word out to emphasize how odd he thought Rick was behaving and maybe even dread at what Rick might ask after everything that had happened in the last few minutes.

Rick took a deep breath and asked quietly, "If you kiss someone, that doesn't automatically mean you're dating. If you kiss someone more than once, on different days even, do you automatically start dating?"

"Rick," Dave's voice expressed both alarm and astonishment. "I know you don't date with the touch issue and all." Dave waved his hand at Rick's entire person to indicate the problem, which didn't make Rick feel any *less* self-conscious. "But you have had relationships in the past, right?"

"Not past the point of the touch and blurt out truths stage."

"Melissa isn't your first kiss, is she?" Dave's incredulity had risen to such a point that Rick was surprised his eyebrows were still below his ears and not hovering in the air above him like a cartoon.

"No," Rick sighed. "There was a woman who launched herself at me at a college party Bobby and I crashed between tours. She kissed me before speaking. And based on last night and this morning, she was bad at it, which is what I thought at the time, even without any points of comparison. And that was before she told me why she did it. Bobby and I left after that. Drunken women looking for military husbands to cheat on while they're off fighting and protecting people is not a scene any of us ever enjoy."

"So, let me get this straight." Dave paused, as if to get his words right. "Last night, at the age of thirty-two, you had your first kiss that wasn't by assault?"

"Yes." Rick gave a firm nod.

"I see." Dave sat there, letting Rick's admission sink in. But when Dave didn't say anything more, Rick's unease seeped past the surface.

"So, is there a way to know if you're dating?"

"There's only one way." Rick stared at Dave, waiting. "You *talk* about it."

"I'd hoped you weren't going to say that," Rick muttered. He'd rather just kiss Melissa and let her say the incredibly sweet things she said between their kisses and on little sighs, like "I like this," or "we should have done this years ago," or whimpering "more." Talking was always the issue in the past.

"And, if you do want to date Melissa rather than just throw her to the curb...." Dave's look at the second comment made it clear he thought the latter option was a death wish regardless of the fact that Bobby wasn't around anymore. "Then, you have to tell her about what happens when she touches your skin. That way, she can make informed decisions about where she goes and who she talks to after being around you."

"Oh no." Rick felt his throat constrict and his eyes opened so wide they hurt. "I didn't think about that at all this morning."

"Take a breath," Dave said. "The other night, she didn't spill everything about us when talking with her friend on the phone. As long as no one asks her something she shouldn't tell them, we might be fine."

Rick's nod was jerky.

"Now, how long were you skin to skin?" Dave asked.

"Something under twenty minutes."

"So, that gives you a window of about forty minutes to account for? Or is there a maximum limit to how long the effect lasts regardless of how long you touched them?"

"I don't know, we've never run tests like that."

"Right. That's something you should find out sooner rather than later." Dave tilted his head and waggled his eyebrows as if to suggest activities that might involve longer amounts of contact. Rick squeezed his eyes shut and pushed the flood of suggestive images out of his head. "So," Dave continued, "who was she around at the coffee shop? Customers? They aren't likely to ask her pointed questions about us."

"Her employee, Tiff I think she said, saw us."

"So, you may have just had your second and, giving allowances for friendly curiosity, first kisses dissected in the guise of friendly gossip." Dave was trying to be supportive, but Rick didn't feel better. "Not the end of the world."

"Unless I'm not a good kisser," Rick said under his breath.

From the way Dave started coughing, Rick knew Dave had heard him and was laughing at him.

"You have nothing to worry about," Dave wheezed out between laughing coughs. "*Nothing*. The way Toby was talking, I think you turned *him* on, and he didn't even get to participate."

Rick didn't know how to take that news. Luckily, he was saved from responding by Jeremy's arrival.

"I've grabbed the security footage from the coffee shop this morning," Jeremy announced the moment he saw Rick and Dave sitting there. "Toby was *not* pleased when I said I'd be deleting it and not sending it to him, unless you want to delete it yourself."

"Toby's going to tell everyone, isn't he?" Rick groaned. At least the dog hybrid didn't know it was only his second kiss, but he still didn't want whatever attention might come from Toby's gossiping.

"On the plus side, he's only going to say good things," Dave pointed out.

"Oh, he isn't going to be talking at all," Jeremy said with finality. At Rick and Dave's questioning stares, his beak actually turned up at the corners from the force of his grin. "I had no idea Susan remembered Bobby's threats to Dave verbatim, but she's making it clear that should he talk about Melissa in a way one of us doesn't approve of, he'll be getting the 'Bobby Treatment' as she's calling it."

"That's probably hot," Dave muttered.

Rick's face hurt from his smile, and Jeremy started laughing so hard he fell against the door behind him. Dave had always thought

Susan was hot, and he hadn't hidden the fact when he first met her. She, of course, never gave into his charm or climbed into his bed. The idea of mixing the "Bobby Treatment" and Susan together was doing weird things to Dave's psyche. Rick and Jeremy were still laughing when Susan came in looking delighted at having scared the living dick out of Toby.

"I can't wait to meet Melissa," she said. "Anyone who drags a Maven into a kiss on their own bike has got to be unstoppable."

"*On* your bike?" Dave asked. "You left that part out. Maybe we shouldn't let him delete it. Perhaps we should watch for, you know, educational purposes first." He winked at Rick. Though the wink looked a little forced since he was joking about Bobby's little sister. Rick suppressed the worry that Bobby would have a problem with him dating Melissa and instead shook his head at Dave's light teasing attempt, trying to put everyone at ease about mentioning Bobby around him.

Chapter 24

Melissa

Melissa sunk her hands into the scalding soapy water and tried to shake her conversation with Jeremy. She had always thought of Bobby as the perfect big brother. The fact that he gave her boyfriends a hard time hadn't seemed extreme to her before, but she also didn't know what he'd said to any of them. She didn't like thinking that he'd messed with the guys she'd dated, but it explained their quick departures from her life. That hadn't been cool of him.

She pulled a mug out of the soapy water and set it in the next sink to rinse. The small kitchen across from the staff bathroom wasn't good for anything more than washing mugs and plates. Having two people in it made moving around impractical. It was the one room in Juniper's Java she hadn't fixed up. It had a double sink and a counter big enough for a large dish rack along the main, off-white wall across from the door. The side walls were only deep enough on one side for a fridge and an oven-stove combo with a microwave above it on the other.

Melissa vaguely wondered whether or not she'd feel more upbeat in the room if she'd made it more welcoming. Unlikely. Washing dishes was a necessary evil, not an activity to savor.

Without any mental distractions, she found herself replaying Jeremy's words over and over again. It made her exceedingly uncomfortable to think Rick had stayed away from her because of something Bobby had said to him. Part of her wanted to talk to Rick about it, but she didn't know if bringing it up would cause him to pull away. She didn't want that. She drained the dish free sink and rinsed the washed dishes before setting them on the rack to dry.

"I'm heading out," Tiffany said as she popped her head into the kitchen.

Melissa turned around, drying her hands, and nodded. She felt like she had over-shared that morning.

Tiffany squeaked, "Hope you get to see your guy later!" with a dreamy look in her eye before leaving.

For the tenth time since Jeremy left the coffee shop an hour ago, Melissa looked at her phone to see if Rick had sent her a message yet. Normally, she didn't cling to her phone and wait on messages, but Jeremy's comments haunted her. Rick had said he'd message her, but would he hesitate because of something Bobby had said to him years ago?

Luckily, while her hands were wet and occupied, Rick had finally sent her a message. He would be back that evening and asked if he could come over when he got home.

When her shift ended, she should have stayed and worked on scheduling, but Melissa headed to her parents' house instead. She hadn't confronted her parents about Rick's revelation that they weren't returning any time soon, if ever. The more she thought about it, the more truth she saw reflected in every interaction since their departure. That, however, didn't make her any less annoyed that they'd taken the cowardly way out.

Since she was, at least for now, living in the house, it was time to make some changes, so when she walked in the door, she took a hard look at the space. She hadn't changed anything except her childhood bedroom because she had just been house sitting as far as she had known. And now, after Rick and Dave had scoured the house, an excessive number of blank spaces lined the walls and empty holes pitted shelves where photos of Bobby had been. Even with the new security system installed, Melissa didn't know if she could bring them back over from next door or not. That was another thing she needed to ask Rick about.

Regardless of if she could have photos of Bobby out or not, she could make several changes on her own to make it feel less like her parents' home and maybe a little more like she lived there rather than was visiting. She started by taking down all the professor and biology plaques and other decorations that signaled she was in her parents' domain. Putting them in boxes would be the best move, but for now, she just tucked them inside her parents' bedroom.

She grabbed her parents' jackets from behind the front door and threw them on her parents' bed. Their shoes that were still out went into their room as well. In order to make room for the meager decorations she had saved from her apartment, Melissa also grabbed her parents' coffee table books, magazines, and the throw blankets and pillows that were more her parents' taste than her own. She added them to the growing pile of resentment in her parents' bedroom.

In her own bedroom, she opened up her closet and pulled out the last two boxes from her apartment. Soon, candles stood on the coffee table, extra-soft organic afghans lay over the back of the couch, and a few pictures of her and her friends she hadn't hung in her bedroom were sprinkled around the living room. In all honesty, her things did not match the dark green couch or striped, yellow wallpaper in the hall, but the rebellious act felt nice all the same.

After heating up leftovers for dinner, she snuggled into one of her blankets to read for a bit. She wasn't too far into her book yet, but the future queen was getting dangerously entangled with an evil witch-king from the neighboring Kingdom who thought *creatures* were below him. The parallels to how the history books portrayed the beginnings of hybrid inclusivity without discrimination weren't exact, but enough that she wanted to know if the evil witch-king would be swayed to the side of good by the future queen or turned into a supremacist caricature.

Melissa moved under the soft blanket that caressed her face. She was so comfortable. Vaguely, she registered she was falling asleep or maybe already had and smiled. Sleeping a little more sounded like a great idea.

"Mel."

She frowned and burrowed deeper into her blanket. Rick's voice sounded a lot like it meant to wake her up. She didn't want dream-Rick waking her up. The past week had taught her that dream-Rick was very friendly and did wonderful things to her ever-increasing heart rate.

"Mel," dream-Rick said a little louder, just above a whisper.

When her hair feathered down onto her neck, she blinked her eyes open to see Rick, real-Rick, with his head cocked to the side. He was staring at her hair trail between his fingers. The look on his face would make an observer think he'd never seen hair before, much less run-of-the-mill brown hair.

"You're back," she said.

He met her eyes and smiled. "I made tea."

"I'll have the chamomile this time," Melissa said.

She sat up and rubbed her eyes before accepting the tea. Rick sat down beside her but left a space between them. With a small scoot, Melissa rectified that situation and snuggled into his side under his arm. Without his jacket, he smelled less like his motorcycle and a little more like the soap she'd used next door the other morning. He didn't tense at her action or comment on it, so she went with the assumption that he liked her next to him.

"How was your day?" she asked.

"Different," he said. He sounded amused.

"How so?"

"It's weird having people talk about Bobby around me, and I'm trying to adjust."

"Is that just from meeting me?"

"No. After I dropped you off this morning, I took a nap and Dave woke me how Bobby used to wake all of us when we were… in certain circumstances." Melissa didn't miss that Rick barely stopped himself from saying something else, but she ignored the awkward correction.

"You mean the," she reached down to the coffee table and did a tap, tap tap, click click click click, tap.

"Yeah. He do that to you too?"

"Yep. He started after you guys got back from your first tour. He'd do it through the wall between our rooms in the morning or sometimes on my window if he had gotten himself locked out of the house in the middle of the night and wanted me to let him in without our parents knowing."

"He never was good at picking locks."

"You are." Melissa met his eyes and willed him to share, but she was also conscious not to push too much. Rick clearly had *reasons* for not sharing or approaching her in the past, and he needed to share when he was ready. She planned to give him many openings to do so, but not ask directly. She didn't want him to push her away.

Rick looked at her from the corner of his eye and said her name in a "I'm sorry" tone. She leaned forward and set her tea on the coffee table and took his as he started speaking.

"Mel, we should tal—"

Melissa pressed herself against Rick and used her lips to interrupt him. She wanted to talk with him. She did. But not in that tone. Not in the classic *I'm-breaking-things-off* tone. Kissing him might not remind him why they should try things out, but even if he said they couldn't try dating, she wanted one more kiss.

The noise Rick made against her lips held so much frustration that Melissa pulled away. If he didn't want her to kiss him, she didn't want to cross that line, but as she moved away from him, he followed, never letting her lips leave his. He followed until her back was on the couch and he pressed down on top of her. His left hand tangled in her hair, pulling just slightly and trapping his arm underneath her. His right hand was braced on the edge of the couch to stop himself from crushing her. Their legs entwined together. He didn't warm up to this kiss like he had that morning. Oh no. This kiss branded his lips against hers with searing heat that would have made her weak at the knees if she had been standing. Melissa melted underneath him and followed his lead now that he'd taken control.

When Rick pulled his head up and looked down at her, both of them breathing hard, Melissa realized she'd slid her hands under his shirt and around his back. His eyes slipped from hers and traveled down. At the tightening of his fist in her hair, she tilted her head back, exposing her neck to his eyes. Rick's head descended and Melissa decided then and there that her neck had to be delicious. Otherwise, why would he be feasting on it until her eyes rolled back in her head?

Her body arched into him, even though there wasn't room for her to go anywhere. Reclaiming her mouth, Rick kissed her with feather-light kisses, teasing her back to coherence. Melissa could tell he was barely able to hold back. His entire body had changed from a frantic *I-need-you* tenseness to just plain taut.

"I think you were saying we needed to talk," she said breathlessly while wondering why she would bring it up when she'd kissed him to stop *the talk.*

"In my head, I had planned talking before kissing," he murmured into her neck.

"Oh, so that wasn't your *we-should-see-other-people* or *it's-me-not-you* tone?"

Rick's head jerked back so he could see her eyes.

"No," he said so emphatically that Melissa couldn't help but smile at him and lift her head to steal a kiss from his shocked lips.

"Well, that's a relief. I'm very interested in not seeing other people," she told him.

"Very interested? Huh?" Rick got a lopsided grin that seemed both pleased and nervous.

"Yeah." Melissa gave into the trust she had in Rick that always let her share things she'd keep to herself. "I've known you forever. I might not know what you actually do with the Mavens, but I know what type of person you are. Regardless of the Mavens' intimidating reputation, I don't have any doubt that you'll help people who need it. You're helping Kate. You drop everything when your mother needs you." She took a breath before admitting: "I've always liked being around you. I've just liked... you."

Whatever tension Rick had been feeling dissipated while she spoke. Given that his lower half was pressed tight to hers, she knew the loss of tension wasn't a loss of physical interest. If anything, he might have gotten harder while she talked even as his body relaxed. He lowered his head and kissed her slowly, like he was memorizing her lips with his own. After a considerable amount of time, Rick pulled up off her slightly.

"Am I crushing you?"

"No," she managed to say. And he wasn't crushing her, but her abdomen did hurt.

Regardless of her answer, he had them roll so that he was on the bottom. It wasn't the easiest of twists to pull off on a small couch, but she'd had boyfriends in the past who'd been less gifted in the kissing department and who had managed the move with more ease. The contrast of Rick's kisses and his less than slick repositioning pulled Melissa out of the moment just enough to ask a question.

"Are you going to tell me what the Mavens do?"

"I'll have to check what I can tell you," he said quietly.

She bobbed her head from side to side.

"Is it going to be okay if I can't tell you much?"

"I mean, I won't be thrilled about it, and I imagine some days I'll be more okay about it than others. I know you're out there doing good things, even if you stylize yourself as a tough guy who will mess up anyone who looks at you wrong. It would be nice to know what you're up to during the day or have a general idea for reference."

"That makes sense."

Melissa inched down Rick's body until she could rest her head on his shoulder. Whatever stress had been on her bruised middle disappeared, and his heat seeped into her, making her relax.

"So, the wake-up tapping made your whole day amusing?"

"Oh, actually it was all the talk about Bobby that happened with everyone, even people who didn't know him because they're newer. On that note, in the future, if we could refrain from kissing in front of the security cameras Jeremy installed at the coffee shop or in front of your house, that'd be great."

Melissa tensed.

"People were watching us?" The creeping feeling of unease that had filled her after the Theo-guy had been in her house was back.

"Hey." Rick's free hand came down to cover her cheek and tilt her head up to look at him. "You said it yourself: we're the good guys. If no one's watching the cameras, we can't come help if something happens."

Rolling her shoulders to relax her body, she nodded. That tracked, even if it was uncomfortable to think about.

"What does that have to do with Bobby?" she asked, not having connected how talking about Bobby and people having watched them kiss worked. Her left hand idly traced lines along Rick's stomach through his shirt.

"My team knows why we're watching your coffee shop. Others could have guessed a connection to Bobby through the name Juniper's Java, but they didn't know you were his sister rather than..." Rick paused and twirled his right hand in the air, "...some random woman."

"So, what you're telling me isn't that you talked a lot about Bobby, but that you talked a lot about me." Melissa didn't feel overly comfortable with that, but she also knew she talked about Rick a lot with her friends. It was one thing for Rick to talk about her with his friends, but he was talking about *teams*. If she assumed his team was made up of his friends, she was fine with him talking to them about her. But talking with other teams, people who he didn't consider friends? That felt weird.

Granted, she had to acknowledge that Tiffany wasn't a friend but rather an employee, and that morning, Melissa had shared a whole lot more than she thought she would have, so who was she to judge?

"I guess most of the talk started from how protective he was in your regard. He told every man and woman in the Mavens not to mess with you."

"Does that mean he told you too?" Melissa couldn't help but ask after talking with Jeremy that morning.

"He never told me off specifically, but I was around when he told everyone else off."

"Do you think he never told you off because he approved?" she asked. The words felt as if they had been pulled out of her as she thought them. Her fingers paused in their path along his stomach. She truly hadn't meant to say them, just acknowledge what he'd said.

"I don't know," Rick sighed. "I was really careful. Bobby started becoming aggressively protective when you started high school, and all our classmates were making comments about you. I was not an idiot. I made sure to not make a single comment to say that you were even pretty."

"You thought I was pretty?" Melissa teased.

Rick gave her a look that she interpreted to say, "You know you've always been pretty."

"What do you mean by 'aggressively protective'?" Melissa made her hand continue its slow trail along the ridges of his stomach, feeling him tense and relax. She couldn't tell if it was her hand or the conversation causing his reaction.

"Let's just say I won't repeat the threats he made. Not even the ones from back in high school. We'll leave them at threats. Solid ones."

Melissa made an unsure noise. The way Rick said it made it worse than what Jeremy had hinted at. She hadn't even managed more than a single date with someone in high school. There weren't guys for Bobby to scare off then as far as she knew. Were the dark looks Bobby shot at people more than him just being moody? She'd never known why he'd looked at people that way, but she had taken cues from it and given those people space.

She gasped as the dots connected. Placing her hand flat against Rick's chest, she pushed herself up enough to look Rick in the eyes. "Are you telling me Bobby had scared everyone so badly that that's why no one who grew up here has ever asked me out?" Most of the people Bobby had given dark looks had, in fact, been of the male variety. She hadn't considered that he might have warned people off *before* she went out with them.

"I remember you dating one or two people from here," Rick said darkly.

Amused at his jealous tone, she settled back in and gave him a squeeze before sharing the truth of the situation. "I never went on more than two, maybe three, dates with anyone from here, even during college. Since no guys asked me out, I asked them. Most turned me down straight away. Those who did go out with me were jumpy and rarely interested in second dates. It didn't occur to me that they were terrified of my brother." A hint of bitterness crept into her voice.

"Well, Bobby was Bobby." Rick's shoulder shrugged under her head.

That was the truth too. He was who he was, and who he was was unforgettable — apparently more so than she knew if he lived on in his threats. Even after he was gone, her memories of him were so fresh, so real, so close to the present that the fact he wasn't around anymore jarred her to the core even as her understanding of who he was turned darker and darker.

Chapter 25

Rick

After Rick avoided sharing just how far Bobby's threats went when he warned people off, Melissa fell silent. Rick let her trail her fingers along his abs over his shirt as he tried to muster the courage to tell her she couldn't lie to him, not if he was touching her or had touched her recently. She deserved to know.

He thought she might be free of his influence; they'd only been touching through their clothes for a while now. He'd been so nervous about her rejecting him once he told her what he could do, but now that she'd admitted she liked him for who he was, gray areas of the Mavens and all, he was more confident she'd still want him in her life. But it bothered him that she might have told him she liked him without intending to because they were touching. He would always force her to tell the truth if they were making skin contact.

Before he found a way to corral his last bit of hesitation and tell her about his touch, her breathing changed, and he realized she'd fallen asleep. He'd never had someone fall asleep against him without the other person having experienced a severe injury, and that was more like they had passed out from pain or blood loss than sleeping. His arm tightened around her, and she murmured. Her hand clenched against his stomach for a second, before adjusting and sliding partially under the hem of his shirt. He knew he should move Melissa's hand away from his skin, or maybe leave altogether, but he couldn't bring himself to wake her.

Instead of leaving, he stayed with her tucked under his arm, her leg crooked over his, and her head rising and falling with his chest as he breathed. Carefully, he pulled the soft lavender throw blanket off the back of the couch and mostly over the two of them. Dave's comment about Rick needing to find out how long the effects of his touch lasted after prolonged contact started breaking through his conscious at the same time he felt sleep pulling at him.

When his phone rang, Rick reached out to the coffee table and put it to his ear without looking at who was calling. Melissa murmured at his movement and rubbed the side of her face against his chest but didn't wake up. They'd fallen asleep with one of the kitchen lights on and the glow allowed him to see most of the room.

"Hello?" he said as quietly as possible.

"I pulled a favor, seeing as it's Mel and all," Neil said without prelude.

Since Neil never called in the middle of the night, Rick was now wide awake.

"Okay," he whispered, looking down at the top of Melissa's head.

"The police arrested Tommy Nolan. If you want to talk to him, you have to do it tonight before he has a chance at bail. Also, there aren't a lot of cops at the station right now."

"I can't break into the police station for a chat," Rick whisper-hissed.

Melissa tensed against him, having woken at the last comment.

"That sounds like a bad idea," she murmured as she shifted up on her elbow to look at him.

"That's not what I meant," Neil said. "Go to the station and ask for Officer Fields. You will have ten, maybe fifteen, minutes to talk to Nolan."

"The police arrested Tommy?" Melissa asked; she'd heard enough to fill in the blanks.

"Sounds like bad timing," Neil chuckled at Melissa's voice. "Good for you two."

"Yeah," Rick said to both Neil and Melissa, no longer whispering. "How'd you explain my need to talk to him and why I should be allowed to?"

"I promised her that if Nolan talked to you, the kid wouldn't dare lie."

Melissa mouthed, *Who?* and pointed at the phone.

"Officer Fields took your word for that?" Rick mouthed, *Neil*, back to Melissa.

"I also promised that you wouldn't rough him up or act too threatening, so please don't make me look like a fool," Neil grumbled.

"Neil?" Melissa said aloud in surprise.

"Hi Mel," Neil said so loudly into Rick's ear that he pulled the phone away from his head. Either his wince or Neil's voice made Melissa smile. Rick took a second to appreciate the sight of Melissa on top of him smiling. "Rick needs to get moving in the next five minutes to get this done before shift change."

"Right." Melissa immediately moved off him.

"Thanks Neil," Rick said, hanging up the phone and silently cursing his friend's timing. He already missed the warm weight of Melissa against him.

"I didn't realize Neil was part of the Mavens."

"He's not."

"But he knows what the Mavens do?" Rick couldn't tell if Melissa was hurt by the notion or plotting to get the information from Neil if Rick didn't tell her more.

"No. He just knows we aren't what we are. Technically, you know a lot more about us than he does."

"Oh."

Rick went to the front door and put his shoes back on. Melissa followed him but didn't turn on any more lights. He was thinking through the time effect. It was a little after one in the morning and he'd gotten to Melissa's a bit after nine but made tea before he woke her. So, from the time she'd kissed him until she woke up, they'd had skin contact for three to four hours which could mean six to eight hours of her only being able to answer questions truthfully if the effects of his touch functioned normally and there wasn't a max time limit to how long the effect lasted. Rick squeezed his eyes closed as a worse possibility occurred to him. What if his touch had a multiplying effect with extended contact? He already knew contact with his blood quadrupled the effect....

"When do you need to be at the coffee shop?"

"I have an afternoon closing shift." That meant she should be free from his influence by then.

"Okay," he said. He could tell her the next time they were together. It wouldn't make any difference right then, and he really didn't have time to talk her through it.

"You gotta go, but I don't want you to." Melissa said as she pulled him down for a kiss before shoving him out the door. Seeing as he had moved them a step away from it rather than making a move to leave, that was for the best.

Rick made it to the police station in less than thirty minutes since he drove at almost twice the speed limit. He'd activated the muted drive on his bike that he used when blatantly breaking the law. Some of the Maven upgrades were really handy.

The police station looked just as drab as usual. Its brick facade and barred windows were weathered and had seen better days. Even the tiled floor inside was worn by a century of footsteps until the green color had faded into a patchy irregular pattern that hinted at frequent paths of foot traffic. Rick followed the most obvious path to the front desk. The officer behind the desk looked like a junior officer who was taking his knocks by getting stuck with night desk duty. Granted, it could just be that as a beagle hybrid, he looked younger than he was. His name tag said Officer Tanner, though his facial expression and pinned back ears indicated it should have said Officer Terrified.

"Officer Tanner," Rick nodded a greeting. "Officer Fields is expecting me."

"And you are?"

"Someone she's expecting," he growled. He didn't know if Neil had given his name or not. Neil wouldn't know the proper protocol for something like this since they'd never discussed it.

Tanner's whimper was barely audible, and when he turned to use the phone and summon Fields, Rick saw the guy's tail was literally tucked hard between his legs. Unable to do anything else, Rick listened to Tanner's quick call.

"Fields, there's someone here to see you." A pause. "Wait Fields, he's big, looks like he could chew up and spit out a tiger." Tanner's lips pulled back in a snarl as he said, "My point? I think you should bring someone with you." Rick could almost hear Fields snapping at Tanner on the phone. "Of course," the beagle hybrid said before hanging up the phone. His tone made it obvious he had just been scolded.

Light footsteps approached, and a perky blond woman walked in. She looked like she belonged in a magazine or should have been one of the pinups Rick had seen in Dave's "Pleasure Pad" before they'd redecorated it. Her police uniform was the same as Tanner's, but it didn't hide that she was gorgeous. The dark navy of the uniform accentuated her light skin and hair, making her look both ready for action and oddly fragile. Neil's comment about not making him look like a fool took on a whole new meaning. Rick had no doubt that Neil had a thing for Officer Fields and thought she was way out of his league, which is what high school and college had taught him, but something Bobby and Rick had never bought into.

Officer Fields gave a stern nod to Rick and waved for him to follow her without stopping to address him as she walked between him and Tanner. The young officer did his best to glare at him with intimidation.

"We have twenty minutes until you need to be out of the building," Fields said. "I'm sticking my neck out here."

"I imagine you need to produce double the results if Officer Tanner's behavior reflects the rest of the department's." Sexism was, in theory, less rampant than in the past according to reports, but the prettier a woman was, the more problems they had with it — both being harassed and treated like they needed to be protected. It wouldn't matter if Fields was the most disorienting hybrid out there or just a human; Rick knew from interacting with her colleague at the front desk that she faced a hurdle to be accepted as a competent police officer. Susan had shared her own struggles with the issue soon after she'd joined his team. A struggle that wasn't over when she had confided in him.

"You can't rough him up. No intimidation tactics." She growled at him, ignoring his observation. The growl was solid, so Rick leaned away from her being human like him. She was likely a dog or cat hybrid, so no worries about her having a *talent* to factor in.

Rick pocketed his gloves as she opened the door to a basic interrogation room. The room had a table in the middle with chairs on each side. Tommy sat on the side facing the mirrored window that held the recording and observation room. He wore the same baggy patchwork sweatshirt he'd been wearing in the photos on his social media, but it looked dirtier. His short gray fur was matted in a few of the places Rick could see. The fact that it was a darker gray than his sisters could just be his coloring, or possibly a sign of how dirty he was. The room didn't smell, so maybe he wasn't that dirty. Tommy's shaking told Rick he wasn't high on Nip at the moment and was instead in need of a fix. Not that he would get one at the police station. He didn't look up at either of them when the door shut.

Fields made a movement with her wrist, and Rick saw the red dot of the camera in the upper corner blink twice. Whoever was on the other side of the glass had stopped and restarted the recording to make an easy-to-save chunk. He wasn't in the shot yet, but Jade would have to call in a favor to get him scrubbed from the recording, even if he didn't show his face. In a different city, just having his back to the camera would be fine, but in his hometown, some officers would be able to identify him from going to school together. His boss was not going to be pleased, but technically, she'd approved the team using the Mavens' resources to protect Melissa and her friend, so maybe she wouldn't be too angry.

Fields reminded Tommy of his rights, but Tommy just stared at his shaking hands. Rick dropped his jacket on the empty chair, keeping his back to the camera, and pushed up his sleeves. Then, he walked over beside Tommy's hunched body. The fur was an issue. Fur muffled the effect of Rick's touch. He either needed to touch the pads of Tommy's hand or his whiskers, and he didn't have much time.

"We need to talk," Rick said.

"Not saying nothing," Tommy answered. His voice shook.

"Tommy, they tried to grab Kate."

Tommy's head jerked up, and he finally looked at Rick. His eyes widened in surprise and then narrowed in distrust till Rick could barely see the slits of the cat's pupils. "What's my sister got to do with this? Or with you, for that matter?"

"Whatever you have gotten into has Theo Barre sniffing around her and her best friend."

At Theo's name, Tommy's shaking got worse. Rick took advantage of the opportunity to "comfort" him. He reached out and squeezed his shoulder, purposely angling his arm so it would brush his whiskers. Tommy jerked away from the touch and grabbed onto Rick's forearm, hissing in scared threat. Tommy's claws were out, and he drew blood. Rick didn't fight his hold or react in any way that showed fear, threat, or pain. He held still while he breathed through his nose as the sharp tips of Tommy's claws sunk in a little further.

Fields stepped forward as Rick said, "I was just going to say that Theo Barre can't get to you here." Rick signaled Fields behind his back to give him room.

Tommy retracted his claws after a few seconds when neither Rick nor Fields made a move toward him. Rick watched as the claws pulled his blood into contact with Tommy's skin, but he didn't encourage Tommy to release his forearm.

Rick waited in silence for Tommy to realize he'd grabbed a scary person. It took another thirty seconds for the knowledge to penetrate. Fields probably thought they were wasting time, but once Tommy finally let go of Rick, a full minute had passed. With just skin contact, that would have given Rick two minutes of truth. With his blood, that time doubled. Since time was of the essence, he wasn't going to quibble about the scratches.

"What did you do that has Theo so interested in you, Kate, and Melissa?"

"Oh shit, you're here to enforce Bobby's threats?" Whatever nerves Tommy had been plagued with quadrupled at the idea of Bobby's legendary threats, which might have aggrandized through rumors for all Rick knew.

"No, just keeping people safe. How'd you get involved with Theo?"

Whatever denial or lie Tommy had opened his mouth to give didn't come out. He'd chosen to respond to the question, and he didn't have a choice in what he said anymore. The only defense that worked against Rick was not talking at all. Since only people he trusted completely knew about his ability, no one just shut up. They always decided to say they wouldn't say anything and then fell victim to his touch as intended.

"I've been taking Nip for years, just the low concentration, you know, for fun. But Theo gave me a free hit, and I didn't know it was stronger stuff than I usually do. The second it hit my senses, I was waxing on about the shit. It was good stuff. I don't remember a lot, but I apparently started describing the unique qualities of the hit in great detail. With my granddad being a sommelier and his girlfriend being a chef, I have a good palate." Though no more sense of smell, Rick thought.

"When I needed a little Nip sooner than I thought I should have, he gave me another hit. It was a different strain, and while high, I described it in detail again. The next time, still for free, he gave me some low concentration stuff like I used to take, and it just wasn't the same." Tommy's voice rose in pitch as he talked and couldn't stop what he was saying.

Rick heard Fields adjust her stance behind him, but he remained focused on Tommy. He only had a few minutes to work with.

"Then Theo offered me a job as a quality control expert and included the good stuff as part of my payment. I took the job but realized they weren't paying me any actual money for taking so many hits of their product. To get out, I grabbed a selection of the stuff they'd left for testing. A *large* selection. I thought I could sell it to a dealer, wean myself back to the low concentration, and get out of there. They're hunting me down because I stole from them."

"Names of anyone you met," Rick prompted.

Tommy shook his head and clearly meant to say no, but again, he didn't have a choice — he'd opened his mouth to answer.

"Theo, Sammy, Troy, and Hughie were the only people I met. Barre is the only one whose last name I got. A few other people came by, but I was whacked at the time. I don't know if I met them, or they just came to watch or what." Tommy's eyes darted around the room like the people he named might jump out of the walls.

"Why are they after Kate and Melissa?"

"Kate? I'd assume to blackmail me into turning myself in. Melissa? No idea. Maybe she's doing drugs or dealing in her coffee shop?"

"She's not," Rick ground out.

"I don't know her that well. Maybe Theo saw her with Kate, and she's his type? I don't know." Tommy was rocking back and forth and becoming more hysterical as the seconds ticked by. He knew he was saying things he shouldn't. Admitting to things he shouldn't.

Rick was not pleased with Tommy's answer. It wasn't that he didn't think Tommy was telling him the truth, but rather that it didn't explain Theo's interest in Melissa specifically. After showing up at the coffee shop that first time, Theo hadn't shown any signs of looking into Kate further. Rick didn't delude himself by thinking it was because Kate hadn't been alone the following days. There was more going on.

"Can you describe Sammy, Troy, or Hughie?" Rick pressed Tommy. None of their names rang any bells from the Wrapper's hierarchy.

"Sammy looks like a lion, but his mane is all over his body. Troy's black ponytail swished and flicked a lot. He was super young, definitely still in school. And Hughie? He looked mean and snarly as a person can be. He was mostly a looming shape that came with Theo one day. I didn't actually meet him, but I heard Theo say, 'Come on, Hughie. The office is this way.' Like they had serious business to attend to."

"Anything else?"

"I'm not saying another word," Tommy choked out.

Rick stood, picked up his jacket, and backed out of the camera's focus.

"We won't get more out of him," he told Fields. She was staring at him with her jaw hanging open. Her shock at the sheer amount of information Tommy had spilled, including pointing fingers at people no one wanted to point fingers at, was painted across her face. "We got to get me out of here before shift change, right?"

That snapped her back to the present. After another flick of her hand, the camera in the corner blinked twice again, cutting the recording into a *very* useful chunk. Then, Fields turned and led Rick back into the hallway.

"Neil sure kept his word with you," she muttered.

"He's as trustworthy as they come," Rick said. It was a fact he knew to his core. Neil had stuck with him and Bobby no matter what trouble they got into. Even after Neil got caught a time or two for their antics because he was slower; he never gave them up. They just got smarter so his speed wouldn't be an issue.

Halfway down the hall, Fields opened a cabinet and pulled out a roll of medical gauze and disinfectant spray. Rick doused his arm, ignoring the sting, and took the gauze and wrapped it around the oozing scratches on his forearm. As they walked, he rolled his sleeves down and shrugged his jacket on.

"What's your deal then?" she asked him. Her face was both impressed and suspicious. "You can't tell me that was normal shit you pulled back there."

Rick shrugged as they reached the front of the building. He looked at the clock and saw he had maybe two minutes before he needed to be gone. He paused by the front desk and a suspicious Officer Tanner.

"A few pointers," Rick said, looking Tanner in the eye. "Do not, under any circumstances, whimper in uniform, pin your ears back in fear, or tuck your tail between your legs. You need to have complete control, or no one is going to take you seriously. Also, never hint that anyone you work with is less than capable because they are a woman or because they're attractive. You'll go nowhere with that attitude."

Tanner pulled back his head and flicked his eyes to Fields but said nothing.

"Nice to meet you, Officer Fields. Tell our friend hi for me."

"Will do," she said to his back as he walked to the door.

"Who was that?" Tanner's voice was incredulous.

"Best interrogator I've ever seen," Fields answered as the door behind Rick swung shut. He still had no idea if she knew his name or not, but at least that it didn't seem like that would be another problem for his boss to handle.

He chuckled as he pulled his gloves on. He wouldn't mind being seen as a great interrogator, but it was best to keep that a secret. Publicity would draw unwanted attention to his *talent*.

Chapter 26

Melissa

"**I** want you to come with me," Kate insisted a second time.

"You don't need me to go talk to your parents," Melissa repeated into the phone as she stared at her empty breakfast plate. "I could meet you at the station after you talk to them if you want me to come with you to see Tommy." It had not occurred to her that Tommy would use whatever limited phone access he had to call his sister and ask *her* to bail him out. Kate didn't have bail money laying around. Their parents were a different story, but Melissa hadn't missed the fact that Tommy didn't call them. She didn't want to be there when Kate told her parents Tommy had been arrested. What she wanted to do was take a hot bath and soak her stiff abdomen until she could move more easily.

"I haven't seen them since before that guy grabbed me in your shop. If it comes up with my parents, I want to have you there as support."

"Fine." Melissa gave in. They had been arguing about it for five minutes. Kate wasn't going to veer from her plan, and Melissa did want to be there for her about the Theo-guy. "Do you want to grab me on your way, or should I meet you at your parents' house?"

"I'll grab you. Be there in thirty minutes."

At times like this, being lifelong best friends was less than fun. If Melissa weren't basically a part of the family, she could have missed the unpleasant family moment that this was undoubtedly going to be. Though, if Bill and Kim decided to post bail for their son, Melissa didn't want them to do so while in the dark. If it came to that, she'd tell them that Tommy was doing drugs, which would be worse than telling them he was in jail.

When Kate pulled up in her vintage blue Beetle thirty minutes later, Melissa could hear an Akdwenian soundtrack playing, even though Kate didn't have any windows open. Shaking her head, she slid into the front passenger seat. Kate's ears were pinned back and twitching — a clear indicator that she was nervous. She was so distraught that she didn't notice that Melissa winced in pain when she contorted her body into the car.

Melissa was relieved to see Kate had picked clothes that could comfortably accommodate her hybrid form's fur since the morning was going to be unpleasant enough as it was for her friend. When Kate didn't offer to change the music like she normally did or at least drop the volume, Melissa resigned herself to a few minutes of discordant chimes, tweets, and piano keys. As Kate pulled away from the curb and turned toward her parents' house, Melissa saw her friend's claws were out as she gripped the steering wheel.

"If you don't calm down a little, your parents will know something is up before we even make it inside," Melissa said as soothingly as she could over the music. Kate rolled her shoulders and retracted her claws, but didn't manage to perk up her ears.

They parked in front of her parents' house, and Kate took a deep breath, finally turning off the music. Her ears almost rose as she exhaled. She tried another calming breath.

Kate *hated* giving bad news to her parents. She had once explained to Melissa that it felt like she was the one letting them down rather than Tommy. Kate knew it wasn't logical, but she hadn't been able to shake the ingrained feeling and all the nerves that came with it. And despite the fact she'd often approached her parents on Tommy's behalf, she still thought he never did anything *truly* wrong. Melissa didn't think Tommy was a bad guy, but he made plenty of poor decisions.

"If you shift, you can hide your emotions better," Melissa reminded her.

"Yeah, but at the first sign of negative adrenaline, my fur and ears will just jump back out."

"Okay, but remember, no matter what happens in there. *You* did nothing wrong. Tommy is the one who got himself arrested."

Kate frowned deeply and her lower lip quivered, but she nodded and rolled her shoulders again before getting out of the car. Melissa climbed out too, noting that they had sat in the car long enough for Bill and Kim to come out on the porch looking worried.

Bill was, as usual, in his cat form. His short gray fur was reminiscent of the Russian Blue he had as a pet in his younger years. Kim, on the other hand, was in her human form. Melissa had only seen Kate's mom as a cat a handful of times over the years and understood why. While Kate's dad and brother had short fur and Kate's was medium in length, her mom's was long, fluffy, and angry looking like her childhood Persian cat's had been when the Crisis hit. Basically, it was not clothing friendly, so she tried to limit her time in her furred state as much as possible. An actual orange tabby wove between their ankles, rubbing its face on them.

"I didn't know you guys adopted a pet cat," Melissa said in greeting. Once she was at the porch, she squatted down and reached her hand out to the miniature cat. It was a perfectly normal size, but having grown up with bipedal hybrids, the little four-legged kitty seemed *tiny*.

"Meowkins just showed up one day and wouldn't leave," Bill said. His deep voice held a rumble reminiscent of a purr, even though he did not look happy seeing his daughter fidget beside Melissa.

"Let's go inside," Kim said, waving them in. "Then, you can tell us what's wrong." There was no judgment in her tone, only concern for her daughter.

Inside, they went to the living room, which opened up to the backyard. It was the entire family's favorite room in the mornings because it was almost completely bathed in sunlight from the large south-eastern facing windows. While Kate and her parents took up seats in the sun's rays, Melissa sat down on the leather love seat that was along the wall specifically to allow guests the option to not be baked alive. Having already ditched her boots at the door, Melissa pulled her feet up on the little couch so that they weren't in the sun either. It didn't matter how plush the carpet was or how perfect it was for mid-morning sun naps, the whole room was already just a little warm for Melissa in contrast to the brisk fall air outside.

"Just let it out, Katie," Kim said.

Kate took a deep breath.

"Tommy's been arrested. He's in jail."

Kim's gasp sounded more like hurt disappointment than complete shock. Melissa had heard her genuinely shocked gasp a number of times over the years, but none of them had sounded quite so sad. Bill crossed his furry arms over his chest and glowered at the carpet between them.

"He called me this morning. He needs bail money."

"Schnook-ums," Kim said to Bill in despair.

"Not a dime," Bill hissed out. His poofed-out tail swished in agitation.

"What?" Kate reared her head back in shock. Melissa tried to sink into the couch and be unobtrusive. Kate's dad had always been easygoing and calm. Not once, even during the year that he taught her high school history class, had she heard him hiss or seem truly upset —like he did now.

"We won't bail him out," Bill snapped.

"But he's in jail, Bill!" Kim wailed.

"Maybe they'll dry him out there," he replied on a growl. Melissa was relieved she wouldn't be the one to break it to Kate's parents that their son was doing drugs. Just knowing that made the room feel a little less stifling.

"Dry him out?" Kate echoed. A frown in her voice. "I've never even seen Tommy drinking."

"Kick the habit, or whatever people say," Bill grumbled.

"What do you think he's doing?" Kate fidgeted uneasily in her sunny seat. She looked at her mom, but Kim was looking at the ground, desolate, and didn't notice. Her dad just snarled at his own thoughts. When Kate's eyes fell on Melissa, they narrowed.

"Why aren't you reacting to this news?" she whisper-hissed. Her pupils were thin slits, and she was bristling just as much as her dad.

Melissa could tell that her friend wasn't angry at her exactly, just shocked and frustrated. When Kate was actually angry, her claws slipped out, and for now, they were still sheathed. However, Melissa thought that maybe she should have driven herself, even if it was only a ten-minute walk back to her parents' house.

"Jail could be great for going cold turkey and setting up a recovery," she said reasonably. "They have rehab programs on the inside. We could ask about them when we go down to the police station."

"You *knew*," Kate said, defeat in her crumpling body. "How long have you known?"

"You remember just the other day, I mentioned he might not be making the best decisions, but I didn't want to say anything until it was confirmed? Well, now it's confirmed." Melissa grimaced.

"We've known for a little over a month, maybe two months," Kim said as if Tommy had wrenched out her heart and stomped all over it, which, in a way, he had.

"He kept needing more money than reasonable for his expenses." Bill's frustrated sigh said it all for Melissa. "One day, when he stayed over, I dug around in his backpack and found drugs. I told him he wouldn't get any more support from us until he cleaned up his act."

"What is he doing?"

"Nip," Bill spat.

Kate's wide-eyed stare tore at Melissa. She was blind to her little brother's flaws. Melissa still suspected that Tommy had just gotten in over his head since he wasn't dangerous to anyone, but Kate had always believed in Tommy regardless of his mistakes over the years; those mistakes, at least, had been minor. This revelation was shaking the ground she stood on.

"I was worried you knew and hadn't told us," Kim admitted. "With you and Melissa going to that party at his place last week. I worried maybe you were...."

"I've never done drugs," Kate whispered. Hurt radiated from every syllable. "What party are you talking about?"

"Last weekend, Jessy Thompson called me up," Kim said. Her brow uncreased as she spoke, likely due to relief that Kate wasn't making the same decisions as her brother. "She said something about her son joining the two of you at a party Tommy was throwing, but that he didn't have his address. I don't remember much about her boy other than he went off to the military after high school, but I thought if he was there, maybe he could keep the two of you out of trouble."

"Rick must have misheard." Melissa scrambled to cover up that she and Rick had broken into Tommy's apartment. Twice.

"Tommy was already missing then," Kate said at the same time. Melissa didn't know if Kate missed the comment about Rick falsely asking about a party or recognized the connection to him helping and skipped over it purposefully.

"Missing?" Kate's dad sat forward. "What do you mean, missing? You say that like you mean more than just not answering his phone."

"I—" Kate's panicked eyes swung to Melissa. Bill and Kim looked at Melissa, too. Melissa sighed.

"One of Tommy's friends came looking for him at the coffee shop," she told them. "He was intense and scared Kate. So, we've been on the lookout for Tommy."

"One of his drug friends scared you?" Kim rose and moved across the room to Kate's side. "Oh, Katie." She wrapped her daughter in a hug, gently petting her arm.

Bill let his wife comfort Kate and gruffly apologized to Melissa for his son bringing undesirable people into her coffee shop. Melissa waved off his apology, reminding him of what the neighborhood used to be like and assuring him that the friend wasn't any scarier than her regulars. This was only true when considering his outward appearance. In truth, Theo was significantly scarier than anyone she'd ever encountered given he had wired her house to watch her and messed with her bike.

"Do you guys want to come with Melissa and me to see Tommy?" Kate asked her parents.

A few minutes later, everyone was on the road and heading to the police station. On the phone, Tommy hadn't told Kate what the police had on him, so none of them knew exactly why he had been arrested.

Melissa was pretty sure he wouldn't have been arrested for having a recreational amount of Nip on his person, so it had to be something worse.

They arrived at the old brick building that housed the police station, and a grey-haired policeman showed them two at a time into a divided room where they could see Tommy. Bill and Kim went in first, but Tommy refused to talk to them when they said they wouldn't bail him out.

When Melissa and Kate went in, Melissa felt bad that his family had to see him like this. Tommy was in an orange jumpsuit that hung loosely on his too-slim frame, and he was shaking so badly most people would think he was close to dying from fright. Though they knew now that he was experiencing withdrawals — bad ones from the look of things.

The moment Tommy saw Kate, his face fell.

"I'm so sorry, Katie. I didn't mean to get you involved in this." He took a step toward the glass wall that divided the bare bones room. Neither he nor Kate moved to sit in the chairs on their respective sides.

"You should have asked me for help a while ago," she half-scolded him. "I'm just happy to see that you're okay."

Melissa stepped to the side then, no longer hidden behind Kate, thinking she'd sit and try to be unobtrusive.

"Melissa!" Tommy yanked himself away from the glass wall like she was venomous, which was a new reaction from him. Normally, he smiled shyly at her and kept his distance. "I don't know why he's interested in you. You have to believe me."

Frowning, Melissa realized she should have asked Rick what he'd said to Tommy. Then she might have some context for Tommy's reaction.

"What are you talking about?" Kate asked, whipping her head back and forth between her brother and Melissa so quickly that the gem-encrusted hoops in her ears seemed to levitate out parallel to the ground.

"Theo should only be after me. Without me, he should just disappear if it has *anything* to do with me." Tommy was so agitated a large police officer came into his half of the room and tried to calm him down.

"Whose Theo?" Kate asked, more bewildered.

"The guy who grabbed you last week," Melissa whispered to her.

"Okay... but why is Tommy apologizing to *you* about him?" Kate asked, alarm painted in her eyes.

"I told you he was seen in town," Melissa whispered while watching the policeman cautiously offer Tommy water. "What I didn't mention was that he was seen in my vicinity, rather than yours, but we don't know why."

"We?"

Melissa paused and then said, "Rick and I." She couldn't tell Kate all the Mavens were involved. That would just bring up questions about what the Mavens were.

Tommy took a few sips of the water, but spilled half of it down his front. He sidled closer to them, pressing up against the barrier that separated the two halves of the room.

"I'm scared," he whispered to Kate when she drew near. Melissa stayed back since she didn't want to send Tommy into more panic at her approach, but she could hear him. "I gave them names. I didn't mean to, but I told them names."

"Told who what names?" Kate asked in as soothing a voice as she could muster. Melissa knew it was Kate's *I'm-seconds-from-losing-it* voice.

"I told them the names of—" Tommy peeked over his shoulder at the guard by the door. "Names of the dealers," he whispered. "No one names them if they get caught. No one. I need to hide. I need to get out of here and disappear."

"Tommy," Kate whispered. "I don't have the money to bail you out."

Tommy's breath became ragged, and somehow, he started shaking more. Then, he collapsed into an incoherent pile of fur.

Kate squeaked, and the guard rushed forward. Melissa focused on Kate and talked her through a breathing exercise to stave off what looked like the start of a panic attack while the guard carried Tommy out. Clearly, Tommy thought someone on the inside was going to kill him, and Melissa needed to get that information to Rick. By the time a guard came to take them out of the visiting room, Kate wasn't great but had some of her fear under control.

While Kate and Melissa talked to Tommy, Bill and Kim had learned that Tommy had been arrested for possession and intent to deal. A quick internet search revealed that convictions could range from six months to three years depending on what drugs he had, how much he had, and how dangerous he was deemed. On the last factor, Melissa guessed he wouldn't get any added time. Despite that, she hoped his sentence would be closer to a year with rehab included in the sentencing. It would put his whole family at ease if he was clean when he got out.

Out in front of the police station, Melissa discreetly messaged Rick and checked the time. It was just after lunch, and she needed to get to work. She could easily call a ride, but she needed to check on Kate first.

"I need to get to the coffee shop," Melissa said, giving Kate an apologetic smile. "I know you have the afternoon shift with me, but maybe you should spend the afternoon with your parents."

"I can't leave you understaffed at such short notice," Kate said despite her distress. "And, working might keep me occupied." She glanced at the station, and her lip quivered as she stared at the bars over the windows.

"We'll come to the coffee shop for a bit too," Kim announced, rubbing her daughter's arm and trying to get her to look away from the station. "Then, if it isn't too busy at the beginning of your shift, you can sit with us." Bill gave his daughter a comforting squeeze to confirm Kim's decision.

As a group, they navigated their way through the lunchtime bustle of people between them and their cars. None of them said anything, but Melissa was relieved to see that at least one of Kate's parents kept her within arm's reach, constantly giving her the silent, reassuring touches she knew her friend needed.

On the way to the coffee shop, Melissa messaged Danny about what had happened that morning with Tommy. Danny immediately responded, volunteering to hang out at the coffee shop and support as needed — either behind the counter or keeping Kate distracted.

Chapter 27

Rick

By the time Jeremy had finished a deep hack into all Barres™'s accounts, Rick had growled at two cat hybrids from Team Kappa in the hallway and actually shoved Toby when he came into the Gamma room to apologize about any unintended jibe he'd made about Melissa the day before. Having faces and profiles to go with the names Tommy had given him did not make Rick feel better. More solid information was good, of course, but not when it went the way it had.

"Jade," Susan said into her phone, "we need you downstairs." Her tone told Rick that he had better calm down quickly or his boss would be questioning him on a lot more than what he'd dragged his team into during their vacation.

Rick squeezed his eyes shut and pushed his worry into a box. He forced his shoulders to relax and leaned against the empty wall space between the handful of forensic machines his team had in their room. He purposely put himself far away from Jeremy and the upsetting results he kept finding, as if distance made a difference. Rick's glower remained, but that, at least, could be expected of him given the circumstances. The rest of his team didn't seem to agree. They *all* sat in chairs clustered around Jeremy, but angled to keep an eye on Rick across the room.

His boss walked in looking like her typical self-contained contradiction. Jade Trigg's black leather pants had white pinstripes that elevated them to elegant dress pants. Her all-black leather vest plunged deep, showing off an excessive amount of plumage. Rick had never seen Jade in her human form in the decade he'd worked for her.

As a bird hybrid, she was breathtaking by anyone's standards. Fluffy white feathers that drew up her head like a pixie cut. A little beak that didn't hinder the expressiveness of her eyes and cheeks. Her scaly feet and hands were light tan and only covered when she was physically astride a bike. She had a sophisticated look that screamed class even when she burned rubber or oversaw a grisly mission. No one knew exactly what type of bird she was, but most of the Mavens had decided between themselves that her parents were a snowy egret hybrid and a snowy owl hybrid — not that either type of bird hybrid were commonly found in any records Jeremy had searched.

"Update," Jade said, looking at the grim expressions on everyone's faces.

"Sammy and Troy were easy to identify," Shawn offered from his spot at the secondary set of computers. "Sammy, or Samuel Rizzo, is a security guard for Barres™. Rick and I saw him patrolling when we scoped out the factory. Nothing officially connects him to Wrappers business beyond Tommy's description of what was most likely Sammy; he's an orange Maine coon hybrid. His record is clean, and his work history isn't sketchy."

"Okay," Jade said. She waved her fingers in a circular motion as if to say, "make this worth my time."

"Troy Phillips, a horse hybrid, is a teenager who fancies himself a hacker," Jeremy continued. Given how good Jeremy was with computers, Rick knew Jeremy meant the kid wasn't too bad, but he also wasn't anywhere near Jeremy's level. "There isn't any mention of him in anything directly related to Barres™, but I dug through email accounts looking for anyone named Troy. Through Theo's Barres™ email, I found another shadier account he uses that doesn't say anything incriminating as far as I can tell. That said, he used it to email Troy a pair of photos recently."

Jeremy clicked on the photos he'd stolen from the email. The ones that had immediately explained why Melissa was on the Wrapper's radar. They weren't anywhere near as graphic as the surveillance of Rick kissing Melissa on his bike had been, but they said more than Rick had known at the time.

Both photos were of Rick and Melissa the night they'd gone to Tommy's apartment together. Rick held Melissa close in one. Her hand fisted in his shirt like she needed him, and her face tilted just so to show she was listening intently. That photo didn't show Rick's face. The second photo, however, did. And in that photo, Rick was smirking like he was about to get lucky, and Melissa was looking up at him with pure anticipation. The two photos were taken when he was suggesting she drive them home on his bike. Not that he'd told his team what the two of them were talking about, and none of them dared ask.

"Implications?" Jade prompted.

"Theo Barre was watching Tommy's place and saw Melissa and I break in," Rick growled. He wanted to gut Theo for capturing that moment and sharing it. It was private. It was the first time he'd really given into the temptation that was Melissa, even if it was for just a few minutes. He didn't want to share that with his team, much less with drug dealers and their associates.

"Why was she with you?" Jade asked.

"She would have gone without me. I made the judgment call to go with her." Silently, Rick added, *and keep her out of trouble*, even if it hadn't worked out that way.

"She has some experience picking locks," Susan offered.

"And she was easier to ID," Jade continued with no judgement. The fact that Jade always focused on the next move, the big picture, and trusted her teams' calls was one of the reasons Rick had stuck around after Bobby disappeared.

"And that's the good news," Dave muttered, looking at Rick out of the corner of his eye instead of focusing on Jade.

Jade's feathery forehead scrunched in clear displeasure. Nothing they had said so far was good, and they all knew it.

"Obviously, they had more difficulty identifying Rick," Jeremy sighed. He'd been working at the computer since before dawn and looked like it. "Three days after receiving the photos, Troy Phillips forwarded the picture with Rick's face, and only that picture, to an email account I haven't been able to get into. I have snagged in-going and out-going email addresses, but again, they aren't emails I can access. Someone is doing *good* security for them. We're lucky that I've been able to finger two or three groups that might be in play."

"None of them good," Carl muttered. He was closest to Rick, and they all knew why; he was the only one who could contain Rick if Rick's aggression turned on them.

"So, we played a long shot," Susan offered, staying on target.

Overall, she and Jeremy were acting the most normal of all of Team Gamma. Granted, they'd been around Bobby for a year or two more than the others, so random moody aggression wouldn't be as jarring for them. Rick didn't know if it was a good thing that he knew he was acting out of character or bad.

"I dug through all known databases to see if any of the groups had someone named Hughie to see if we could find the last person Tommy named," Jeremy said. "One does. Hughie is the new head of the Minfried crime family."

Jade's eyes narrowed. The year before, in Rafity City, they had taken down the former crime boss, Jeffrey Minfried, at the request of a government agency; only Jade knew which set of letters had hired them. The case against Jeffrey Minfried was impenetrable. Rick had done the interrogation himself. The hamster hybrid had admitted to ordering hits, completing a few himself, and given enough information about the flesh ring he ran that it collapsed not long after his arrest. No major players were left. None.

"What's Hughie's connection to the crime family?"

"Jeffrey had an older, very clean, half-brother who was raised by his mother rather than in the family," Dave said in mock delight from his seat next to Shawn.

Jade's beak pulled down in a frown. None of them were happy to have missed something, but even if they'd known about Hughie at the time, they wouldn't have had reason to dig deep into him. And Jeremy had needed to dig *deep* for the red flags to start popping up. On the surface, when they took down the Minfried enterprise, Hughie looked like nothing more than an intimidating business mogul. But that was only on the surface.

"He isn't so clean now," Rick said.

"Hughie's connection to the Wrappers is Allison Barre; they got their MBAs at the same university and their cohorts overlapped. This morning, Hughie visited his little brother in prison. The video," Jeremy played the clip he'd pirated from the prison security system, "shows Hughie sliding Jeffrey a dark-looking piece of paper that could be a printout of the photo Theo took."

"So, you think Rick has been IDed back to his hometown and a connection made to Melissa," Jade concluded.

"And depending on what he saw or knows," Rick said, "they might think Melissa is involved more than she is."

"Why?" Jade prompted him. Everyone else's eyes turned to Rick.

"If we assume he saw us go into Tommy's apartment, then he saw me, now known as the guy who interrogated Jeffery Minfried, with a woman who picked a solid lock in less than thirty seconds."

"Seriously?" Susan said. Rick could almost see her manufacturing a reason to meet Melissa rather than waiting for it to happen naturally, which was, to Rick's knowledge, her current approach.

Shawn whistled in appreciation.

"Bobby was shit with locks," Dave commented.

"Then," Jeremy added, "he either knows or is bound to find out soon that all the wiring he put up in her house and the trackers on her vehicles were disconnected before they recorded a single shot or showed any movement."

"Maybe we should have left the cameras up and had her do innocuous things," Carl said.

"I'm not having her recorded in her own home," Rick snapped at Carl. A second of fear flicked through Carl's eyes, and Rick squeezed his own shut and took a deep breath.

Bobby had always been the one who put fear into other people with his threats and, not that Rick had liked it, his follow through. If it was for "good," Bobby could justify any action. He had no limit except what Rick had managed to impose when he was Bobby's sounding board or literally holding him back from meting out "justice."

From Carl's reaction, it was clear to Rick none of them knew if he was any different from Bobby now. They didn't know where he stood, what his limit was, or how deeply Melissa skewed his breaking point from where it might be in any other circumstance.

Jade gave Rick an assessing look but didn't speak right away. Rick wondered what she had heard through the grapevine after yesterday's video debacle. She knew his past. She knew, in the decade she'd employed him, he'd never been caught or heard talk of him with anyone like in the photos. Rick didn't know what was in his file when she plucked him from the army and he convinced her to bring Bobby along for the ride as an asset. But Jade and his team all knew he couldn't turn off his touch. It was a constant in his life. For him to be acting like he was, she'd have to be an idiot not to realize that Melissa was more than just Bobby's little sister to him. And Jade was not an idiot.

"We assume the worst until we know differently," Jade said to the room at large, though she kept her eyes on Rick. "Melissa is family, with or without Bobby at our side. He's in our hearts. He's in our blood. We will provide security." She paused and smirked. "I'm assuming that will mostly be in the form of Rick glued to her side."

A few tentative chuckles drifted from his team. Rick just gave her a tight nod, not dignifying her teasing with a response.

"Anyone who the Wrappers or Minfrieds might think they can leverage to make Melissa cooperate should be protected, too. Might they have seen her in close contact with anyone in particular?"

"Kate Nolan, Tommy's sister," Jeremy said. "We're involved because Kate was approached, if they assume we weren't involved prior to that."

"I'll cover her tonight," Dave offered. Rick saw Susan narrow her eyes at Dave's casual offer to look out for the girl.

"How about you provide security?" Susan said. "*Covering* her with yourself isn't part of the job description."

Dave batted his eyelashes at her in faux innocence.

"If the Wrappers and the Minfrieds don't show any interest in the next two weeks now that Tommy is in police custody, we're in the clear," Jade finished, ignoring Susan and Dave's typical ribbing. Rick and his team nodded in agreement. "I'll get back to work, and you can all get back to your questionable use of vacation." She turned at the comment and left. They would iron out the details on their own.

Chapter 28

Melissa

"*Wait for me. Kate, too.*" That was all Rick's message said. What did he want to tell them? Did it have anything to do with Tommy thinking his life was in danger?

Melissa hoped they didn't have to wait long for him to show up and tell them. As it was, she'd already closed the coffee shop for the day. It wasn't particularly late since she closed in the early evening on Sundays, but Rick hadn't said how long he'd be.

"So, why again are we all waiting for Rick?" Danny asked for the third time as they all sat down at one of the coffee shop tables. They had already prepared everything for the next day. There wasn't anything left to do.

Melissa bit the side of her lip. "He didn't say why we needed to wait."

"I mean, I get why he wants *you* to wait for him." Danny winked at Melissa. "But with Tommy found, it's not like there's any reason for Kate and me to stay too."

"Found?" Kate muttered. "Arrested." She'd moved from the panicked and distraught stage to the annoyed stage. She was worried about Tommy's safety after his admission and how he'd broken down, but she wasn't scared for herself anymore.

"Right," Danny said while watching Kate.

"Let's just assume it's safety related."

"Safety related?" Kate repeated. Melissa wanted to kick herself. She hadn't meant to imply that it was about Tommy's safety. Because really, it wasn't like they could do anything about that.

"You think Rick, a member of a motorcycle club, is coming here to talk to us about safety?" Danny asked to clarify.

Melissa fought the urge to roll her eyes. The Mavens were so far from being the motorcycle club they pretended to be that she wondered how they kept everyone believing it.

After about thirty minutes of Melissa dodging her best friends' questions and avoiding saying much of anything about the Mavens, Rick finally knocked on the window of the locked front door. Melissa could tell it had been a long day, if only because Rick was wearing the same clothes she'd snuggled against that night. Whether or not he'd slept was anyone's guess after his comment the other day about being awake for over twenty-four hours. She instantly got up and went to unlock the door for him. She heard Danny and Kate's chairs scrape along the floor as they also stood up from the table.

"Who's with him?" Danny asked from behind her.

"Hi," Melissa said as she opened the door. She automatically bounced up and gave Rick a quick kiss as he stepped inside. He looked surprised, which confused Melissa. How had his girlfriends greeted him in the past? Still, he wrapped an arm around her, pulling her against his right side.

Sliding her hands under his jacket, she encountered a gun in a holster hidden on his far side — that was new. Stopping, she flicked her eyes up to Rick's and he tipped his head in response, which told her nothing. Biting back her questions in front of her friends, she dropped her hands a little lower, below the gun. Melissa knew whatever the Mavens did was more dangerous than being mechanics, but Rick hadn't been carrying a gun before. Something must have changed.

"Do I get a kiss too?" Dave called from behind Rick. He was still standing outside. She'd completely forgotten about Dave when her hands encountered Rick's gun. At Dave's comment, Rick moved them out of the doorway and glared at the cheetah hybrid he worked with.

"Not from Melissa," Dave said, holding his hands up like he was warding off the devil. "Never Melissa. No offense," he said to her. "I just—"

"Bobby?" she asked. It was the first time since they were kids that she'd said her brother's name with a measure of disgust.

"Yeeah." Dave drew out the word, and his eyes were seeing something uncomfortable that wasn't in the coffee shop. After an awkward moment, he shook himself out of it and looked over at Kate and Danny. "I was asking if *I* get a kiss from one of these two lovely ladies." He waggled his eyebrows at the pair.

"Dave, these are my friends Kate and Danny." She made the introductions, even though Dave already knew who each of them was. "Girls, Dave."

"You came in before," Kate said.

"I did." Dave grinned at her, obviously delighted she remembered him.

"Was I here?" Danny asked. She rubbed one of the spiral horns that poked out of her blond hair as she looked at the speckled cat with narrowed eyes.

"No, Tiff and Ilona were," Melissa said.

"Ah."

"So, why are we waiting here for you?" Kate asked. Melissa looked over and saw her friend's face was scrunched with worry; half her whiskers drooped, and the others shot up at an odd angle. "Did you have something more about Tommy?"

"Right," Rick said. "I know Tommy has been found. I'm sorry that wasn't better news," he added to Kate. She nodded. "But I don't have any more information to share about your brother. I just want to make sure everything is fine, and no one bothers his family and friends."

"So, you two are… what? The motorcycle club version of a stay away sign?" Danny quipped.

"You mean this Theo-guy might still be interested in us?" Kate asked. Her hands fidgeted with the slanted hem of her shirt.

Rick looked down at Melissa. His eyes asked her what she'd told Kate.

"Tommy flipped out when he saw me," she told him. "He started apologizing profusely to me about Theo. Apologizing like he was scared for his life."

"Hmm." Rick's eyebrows bounced like he saw the logic in Tommy's reaction.

"Why 'hmm'?" Melissa mimicked him.

"Makes sense," Rick shrugged against her.

"Why?"

Dave snorted. "Bobby had the whole town terrified?"

"Would you expect anything different?" Rick asked Dave, clearly frustrated by that fact. Melissa hadn't even considered that Tommy's reaction to seeing her had been related to Bobby. She was becoming more and more certain her brother was why Rick had kept his distance and had planned on continuing to do so if she hadn't made the first, second, and third moves.

Her frustration growing, Melissa watched Dave as he considered Rick's question. After a second or two, he nodded as if it made complete sense that the entire population of Granberg feared her brother. Her *dead* brother. Melissa felt a growl climbing up her throat.

"I don't get it," Danny said.

"I don't either," Kate volunteered.

"Bobby," Melissa snapped, "it turns out, didn't like the idea of me dating and made it extremely clear to everyone to stay far away."

"Seriously?" Danny asked. She didn't have any siblings and had never ceased to be caught off-guard by the now-amusing squabbles Melissa and Kate had with their siblings growing up. From the *what-the-hell* look on her face, she found this to be a less than amusing facet of having a sibling.

"At least that explains things," Kate huffed, shaking her head. At Danny's questioning look, she continued: "Remember how we found it odd in high school that, despite Melissa being, well—" Kate gestured at Melissa to reiterate her age-old argument that Melissa was attractive even when she had trouble believing it when growing up, apparently thanks to Bobby. "No one asked her to dances or out on dates. *No one.*"

"That's true. I remember the time—"

"Okay," Melissa said loudly in order to cut off whatever mortifying high school memory that included her failing spectacularly with boys that Danny was about to recount. Dave and Rick had the gall to chuckle.

"So, to make sure Theo, or one of his friends, doesn't follow up, Dave's going to hang out at Kate's tonight, if she has no objection," Rick announced. Melissa squeezed him in thanks for getting the topic off her.

"Is that necessary?" Kate's voice rose in alarm.

"Probably not," Rick said. "But you're important to Melissa, so I want to make sure you're safe."

Danny and Kate both looked at Rick like he was the most heartwarming thing they'd ever seen. They might have sighed a little.

Melissa barely heard Dave grumble, "How am I supposed to compete with *that*?" She hid her smile against Rick's shoulder. She didn't know if Dave was actually interested in Kate or Danny, but if he was, he would have to move past the player tendencies she had heard about in order to beat the romantic hero image Rick was projecting.

"It'll make sure Danny is safe, too," Melissa pointed out, nodding. "She was here when Theo came by."

"How does this do that?" Dave asked, looking at Melissa like she'd skipped something important.

"For now, Kate and Danny are roommates."

After a few more details were sorted out and thankfully no more questions about why a motorcycle club was providing protection, they all left. Dave followed Kate and Danny home to an address that Melissa was sure he already knew. Rick rode beside Melissa as they headed back to her house. He hadn't said it, but Melissa had no doubt that Rick was her protection detail.

With Tommy out of the picture, Melissa wanted to think everything was over, but if it was just about Tommy, why would Theo have put cameras in *her* house and a tracker on *her* motorcycle? Why would Rick be carrying a gun when he hadn't had one before?

They both pulled into Melissa's driveway, and Melissa watched as Rick wheeled his bike into the garage to the spot where Bobby had parked his bike when he was alive. Closing the garage behind them, Melissa felt Rick's presence as he followed her into the kitchen.

"You going over to your place?" Melissa asked, waving vaguely toward his childhood home. She had understood that Dave was staying with Kate and Danny for protection, but she didn't want to be presumptuous and assume Rick was spending the night snuggled against her.

"No." His answer was cautious and slow.

Inside her head, Melissa bounced on her toes and fanned herself in anticipation. In the middle of the kitchen, all she did was smile and say, "Alright."

Rick stayed by the door they'd just come through, like he didn't know what to do. Melissa was a little concerned that Bobby's supposed threats were messing with him, but she was used to having to make the first move, or fourth as the case was.

She walked over to him and placed her hands on his chest. His eyes dropped to her lips, and she nearly laughed at the dichotomy of how cautious he was and how much he wanted to devour her. Her hands slid up his chest, working their way with deliberate slowness to wrap around his neck, but they encountered a strap, reminding Melissa that they needed to talk about the weaponry in the room.

"Do you want to tell me why you're carrying a gun today when you weren't the last few days before, during, or after dinner?" she asked.

"Dinner?"

"I haven't eaten, and I'm assuming you haven't either."

"After?" he suggested as if asking if that was okay.

"I'll see what I have in the fridge." She stepped away, reminding herself it might be prudent to have dinner before making out in the kitchen and forgetting that she didn't know everything. Answers before making out, she chided herself.

"If you don't mind," Rick spoke faster than usual, "I'll jump in the shower."

"Do you want to go grab a change of clothes from your mom's house?" Melissa asked, giving him another once-over. He looked good, even if he was in the same clothes.

"I can't go back there until this is finished, Mel." He stated the fact like it should have been obvious.

Melissa blinked at him.

"This?" This meaning the two of them?

"I can't be seen connected to my mother's house. That would put her in danger. I can't go there until either this thing with Theo and his associates is taken care of or determined not to be a factor anymore."

"But you can be seen connected to *this* house?" That didn't sound logical. Melissa knew Rick wouldn't want to put her in danger any more than his mother.

"I guess we're going with before dinner," he muttered before answering her question in an authoritative tone Melissa associated with briefing subordinates and team members in movies. "I've been connected to you and hence this house. The night we went to Tommy's apartment, Theo snapped pictures of the two of us."

"And you have that no photo thing," Melissa said slowly, pushing past Rick's all-business tone and the paralyzing fact that the Theo-guy had taken photos of them — likely of them and mild PDA if walking pressed against someone while they whispered in your ear counted as PDA.

"There's a chance that Theo was watching you before the day he broke in, which means he might have seen me going in and out, both here and next door, which is why I'll also be watching my mother's house from here. There's just as much of a chance that he didn't see me next door and hadn't started watching you. It would have taken a day or more to figure out they couldn't find me in any databases."

The way Rick laid out the facts made Melissa wonder if Rick was in charge of his "team." But she wasn't on his team, so she asked, "If they can't ID you, what's the problem with them having a photo?"

"The people they sent the photo to might connect me to a job I did last year," Rick said. Melissa could tell he was picking his words with care. "There's a strong likelihood that the photo has been or will be shown to someone who, even if they don't know who I am beyond the first letter of my name, will not have friendly desires in my regard and hence in *your regard.*"

"In my regard? You think they'll hurt me to get to you?" Melissa's heart was racing and not in the way she had anticipated a few minutes earlier. None of what he was saying had anything to do with Tommy's debacle, and it sounded so much more serious than dealing drugs.

"It's possible they will think you helped me with that job." Rick stepped forward and pulled her against him. His hand rubbed up and down her back as if trying to soothe her and encourage her breathing to slow to a more regular rate. It wasn't working.

"Why would they think that?"

"I may have downplayed how easy it was to pick Tommy's lock," he admitted.

"What does that mean?" She stared up at him with wide eyes.

"It means that if Theo watched you pick the lock, then he'd assume you had serious training in the lock picking department. Serious. Professional. Skills."

"This sounds bad," Melissa said. Her whole world was tipping upside down because she got lucky picking a lock? No one in her life had ever been dangerous. Even people who scared others weren't actually dangerous. The way Rick was talking about this made it clear *this* was really bad news.

"It's not great." Rick tipped his head down to hers and touched their foreheads together. "But I'm going to take care of it." It sounded like a promise. Almost like he was promising to take care of her.

After a moment, he pulled her head down against his shoulder. As he continued to hold her and rub her back, Melissa felt the tension slowly leave her body as his warmth sunk into her. He'd take care of it. She believed him. She just didn't want to know the details and was thankful that he likely wasn't allowed to share them.

Chapter 29

Rick

Rick could hear Melissa in the kitchen when he left the bathroom. Instead of heading toward her with a towel wrapped around his hips and nothing else, he headed toward Bobby's room. Rick knew Bobby's room was intact and full of clothes. He hadn't personally gone in, but Dave had when he'd checked the house. Apparently, the room looked like Bobby would be back any day, but dusty.

Normally, Rick would have had clothes at work he could have grabbed and brought with him, but with it being his vacation, he'd had the bright idea to take everything to his apartment to wash and switch out. Riding an hour farther away before coming back to Granberg was not something he had time for. He did have the clothes for his visit next door, but thanks to Theo and now the Minfrieds, those clothes weren't an option for the time being.

Standing in front of the bedroom door, Rick tried to convince himself to open it. Logically, he knew Bobby's clothes wouldn't be the best fit since his shoulders had never reached the same breadth as

Rick's, but they'd be better than the clothes he had been wearing for close to forty-eight hours straight. He just needed to go in and grab sweats and a shirt. He could do this. He could.

"Rick?"

He looked down the dimly lit hall and saw Melissa watching him. Her hair glowed from the light behind her in the kitchen. He couldn't make out her expression.

"What are you doing?" she asked, taking a step into the hall toward him.

Rick looked back at the door in front of him and knew he couldn't do it. He pointed at Bobby's door, and no words came out of his mouth when he moved it. His mouth was dry, so he tried to swallow. He didn't succeed. On his second attempt, he managed, but barely.

"Clothes," was the only word he was sure came out when he tried to answer Melissa.

Melissa walked to where he stood frozen, still pointing at Bobby's door like it was an apparition. She reached out and took his hand, turning him away from it. She walked backwards, leading him away from the room that was a mirror of his own across the lawn.

When she stopped by her bedroom door and put her free hand against the bare skin of his chest, he remembered he was only wearing a towel. She pushed gently against his right pec, and he yielded, turning so his back was to her bedroom door. He hadn't missed that the door was ajar and her room looked nothing like it had when they were growing up, except for the bright pink wall.

Despite having taken a cold shower, Rick could feel a sheen of sweat break out over his body as he waited for Melissa to push him into her room. He'd made a point to avoid her room for the past decade and the vivid images of her in it that his mind would paint. It had been bad enough when she'd come to his room with Bobby and sat on his bed those few times over the years when they were both in town.

"I'll grab some for you," Melissa said quietly. She removed her hand from his skin and walked back toward Bobby's room.

Clothes. She was getting him clothes, not ripping the towel from his body and pushing him down on her bed. Rick licked his lips and tried to tamp down the disappointment that came from her helping him cover up, even if that was the smarter idea. He was supposed to be providing her with security. Latching on to that idea, he watched Melissa come back out of Bobby's room with a selection of clothes.

"I don't know what the story is here." Melissa waved what looked like a men's underwear package, "but it's unopened." Rick took the stack of clothes from her and groaned when he saw what the package was.

"It was a gag gift exchange."

"That leaves no question about who brought it, I guess," she laughed.

She headed back to the kitchen, where something smelled delicious. Rick went back into the bathroom and opened the dreaded black boxer-brief package. He fervently hoped they didn't all have Dave's grinning face all over them. They didn't. Rick wasn't sure the pink phrases on them — "Ride Me," "I love pussies" with Dave's face on the butt, and "Surprise Inside" — were much better though. There was no way he was going to wear Dave's face, which left "Ride Me" and "Surprise Inside" to choose from.

Rick closed his eyes and picked one. He pulled on the pair of black gym shorts without opening his eyes so he didn't have to know which phrase he wore. The long-sleeve shirt Melissa had included had absolutely no chance of fitting over his shoulders and arms; he had to go with a blue tee-shirt that said "Burning Rubber" and had skid marks from a fast turn on it. It was a very high-school-Bobby shirt. It felt weird leaving the bathroom in a tee-shirt and shorts. He doubted he had had this much skin exposed around anyone since he was eleven years old.

"Dinner," Melissa called from the kitchen.

Rick walked down the hall and saw Melissa had set the kitchen table with food. The lights were mostly out, and she'd lit candles on the table. Rick felt extremely underdressed. Discreetly, he set his gun and holster on an empty chair as he sat down across from her and took in the plate: chicken with herbs, green beans, rice, and a cup of what was likely a vegetable soup.

"You made all this while I showered?" he asked.

Melissa's gaze lingered on the scratches he'd gotten from Tommy, but she didn't ask him about them. Instead, she said, "The rice was already made. The soup too. I just had to reheat them. The rest was simple."

As they ate, they talked about recent movies they'd seen and a few current events. Rick started to relax. The entire conversation was light, and he wasn't worried about accidentally brushing against her and then her saying something about just wanting a one-night stand in order to make a friend realize what he was missing out on. They had already passed that hurdle. Melissa liked him for who he was, which was a revelation in and of itself.

It wasn't until the dishes were put away that Rick felt the evening shift back to a complete unknown. He didn't know what was next, if anything. Falling back on what he'd heard about from Bobby's, Neil's, and the Mavens' dating stories, Rick suggested a movie. That seemed relatively safe. His friends had mentioned watching movies on dates. He could put his arm around Melissa and maybe kiss her some more, but be ready to act should anyone break in. Melissa readily agreed and popped in a classic: *Opposites Collide.*

The movie came out several years after the Crisis and blended genres like the world had blended genes. The plot was a rewrite of *Romeo and Juliet* as a detective investigation. Rick thought it was a great movie choice. Not only was it entertaining, but he knew the story in and out, so he could split his attention between monitoring the house and just soaking in Melissa. At least that had been his plan.

His vantage point with her under his arm gave him a glimpse down her V-neck shirt; the rise and fall of her chest was mesmerizing. He tried not to look because that wouldn't be good, right? But with her attention on the screen, the temptation was too much. He couldn't help but keep stealing glances. To make matters worse, she smelled like his favorite coffee blend, the one she always made him.

Ten minutes into the movie, he realized his miscalculation. He hadn't considered the fact that Melissa also knew the movie in and out. Her focus was more on his thigh than on the screen. Her fingers drew circles on the incredibly thin material of the gym shorts he had on. Rick's heart rate picked up, and he knew he was going to embarrass himself if her fingers wandered a little more. He should have put his jeans back on. They would have made his reaction to his view, her hands, and her body against his less obvious.

Twenty minutes into the movie and Rick was deeply conscious that Melissa liked petting and touching him. She'd moved from drawing circles on his thigh to dragging her fingertips up and down his leg. Sometimes, they fluttered against him like a feather, but other times they were firm and nearly massaging. Regardless of the pressure she used, if she let her fingers drift an inch to the left, she'd make contact with the hard outline that was bulging against his shorts. He was certain she'd heard his breath catch when she'd passed a hair closer to his hard-on. He'd seen the corner of her mouth hitch up. Rick was in over his head. He didn't have experience with dating games.

After another five minutes of excruciating teasing, Rick grabbed onto the small shred of coherency he had and retaliated. He bent his arm over her shoulder and slid a single finger along her neck, down her throat, to the tantalizing curve of her breasts until he reached the V of her shirt. Melissa's hand froze for a split second before continuing its caresses. Her chest rose and fell more rapidly, and he retraced his finger's path.

Melissa at least made some semblance of watching the movie since her head was facing forward, but Rick was only aware of the flashes on the screen when they flickered across her skin. He didn't know how much time passed with her skin sliding against the pads of his fingers, but if she hadn't moved, he would have continued indefinitely.

When Melissa turned her head toward Rick, she caught him staring at her chest. He braced himself for something. A scolding, perhaps? He'd never blatantly stared at any woman's chest, but he also didn't get to caress anyone anywhere. Instead of receiving a rebuke, Melissa's lips transformed into the smile she had given him in front of her coffee shop. It held so much erotic promise Rick felt his lungs seize.

Transfixed by her expression, Rick was completely unprepared for her fingers to skip lightly over his dick. Unable to breathe, the rest of his body tensed, and he was sure he looked like a deer staring at headlights. Her hand continued up his body until it reached his neck and pulled him down for a kiss. Without releasing him, she tipped back slowly, and he followed her lips until she was flat on her back and he was over her.

Silence and darkness fell around them, and Rick snapped his head up, breaking their kiss. The movie was over. The credits had even finished. He hadn't seen more than the first five minutes. His whole body hurt from wanting Melissa and being pressed down on top of her. He had never understood why people kissed so much before; now, he had no idea why people didn't kiss more. Rick rolled to the side, between Melissa and the back of the couch. He almost had his bearings but needed more space to think.

Melissa grabbed the remote and turned off the TV. As his brain started functioning again, he remembered that he was supposed to be protecting Melissa, not devouring her. Though, the latter was all he wanted to do.

After lifting her head and stealing another kiss from Rick's more than willing lips, Melissa slipped off the couch, saying she'd be back. Rick took deep, steadying breaths, trying to get his body back under control. He listened to Melissa brush her teeth and get ready for bed, trying to suppress the memory of the sounds she'd been making as they kissed and the moaned "yes" that had slipped out of her mouth and into his when his hand had cupped her breast and his thumb stroked over her nipple.

By the time she came back to the living room, Rick had moved to a seated position and was determined to somehow switch into work mode. He needed to keep her safe. When she told him she'd set out a toothbrush for him, he nodded. This was good. She could go to bed, and he could relive the last hour and forty minutes over and over while he kept watch. With that plan in place, he went and brushed his teeth.

Stepping out of the bathroom was a mistake. Melissa was leaning in her doorway right in front of him. His eyes, of their own accord, slid down her body, taking in her short, burgundy silk nightgown with tiny straps. The straps transitioned into a lacy edge that molded to her chest before cascading down her hips. When his eyes managed to make their way back up to her face, she had that smile again. Any semblance of control he had gained in the ten minutes they hadn't been touching evaporated.

She took a step backward, and he automatically took a step forward. Her smile grew. Another step and he followed. Her hands reached forward and under his shirt, sliding it up and over his head. When she pushed him onto the bed, thinking was long gone. This was nothing like he had imagined it would be. She was so confident and in control.

Watching her climb on top of him and up his body on her hands and knees over the bulging tent in his shorts was surreal. When her lips dipped down to meet his, he lost himself in the feel of her mouth and the pressure of her hips on his. It wasn't until a moan broke free from Melissa that he realized his hands were under her nightgown, grabbing her ass as she rubbed against him.

"You'll tell me," he urged, "what you like. Won't you, Mel?"

"Of course," she moaned into his ear.

She proceeded to do just that. She told him how she loved his hands caressing her. How sliding just like that was perfect. How she liked to be squeezed. How she liked to be stroked. Rick trusted every word that fell from her lips, subconsciously registering it was the absolute truth. He really, really wanted this to be good for her. *He* wanted to be good for her.

When she sat up and pulled off her nightgown, her body seemed to glow in the faint light as she ground her hips against his shorts. His determination to satisfy her was the only thing that kept him from coming as she pressed down harder against him. The bruises across her middle snagged Rick's attention, but when she told him to rub her clit, he instantly refocused. He followed her orders exactly, bringing her to a shaking climax on top him that he felt through his damp shorts.

Coming down off her high, Melissa looked both surprised and delighted by the turn of events. Rick had no idea how what just happened had differed from or exceeded her expectations, but he hoped he got to attempt a repeat performance. Many repeat performances.

Just as he was processing the thought that he should see how her bruises were feeling, Melissa fell forward, catching herself before their bodies collided. Then, she kissed him. The wicked glint in her eye had returned. When she started tracing her tongue down his body, his hands gripped her sheets for dear life. He watched her as she tugged his shorts off, wondering how long he was going to last. He already felt ready to combust.

Her burst of laughter caught him off-guard.

"There's a 'surprise inside,' is there?" She smiled and dragged a finger across the words on his underwear.

"It was that or 'ride me,'" he said breathlessly.

"*That* I can do."

At a loss for words, Rick watched Melissa crawl back up him, her breasts dangling tantalizingly close to his mouth as she reached for something past him. He flicked out his tongue, barely catching the tip of her nipple, and her delighted gasped filled the room. Before he could repeat the action, she climbed off him and prompted him to lift his hips.

Staring at her exquisite form kneeling next to him, he did as he was told. When she whipped his boxer-briefs down his body without warning, he felt embarrassment course through him. He'd never been naked with a woman, and now he was completely exposed to *her* — the only person who saw through his standoffish, tough-guy act and trusted him on every level. He'd liked her since high school, but never imagined he'd be here now.

"A surprise indeed," she whispered before reaching out and grabbing him.

Rick's body arched up and into her hand. She let go, and he heard a tear before she rolled a condom over him. She climbed back over him and kissed him until his head spun.

"Are you ready?" she asked, her breath coming in gasps.

Rick nodded, even though he would never be ready for Melissa. She was the spitting image of sinful delight when she was naked and straddling him.

Slowly, she slid down, encasing him. Rick fought to hold still, but his hips revolted and bucked up against her. Melissa lost her balance and caught herself with her hands on his chest. Her breathless laugh and rocking hips took away any thought that he'd done something wrong or possibly hurt her.

"Tell me what you need," he told her again.

As he followed her directions to give her exactly what she wanted, a wave of possessiveness hit Rick hard. He loved seeing her completely free and grinding down on him. He hated that anyone else might have held her, and he was certain some of her exes had. It occurred to him on a thrust that it might be a good idea to kill them. Every single one of them. A very, very good idea.

Chapter 30

Theo

With the dipshit in prison, there wasn't anything to gain by pursuing him. Theo had made it more than clear to the dipshit when "hiring" him that if he talked, he'd die behind bars before a month was out. It didn't matter that the Wrappers didn't have that pull yet; the dipshit didn't know that and believed his threats. The dipshit wouldn't talk. There was nothing to do about him until he served his time and got out. Then, Theo planned on getting his hands back on their taste tester.

Humming to himself about what he would do to the dipshit in the future, Theo turned on his laptop's Bluetooth and set it to search for the recording box connected to the cameras he'd left around the girl's house. He didn't want to spend more time than he needed sitting in his car on her street, but everything was looking up.

The girl and her mentor had become more interesting once Hughie got back to Allison. The mentor was apparently a Fed, and Hughie wanted to get his hands on him in a bad way. Hughie called him "R," and Allison had assured Hughie she'd get the guy for him in exchange for a few things. Theo was looking forward to the opportunities that were opening up because of their connection to Hughie. He didn't even care that Hughie creeped him out; Hughie was an entire flight away.

Smiling to himself, Theo twisted the itchy braided bracelet on his wrist. It had taken a few attempts to successfully connect to the video backup, but what mattered was that he could tell his sister exactly where the Fed was; he had watched Melissa and R pull into her garage from his car on the street. With his laptop perched on the dashboard buffering, it wouldn't be too long before the recordings from the cameras he'd placed inside seventy-two hours earlier started down-loading. If they were lucky, something in the footage would give them more than the letter R to work with.

Allison had shared that while the girl was of interest in that she might also be a Fed, Hughie wanted R at any cost. Neither Hughie nor Jeffrey knew how the Minfried family business had been taken down or how Jeffrey had landed in an interrogation room, but the guy inside the girl's house knew.

With Hughie in control, the revamped family business was now more successful than ever. Having an MBA in charge paid off for them, too. In less than a year, Hughie had rebuilt the Minfried busi-ness into something toothier than what it had been. Now that his hands were dirty, the hamster hybrid wanted answers to make sure the family empire didn't collapse again.

Allison was adamant the Wrappers be the ones to bring R to Hughie. And not just because she'd promised him she would deliver the Fed to him. Hughie was good for business. Theo's sister had gone into great detail about how they could all benefit from a partnership. She had skills Hughie needed to brush up on, and Hughie had more business experience for her to mine and even torture techniques that Theo could learn from.

All Theo knew about this Fed they were after was that he had been the one to ask Jeffrey questions in the interrogation room. That R had gotten answers from Jeffrey did, however, make Theo uneasy. The former head of the Minfrieds was slick. Nothing stuck to him. It was like he scrubbed oil into his pudgy fur and filled his cheek pouches with it. The fact that he was nailed in an airtight case meant the Minfrieds had missed something *big*. And they thought R was the key to figuring out what had gone wrong.

Theo wouldn't have thought it possible if he hadn't met the man, but Hughie was even slipperier than Jeffrey. He'd spent considerable time with Hughie when he came in to check out the dipshit and chat with Allison. Just being around him made Theo uneasy, even though the man was nothing but polite to him. Still, Theo was looking forward to watching what Hughie finally did to the Fed once they had him. Allison had insisted on that when she made her deal with Hughie. Theo knew Hughie was in a different league than him. His sister even called him "a creepy fuck. A wealthy, well-connected, creepy fuck." She'd said that with enough admiration that Theo had felt a little nauseous.

In straight business terms, if the Wrappers came through with the Fed, Hughie had promised to pay them in the combined weight of himself and Theo in any drug of their choosing. Theo was large by anyone's measure, but Hughie was a stout hamster that was half as wide as he was tall. That meant a buttload of free product for Matt to treat and for them to deal. If the Wrappers tacked the girl in on the deal, they got the girl and Allison's weight in a second drug of their choosing. Both were small and delicate looking women compared to Theo and Hughie, but it wasn't an offer to sneeze at.

Theo's computer dinged sooner than he'd expected. He frowned; the recording download had gone too fast. There were only three hours of footage from each camera. A growl rose in his throat. He must have underestimated the girl if she knew cameras, too. But why did she and the Fed come back to her place like it was safe? That was suspicious. It gave Theo pause.

Fast-forwarding through the footage, he saw a single person walk through the house. Himself. That meant she disabled them before even going inside. He was certain she didn't have any security set up in there. He'd been careful. If he missed something, he had a problem. It would mean he was caught by *her* cameras. What Fed had her own house wired with cameras without other security measures?

Carefully, Theo got out of his car. He sniffed the breeze to check if any people were out in the night. Finding no traces in the air, he padded toward her house. The front left window had the curtains pulled, like all the windows, but flashing lights indicated the TV was on. That didn't necessarily mean the girl and Fed were watching TV. It just meant it was on.

He worked his way into the backyard and dug up the drive he'd hidden. Given the way she picked locks and disabled cameras, he was leaning more and more away from her being *just* a mentee. The girl and Fed might be full partners, colleagues, people that he wouldn't mess with under normal circumstances because people would notice.

Back in his car, Theo dialed his sister.

"Tell me you have eyes," Allison said.

"The girl and Fed are inside the house. She disabled the cameras and trackers, so I haven't got a clue what's happening."

"But you know where they are." The thoughtful comment floated in Theo's ear as he waited for her to give an order. "Watch the house for the night. I'll gather people for a snatch. If you can track the Fed when he leaves, do it. If not, stick to the girl. He's invested in her if that picture is anything to go by. If they're together again tomorrow night, we'll grab 'em both."

Theo smiled. He was looking forward to finally getting to do something hands-on. And with his sister planning it? No one would find enough information to pin anything on them.

Chapter 31

Melissa

The high of waking up with Rick was dampened by the gleam of his gun on the nightstand. It gave Melissa too much to think about, and none of it was good. Her mind spun and imagined the worst things she had read about the military while Bobby and Rick were enlisted — explosions, torture, wounds. Then her imaginings took the scariest real-world movie and TV show plots in the most dangerous situations and put Rick slinging a gun on his motorcycle right in the action. As her thoughts got darker and darker, Melissa nuzzled closer to Rick.

The next second, Rick was over her. He pinned her hands above her head, and his free arm extended toward his gun on the nightstand, which was thankfully out of reach. Melissa's abdomen clenched and shot a twinge of pain through her as her heart did its damnedest to strangle her. If she could have, she'd have screamed.

Rick blinked at her in confusion, unseeing, as her chest collided with his over and over as her lungs ran a race to get air and her heart slightly loosened its hold on her throat. Each breath hurt with her body stretched out like this. She did the only thing that came to mind since no way were words going to come out of her mouth.

She tapped a knuckle on the wall that her room shared with Bobby's room. Then, she tapped it twice. When her knuckles drummed a fast click, click, click, click, Rick shook his head, clearing it. Melissa gave a final tap to the wall to finish Bobby's *pay-attention-to-me* code.

Rick wrapped her up in his arms and rolled onto his back, pulling her on top of him. She let his hug sink into her skin and calm them both while her breathing returned to normal and her abdomen stopped hurting.

"Sorry," Rick mumbled into her neck.

"You know, you're going to have to clarify what 'certain circumstances' you find yourself in that a coded tap is a better way to wake up than an embrace." Melissa tried to sound playful, but her voice came out scared.

"I'll ask today what I can tell you," he said, his arms tightening around her. "When do you need to go into work?"

"Soon," she said. "I have a few interviews to do with potential employees." She squeezed her eyes shut and pushed the last few minutes from her mind. Instead, she focused intently on the night before. With her mind filled with much better thoughts, she said, "Take a shower with me?"

His hips bucked beneath her.

She laughed a little. "I'll take that as a yes."

Two hours later, Melissa forced herself to focus on the interview questions in front of her and not on remembering making out in the shower while she and Rick got each other off. It was, by far, the best shower she'd ever had and did a fantastic job of erasing her less than stellar wake-up.

Melissa didn't care in the least that she got into work a half hour later than she intended. She arrived there in time for the interviews, so no harm done. The opposite of harm, really. Her entire body was feeling rather spectacular, in fact.

"Melissa," Ilona called from the front, "are you ready for Pam?"

"Send her back," Melissa hollered from the red armchair in the staff room.

The hedgehog hybrid she'd noticed the week before trundled down the hall. She wore brown sandals that allowed for her longer toes, an athletic-looking blue skirt that could stretch around her spiky back without puncturing, and a brown blouse Melissa knew had to be made of flexible material as well. Pam had a yellow flower tucked into the spikes near one of her tiny ears. She practically blended into the floral chair she sat in for the interview.

The second interviewee was a young man, Aaron, who explained he liked the idea of working in her shop because he'd seen a mouse hybrid behind the counter. He was adamant that he didn't want to hit on her other employee, but rather that he didn't see many rodent hybrids being welcomed in any place that served food, even in Granberg.

Confident and polished, he was basically the opposite of what most people expected when they met a rat hybrid — dirty and untrustworthy. Stereotypes were rough to shake. Melissa guessed at least one of his parents or grandparents was a scientist; however, she might be latching on to the more positive, post-Crisis stereotypes of rats, which was that they were intelligent and dedicated like the scientists they had fused with. In either case, she had to admit it would be nice having another guy on staff. Nick might enjoy working with a male barista from time to time.

The third interview was with a young woman named Olya, who started her interview by sharing that she wasn't a hybrid, which, by law, Melissa couldn't have asked if she wanted to. Not that Melissa cared if her employees were hybrids or not. Olya explained she was looking for a job because she wanted controlled interactions with other people. She came from a more anti-hybrid area and hadn't fully understood the culture shock she'd experience in Granberg where hybrids were in their hybrid form, even if they weren't of the cute and furry variety. Melissa doubted Olya realized how sharing such things might make her a less than ideal hire.

The last interview that day was a hermit crab hybrid who gave Melissa the chills. It wasn't his legs or pincers that put her off. It was his leer. After he left, she checked how he struck Ilona and Nick out front to make sure she wasn't overlooking a personal bias. Ilona confirmed the creeping eyes. Nick had also noticed the crab checking out customers while he waited for his interview.

"What about Pam, Aaron, or Olya?" Nick asked.

"Pam was sweet, but too timid," Melissa said, wondering why she was sharing. "Aaron had all the right answers, but his image was more upscale than..." She gestured to their casual clothes, seeming unable to stop talking.

"Unless it was just interview clothes," Ilona said.

"That's what I'm trying to figure out," Melissa answered with a frown as her mouth kept moving. "And Olya isn't comfortable with Granberg's diversity, which won't make for the best customer service experience."

Normally, she would have just told Ilona and Nick that Aaron was her top pick of the day, but there were another half-dozen candidates to interview; her job announcement had been in the window for four days and online for two. It wasn't far-fetched that she would share her thoughts with them, but she hadn't planned to when she opened her mouth to answer them. For that matter, she'd been chattier in the interviews, too. Not overly talkative, but more than she remembered from past interviews. Her own actions were throwing her off.

As Melissa rubbed her forehead, the bell over the door jingled and she heard a motorcycle race off. Looking up, she saw Kate and Danny walking to the counter, laughing. Melissa hadn't seen Kate look so relaxed since before Tommy's whole thing started. She was even wearing a new necklace that struck Melissa since Kate didn't normally wear chokers. In all honesty, since the Crisis hit, chokers made too many people think of animal collars no matter how trendily designed.

"Come to enjoy the general splendor of your workplace?" Melissa joked as Nick made his co-workers their favorite drinks.

"We were told to 'hang and wait for further instructions,'" Danny whispered dramatically.

Melissa's phone flashed then with a message from Rick: "*Gotta take care of something. Not sure how long it'll take. Sit tight.*"

Whatever had pulled Dave's attention away from Kate and Danny must have also ensnared Rick.

Melissa spent the next two hours trying to figure out why she was sharing more than she intended and how Dave must have delivered his orders to "hang" that had left Kate and Danny giggling so much over their coffee. Eventually, she asked Ilona to flit out and grab lunch for everyone before her shift ended. Melissa wasn't sure if she, Kate, or Danny were supposed to literally stay in the coffee shop or what.

Stretching her arms overhead, Melissa sat back in her seat at the small corner table and looked over the paper in front of her. She had just finished another week of scheduling, hopefully the last one without a new hire. While her arms were up in a full stretch, the coffee shop's noise level dropped dramatically, and Melissa looked up from her work. In the middle of the room stood a blonde with double French plaits. Her pink shirt had the ghost of an even pinker pony on it. Her tight jeans hugged her curves provocatively. Boots that Melissa would die for finished the look.

"Well?" the woman demanded the room at large. Melissa realized she must have already shouted something. To Melissa, silence was more shocking than any shouts in her book of coffee shop noises, especially since her employees had been playing the ASS game for the last three hours and the last shouted number had been forty-three; it was a busy day.

"I said, who's ready for a girls' night?!" She stamped her feet in delight and looked around expectantly. The many customers at the tables throughout the room searched for who she was addressing since it apparently wasn't them.

Melissa stood up because clearly the woman needed someone to talk to, and it was her coffee shop. When the woman saw Melissa, she bounced in excitement. Melissa, who was used to fake intimidation, not aggressive friendliness, hesitated.

"You, me," she said, pointing at Melissa, then herself, before spinning and around and pointing at Kate and Danny, "and you two. Girls' night!"

Kate and Danny looked terrified of the crazy pink pony lady in front of them who had just decreed they were hanging out with such glee that any sane person would back away fast.

Pink Ponies.

"Susan?" Melissa guessed.

Crazy pink pony lady's smile grew. "They said you were sharp."

"Oh, yes," Melissa laughed. A glint in her eye. Pink ponies indeed. "But you have to tell us what he did in revenge for decorating his apartment in your signature style." Melissa gestured at the pink pony shirt. The blonde snorted, and Melissa pulled her over to Kate and Danny to make introductions and explain that Crazy Pink Pony Lady, aka Susan, was the "further instructions" they were waiting for.

As night fell, Bethany joined them at Melissa's parent's house after work. Pizzas were ordered. Wine was poured. Sleeping bags were strewn across the living room floor where the coffee table usually sat, though Bethany chose to hang a removable bar in the doorway — she'd hang upside down to sleep as she usually did.

"Did Dave behave last night?" Susan asked Kate. Her look said, hit me with the hard truth.

"He was more than flirtatious at the beginning." Kate shook her head at whatever Dave must have done.

"Jeremy cramped his style." Danny flipped her hair and smirked.

"He called Dave?" Susan asked, tipping her head so her braids hung askew. Melissa guessed she was wondering what Jeremy might have called about. He likely knew Dave was providing security.

"No, he showed up with our dinner delivery that somehow included his own." Kate's whiskers drooped as if puzzled by how Jeremy had done it. Melissa wasn't going to question anything the bird — who had removed cameras and wired her house with security — did.

"He just showed up?" Disbelief filled Susan's voice.

"Yeah," Danny said, wiping a drop of wine off her scaled lip with a napkin. "At first, Dave growled at him in annoyance, but later, Dave seemed thrilled to have him there. Dave was a bit all over the place."

"Huh." Susan blinked at the vegetarian slice of pizza in her hand.

"Tell us your version of redecorating Dave's apartment," Melissa said. Curiosity was eating her alive. "Why'd you do it?"

"You agreed to redecorate a guy's apartment?" Bethany wrinkled her nose. "That sounds like a nightmare."

"'Agreed' gives the wrong impression, and it was a nightmare — for Dave," Susan's evil plotting smile pulled everyone in a little closer. "I'd known him for about two years and had had it up to here," she flourished a hand *way* above her head, "with his womanizing ways. He was either practicing pickup lines on me, being overly solicitous, or making crude comments about women he was seeing."

"Yuck," Kate said. Her mouth moved like she was trying to get rid of an unpleasant taste.

"I'll say," Bethany agreed.

"Mmhmmm." Danny nodded.

"Bobby," Susan nodded to Melissa, "suggested I take out my frustration with a prank rather than taking... more permanent action."

Melissa snorted.

"The timing couldn't have been better. My parents had insisted I clean out my childhood bedroom, and instead of donating the toys and decorations, I decided to *repurpose* them. I had to buy a few additions, like hot pink king-size sheets, but it was totally worth it. We broke into Dave's 'Pleasure Pad,' as he liked to call his place while he was out picking up women. Pink pony figurines, posters, photos, plastic dishes, you name it, we put it in Dave's place. I even took all his white clothes and threw them in the washing machine with a red shirt I knew would bleed like crazy."

"You didn't!" Danny laughed.

"Oh yes, and then we put up cameras to catch his reaction. I keep a photo on me at all times, for this exact type of shaming." Susan said, swiping through her phone with a pleased grin.

The picture was priceless. Melissa had seen the photos of what the place looked like, but they only set the scene for the reality that was not one picture on Susan's phone, but an entire collage. There was Dave slack jawed; Dave glaring at the room in annoyance; Dave looking at the ceiling like it would save him; then, Dave looking like the ceiling just accosted him further.

"Why's he looking at the ceiling like that?" Kate asked.

"That was because of one of my additional purchases." Susan's face was turning red. "One of the guys helping me found it. I honestly didn't know there were posters of that size with that... type of content, but it was the perfect thing to adorn a 'Pleasure Pad.' For a little extra money, the creator even tinged the pony pink."

"You mean *that kind of content?*" Bethany's words were laden with meaning.

"Yup," Susan squeaked.

"Oh my," Danny said.

"Something had to be done." Susan tried to shrug but looked slightly aghast at what she'd wrought.

"But it doesn't end there," Melissa said, feeling enlightened about the story. "He retaliated, right?"

"That can't be good," Kate muttered.

"He did retaliate," Susan said, giggling. "Between us?" She paused and looked at each of them until they nodded. "It was so hard to pretend to be angry at his prank. Do you have any idea how hard it is to scowl when you're trying not to laugh and skip about? But I had to make him think his retaliation was successful or he might have actually done something bad."

"Of course." Bethany's nod was filled with firsthand experience. Her little brothers were menaces as she told it.

"So, what did he do?" Danny asked.

"I don't know how he did it without being noticed," Susan admitted.

"He mentioned that Bobby helped. One of them must have acted as a distraction."

"Bobby helped?" Susan sat up straighter. "That sneaky bastard." Her eyes narrowed like she was plotting revenge for the betrayal. Melissa watched the moment of realization hit Susan, and she'd just called her host's dead brother a bastard.

Melissa waved the comment off. She'd felt that way plenty of times when he'd pranked her growing up. Just hearing anyone talk about him like he had existed once was a comfort.

"Anyway, while I was out on a distance run, really working my muscles hard, he managed to tamper with my shampoo. I came back, hosed off, as to not leave muddy hoof-prints everywhere, and jumped in the shower. The prank was well planned. I was exhausted and not paying attention, which honestly worked out for the best. I didn't notice that the soap suds weren't white or, you know, muddy white. It wasn't until my final rinse after a *second* full body scrub that I noticed pink bubbles on the wall."

"He made you a living pink pony?" Melissa breathed out.

"Yup," Susan said. "I'm a Palomino, nice and golden, with a blond-white mane and tail. After that shower, I was a dusty pink with a hot pink mane and tail. If I hadn't been in my horse form at the time, I just would have had the hot pink hair, but with the pink coat, the effect was something to see."

"Was Dave delighted with his success?" Kate asked, shaking her head.

"Oh yes, but it gave me the perfect ammunition to quip that despite his love of pink ponies, he wasn't ever going to have one in real life. Then, I stomped away like I was pissed."

"How long did it last?" Bethany asked, looking at her own pure white hair. Melissa imagined it would soak in dye even faster and deeper than Susan's light blonde did.

"I wanted to make sure Dave thought he'd bested me, and I loved the humor of being the pink pony that I had obsessed over as a child. So, I *may* have used the shampoo until it ran out."

Everyone laughed and finished their drinks, the night winding down. When Susan came back from brushing her teeth, she came at a mad dash.

"Please, please, please, tell me I can have these!" She waved around the three pairs of boxer-briefs Melissa had not peeled off Rick the night before. Dave's face swished around in the air. "I've been trying to come up with a new prank for years. Without Bobby's help, I've been stumped. I've only done small things. I'll have to save these for something special."

"Sure," Melissa said. If she could fill Susan's Bobby-prank deficit, she would.

Chapter 32

Rick

Rick pushed his head harder into the headrest as Shawn took over at the wheel. They'd been on the road since before noon. Sitting in an SUV, no matter how discreetly tricked out, was not doing Rick's mood any favors. No amount of luxury interiors, souped up engines, or non-street legal weaponry could make him feel better. He wanted to snap at Jeremy for finding the intel and at Jade for sending them to investigate it.

Driving hours away from Melissa to go see what Allison Barre and Matt Helms were doing in Rafity City was, he could admit, strategically a good move, but not one that needed *him*. Jade could have sent someone else on his team or sent someone from Team Kappa or Team Delta.

The only saving grace of the drive was Melissa's late-night message saying she needed his help coming up with a good prank Susan could pull on Dave. Whenever Rick glanced in the backseat of the SUV to check on Dave — who was passed out and drooling — Rick's determination to find a good prank grew. His motivation wasn't anything all that friendly; but between the bruises he remembered encircling Melissa's middle and the guilty reminder about the differences in their protection details the night before, Rick's prank ideas were a little meaner than normal. Unlike Rick, Dave had actually performed his protection detail by keeping watch all night rather than basking in his protectee's attention — naked attention — and falling asleep next to her.

Maybe it was for the best that he would be several hundred miles away for the next day or three. Between seeing Melissa riding him whenever he closed his eyes or her dripping wet in the shower panting, he was actively thinking about how he could put Bobby's deadliest threats to use against her exes. And there was the fact that Shawn and Dave had had to literally shove him into the SUV when it sounded like one of the guys might be assigned Melissa's overnight protection duty. Rick needed to get his head on right.

He knew Susan's desire to meet Melissa in person was not the sole reason she was at Melissa's that night. He'd seen Dave shoot a message to someone about his state of mind. His team had to be wondering if his and Bobby's protective streak stemmed from Melissa herself in some way. Rick had no intention of confirming it if their suspicions turned that way; though he might not have a choice much longer if that ended up being the "good" or "right" thing to do. Especially if he kept letting Melissa touch him, and vice versa.

"Home, sweet home," Shawn murmured as he pulled off the road and into a long driveway that led to the safe house of a certain government agency his team didn't need the specifics of. The dashboard said it was four in the morning.

Rick stretched his neck, mentally braced himself, and tapped Bobby's wake-up code on the dashboard. Dave made a distinctly feline sound as he stretched and sat up, calm as could be. When he looked around and saw Rick, he tensed, darting his eyes to the fluffy white dog hybrid in the driver's seat.

"He did it," Shawn said, shaking his head and holding his hands up.

Dave's eyes were comically big at the news. Rick felt uncomfortable about how on edge he'd made his team all these years about Bobby and how keeping little ticks like the special wake-up tap could be good for all of them.

"Well, I'll be," Dave muttered before getting out of the car.

Inside the safe house, they planned their first moves. Dave would go take over from a local contact that was monitoring the hotel where Allison Barre and Matt Helms had made a reservation. After sleeping for a bit, Rick and Shawn would come take an afternoon/evening shift but stagger their arrival to make sure they had a two-person watch running for most of the trip.

"What did I miss?" Rick asked as he joined Dave, who was "reading" a newspaper at a corner bus stop while watching Allison and Matt have lunch. Rick almost asked Dave why he was in his human form — not his preferred state — but Rafity City wasn't the most hybrid-centric of cities, making the question moot.

"They've been sightseeing."

"Sightseeing?"

"Yes, this morning we visited the Museum of the Ancients that has all the archaeological findings like cave paintings, the Temple of Setsuni to pay our respects to the newest Lord of Dog Hybrids who prowls fences to bestow success and seduction upon their followers — I shifted to blend in better, but I still felt uncomfortable in there

— and we admired the Wheel that the Minfrieds had built to mark their city. The last was my personal favorite," Dave admitted.

"At the foot of it, they had a lot of miniature wheels for kids to play on and even a few larger ones for adults to run in. I was tempted to do a time trial, but..." He shrugged at the obvious reason — he couldn't do so and maintain his cover as a run-of-the-mill hybrid rather than a rare cheetah hybrid.

"They didn't bump into anyone?"

"Only if you count each other. I know she's supposed to be the head of the Wrappers, but to all appearances they're on a romantic getaway. They're holding hands constantly, gazing into each other's eyes, and exchanging meaningful looks. He's petting her constantly like he can't keep his hands off her."

"Rafity City isn't the most romantic of places," Rick said. It was just a typical city, a bit grimy and not the greenest of places. Most people stayed in their human form, but there were some people in their hybrid form walking about, just nowhere near as many as in Granberg.

"The restaurant they're in does look swanky."

Rick had to agree. The red velvet chairs looked plush, and the pure white tablecloth with actual candlesticks created a certain ambiance. Allison and Matt had their hands entwined on the table and were engrossed in an animated conversation.

Allison looked much the same as the last time he'd seen her when he and Shawn set up the surveillance at the Barres™ factory. Her gray hair was pulled back in a ponytail, and she was wearing CEO casual — basically, what Rick could see of her clothes hinted at business and looked expensive.

This was, however, the first time Rick had a good view of Matt Helms. He wore a gray button-up with the sleeves rolled up. His brown hair was longer on top but styled into a swoopy look male models sometimes had. There was nothing about him to draw attention, which just made Rick even more suspicious of him.

It was a shame they couldn't get inside the restaurant and listen in on whatever the two were talking about. Not only were he and Dave not appropriately dressed for the restaurant, but there were only couples inside.

Rick couldn't manage that cover story, and they'd tried a few times —both with the men and the women on their teams. He just couldn't bring himself to touch them enough to make the relationship believable. If Shawn were here, he might be able to pull off a couple with Dave, but the point was moot; Shawn was sleeping, and they didn't have any ears inside.

"So," Dave said as they loitered by the bus stop, where they were just able to keep Allison and Matt in view through the restaurant window. "You seem well rested after keeping watch over Melissa." Rick knew Dave's innocent commentary was anything but.

"We watched a movie," Rick said, trying to brush Dave off.

"Did you now?" Dave grinned in delight. His shaggy, dark hair fell in front of his eyes when he looked over at Rick.

Rick tried not to blush under Dave's scrutiny but wasn't sure if he succeeded. He was in uncharted waters.

"What movie?"

"*Opposites Collide.*"

Dave covered his mouth to muffle his laughter. "Good choice. Yours?"

"Hers," Rick said cautiously.

Shaking, Dave doubled over and held his stomach as he continued to attempt near silence. His antics drew attention to the two of them, not from the restaurant thanks to a bus that had stopped to drop passengers off, but still not ideal.

"Why is that funny?" Rick growled.

"Everyone, and I mean *everyone,* has seen that movie. It's a movie that's easy to put on when you have no intention of actually watching."

"So it was intentional," Rick muttered, more to himself than to Dave.

"Oh man." Dave put his laughter aside and lowered his voice. "Do you need…" he darted his eyes back and forth as if watching for eavesdroppers, "any explanations? Tips? Techniques?"

Rick dragged his hand down his face, which he knew was becoming red with embarrassment.

"I acquitted myself just fine," he mumbled.

"On your first time?" Dave stared at him in surprise. "Are you sure?"

"Yes, I'm sure." Rick looked up at the sky, wishing it'd fall and squash Dave.

"How can you be sure? It's not always easy to tell if you don't have experience."

"She *told* me what she liked." Rick stared at Allison and Matt, leaning their heads together behind the candle. Melissa might like a date like this once everything was taken care of. He could do that. With her, he could do that.

"Wait. She *told* you what she liked while you were touching her?" Dave's attention was fully on Rick rather than on the head of the Wrappers and the man that Rick knew had to be the key to the Wrappers never getting caught.

Rick jerked his head once to affirm Dave's comment.

Dave let out a low whistle before saying, "Then, you did just fine. Probably better than fine."

They stood there in silence, or in as much silence as you can have on a street with a medium amount of traffic. Rick hoped Dave's mind had moved on, even if his own hadn't. He was itching in his own skin. He wanted to get back and see Melissa, hold her, kiss her, do everything she liked.

"And she isn't self-conscious about literally not being able to lie or obfuscate the truth when you're together?" Dave asked.

Obviously, Dave hadn't moved on. Rick was more than happy to see Allison and Matt walk out of the restaurant, and he used work to ignore the question.

"They're moving."

He didn't want to think about the fact that he hadn't told Melissa what his touch did yet. Once he told her, he'd have to tell her about her own touch, and he didn't want the information to change her like it had him. At least he'd made a point to inch away from her after she fell asleep, so she hadn't soaked in his touch all night. Granted, he'd woken with her against him and then they'd had that mind-blowing shower, so he wasn't sure how long she'd been under his influence after they parted. He felt rather guilty about that.

Allison and Matt continued their sightseeing tour of the city. They hit the city's Crisis Memorial that honored everyone who had died forty-five years earlier. It was one of the odder memorials Rick had seen. It separated those who had died by what prompted their death — lack of new medical care, trying things that weren't okay in their new forms, persecuted because their hybrid form was creepy, attacked because others didn't accept hybrids, etc.

During that attraction, Shawn, in his human form with stark black hair that contrasted with his hybrid dog form's white pelt, came to relieve Dave. Then, the two lovers strolled hand-in-hand beside the Rafity City Lake and laughed in the dappled sunlight that fell through the trees. Rick had to admit, watching the two of them, the city was starting to look a lot more romantic and a lot less dreary.

As the dinner hour approached and the Wrapper's trip to Rafity City was looking more and more like a coincidence, Allison and Matt jumped in a tram car. Rick and Shawn climbed aboard through a different set of doors. For the first time in their day's surveillance, Rick was supremely conscious of the fact that Allison and Matt had seen the photo of him, and they were all riding in the same tram car. He plucked Shawn's hat off his head and put it on his own as he hunkered down in a seat. Shawn automatically leaned over to block him further from view. It was a common move their team pulled since Rick only had one face, unlike the rest of the Mavens — all of whom were hybrids. He and Bobby had been the only humans on any of the teams.

Allison and Matt disembarked in a ritzy neighborhood. Rick and Shawn had no choice but to get off the tram, too. Allison and Matt turned left. Rick and Shawn turned right. Rick had his phone in his hand, camera on facing him, and watched Allison and Matt round the opposite corner before he and Shawn turned around. Shawn peeked around the corner just in time to see the two enter the third house from the far end of the block.

"Jeremy," Rick said into his phone. "I need to know who lives on Sunflower Road, five houses away from Wicker Street on the right."

"On it."

Rick listened as Jeremy's fingers tapped away at a keyboard.

"4587 Sunflower Road is owned by Minfried Millinery," Jeremy's voice fell as he spoke.

"So much for it being a romantic getaway," Rick muttered. It was what they had expected — the Wrappers were meeting up with the Minfrieds — but having their thoughts confirmed didn't give them any satisfaction.

"You can't loiter in the area," Jeremy warned. "There are a lot of street cameras. You two need to move out of there."

Rick waved Shawn to follow him, and they strolled down Wicker Street until they hit the next tram stop. Jeremy muttered in Rick's ear the entire way.

"Okay, I got into the cameras. I'll tell you when they leave and what direction they go. I just have to call Carl and send him to Granberg so I can stay and monitor this."

"I thought Susan was taking care of everyone there," Rick growled.

"She isn't doing it every night," Jeremy said reasonably. "Carl has no intention of making any moves on anyone, much less a woman with no sense of self-preservation. He still isn't over breakfast the other morning. She just introduced herself like she wasn't in any danger."

Rick grumbled as he hung up to let Jeremy make the call. Most people were terrified of Carl in his human form and even more so in his hybrid form. That Melissa treated him as harmless did not surprise Rick in the least.

Chapter 33

Melissa

Melissa knew something was up. She'd barely heard anything from Rick for two days now. She understood he was off on a job with the Mavens, but all his messages had been curt. Mostly just letting her know he got her messages or that he wouldn't be back that day.

Maybe she wasn't supposed to message him when he was doing a job. Or did he not want her messaging him at all? That didn't seem likely since he hadn't said as much, but she couldn't rule it out. If Susan had been coming over again Tuesday night, Melissa would have asked her, but Susan wasn't the one sent to watch them. Carl was.

The girl's night with Susan had been fun. It hadn't felt like a security detail. Carl, on the other hand, was a bodyguard on duty. No doubt about it.

To say that Carl took his protection detail much more seriously than Rick or Susan had would be an understatement. He patrolled around the house, both outside and inside, making it feel like he was circling in for the kill, even if his focus was outward. He kept looking at Melissa out of the corner of his eye and stayed away from her like she might bite. His behavior raised the hairs on Melissa's neck. Making matters worse, this was the first time Kate and Danny had met him, so they were doubly skittish. None of them knew why Carl was scared of Melissa — and that was how he was behaving.

None of Melissa's guests were happy when she dragged them into Carl's SUV at the crack of dawn. But their displeasure had been nothing compared to the shock on Greg's face when she walked up to him at the cliffs for their weekly climb with an entourage that included a man that could rip him to shreds.

"What's going on, Melissa?" Greg took in Carl's overly muscled frame, which was not remotely hidden by his leather motorcycle jacket.

"Good morning," she replied, trying to suppress her annoyance. She'd heard nothing from Rick all night, and Carl had literally flinched when she'd passed him a travel mug of coffee. It wasn't a great morning. "Meet Carl. He's being insufferably dedicated to his assignment."

"What's his assignment?" Greg asked, eyeing the bald man.

"Me."

"And us," Kate offered, dragging a slow-moving Danny forward.

"I'll go first," Melissa said, tightening her harness. She did not want Greg asking about why they had a protection detail from a motorcycle club. She did not want to deal in evasive answers that morning, especially when feeling so testy.

"Sure," Greg said uncertainly.

Melissa started climbing while Kate and Danny trudged up a small mound of dirt that would get the first peek of the day's sunshine. After a few movements, Melissa purposely opted to go to the right and take an easier route up. The pain in her middle wasn't debilitating, but it didn't feel fantastic either. But movement was supposed to help, right?

"You know what you're doing?" Carl asked Greg below her.

"Yeah." Greg said with a *back-off-buddy* tone, likely taking his cues from Melissa's own frustration.

Focusing on her climb became nearly impossible as Carl ignored Greg's dismissive tone and continued talking. He didn't know Greg was wearing a headset in his other ear. Since neither of them had held a conversation with a third person while the other climbed, Melissa hadn't realized the microphone was sensitive enough to pick up more than Greg's voice.

"You don't like me."

"I don't know you," Greg retorted, telling Carl to get lost with his tone.

"You're protective of her," Carl observed.

"Yeah. She's my friend. I'm protective of all my friends."

"So, it's not just Melissa."

"No." Greg was offended at the insinuation. Melissa rolled her eyes and held in a small groan as she reached for the next handhold. For all of his bachelor ways, Greg hadn't ever shown interest in being more than friends with her. And Melissa would not have put Greg in much of a protective category to start with, other than his random comment the week before about researching any sketchy boyfriends. "Why would you think that?"

"Her brother was crazy protective of her, and Rick is heading that way."

Melissa froze in her climb, and she knew Greg realized then that she could hear both sides of the conversation. However, he made it clear that his loyalty was to her, not Carl and not Rick, by continuing to gather information.

"What do you mean?"

She held back a smile at the fact that Greg didn't care in the least that the conversation was not meant for her ears.

"Bobby threatened us all off a long time ago. None of us have forgotten, but over time, fear wanes." Carl paused, and Melissa forced herself to keep climbing lest he get concerned about her static position. "I thought Rick was going to tear me to shreds when I offered to watch over Melissa and her friends while he was out of town."

"Huh," Greg said. It was a thoughtful "huh" and not one that settled Melissa in the least. "You know, I don't know exactly what's going on between Melissa and Rick, but it sounds like he's acting like half of her exes did."

"How so?" Carl's question echoed Melissa's own thoughts.

"Her relationships, since I met her, have ended on remarkably friendly terms. Half broke it off with her because they thought she was too good for them, which was true. The other half, she broke up with because they got upset when she hung out with me or Ted and sometimes when she just talked with guys in passing."

Melissa paused at the top of her *should-have-been-easy* climb and blankly stared out at the view, thinking about Greg's assessment of her relationships. The guys that broke it off with her hadn't told her she was too good for them, but the sentiment might have been there. The guys she broke up with? She had just thought they were jackasses and were trying to control her. When she thought about it, they only tried to control her around other guys, so Greg was probably right. And, when she'd bumped into them after their breakup, they were nice to her, but not in a *let's-get-back-together* way.

"But if Rick is in the possessive half like Carl is indicating," she said into the headset, "why hasn't he been messaging me more? He's barely said anything to me since...."

"Since...?" Greg asked cajolingly when her voice trailed off.

Melissa looked down and caught his eye. Carl's head turned to Greg at his strange-seeming question.

"Melissa," Greg sighed in a mixture of consolation and disappointment. "If he hasn't been messaging you, he isn't worth your time."

Squeezing her lips together as her heart clenched, Melissa pushed down the feelings that were bubbling up. Looking down at Greg, she saw Carl's face turn skyward, but she couldn't make out either of their expressions. She had a good idea of what Greg's face said, but Carl's was a mystery.

"Lower me down," Melissa muttered. There was no way she was climbing down today. Going up was probably more than she should have done in the first place, but she had needed space from Carl's weird behavior and hadn't thought it through.

"Who are you messaging?" Greg's voice was suspicious, and Melissa looked down to see Carl focused on the phone in his hands. She had a good idea of what Carl might be saying, just not if it was to Rick or to another Maven. She hadn't signed up for a slew of new older siblings; though in this case, she didn't know if Carl was looking out for her or for Rick. She groaned aloud as she hung in the air, slowly descending. Greg's humph in her ear didn't settle her nerves.

Back on the ground, Melissa ignored Greg's worried looks and sent him up the wall on his climb with the threat that if he didn't start right away, he'd be late for work. Carl stood nearby looking uncomfortable while Greg pushed himself harder than normal, forcing Melissa to focus on his climb and nothing else. When Greg slipped and jerked the belay rope, Melissa's grunt was more pain induced than surprise, but luckily it only happened once.

After Greg's speed climb, she relinquished her half of the headset and shook the sun-basking tangle of Kate and Danny awake. Carl followed her closely to the car. Just before the girls climbed in with them, Melissa turned to Carl, who moved a few inches away from her like being too close to her would get him killed.

"At least we know why you're acting terrified of me," she said. "Relax. Rick won't do anything to you for ensuring I'm okay. Maybe he'll hug you."

Carl snorted at her comment but settled in a bit. When he dropped the three of them off at the coffee shop, he still wasn't relaxed, but he no longer flinched when Melissa moved in the seat beside his, which was an improvement.

Barely an hour later, Jeremy came through the coffee shop doors. Kate and Danny waved at him from behind the counter, and Tiffany leaned in toward them.

"This is his third time here. He's going to become a regular. I know it. How do I look?" Tiffany didn't wait for an answer. "I'll take him a drink. What do you think he likes?"

"Pineapple iced tea," Melissa said absently, stuck on Greg's comment that Rick wasn't worth her time. She definitely thought the opposite, but she'd been wrong before and his abrupt messages were a red flag. Though a red flag that she'd never personally encountered before. If he couldn't message because he was working, he would have said something, but he hadn't. Bobby had always let her know when one of his "mechanic jobs" needed his entire focus. Logic told her Rick would have let her know, just like he had when he was going out of town for the day. It was hard to stomach the idea that he might be brushing her off, but what else could it be?

Danny made up Jeremy's drink, and Tiffany ran it over to him.

"She's feather-struck," Ilona scoffed from the cash register. "You guys know all her prior boyfriends have been birds? I think she enjoys being prey."

The last observation made Kate choke on her sip of water. She coughed so hard her fur poofed out and her ears pinned themselves tight to her head.

"Then wouldn't she be into cats?" Danny asked, as she patted Kate's back to help with the cough.

"Birds and cats do have a lot in common, but Tiff doesn't have feathers. She wants what she doesn't have." Ilona continued, meaningfully dragging one of her own wing-feathers through her beak before laughing. Kate had stopped coughing, but not enough to join in Ilona's provocative banter.

"And what do you like then?" Melissa said with a shake of her head, turning the tables on Ilona. Focusing on the present and the people around her was a much better use of her time than dwelling on whatever was happening between Rick and her. "What don't you have that you're... taking wing for?"

"Me? I like *variety*." Ilona swished her hips in a saucy move as she spoke.

Tiffany walked back behind the counter, not noticing that Danny's scales were wet from laughter.

"He remembered my name!" Tiffany squeaked.

"See." Ilona nodded like she held the world's answers behind her feathery gaze, and Kate started coughing again as a laugh tried to overtake her.

After a while, Jeremy caught Melissa's eye, and she walked over to him.

"Tiff was delighted you remembered her name," she told him, checking for a response.

"I made dossiers on all your employees," he said matter-of-factly.

She plopped down in the empty chair at his table. "What?" she asked. This had to be an alternate dimension.

"Like I said, nothing we wouldn't do if you were my little sister."

Melissa stared at him while that sunk in.

After a minute or two, she noticed he hadn't even looked at her since she sat down. He wasn't looking at Tiffany either. No, he was analyzing the far corner where three guys were huddled at a table.

One guy, a human at least in form, had on a macrame necklace and looked like he was a college kid. The other two were younger. One was a teenage frog hybrid who looked unhappy and agitated. The other was a billy goat hybrid who was clearly trying to brush his froggy friend off. At a second look, the college kid didn't want the frog there either.

Melissa wrinkled her nose at the scene. It'd been a while since she'd seen such groupings in her coffee shop, but she knew what to do about it.

She stood up, promising Jeremy she'd be back in a moment, and walked straight over to the group. The college kid started shoving a variety of colored candies into his bag as Melissa stopped at their corner table. She leaned in, her right hand on the back of the goat hybrid's chair and left hand brushing over the college kid's wrist as she tapped one of the colorfully wrapped candies.

"Worried I'm going to scold you boys about having sweet tooths?" she asked, puzzled.

"I think you're right, Conner," the billy goat said to his friend as his ear flicked against Melissa's arm a few times. The frog hybrid, Conner, was so relieved he slumped against the wall, which would seem like an extreme reaction to most people, but it was how these incidents always went.

"Yeah," the college kid said, looking like he knew better. "You kids gotta think about your... teeth."

Conner looked at the college kid with narrowed-eyed suspicion but dragged the goat hybrid right out the door. The college kid swiped up the rest of his sweets and left too; Melissa noticed he went in the opposite direction than the teenagers had. Shaking her head, she turned around to see Jeremy standing a few feet away. His beak was hanging open.

"Are you okay?" she asked him.

"What just happened?"

"Nothing too unusual. The fact that it was candy was the oddest part. I expected to find the teenagers buying a dirty magazine or something like that from the college kid. It's been a while since that's taken place here. Instead, it was just candy."

"And they... just left?"

"Yeah." Melissa took Jeremy's lightly feathered hand and led him back to his table, telling him to finish his drink.

He did as she directed, but he had become even more flighty than Carl the night before.

What was going on?

Chapter 34

Rick

With no idea what happened during the four hours Allison and Matt were inside Hughie Minfried's house, none of the Mavens were in a great mood as they started their drive back to Placerville the next morning. Allison and Matt had hopped on a plane back to Lunser at the crack of dawn, and there were other agencies watching Hughie, so there was no need to stay.

Rick desperately missed the ease and expediency of flying. He hadn't flown commercially since he'd joined the Mavens — it was too hard to scrub their images from the security cameras — and military flights were rarely options unless they were leaving the country. Hours of driving loomed ahead of them and despite having taken most of the night shift, Dave was awake and chatting up a storm with Shawn about the different strategies sports leagues used to ensure equal play with a slew of hybrids in the mix.

"Clip Clop," Dave's phone sang out in a recording of Susan's most sarcastic tone. Rick watched Dave as he read Susan's message. Whatever it was, it wasn't good. Dave's head fell back against the headrest, and he asked the ceiling, "Why me?" before waving Shawn off and climbing into the back with Rick.

"Did something happen to Melissa?" Rick's mind spun through all the possibilities and how he might have to kill Carl. Rick reasoned it couldn't be too serious if Dave was just looking pained by being the messenger. Maybe a minor cut or a stubbed toe; it had better not be broken bones or more bruising. She'd still have the bruises on her abdomen from where Dave had grabbed her for days to come. Rick's hand balled up into a fist at the thought.

"It's more about what isn't happening," Dave said, watching him carefully.

"What's not happening?"

"You don't sleep with a girl and not message her for several days." Dave's eyebrows rose meaningfully as he ignored Shawn jerking the steering wheel to the side when he spoke.

"I've messaged her." Rick was more confused than upset that Dave had just told Shawn that he'd slept with Melissa.

"You've messaged her? What did you say? How often have you messaged? Did you squeeze in an actual phone call during this trip? Because I know you had the time to. At the early stages of a relationship, communication is key. A lot of communication, and not just the physical kind."

Rick blinked at Dave. He was sure Dave hadn't seen the same girl for more than a week in his entire life. He always moved too fast. Rick couldn't believe Dave, of all people, was giving what sounded like good advice.

"I—" Rick trailed off, thinking through his messages. He'd sent more than he'd sent in the past, but they hadn't sent messages before, so one was, technically, more; and he was certain he'd sent six, if not seven.

Dave slumped down in the seat and held out his hand.

"Give me your phone."

Rick handed him his phone and considered being sick.

"Wait, how do you even know my messaging has been inadequate?"

"Melissa said something to one of her friends." Dave opened Rick's messages. Melissa wasn't at the top. He'd coordinated with the Mavens a number of times since his last message to her. "And Carl overheard the conversation. Melissa has been advised that you aren't worth her time because you're blowing her off." Panic churned in Rick's gut. Dave continued: "Carl messaged Jeremy. Jeremy discussed it with Susan. Susan ordered me to 'give guidance' on the subject."

Rick swallowed hard. Everyone on his team now knew he'd had sex for the first time and fumbled post-coital messaging protocol, which was fan-fucking-tastic, but that wasn't what mattered. What mattered was that he needed to fix things with Melissa somehow. He really hoped that was still a possibility.

"Okay, so first thing," Dave said, tilting Rick's phone back at him. "Look at the number of messages she has in comparison to yours and the general length."

Melissa had sent him twice as many messages and they were all significantly longer than his. As Dave scrolled through their conversation, Rick noticed that Melissa's messages got shorter and less frequent. That didn't seem good.

"Now, I'm going to pretend I didn't see this message that you two are going to help Susan pull one over on me." Dave gave Rick a *good-luck-with-that* eyeroll. "But you can tell she's expecting more from you in the messages."

"How can I tell that?"

"She's left a lot of openings. Look at this earlier one that tells you what she did that day and wishes you a good day. You could of course offer up details about your day if available, but her message also leaves enough vagueness about her own day that you could ask her follow up questions, showing you're interested in her life, even if you can't share about your day. You didn't do that."

"How can I fix it?" Rick asked. He didn't want to lose Melissa.

"Let's start by sending her a nice update." Dave's fingers flew across the phone, typing out a message to Melissa, but thankfully, he turned the phone to Rick for approval before hitting send: "*On my way back, but I won't make it to Granberg until tomorrow afternoon or evening. I'd love to take you out somewhere.*"

"That's like five times as long as any message I've sent her," Rick observed.

"Yeah." Dave hit send and pulled out his phone. "Let's take a look at my message chain with Susan, just as an example of communicating with women in a fashion that promotes continued conversation."

Rick met Shawn's eyes in the rearview mirror.

"She's required to speak to you," Shawn pointed out.

"Yes, but Rick can see the difference in how I send her messages and how I send them to him."

Rick looked at the lengthy exchanges without reading the content. Dave sent Susan messages that made the length of this latest message to Melissa appear paltry. The contrast with Rick's messages to Melissa was even starker given that Dave thought Susan was hot, but she'd made it clear that if he made another move on her — real or joking — her hooves would be stomping on his most precious appendage.

A few minutes later, Dave and Shawn assured him that not all hope was lost when he got a frosty "*Sure*" from Melissa. As the car barreled down the freeway, either Dave or Shawn, depending on who was awake, acted as his messaging guru. By the time they pulled into the garage behind Trigg's Triad, Melissa was happily messaging away with him; both Shawn and Dave confirmed he should believe the smiley emoji.

Rick's feeling of relief dissipated when they went upstairs and found the rest of their team and Jade waiting for them. Jeremy sat in front of his computers with Susan and Carl huddled around him in chairs they'd stolen from the conference table. They were all looking at him as if he'd betrayed them, and Jade was seconds away from screeching at him.

"If we're all here," he said before things got underway, "who's with—"

"Felicia will be waiting for Melissa and her friends when it's time for them to leave the coffee shop," Susan said, frowning. Rick approved of the choice. Felicia had a lot of skills that she put to use on Team Kappa's missions. Melissa would be in good hands. "It's noteworthy that not a single man on any of the other teams will risk crossing you to protect her."

"Even if she is aware you're scaring everyone shitless," Carl muttered with clear unease.

"That's why we're all here?" Rick looked around at everyone. "*More dating advice?*"

"No. What the hell is going on in Juniper's Java?" Jade yelled. Her temper had flared, which was new. She was always even-keeled and controlled. Not once had Rick ever heard her raise her voice unless there was gunfire or other loud noises in the immediate area. The white feathers on her head were even standing up in a sharp crest that looked knife-like compared to Jeremy's poofy crest next to her.

At Jade's outburst, Jeremy flicked on several recordings from the last few days inside Melissa's coffee shop. Dave and Shawn pushed past him to get a better look. Each one was of Melissa calming an upset or angry customer. Seeing it once, no one would notice anything. But with all the recordings, it was a pattern. Nothing major happened in them, except for the one in which she interrupted a Wrapper drug deal in the corner of her shop without so much as a harsh movement or word.

Rick watched and took in what his team and Jade might know. He hadn't considered they would pick up on something when they were monitoring the security cameras. He honestly hadn't given it a single thought. His team's eyes flicked between him and Jade's irate stance as he took his time thinking about what to say; there was no way to avoid the conversation now.

Screw it. If he had to share this, then he damn well was going to get some answers.

"How sure are you that Bobby is dead?" Rick asked, staring Jade in the eye. The rest of his team sucked in air at his comment.

"Are you serious?" Jade looked at him like he'd lost it. "He disappeared four years ago. There was absolutely no trace to follow. After the job he did, you know the *only* reason he wouldn't resurface is if he was too far underground to dig his way out. Literally."

"When you recruited me and I asked you to hire Bobby too, what did you see in his file?" Rick asked instead of acknowledging anything his boss had just said. It was more or less what she'd said to him three years ago, but not phrased nearly as nicely. She couldn't comprehend why Rick wouldn't accept Bobby was dead.

She frowned and answered anyway: "Nothing of note. He did fine, not great. Nothing hinted at the potential he demonstrated as a Maven. Even the first time I met him, he seemed singularly unremarkable."

"But the second time," Rick pushed, "after I told him he needed to be noticed by you? After he approached you himself."

"What's your point?" Jade eyed him with suspicion. He had never told her he broke the NDA he'd signed when she'd hired him before he had even worked a day for her. Telling Bobby to be noticed by her was a direct violation.

"I have this *talent*." He waved his hand in the air when he said talent.

Jade's head moved ever so slightly forward and waggled as if to say, "not news to anyone here."

He took the plunge: "I haven't met a human who doesn't have a *talent*."

"What do you mean?" Jade asked, looking at Rick like she could crush him with a single one of her feathers. If he hadn't grown up with Bobby, the look would have been intimidating. It was clear his entire team was both confused by his comment and trying to figure out if their boss was about to kill him. Rick doubted they'd side with him; he'd been acting too erratically the past week.

"When I touch people, they tell the truth. When my mom repeats the same information more than twice, you never forget it. My dad? Who knows? I've never bothered to meet him. If Bobby doesn't want you to notice him, you won't notice him. Period. The only humans who survived the Crisis without the assistance of their beloved pets, were people who already had a special ability or developed one from the Crisis."

"You're trying to say that Bobby was only memorable if he wanted to be?" Jade asked. Her doubting frown morphed into dubious consideration.

"The only thing anyone in Granberg remembers about Bobby is that he would tear them to shreds if they touched his little sister. No one there remembers him beyond that. Melissa does, yes, but he wanted her to see him differently. Her parents can't forget who Bobby wanted them to see him as. My mother remembers him as a good and loyal friend to me, but little else about him. He wanted each person to know him in a certain way. Neil and I were his best friends who, I surmise, Bobby wanted to see him fully. If he wanted to disappear? I'm not convinced we'd find a single clue to prove he was alive. Why do you think no one ever saw us or remembered the team after we completed a job *with Bobby*?"

Jade made a noise that sounded a lot like, "Huh."

No one on the team said anything as what he said sunk in. Rick watched Jade work through the jobs Bobby was part of in her head. He could tell she didn't have a counterargument. Not a single job Bobby had been on had ever even hinted at coming close to being traced to them.

"Why wouldn't he tell us?" Dave asked.

"If he knew," Rick said, "he didn't tell me, and I *asked*." Bending his moral code, Rick had touched Bobby and asked when he was sure Bobby didn't know they'd had skin contact. Bobby didn't know.

"You're saying all humans can do *something*?" Carl asked. "My dad, he's human. He can do *something*?"

"I was told it's rare to have a *talent*," Rick said. "And if you look at the data, it is. But that's only right if you look for *talents* that have a disruptive effect. I was literally breaking up couples before I knew how to speak. Some *talents* are things people just think the person can do suspiciously well. If students attend every one of my mother's lectures, they have a 100% pass rate. People would notice this if all students attended lectures, paid attention the entire time, and stayed awake in class."

"Hmm," Carl said thoughtfully, like he'd come upon an idea.

"What's this have to do with what happened in Melissa's coffee shop today?" Susan asked. "What did she do?"

"You all saw the recording," Rick said. "She touched them."

"Touch? Like you?" Shawn said.

"Dude," Dave hissed. His voice was full of the pain of betrayal. "She's been touching all of us. She's been touching you *a lot*. What the fuck is she doing to us?"

"She makes you want to be good," Rick admitted. "To do the right thing. To be the best you can be."

"You attribute your moral compass to her," Jeremy observed.

"She was around a lot growing up," Rick explained, spreading his hands out as he laid it down for them. "I didn't realize it until later, but she'd touch me, then tell me the truth, that she just wanted more time with Bobby or just to watch us play a game. Bobby and I knew she was telling the truth and let her hang out with us."

"How long does her touch last?" Dave asked.

"I'm not certain it has an expiration date," Rick muttered, not looking Dave in the eyes.

"When did you figure it out?" Shawn asked. He was the only one other than Jade who hadn't met Melissa in person, who definitely hadn't been touched by her.

"Around the time I picked up on the fact that Bobby could control what impression he gave other people. My hunch was confirmed when she opened Juniper's Java, and the neighborhood turned around. She touches just about everyone who comes through. The residents with criminal records? Suddenly, they just stopped committing crimes. After a few months of visiting her coffee shop? They started fixing up the neighborhood. After a year? They started helping out in the community and volunteering all over town."

"That explains the lack of town programs to clean up the neighborhood," Susan muttered.

"That doesn't explain Bobby," Jade said. "She must have had contact with him way more than you, and we all know his moral compass was not *direction sensitive*."

"I think it has to do with the amount of touch and the timing. Melissa's long-term friends are all *good* people."

"Explains why she thinks no one means anyone else harm," Jeremy muttered.

"Lindsay and Jonathan Juniper would have touched Melissa more than anyone else," Rick continued. "They have dedicated their lives to mapping the hybrid genome because they want doctors to be able to help any hybrid that crosses their path in the future. They're practically saints."

"Then why wasn't Bobby?" Dave asked. "I loved the guy, but he was scary as shit."

"He had a ton of contact with Melissa when he was a toddler and young kid. Way more than me." Rick swallowed down his apprehension. "I think that much contact before puberty twisted him. Rather than being pushed to be good or the best he can be, he's pushed to protect good as he sees it.

"The change started when we were seventeen and our classmates started saying shit about how hot his little sister was. Bobby, Neil and I had existed on the fringe of our class groups at that time; I was focused on making sure people didn't touch me and Bobby and Neil were on board with that. But when he made it clear Melissa wasn't available for any of our classmates in any way, shape, or form, everyone looked at us differently; they noticed us all the time and gave us a different kind of space. In the army, he went deeper down that path. I've checked him on a few things when I thought he was acting on a threat that went a little too far, but he never hurt anyone that was definitively *good*. I made sure he didn't."

"And her past boyfriends," Carl said, "they either thought she was too good for them or tried to stop her from interacting with any guy, including her close guy friends. So, intimacy might influence things."

Rick squeezed the back of his neck before admitting, "Given the direction of my thoughts since Sunday, I'd say that's... that's a distinct possibility."

His team looked at him with a mixture of caution and sympathy. If his and Melissa's relationship continued, they would both need to track what, if anything, changed in both their personalities. Rick had no idea if his touch could have long-term or intimacy-related effects. He hadn't touched others with any regularity since he was eleven and never intimately.

"So," Jade looked at Rick like she was going to rip him to shreds with her talons. "You're saying Bobby might be out there, actually doing the things he threatens people with in the name of good, but without a check on his warped conscience, and you're just mentioning this now?"

"How would it have helped earlier? Even Neil isn't sold that all humans have *talents* and he knows Bobby almost as well as me," Rick said, finally slumping into a chair. Neil hadn't completely blown off Rick's theory, but he had said Rick was making a lot out of nothing. And if Neil wasn't on board, why would his team believe him? "If Bobby doesn't want to be found, we won't find him," he finished in a resigned voice.

"Would have stopped us from questioning your sanity for that first year after he disappeared," Carl offered, shaking his head.

"It could have informed more of our jobs," Jeremy put in.

"I always check the humans out personally," Rick said. "I've told you every time that I found a person who had a *talent* of significance." All six times in the past decade. "This is why I'm way more suspicious of the humans we encounter. Like this Matt Helms guy, he is in way too deep with Allison Barre to be impotent. I don't know what he's doing, but he has to be doing something to keep the Wrappers up and running regardless of the attention they garner."

"You have been saying that," Shawn said thoughtfully.

Jade stared at Rick like she was planning to gut him and fly his entrails to his mother. Considering Bobby had made that threat to several people, with Jeremy as the messenger, Rick didn't consider it very scary.

Anyway, there was nothing that Jade could do to him that would match what Bobby would do when he found out he'd slept with Melissa. If, of course, he was right that his best friend was indeed alive.

Chapter 35

Neil

Neil strolled down the tree-lined street that held Juniper's Java and shook his head. He never got over how the area had turned around.

He didn't come to this neighborhood all that often; he preferred to stay near his pond. It just took too long to cross town on foot, and the town's buses, while good, weren't amazingly convenient in their routes. Over the years, Melissa had been over to his restaurant more than he'd been to see her. She generally came with her friend Ted, an octopus hybrid who moved to Granberg for college. He was a cool guy.

Given how spread out Neil's visits had been over the four years she'd been open, each visit to the neighborhood had been a shock.

The first time, trash rolled down the street and piled in every corner. Graffiti covered every building except Melissa's coffee shop, but she had had it freshly painted for the opening; it was only a matter of time before it looked the same. Neil's skin had crawled at the drug deals taking place in broad daylight and the sheer number of people carrying unconcealed weapons.

On his next visit, he didn't see a single drug deal, weapon, or piece of trash. On his third, the graffiti was gone; every building had a fresh coat of paint.

On his fourth or fifth visit, he saw a guy, who on his first visit had held another guy pinned against the wall, *help* an older lady carry her groceries; the guy even nodded hello to Neil with a smile as they passed. The entire area was thriving.

Melissa had really gotten in on the ground floor. Neil was relieved the area had improved and none of them had to worry about what Bobby would have done if he were alive and something happened to Melissa while working. Rick insisted the neighborhood had improved because of Melissa, but Neil wasn't the one who'd been secretly in love with her for most of his life. Rick was just wearing rose-colored glasses.

As normal, all the tables in front of Juniper's Java under the trees were full, mostly of young, college-age kids taking advantage of the fall air, but there was a business meeting happening at one table and a young pup out with his grandmother whose fur had gone gray. Someone had even brought their pet cat to the coffee shop on a leash, which wasn't a sight he saw every day.

Neil made his way through the tables. A few of the older college girls gave him an appreciative once-over, which he ignored. He'd learned his lesson a long time ago; when a woman discovered that his leisurely pace had nothing to do with acting laid-back and everything to do with an inability to move faster, she'd be gone before he could turn around and look for her. Shaking his head, he walked inside, finding the coffee shop over-staffed.

"Hey Neil," Melissa waved from behind the counter where she was leaning against the wall.

He saw Kate wave as well while she grabbed a pastry. A lizard hybrid he'd seen around Melissa growing up looked at him curiously from the cash register. The young man behind the espresso machine didn't look up at him, and the mouse hybrid he'd seen behind the counter the week before hurried past him like she was late for something. He didn't think he'd ever seen more than four employees during a rush time; five, at the current lull, wasn't practical.

"Hey."

"What would you like today?" the lizard hybrid asked him. Her once-over had turned into an eyeball inquisition. If he was on her food chain, it would have been unnerving. Her name tag said "Danny."

"I'll have a fly mocha with an extra drizzle of chocolate." Neil shifted his eyes to Melissa while the lizard started making his drink. "Do you want to grab some late afternoon ice cream? I heard good things about the place two doors down."

"Sure." She pushed off the wall.

"Melissa," Kate said in warning.

"I'm just going two doors down. No one specifically said we can't leave the premises."

"Still...." Danny muttered as she passed Neil his drink. "Do you think you should check?"

"What's going on?" Neil looked between the three women. He noticed the young man behind the espresso machine looked as perplexed as Neil felt.

"Rick is being overprotective," Melissa said, rolling her eyes.

Neil laughed. "Do you find that surprising? He's been keeping his distance for over a decade. And with Jessy hounding him to ask you out? I can easily imagine him taking things a tad too far." He took a sip of his fly mocha and thought that Danny must like flies a bit more than him. It was too heavy on the fly flavor, but the extra chocolate was just right.

"We so told you," Danny said, bouncing up and down with a speed that made Neil envious.

"It wouldn't hurt to call," Kate said.

"I'm not calling," Melissa said with finality. She walked around the counter and hooked her arm through his. She leaned in and whispered, "I also know the cameras out front reach three doors down, so we'll only be out of sight while in the ice cream shop."

Neil shook his head. It was hard to believe that with Tommy Nolan caught Rick was still insisting on cameras and what sounded like constant escorts; that was overkill.

"At least you're being considerate," Neil joked.

They made their way out of the shop at Neil's speed and turned to the right toward the ice cream shop.

"So, tell me," Neil said after another sip. "Other than his overprotectiveness, which I imagine will dissipate with Tommy taken care of, how are things going?"

"He left town for *reasons*," Melissa said, looking up at him through her lashes as if he knew what she meant. Clearly, Melissa was aware they both knew that whatever the reason was, it had nothing to do with being in a motorcycle club. Neil just tipped his head in acknowledgment. "And then, he didn't message me much until yesterday, but I don't know if he could before. It's too early to know how things are going, I guess. He's supposed to get back tonight."

"Is Jessy elated?"

"I don't know if she knows. She wasn't fazed when I came out of Rick's bedroom the other morning. But considering Rick and three of the Mavens were over at my parents' wiring the place, she already knew I was there." Melissa shrugged. Neil barely held in his choking noise when Melissa casually commented she'd spent the night in Rick's childhood room directly across the hall from Jessy's room. "That was all before anything really started. I do know he hasn't been home since he and I talked about being exclusive."

"Because he's been at your place every night," Neil surmised.

"No, because he can't go into Jessy's house until the fallout from Tommy's debacle is done."

"The fallout?" Neil looked down at Melissa with his face scrunched in confusion, and they paused in front of the ice cream shop.

Melissa opened her mouth to say more, but a sweatshirt covered arm shoved Neil away from her. Purely by chance, the arm brushed Neil's hand and his fingertips snagged on a cord of some sort. This pulled the man who shoved him a foot away from Melissa until the cord snapped, but Neil had too much momentum to stop his backward movement. Melissa screamed in what sounded like pain as a sunglass-wearing dog hybrid in a ripped leather jacket put his shoulder into her stomach and threw her over his shoulder in a fireman's hold, barely slowing down.

They were all several feet away by the time Neil's ass hit the concrete and he fell onto his back, spilling his fly mocha all over him. As the shock of pain reverberated through him from his fall, he shifted automatically. Stuck on his back, propped up weirdly on his shell spikes, and covered in his drink, Neil saw them stuff Melissa into a white van and disappear down the street.

Neil tried to move and groaned. He hoped nothing had cracked from the fall. He hadn't been knocked down like that since high school; his tail bone had grown accustomed to no longer being assaulted. Around him, people had gathered, and one person was already on the phone with the police.

"Officer Fields," he said loudly. "Ask them to send Officer Fields." He didn't want to admit to anyone what had just happened, but he knew she wouldn't laugh at him or give him pitying looks. She never had, and he didn't think she'd start now, even if his clothes were riddled with holes from his spikes. There were plenty of officers in Granberg who Neil had gone to school with, and he didn't want to deal with their smug, knowing smirks.

Neil focused on his breathing and ignored the offers of assistance to help him get up. As he got the pain under control, he shifted back to his human form and fell over a foot to the ground. His saving grace was that someone's shoe had stopped his head from cracking against the concrete. He almost shifted back but managed to hold his human form. He hadn't taken his spikes into account in the fall. Last time he'd done the shift on his back on a hard surface, he hadn't had the blasted five-inch spikes protruding from his shell.

Even more slowly than normal, Neil sat up. His body protested the achingly slow movements, but he ignored the pain.

His phone rang.

Neil looked at the caller ID and didn't recognize the number. He glanced toward Juniper's Java and answered as a squad car rolled up along the curb.

"If you could convince whatever police officer comes to talk to you to do so in the staff area of Juniper's, do it." Jeremy's voice said without preamble. "That way, we can get the intel at the same time." In the background of the phone call, Neil could hear what sounded like a violent scuffle if the grunts and breaking furniture noises were any indication.

Neil let his gaze drag up the navy blue-clad legs in front of him until he reached the concerned, dark brown eyes of Officer Fields. Billi looked great, but then she always did. He hoped he didn't smell like flies and just smelled like coffee or chocolate.

"Officer Fields," Neil said with his phone to his ear.

"Mr. Polski," she said back in her normal formal demeanor. "Who are you on the phone with?"

"You'll know if I do," he said into the phone and hung up. Neil started standing up slowly. "An acquaintance who'd like to listen to whatever I can tell you."

"To listen? A woman was abducted less than ten minutes ago, and someone called you about wanting to listen in?" Her tone demanded explanations he didn't have.

"Melissa's my best friend's little sister and the girlfriend of the interrogator I sent you."

Billi paused. "He was helpful," she said, before muttering: "He mentioned a Melissa in the interrogation room." Her eyes flicked to the phone in his hand. "Does he want to listen in on the phone?"

"Melissa owns Juniper's Java." Neil glanced past her toward the coffee shop. "We can use the staff room. It's private."

"How will that help?" Billi's hands were on her hips. While she was considering the offer, she wouldn't just go along.

Neil glanced at the people around them meaningfully before looking at her again, trying to convey that he couldn't say where they were. Billi sighed and told the young, uniformed beagle hybrid with her to question the bystanders then find her to combine their reports.

Neil's return to the coffee shop was less climatic than he anticipated. The commotion from the shove, snatch, and Melissa's scream had reached the coffee shop, which was now empty. Kate, who was now covered in fur, and Danny, who was petting her in their mutual worry, stood when Neil and Billi became visible through the coffee shop windows. The young man from earlier was just flipping the sign to closed, but he let Neil and Billi enter.

"We're going to use the staff room," Neil said somewhat uncertainly.

"They said it was a dog hybrid in a ripped jacket and sunglasses that grabbed her," Kate mewled immediately. She'd clearly stress shifted from everything happening. "It has to be the same person who grabbed me last week. He was wearing a ripped jacket too."

"No one reported a prior kidnapping," Billi said in reprimand, obviously thinking they could have stopped Melissa's kidnapping if they'd known.

"He just grabbed her wrist and asked about her brother," Danny said in Kate's defense.

"Your brother?" Billi said.

"Officer Fields, this is Kate *Nolan*," Neil cut in to shorten things. Billi gave him a tight nod; she caught the connection. "If we could talk about this in back—"

"First, I need to get their statements," Billi said. She was all business, like always. She hadn't even blinked at his punctured clothes or at the fact he was covered in coffee. No reaction to him as an individual. At. All.

"Can you describe the man?" she asked Kate.

"It was Theo Barre," Neil said. "That's who grabbed Kate before, and if she's right about the dog hybrid being the same person, it's who grabbed Melissa just now."

Billi's entire body turned to him.

"Excuse me?" she said with more attitude than he'd ever heard her use.

Slowly, Neil pulled out his phone and called the number Jeremy had used to reach him and hit speaker.

"I can't get her into the staff room. Is this okay?"

"Yeah. Kate, Danny, and Nick, could you go to the staff room and close the door, please?"

"Absolutely not," Kate said. Her eyes were narrowed in suspicion despite her distraught state, and Neil wondered if she recognized Jeremy's voice from his single coffee shop visit. "Whatever my brother has dragged Melissa into, I want to know. I'm not sitting this out."

"I'm staying, too," Danny agreed.

"Nick," Jeremy said as if it pained him. "If you would go in the back or just go home, that would be great."

Nick stood there for a moment before shaking his head no and crossing his arms.

"Who is this person and how does he even know what's happening?" Billi growled at Neil in overt irritation. Neil thought it was an inopportune time for his heart to start racing, but he searched for a way to explain when he didn't know what he could say.

"Officer Fields," Jeremy said before Neil thought of an explanation. "I'm a friend of the interrogator. I just sent two recordings to your phone. The first is of Melissa's kidnapping, and the second is of her interrupting a Wrapper's drug deal yesterday morning."

"She did what?" Kate said as Danny asked, "A drug deal?"

Neil couldn't imagine Melissa coming out on top when breaking up a drug deal, and he dreaded seeing the footage. No matter what, he knew it wouldn't be pretty.

"Cameras," Billi muttered to herself as she pulled out her phone and looked around the coffee shop.

Billi angled her phone so Neil could watch the recordings with her. He wasn't sure Melissa really broke up a drug deal, but the candies looked right, as did the expression on Conner's face. Neil had helped the teen frog hybrid kick his drug habit before he got addicted, but the frog, who now worked for him, had mentioned to Neil a few days ago that he was worried about his friend Timothy, who had to be the goat hybrid in the video.

As they watched, Neil lifted his arm to rub his neck. Not only did he ache from the jarring falls, but he couldn't relax his body while Melissa was unaccounted for. He couldn't help but blame his slowness for how easy it was to grab her. As his hand came up, he noticed he was clutching a lanyard or something. His attention focused on the cord in his hand, and he felt on the cusp of something.

"Does this look familiar to you?" he asked Billi.

"What?" she glanced at the knotted hemp.

"I think it fell off one of the kidnappers. The one that wasn't Theo Barre."

"I think the Theo-guy had one of those around his wrist when he grabbed me," Kate said. "It also looked like a thinner version of sisal rope used on the scratching columns I installed in my apartment."

Billi backed up the video of the drug deal from the other day. She zoomed in on the young dealer.

"He has one around his neck." She pointed at the necklace on the kid.

"Is it a marker for the Wrappers?" a woman's voice that Neil didn't recognize said from his phone. Kate and Danny's faces perked up a little at the woman's voice, so they might have met her.

"There haven't been any common traits noted before," Billi said to the anonymous voice.

"There's no insignia on it." Neil looked at it closely. "There's nothing noteworthy about it. It isn't well-made, to be honest."

"So, if I made a lousy bracelet and wore it," Nick spoke for the first time, "I'd be mistaken for a drug dealer?"

"That's it," Rick's voice chimed in for the first time on the call. Neil saw no understanding in Billi's eyes either and frowned. "It's not about what it looks like. It's about *who* made it."

"Is there any way to confirm that?" Jeremy asked.

Neil glanced at everyone else in the room. They had all recognized Rick's voice, but none of them had a clue what Rick was talking about. Neil had a sinking suspicion that he knew. Rick was using the tone he only used when talking about *talents*.

"Is there anything else of pertinence Neil can tell us?" another unknown woman's voice asked sharply.

"No?" Neil said.

The phone went dead. He looked at Billi and knew *his* inquisition was nowhere near over.

Chapter 36

Melissa

Delicacy was not either of her abductors' middle names. The dog hybrid, who she assumed was Theo given his ripped jacket and sunglasses, jerked his shoulder into her gut and directly into her bruises in order to heft her off him and into the stripped interior of their van. Her pained groan probably sounded overdone to her abductors, but there was nothing she could do to stifle it. She collided with the hard metal with enough force to daze her. It was all she could do to just draw in the metallic-smelling air around her.

"Fuck, man," the human-looking man cursed as the van sped away. "The surfer dude snagged my bracelet."

Melissa fought both the need to vomit from having a shoulder jab into her and the temptation to slip into unconsciousness after being slammed into a metal van floor. She knew that whatever injury she'd suffered from Dave grabbing her seven days ago was going to be paltry in comparison to her upcoming days, assuming she got to see those days.

"Just get a new one," the dog hybrid said as he pulled her hands behind her back. Shooting pain radiated from the shoulder she'd landed on. Her sharp cry didn't stop him from what he was doing, and he slapped a thick pair of cuffs on her wrists.

Melissa had only seen cuffs in movies. There were a few different types if media could be believed: military grade cuffs that could withstand a bombing so there'd be cuffed skeletons afterwards (Melissa doubted these existed); standard police issue cuffs that were utilitarian and easily cleansed between uses; bedroom cuffs that were velvety and colorful but had an auto-release should someone leave for too long; and among these, they all came in a variety of hybrid specific versions should shifting factor in.

Given the fuzzy feel of the cuffs against her wrists, she reasoned her new jewelry was of the bedroom variety. Taking small, measured breaths to fight her panic and manage the pain from being grabbed, she valiantly hoped the handcuff selection reflected that they were the most readily available and were not a reflection of her captors' intentions. Needing to reduce her nausea, Melissa forced her body up into a sitting position. The dog hybrid took this as the right moment to slap a pair of fingerprint-locked leg cuffs on her as well. The fluffy purple cuffs covered about half of her calves, and looked ridiculous against her jeans. Unable to move much at all, Melissa's gut clenched, sending a stab of pain through her body.

"Maybe we can get it back, instead," the man who had lost a bracelet said.

Whoever was driving snorted at the idea. Melissa had no idea why he'd want to go back to the scene of the crime for a bracelet. Was it expensive? Did it have an identifying aspect to it? Maybe it could help Rick and the police find her. She was sure that the ice cream shop was in range of the cameras Jeremy had slapped up, so everything would have been recorded. That had to be in her favor. Or maybe it made her a liability. She squeezed her eyes shut.

As her thoughts spun, her nausea multiplied until she could taste the vomit climbing up her throat. She had known that it wasn't great that she'd been targeted in any way by Theo, but she hadn't realized things could go this far. Rick had *not* been overprotective. He hadn't been protective *enough*.

"Do you know what your sister will do to me if the authorities figure it out?" the man snapped. The dog hybrid before her smiled a little, like he couldn't wait to watch if that happened.

Melissa chose not to ask either question that popped into her head: what might the authorities figure out or what will she do to you? Neither answer would increase her likelihood of survival. In fact, speaking at all seemed like a bad idea. She was certain she'd throw up if she opened her mouth. When the van seemed to spin a little, Melissa realized she had stopped breathing. It took a lot of effort, but she forced air in and out of her lungs regardless of the pain.

It hadn't escaped her notice while she was trying to breathe that the dog hybrid was watching her intently and held a gag in his hands. She squeezed her lips together and gave him a little wide-eyed nod, trying to communicate that she was terrified and would keep her mouth shut. She really didn't want the gag-of-unknown-origins-and-cleanliness in her mouth regardless of how gentle he was in the process of gagging her — not that anything he'd done so far had been gentle. He narrowed his eyes at her and frowned before yanking his sunglasses off and revealing a pair of cold brown eyes.

The way he looked at her did not bode well. The complete lack of humanity in his gaze sent goosebumps down her body. Just looking him in the eye, she could feel her chances of being released or rescued alive dwindling.

While the man climbed upfront with the driver to bicker about the bracelet he was so worried about, the husky hybrid placed a hand on her upper-back and shoved her forward away from the van wall. He pulled her cell out of her back pocket. In front of her, he pulled out the battery, snapped the SIM card in half, and then grabbed a hammer from who knew where in the van and smashed the phone until it was in little bits. Then he continued scrutinizing her in a way that made her fear she could be on the receiving end of the hammer any second.

"Any other tracking devices you want to fess up to now?" he asked in the silence that now reigned in the van.

"There was a tracking device in my phone?" Melissa couldn't help but ask. TV shows told her that taking out the SIM and battery should have been enough to disable any GPS, but if there had been a tracking device in there too…. Her eyes bugged out as she looked at the little pieces that might have helped Rick find her with all due haste.

Whatever her kidnapper expected, it wasn't her utter devestation. His head reared back, and he shifted to his human form, confirming his identity as the guy who had grabbed Kate's wrist, aka Theo. He put his sunglasses back on but continued to look at her with a deep frown as if she was a puzzle to figure out — a puzzle that might just be poisonous.

Melissa remembered then that Rick had said she might be considered a colleague or a threat all on her own just because she'd gotten lucky with a lock. Was it better to tell Theo that he had it all wrong or not to say anything at all? If she said something, would he even believe her? Unlikely.

The van sped over a bump that forced a pained squeak from Melissa's lips before she tipped over, unable to keep her balance. When her shoulder rammed into the van floor again, a groan tumbled out. Without being able to move her legs in the cuffs, she was stuck on her side, bouncing on her shoulder.

Theo typed something into his phone and then continued to watch her as she did her best not to make a sound as they sped over more bumps in the road. He made no move to help her sit up and Melissa didn't know if that was a good or a bad thing. The mere thought of him touching her made her break out in a cold sweat, but if he helped her up then he might have a shred of human decency in him. The more he looked at her, the more certain she became that decency wasn't one of his qualities and the less she wanted to be in his vicinity. Nothing good could come from being around him. She wished she could squirm away, but there was nowhere to go.

After a while, the van slowed down, and before it came to a full stop, another husky hybrid jumped inside and growled at her. Melissa sucked in a breath and a cold fear washed over her body. This woman, whoever she was, was much scarier than Theo. It might have been her sleek clothes and fancy perfume that contrasted so strongly with the aggressive snarl on her face. Or maybe being kidnapped made everyone threatening.

The woman didn't say anything but passed what looked like a security wand to Theo. Theo took the wand and waved it all around Melissa as the van continued on its merry way like it wasn't driving to a dock where she would be drowned. She fought down a new wave of fear as her mind came up with a realistic rendition of what it would be like to go swimming with the fishes like in the old mafia movies. She fought to keep her breathing even and not give away how terrified she was, but she knew she was failing. Every sharp inhale felt like a knife was stabbing into her side.

"Nothing," Theo told the other hybrid.

"Nothing?" she asked.

"Nothing," he said again.

Melissa wasn't positive what the wand had looked for since it hadn't made a sound. If it were a metal detector, it would have dinged at the metal fasteners on her boots. If she had to guess, it was for the supposed tracking devices on her person.

Tears slipped from her eyes. There weren't any tracking devices. There was no way for anyone to know where she was being taken.

Both Theo and the woman continued to look at her like she was an ever-growing problem. But if having her was a problem, why'd they bother grabbing her?

Minutes ticked by in near silence, only broken by the rumble of the van hitting potholes and bouncing over other bumps. Melissa tried to hold in the pained squeaks that each jostle elicited, but a few escaped her. Each movement Theo and the woman made caused Melissa to flinch and then groan; her body hurt so much. At one particularly violent bump, her head slammed into the van floor, and her vision blurred for a moment. Valiantly, she clung to consciousness as if being awake might somehow help her get out of this alive. She put all her energy into breathing as normally as possible and not moving. If an opportunity arose, she needed to be ready to take it. Not that she could even manage to sit up at the moment, but somehow that fact didn't seem important to her hyper awareness.

By the time they stopped again, she guessed they had driven over thirty minutes but less than an hour. That meant there were a lot of places they could be. She looked at Theo and the woman, whose eyes had never left her, and swallowed hard. Theo was flipping a syringe in one hand and had a purple blindfold that matched the cuffs around her ankles in the other.

"Blindfold or a little shut-eye?" Theo asked her.

She felt the blood drain from her face and managed to croak out something like the word blindfold.

The woman growled at her response. It was a very unhappy noise.

"That's my point," Theo said back to her.

Melissa looked between the two and could tell they hadn't liked her response, but she didn't know why. Did they honestly think she'd pick to have unknown drugs injected into her with a suspect syringe? Who would pick that option? For now, the best thing she could do was not upset them. Somehow, she knew beyond a shadow of a doubt that anything could set them off and get her stabbed with the suspect syringe. Her nausea resurfaced at full force, and she pushed it down. With supreme effort, she focused on controlling her breathing to the best of her ability, which was an exercise in futility at the moment.

Finally, Theo rummaged through a box and dug out a black cloth bag. He put it over her head and secured it around her neck tighter than necessary. Tears slid down Melissa's face and her shoulders shook as terror overtook her. A whimper of fear slipped out. Nothing about this was good. She had just enough presence of mind to notice that the bag smelled freshly laundered. Noting that was surely a sign of sanity slipping away. It was a minute or two before someone hefted her over their shoulder, eliciting another pained shriek from her, and carried her out of the van.

She didn't know where she was or how long they had carried her, but at some point, she blacked out, either from the blood that rushed to her head or as a coping mechanism to block out the experience. She didn't want to reflect on which it was.

Hands with a hint of fur gripped her upper arms, and she heard displeased noises from behind her. Melissa wasn't ready to open her eyes and risk finding out that she was still suffocating inside a bag, but she did it anyway. More frustrated sounds came from somewhere past the closed door that came into view as her eyes blinked open; the bag over her head had been removed. She felt a second pair of thick, fuzzy cuffs slide around her forearms as the ones at her wrists were released. The new cuffs slid down to her wrists and tightened, but not quite as much as before. A large, shaggy, orange tabby hybrid crouched in front of her and switched the cuffs on her legs as well. Melissa focused on his ear tufts, trying to block out the new red cuffs and the gray room she was in — a room only contained her in a chair at its center and the cat hybrid cuffing her. Dread settled deep in her gut. This looked like a place people were brought to in movies to be tortured. A place where the blood would be easy to wash away.

"I'll see if I can get you something to eat," the cat hybrid said, as if giving her an apology.

Melissa nodded in response since her mouth was dry but cut the action short when the room tilted a little.

"Ah Akdwen," he murmured as he kept her upright in the chair when she would have fallen off.

Melissa didn't know what his prayers to Akdwen meant for her future. She really should have checked if the hybrid cat god had more significance than flexibility and ferocity when she thought of it the other week. Melissa only vaguely remembered Kate talking a few years back about the different in-circle interpretations. The most worrisome at the moment were the ones that applied to a flexibility of morals and a bloodthirsty ferocity to destroy the weak. Others were more benign and had used those same two aspects to mean physical health and dedication to the task at hand. Kate and her family adhered to the latter.

None of that helped her at the moment. Overall, she was wondering about her mental stability in general with the random things she was thinking about.

After several unsure minutes, during which Melissa kept tipping to the side, the cat hybrid grabbed rope from somewhere behind her and loosely wrapped it around her middle and the chair, but under her cuffed arms. She couldn't decide if being tied to the chair was better than falling to the floor. Not that she could move in either case. Everything hurt. Breathing hurt. Passing out again was looking more and more merciful as her imagination came up with a heart-stopping snapshot of her sitting in the chair in a pool of her own blood.

"At least you won't fall off for the moment," he said, appearing unsure. He loitered for a few more minutes before departing. Melissa blinked at her feet, reflecting that maybe they'd drugged her after all.

Chapter 37

Rick

Rick's normally logical thought process stopped the second Shawn cussed and told Jeremy to track a white van that had just left Juniper's Java with Melissa inside.

By the time Rick made it to the door, Dave had gotten his speedy ass between him and the hall. Rick tried to plow through Dave, but Dave's claws bit into Rick's arm enough that Rick couldn't just surge forward. He had to extricate himself without being totally mauled. He had to get to Melissa. From the depth of Dave's claws in his arm, Rick knew they weren't fully extended.

Mentally putting a pin in the pain, Rick turned to Dave and threw a punch at his teammate without holding back. Nothing was going to stop him from saving her. His fist collided with Dave's jaw, knocking him back, but Dave kept his hold on Rick's arm. Crashing his elbow down into Dave's shoulder, earned Rick a grunt but nothing more.

When Jeremy called out that he'd lost the license-plate-less van when it drove through a tunnel in town *with four other identical vans,*

Rick stopped caring if he lost his arm. He had to reach Melissa imme-diately. He threw himself toward the door.

Dave must have felt the feral change in Rick's movement because he retracted his claws before they severed something irreparable. But Carl was there. He grabbed Rick from behind before he was able to get into the hallway. For a second, Rick knew Carl was going to phys-ically snap him in half. He'd seen Carl do it before when things had gone wrong on a mission. Some rational part of Rick's brain asserted itself; he stopped struggling against Carl's hold, letting his teammate half-drag, half-carry him over to the windows and as far from the door as possible.

Panic continued to surge through Rick, but there was nothing he could do. He couldn't get away from Carl. At least, not without being too injured to help Melissa. Seconds ticked by, and the fact he didn't know where Melissa was slowly sank in. Leaving and going to her wasn't an option. Not until they uncovered where she was taken.

When it was clear Rick wouldn't rush the door again, Carl released him. Jeremy set his phone down from a call Rick hadn't noticed he'd been on and returned his attention to his computer screens. Susan slipped back into the room holding two first aid kits; Rick hadn't even seen her leave for them. She passed one to Shawn before heading back toward Dave, who stood in the doorway looking pissed but not saying a word.

Rick took off his shirt and forced himself to stay still as Shawn stitched up the four deep scratches in his left arm. Each time the needle pierced his skin, Rick clenched his right hand into a fist until his nails bit into his palm. Focusing on the thread pulling through his skin was better than watching Neil's painstakingly slow progress on the screens. Waiting for Neil to make it up off the sidewalk, convince Officer Fields to relocate, and then stroll past a shop and a half was an agony Rick wouldn't wish on anyone. He'd never held his friend's pace against him before, but patience was not Rick's friend today as he cursed Neil in his head for being a damn turtle. Moving slowly was a sure-fire way to get killed.

Minutes later, Jade pushed through Dave *and* Carl, who both flanked the door in case Rick made another ill-advised attempt to leave. She was pissed and glaring at Rick; her eyes barely flicked to the stitches Shawn had almost finished. Rick gave her a grim nod; he'd wait for a plan to be made. Maybe.

"Update on Melissa," Jade said. Her tone had its typical no-nonsense quality that kept people on task. Her feathers weren't ruffled in the slightest. If she wasn't glaring at him, Rick would say the day was just another stroll in the park for her.

Neither Carl nor Dave responded since they had touched Rick's skin and, Dave more than Carl, Rick's blood. They wouldn't have much control over what they said. Susan glanced over at Jeremy but continued to check Dave's injuries. Dave handled the check by alternating between grinning at Susan's hands on him and wincing when she found a bruise and purposely pushed on it in retaliation for looking a smidge too pleased about her attention. Hand-to-hand combat wasn't Dave's best skill, but he had been the only one fast enough to get between Rick and the door.

"No chance of tracking the van," Jeremy said. If he was frazzled, he hid it well. "Waiting to get info from Neil once he gets into the coffee shop."

"Do we know the officer?"

"Officer Fields let me in to interrogate Tommy Nolan," Rick supplied. He'd managed to make his voice stay normal, but he knew no one in the room believed he was calm. "She'll be inclined to cooperate," he added.

Jade's eyes stayed on him as Shawn secured a wrap around his stitched-up arm. When Shawn threw away his gloves, Rick put his ripped, bloody shirt back on. The less skin exposed, the better. For whatever reason, Rick felt satisfaction at forcing Dave and Carl to be silent, knowing that they would share more than they intended for the next ten to fifteen minutes. It made him feel like he'd done something, even if he hadn't done anything to help Melissa yet.

"Neil's calling in," Jeremy said. He answered the phone and put the call directly on speaker.

As Neil and Officer Fields watched the videos Jeremy sent, Jade reviewed the information on the second kidnapper — Mich Graff, a mid-level dealer for the Wrappers. Jeremy had identified him from the video in a matter of seconds since they had all the Wrapper profiles downloaded. None of the information in Graff's profile had struck Rick as particularly helpful in finding Melissa.

"Good to know her employees love her," Jade murmured, discontentedly looking at the screen with Melissa's coffee shop where even Nick, who Rick didn't know, refused to leave.

Rick realized Jade was evaluating Melissa as much as she was evaluating him. He'd thrown them a number of curve balls in the last two weeks by dragging the team into work during vacation and now being less than stable when a threat to Melissa was at hand. Not to mention that he hadn't shared his theory about humans in general, or specifically about Melissa and Bobby, before Jade forced his hand. He didn't know what Jade would make of Melissa, but he wasn't going to worry about that until he had her back.

When Neil held out a strip of brown cord and asked Officer Fields if it looked familiar, Jeremy zoomed in on the bracelet. At Kate's revelation that Theo Barre wore one, Jeremy pulled up the picture of the dealer in the coffee shop from the day before and any other photos of suspected Wrappers he could snatch from databases.

Rick moved to look at all the photos Jeremy threw on the screen like rice at a wedding. Jackets made it hard, but he saw three others with a similar accessory.

"Is it a marker for the Wrappers?" Susan asked from beside Dave. She couldn't see the photos from across the room.

"Allison and Matt," Shawn whispered so the phone wouldn't pick up his addition, "they each had a brown piece of jewelry. Matt had a thick armband I thought might have been a tattoo peeking out from under the sleeve of his shirt one day, but it was the right color. In Rafity City, Allison wore an intricate necklace and a ring that same color."

"That's it," Rick said. "It's not about what it looks like. It's about *who* made it."

"Is there any way to confirm that?" Jeremy asked him, grouping the images that had jewelry of the right color.

"Is there anything else of pertinence Neil can tell us?" Jade asked loudly to cut off any further discussion while five people listened to them in the coffee shop.

At Neil's uncertain "No?", Jeremy hung up.

"Explain," Jade said, staring at the info Jeremy was pulling up on Matt Helms since they all knew Rick was talking about Matt, just not why or how he could factor in.

Rick took a deep breath. He needed to show Jade he was level-headed. He needed to focus on the details that would lead to answers. That would get them closer to finding Melissa.

It had to.

"I'm thinking Matt makes the bracelets or whatever and it gives the item special qualities. What if being near the bracelets lets the drugs actually be candy? It's only after people have bought the 'candy' and left the area of the bracelet's influence that it reverts to its natural state — drugs."

"Have you come across any other similar *talents*?" Shawn asked. He sounded dubious.

"You remember a few years back when I had us switch to a different windshield specialist?" Rick asked, glancing at Jade. Her brow furrowed, making her fine feathers crunch together oddly. Rick swallowed hard. He was digging himself into a deeper hole.

"From a hybrid glass specialist to a human one," Jade said with a lightness that made everyone fall silent, and the apprehension in the room rocketed up another notch.

"Yeah," Rick said, purposely not looking at Jade. "Absolutely nothing can penetrate them from the outside, but we can still shatter them from the inside if we're trapped after rolling the vehicle or something. But otherwise, they're unbreakable."

"Seriously?" Dave snapped, speaking for the first time since touching Rick.

No one else said a word as they all seethed. It's not like Rick had any proof that it was the person making the glass rather than some other factor, so why should he have said something no one was going to believe anyway? Nothing Jeremy was pulling up about Matt would prove Rick right or wrong about him, either.

"We can test my theory. Have Officer Fields bring the bracelet back to the station and hold it near some confiscated Wrappers' drugs and see if they resolidify into candy," Rick reasoned. "That will tell us if the bracelets are why none of their dealers are ever caught with anything but *candy*. If we can get confirmation, we can grab one of the Wrapper's dealers and offer them a deal if they can tell us where Melissa was taken."

"Can we trust her?" Susan murmured, holding an irate Dave in place with a hand on his chest.

"If Neil trusts her, we can too," Rick snapped. He shot her a look that would have made most people flinch, but she just shrugged at him like she hadn't been stabbing daggers into him with her comment. They needed to find Melissa quickly. If the Wrappers thought she had training, who knew what techniques they might use to make her talk. Rick would have felt sick about Melissa being tortured period, but when she didn't know anything? The guilt pounding through him from putting her in danger was beyond anything he'd ever experienced before. "We have to do something."

"And we are doing something," Jade said in an icy tone that silenced Rick. "Call Neil back. Officer Fields isn't done with him regardless of him not knowing anything about us. Right, Rick?"

"He knows what I can do and that we aren't a motorcycle club, and the latter he only knows because Bobby and I wouldn't join one." Rick paused. "And, he's also aware of my theory about *talents*, even if he doesn't believe it."

"No one will direct discussion in that direction," Carl pointed out. He was a silver-lining type of guy sometimes.

"If Fields doesn't have access to a sample of the drugs," Jade continued, "find out if she can procure some or if we need to send someone out to do it. In the meantime, Jeremy, dig into any buildings the Wrappers might own that Melissa could be held in. Rick, what might Melissa reveal about us if she's thoroughly interrogated?"

Taking a few bracing breaths at the horrific images that flit through his mind at the realities of what "thoroughly interrogated" would mean for Melissa, Rick ran down everything he thought she might know. Since he hadn't talked to Jade about what he could tell her, there wasn't much in the way of specifics.

She knew the Mavens weren't what they seemed. She had a vague idea about what resources the Mavens had because of the information they had discussed when looking for Tommy. She was aware the Mavens weren't in any databases. She had no idea if the Mavens were part of the military, a government agency, or privately contracted for cases. While she did know Dave was a cheetah hybrid and she'd met everyone on their team but Shawn and Jade herself, she didn't know Rick could force people to tell the truth.

After running through the sheer lack of knowledge Melissa had, there was nothing to do but wait for more intel. While Rick briefed Jade, Jeremy established that Officer Fields couldn't get her hands on any confiscated drugs with any type of speed as she wasn't in narcotics. Neil, on the other hand, cryptically offered to make a call. Even Rick didn't know how Neil planned to help.

A half hour later, Neil called and updated them, unnecessarily, considering he was in the coffee shop and they had listened the whole time; he had sent his employee Conner — the teenage frog hybrid that had greeted Rick when he was last at the Pond Side Grill and who was apparently the same frog that was in the video of Melissa interrupting the Wrapper's drug deal — out to buy some drugs. If the kid could get his hands on them, Neil and Officer Fields could test the bracelet on the sample to see if anything happened.

Jeremy was still systematically sorting through locations that might be viable places to hold Melissa, but not fast enough for Rick. He wanted to be out there looking for her. Deep down, he was sure that was the right thing to do. Since Jade and the rest of his team didn't agree though, Rick wondered if he was having a Melissa-induced judgement issue. If he was, he hoped it only extended to situations that involved her rather than to all situations.

While they waited for Jeremy to find something and listened to the interminable tapping of keys and whir of electronics, the team watched Rick to make sure he was accounted for.

"Too bad she wasn't in a bikini," Dave muttered into the tense silence.

"What?" Rick snapped.

"Melissa. It's too bad she wasn't in a bikini. It's hard not to touch a woman's skin when she's in a bikini."

Susan smacked Dave's arm at the womanizing comment. She must have hit one of the bruises Rick had given him because he winced more than he should have from the light hit. Rick couldn't refute his logic though. If there had been skin contact when they had grabbed Melissa, they might not have managed to get her in the van. They would have recognized they weren't doing something *good*.

The computer dinged with an alert, and they all looked at Jeremy. His feathered fingers were flying over the keyboard with a speed anyone would envy but only made Rick's heart rate increase.

"One of Hughie Minfried's private planes just took off," he informed the room at large. Rick didn't know Jeremy was monitoring the Minfrieds' aircrafts, but Jade must have suggested it. She had an acute aerial awareness that made most pilots and airborne attacks look like children rolling around in the mud. "No documentation of who's on board," Jeremy rattled off. "Not even the pilot's name. No flight path logged either. Clearly, the goal is to stay under the radar."

Rick couldn't breathe. With what they had found out about just Theo Barre, things were not looking good for Melissa in the interrogation department. Theo Barre had been dishonorably discharged for having had a little too much unsanctioned "fun" with a fellow soldier before he hired his skills out to drug dealers. What he knew was not to be scoffed at. He enjoyed leaving a mark. He enjoyed making it hurt. And he'd already had Melissa in his grasp for almost two hours.

If Hughie was in the mix, things got a whole lot worse. He had served as well. It was part of his previous upstanding citizen facade, but it only held up to a passing glance. If someone looked at what type of work he did in the military, they wouldn't ever challenge him in a boardroom. He made waterboarding look like a day at the spa. Rick could only hope that when they tried to break Melissa, they used their bare hands. If they touched her skin, they wouldn't harm her. Much.

Now, he wished she *really* had been captured in a bikini....

"If he's coming here, we'll know it," Jade said. "Shawn, activate the trackers you installed on the Minfried planes."

Even if he tried, Rick couldn't thank Jade enough for skating around the edge of the law. He doubted she'd done it for Melissa's protection. Rather, he figured she didn't like that they took down the Minfried Crime Organization only to have it back up and thriving so quickly.

"If he heads in our direction, we'll be waiting at the airport when he lands. Then, we'll follow him if we haven't located Melissa yet," Jade said.

If Hughie's private plane was as fast as a commercial airplane, he could be in the area within three hours. That gave them three hours to keep digging for information.

Three hours that Melissa would be subjected to Theo Barre's sadistic whims.

Three hours for Rick to agonize over what might be happening to her.

Three hours that he had to trust his team was doing everything imaginable to find her.

Three hours not to kill any of them because they'd let this happen.

Three hours to wonder how Bobby would have killed them all if he were there.

Chapter 38

Melissa

Melissa's heart beat so loudly she barely heard Theo's next words even though he crouched just inches away from her. His forearms rested on his knees, and all Melissa could focus on were the scalpel and needle he held in his hands; he slowly twisted them one way and then another to make them glint in the weak light of the room. Each movement made her gut clench in panic. She hurt all over from being wrenched around during the kidnapping; she didn't think she could survive much more. And from what Theo was saying, he had a lot of plans for her. Plans she didn't want any part of.

"If you agree to help us, I won't do any of that," Theo rumbled. "I want to do those things to you, but if you help us, I won't."

She knew he wanted to pry her fingernails off with that scalpel. He wanted to take the needle in his hand and gouge her bare nail beds before rubbing salt into the wounds. His voice was coated in a sick desire as he'd described it to her; he'd even described how it'd make him feel. Melissa's eyes brimmed with tears. She fervently wished she hadn't eaten the food the orange cat hybrid had brought her because she knew she was going to vomit-cry before Theo even started on her. He hadn't even touched her yet, and she thought she was going to be sick.

"Just tell me what you know about R," Theo coaxed.

"Your what?" Melissa squeaked. She desperately wanted to answer his question, but how could she tell him anything if he didn't finish his sentence?

Theo stopped twisting the scalpel and the needle about and let his hands drop so they hung from his wrists limply. Melissa pried her eyes up to his face, swallowing down the bile in the back of her throat. Theo was looking at her like she had said something nonsensical. But she didn't have any information about anything of his. She tried to pull air into her lungs as he narrowed his eyes at her, but her lungs weren't cooperating. She was only getting the tiniest puffs of oxygen. To answer his questions, she needed to stay conscious.

"Tell me what you know about R," he repeated. This time, he pushed the scalpel against the inside of her knee in threat.

Melissa's vision tunneled until all she could see was the sharp edge cutting her jeans like butter. She whimpered. With herculean effort, she managed to push out a sentence while she held herself as still as possible: "Tell you about your what?"

He pulled the scalpel away from her leg, and Melissa drew in a gasping breath as she sagged in the ropes that held her to the chair. It didn't matter that the ropes dug into her bruised middle; her adrenaline muted most of that pain anyway. Her vision cleared, and she stared at the door past Theo. That was her way out, one way or another. The problem was that she was pretty sure she wouldn't be walking out of there. They would be carrying her lifeless body through that door when Theo finished with her. This was it. She had no idea why she had thought Theo was harmless before. Theo was the poster child of *not* harmless. Rick had been very, very right to worry about his interest in her.

"R," Theo said, as if speaking to a half-wit, "is the guy you broke into Tommy's apartment with. The guy that parked his motorcycle in your garage the other night."

Understanding coursed through her, and her eyes widened. R was what they called Rick. The first letter of his name. Not "our" like she thought Theo was saying. Shit.

"So, let's start off easy," Theo said. His sadistic grin was back; he knew he had her. She'd given away that she finally understood what he was talking about. "What's his name? How can we get our hands on him?"

Melissa shook her head. She was breathing so hard the edges of her vision were darkening again. She couldn't betray Rick to these people. He was out there doing good things. She knew he was. Besides, she couldn't share anything beyond his name. Rick hadn't told her anything. She couldn't even give Theo Rick's phone number since he'd destroyed her phone. She had no idea that Rick's *jobs* dealt with stuff like this. For all she knew, being cuffed and tied to a chair was just another day for him.

As the second of silence drew out into another, Melissa realized that when Theo actually started hurting her, she *would* say something. She knew his name, which was more than Theo knew. She might not know Rick super well *now*, but she knew his past. She could give them his mom's name and that would be worse than giving them anything about Rick. The mere fact that she'd thought about what would be the worst she could reveal meant it was at the forefront of her mind. She couldn't do that to Jessy or to Rick. But she also knew she wouldn't make it to the other side of this ordeal without revealing something. Maybe even everything.

"Maybe I won't start with your nails," Theo mused.

He set the needle down on the piece of fabric next to him with other metal implements Melissa refused to look at and process. He reached forward with the scalpel and dragged its cold, flat surface down the side of her left arm. Melissa wouldn't have dared flinch if she could have moved, but the cuffs behind her back held her arms too securely for a flinch. She also wasn't sure she could move her left arm even without the handcuffs; it had stiffened up and throbbed grotesquely from when she landed on it in the van.

"Maybe I'll start with cutting down your arm. A slice here," he drew the scalpel down, "and here." He drew it down a little farther back on her arm. "Then, I'd do the same here." This line was at the top of the last two lines he'd drawn. "They wouldn't be deep cuts. Just enough to make you bleed." He gave her that creepy-pleasure-filled smile as a shudder wracked her body. "I'd peel the top edge down until I could grab the flap of skin. Little by little, I'd reveal the muscle beneath. Then, I'd make another cut here."

He dragged the flat of the scalpel down her arm just a little farther back and kept talking, but his voice was too distant to make out. She didn't know if he talked for a few more seconds or an hour, but her chin was lifted with a cold metal surface.

"No passing out on me," Theo chided. "Let's try a different question. How long has he been a Fed?"

"A Fed?" Melissa echoed, making Theo's frown return. She hadn't known Rick was a Fed. Did Feds have motorcycle club covers? In movies and TV shows, they wore suits. She hadn't seen Rick or Bobby in a suit since their senior prom. She remembered her mom and Jessy forcing them to stand together for a photo. That photo had been in the hallway of her parents' house before Dave took it down to hide before Theo broke in.

She missed Bobby so much. If he were alive, she knew he'd have stopped this somehow before it reached this point. Melissa couldn't explain how she knew that, but she did.

A tear finally broke free and rolled down her cheek. She wasn't going to make it out of this alive. She was sure of it. At least she'd see her brother soon, even if she never saw anyone else again.

Theo looked at her with something akin to glee as he placed the tip of the scalpel against her arm. He was finally going to start. Melissa wondered if he felt her hopelessness rise to the surface. Before he pushed the scalpel into her skin, his free hand raised up to brush her tear away with the back of his finger. Her whole body wanted to recoil from the gentle slide of his skin on hers, but her body had locked solid at the touch.

His brow furrowed deeply at her as another tear fell. The pressure from the scalpel lessened on her arm as he brushed the second tear away, too. Every fiber of her body wanted him to stop touching her, but there was nothing she could do.

Melissa couldn't stop the torrent of tears that overwhelmed her. She had tried so hard not to cry since she'd woken up in the gray room. She'd tried to hold it together while Theo promised to hurt her. But she knew there was no escaping what he was going to do. Whatever shred of decency Theo possessed made him set the scalpel aside and use both his hands to wipe away her tears. She didn't know how long it took to cry herself dry, but the tears eventually stopped though her short, choked sobs didn't. Each jerk of her body sent pain through her. Theo continued to hold her face for a moment, and she had no idea what he was waiting for. Then, in one sudden motion, he released her and stood up.

Keeping her eyes shut, Melissa tried to listen for the inevitable clink of Theo's scalpel when he picked it back up, but she couldn't hear anything over her own jagged gasps. The first cut would come out of nowhere if she couldn't pry her eyes open to see it coming. She fervently wished she'd died in the van when Theo had thrown her into it.

Melissa's head hung down, and she finally forced her eyes open. All she could see was a blurry image of Theo's feet as he stood in front of her. He didn't move. After several agonizing minutes, she looked up at him. He was staring at her like something was wrong, but she didn't know what. Then, he turned and left, shutting her in the little room all alone.

Melissa fought for control of her breathing. She needed to calm down before he came back and *started*. If she was going to die here, she had to at least figure out how she'd stop herself from answering Theo's questions. But no solutions came to her. She had no experience with any of this and movies and TV shows just said the character had *training*. Melissa had no training, and no way to get any before Theo returned. The longer Theo was gone, the more her mind raced. Calming down was a hopeless endeavor.

But as time stretched and she waited, her breathing almost returned to normal, though every sound in the hall outside the room made her jump and her body hurt. She waited and waited, but no one returned.

Just when she started to think Theo wasn't coming back, the latch on her door creaked. Her heart tried to launch itself through her brain, but it wasn't Theo returning to start on her. It was the orange cat hybrid who'd fed her. He was holding the purple set of cuffs she'd worn originally. She wanted to cry, but didn't have anything left in the tank. If they would have been tears of relief or despair eluded her. When he touched her arm, she whimpered. She heard him muttering under his breath, but she couldn't make out the words. He changed the cuffs on her wrists with as much gentleness as he could. Then, he moved around her to crouch near her leg cuffs. Melissa made a point to stay as still as possible since even the smallest movements caused by changing her cuffs were nearly unbearable. He looked up at her as he nibbled on his lower lip, revealing a long canine.

Voices slipped in through the door he'd left open. Theo's voice made her break out in a cold sweat. Another man spoke, and the feminine voice of the husky hybrid from earlier joined the conversation.

The orange cat hybrid stood up abruptly and hurried out into the hall without a word. When he shut the door behind him, the voices cut off.

Melissa hadn't heard much, but she had heard enough. They were discussing her. It was only a matter of time before they came back and finished what Theo had started.

Chapter 39

Theo

"What do you mean, you don't think we should torture her?" Allison snarled in Theo's face. Theo barely stopped himself from flinching. It had taken years to train himself not to back away from his snarling sister. "I do not keep you around to think. Just do what I tell you!"

Her snarling was worse than normal. Then again, rarely did he refuse an order. Especially not an order that had been, until a few hours ago, something he was looking forward to. After wiping away the girl's tears, Theo knew, deep down, that he shouldn't torture her. He'd tried to force himself to go back in there and start several times, but he just couldn't do it. If Allison hadn't insisted on complete radio silence, Theo would have brought the problem to her attention sooner, but there was nothing he could do about it now.

Looking past Allison, Theo saw Hughie's impassive face — stout and stoic in contrast to Allison's bared teeth and angry eyes. The hamster hybrid showed no reaction to Theo's comment or his sister's outburst. In fact, he hadn't shown a reaction to anything yet. Not the bare concrete factory basement they were in or the half-conscious girl they were holding. No reactions. That worried Theo. He didn't even know how long Hughie had been there.

"I just know it isn't a good idea. It isn't going to help any of us," Theo replied.

It was the same feeling he'd had that the dipshit's older sister wouldn't be useful and that he shouldn't do anything inside Juniper's Java. Shit, he hadn't felt great grabbing Melissa — if that was her name — two doors down from her cover coffee shop, but it was the first time she had been outside without an armed escort.

Clearly, her agency thought she was valuable enough to assign a protective detail to, which made him wonder what had tipped them off that she'd been made? And if they knew her cover had been blown, why hadn't they pulled her out? They had to want intel on who had made her. He didn't like it.

That said, Theo hadn't been willing to gainsay his sister. What she said went. He'd grabbed the girl like she'd told him. But something had changed. He couldn't believe he was fighting his sister on this. But the girl shouldn't suffer through anything. The sheer foreignness of the thought made him almost more uneasy than the thought of torturing the girl did or what Hughie might do to him as a favor to his sister.

"I don't have any issue making a woman talk," Hughie said in a deep squeak that gave Theo chills. Theo had to admit he was envious of the way Hughie could unnerve someone with just his voice. It was that scary calm that slid under your skin and poked at your nerves. Allison couldn't manage that level of intimidation without showing her anger.

"I don't either." Theo shrugged. He'd roughed up a lot of women who needed to cough up the dough for their nasty habits. He'd never had a problem with it. In fact, he'd always enjoyed it. "I just know that torturing *this* girl won't be the right move."

"You think there's another way to make her cooperate?" Allison growled.

Theo felt the blood drain from his face and was happy that he wasn't in his hybrid form at the moment because he wouldn't have been able to untuck his tail. After Allison growled in his face, something bad always happened to him growing up. Now wouldn't be any different. So, he said nothing and waited for the shoe to drop.

"Something other than torturing to get her to give up the guy she's fucking? Asking didn't work. Threatening her didn't work. She doesn't have any family in the area we can threaten, and the few friends we've identified don't go anywhere without an escort. Do you think we can offer her a lollipop and she'll sing a different tune?"

Hughie's eyes narrowed at Allison's last sentence. Like something had clicked for him.

"What type of hybrid is she?" Hughie asked with a thoughtful voice that grabbed both their immediate attention.

"She's not a hybrid," Theo said, praying Hughie would distract Allison and she'd forget about taking her anger out on him or, worse, asking Hughie to do something to him.

"And you don't make any of your product in lollipops," Hughie continued.

"But we could give her something else," Allison nodded along like it was her own idea. "Humans tend to like the classics. None of the new stuff we pedal."

Theo thought the idea might have merit. "But does drugging her against her will count as torture?" he murmured to himself.

"What is wrong with you?" Allison looked at him like he was off his rocker. His sister didn't understand that no good would come of torturing the girl.

"Human, you say." Hughie looked down the hall at the door to the girl's room. For the first time, he looked hesitant about what lay beyond. Theo's entire body tensed. "Tell me every interaction you've had with her."

"How is that going to help us pick a drug that'll make her talk?" Allison asked, more intrigued than confrontational.

If it would get around torturing the girl, then Theo was on board; he'd just have to find another target to work over to make sure he was okay. Pushing that thought away, Theo started with the dipshit's little sister and ended with him pacing in the hallway outside the girl's room after she cried.

"And you say you've never had a problem torturing anyone before?" Hughie confirmed. "This feeling you have that torturing her won't help; have you had any other similar feelings?"

"Yeah, after trying to grab the dipshit's sister." Theo was relieved that Hughie was listening to him. Allison never would have.

"Interesting." Hughie smiled down at the room the girl was in. It was a calculated smile that Theo didn't think boded well for his new stance that not everyone should be tortured. "Allison," he said, "she's like your boy, Matt. Why else would the Feds recruit her and keep guards on her?"

Theo watched his sister's face twist in thought. Swallowing hard, his mind flashed back to the first time he met Matt — back when his sister was trying to get on his good side and being the perfect doting girlfriend — and then to the next time he saw Matt; by then, Matt was at her beck and call like a broken dog. More than once, Allison had said Theo's crude approach had its place, but there were better ways. Then, she'd ruffle Matt's hair. Dismantling a person — his sister had gotten very good at that in the last decade. It had only taken her two months to go from buttering Matt up to having completely rebuilt him.

Unease swept through Theo. Normally, he didn't give two shits about who his sister messed with as long as she didn't turn her penchants on him. He was even more okay with her targeting whoever she wanted when she doubled Barres™ production facilities because the new half was dedicated to supplying the Wrappers and giving his own pastime an easy outlet. But dismantling this girl crossed the line for some reason.

Something was really wrong with him.

Allison picked up her phone and purred, "Matt, darling, I need you to come to the factory to help with something." When she hung up, she eyed the door the girl was behind with caution. "What do you think she can do?"

"Best guess from Theo's interactions? Convince people not to do something they were going to do," Hughie said.

"Through what medium?" Allison asked. She tapped her lip as she thought. Theo guessed she was replaying his interactions to see how the girl had changed him.

Panic rose in Theo's gut.

The girl had changed him. And no one was addressing it.

Completely ignoring Theo's existence, Allison continued, "Matt masks the essence of a substance through hemp work, but it requires a lot of focus on his part to put his work to our business. He's found it easier to alter perception and hide minor imperfections."

Theo itched at the bracelet Matt had made him. He disliked the idea of wearing anything that exerted an influence on him or on something around him. The bracelet was the latter, and he hadn't realized there might be people that could do the former. Or do either at all without an intermediary like Matt did.

"Hide minor imperfections?" Hughie said, studying Allison in a way that made Theo not want to be there for other reasons.

"It's good, isn't it?" Allison said. She fluttered her eyelashes and rested a hand on her chest in a coy maneuver that made Theo queasy. Her movement drew Hughie's attention to the now invisible birth-mark that used to stretch across part of her chest. She had always hated it and had sworn one day to get it removed. Whether or not Hughie remembered the birthmark wasn't something Theo wanted to know.

"So each piece you're wearing does something different?" Hughie asked, moving his bulk to get a closer look at her.

"Yup. It's the ring," she flit her hand with the hemp ring through the air, "that you're admiring at the moment."

Hughie caught Allison's hand and peered at the ring Matt had made. It was nicer looking than the bracelet on Theo's wrist. Maybe his damn bracelet itched so much because putting his skill to the drug trade didn't come naturally to Matt.

As Hughie continued to flirt and peruse the different hemp jewelry pieces on his sister's body, Theo turned away and stared at the door between him and the girl. He wasn't sure holding her in the factory was a good move. Perhaps they should relocate her? But how could they if she made them not want to do things?

"So, how do you think she works then?" Theo asked the pair behind him as a door opened to his left, and Matt walked in looking like he rolled out of bed and came directly to his handler without a thought for himself.

"Matt, darling," Allison said as Hughie continued to hold her hand, "how would we go about isolating and identifying others with skills such as yours?"

"I'm not sure, love," Matt answered in that *I-want-to-please-you* voice that grated on Theo's nerves. "I don't know if I've met anyone who had a skill like mine. You were just so gifted at recognizing it." Blech. The suck up.

"We need more reference data," Hughie declared.

"Has anyone else been in to see her?" Allison asked.

"Sammy," Theo said before padding off to find the over-sized cat hybrid. He was too anxious about figuring things out to wait for Allison to tell him to get the guard. Sometimes, she preferred him to be proactive, and other times, she wanted to order him around like a lackey. He never knew which mood she'd be in, but tonight he didn't care. He just needed answers.

The guard was easy to find; however, Theo thought he looked nervous. Hughie probably put him on edge. He was the only new element present.

"Are you feeling any different?" Allison asked Sammy when he stood before her.

Sammy's attention was on Hughie though. Theo guessed Sammy was trying to figure out why a hamster hybrid — no matter how large — was setting off his instincts and making him feel like literal prey. At least, that had been Theo's first reaction to meeting Hughie.

"What do you mean, Ms. Barre?" Sammy asked, finally focusing on Allison.

"Is there anything you'd normally do that you feel you shouldn't or wouldn't be willing to do suddenly?"

"No," he said.

"Tell us, in detail, what interactions you've had with our guest," Hughie ordered.

Sammy did as he was told and was dismissed to help the girl to the bathroom again. Theo preferred to work without those particular bodily fluids. Not that he thought he'd be doing any work that night anymore.

"So, Sammy hasn't been influenced like Theo has," Allison concluded.

"The difference being that our guest hasn't spoken to Sammy," Hughie continued.

"She didn't get a chance to speak to you when you guys picked her up, did she?" Matt worriedly asked Allison.

"She said a word or two in my presence, but never spoke directly to me. There could also be factors controlling when she can exert her skill, but how do we identify them and control someone who has influence through speaking?" Allison pondered.

Theo stood there and stared at Hughie and Allison as they discussed how to control their "guest" and turn her to their purposes. Matt stood devotedly beside Allison and added in a few tidbits here and there as if Hughie wasn't holding Allison's hand and rubbing his thumb back and forth along her wrist. The image of the three of them set the alarm bells in Theo's head into overdrive. His sister was about to do something atrocious that only he would notice.

No one was concerned that Theo was sweating in the cold basement. His panic at being influenced by their "guest" had grown exponentially as no one even seemed to think that what they were discussing was wrong.

Theo knew they couldn't torture the girl. That would not be good. But what they were discussing? Even he didn't have the stomach for it.

Chapter 40

Rick

Rick smashed the chair he'd been sitting in on top of the table. Chair legs flew through the air. Late night coffee cups slid to the sagging middle of the table. Even with the entire team in the room, no one offered him a comforting hand or word, which pounded in harder that Melissa would have. She never hesitated to reach out to him. Sure, she didn't know why he had been standoffish for most of his life, but she wouldn't let him suffer alone if she were there.

And now?

Now, she was going to have to deal with Theo *and* Hughie since Team Kappa had managed to both confirm that Hughie disembarked at a tiny airport between Placerton and Lunser and then lose him. He wasn't in the car that left the hangar his plane parked in, and he wasn't with his airplane. They had no idea where he was other than likely with Melissa by now; his plane had landed an hour ago.

Not looking at anyone, Rick sucked in a breath that felt like it was passing through a stirring straw. He repeated the action.

In his head, he heard Shawn's voice guiding him through a breath-ing meditation like he had earlier when they continued to hit dead ends in their search. Whether Shawn was talking him through an-other breathing exercise at the moment or if it was all in Rick's head didn't matter. Results mattered.

Jade had made it clear in the last couple hours that if Rick couldn't pull himself together, not only would he be benched, but his whole team would be too in order to make sure he stayed out of the way.

Feeling like he was tugging sharpened rake tines through his guts, he squashed down the fact that it was *Melissa* who was kidnapped. He needed to treat this in the same level-headed way he treated any other mission.

He focused on the cold, smooth feel of the back of the broken chair still in his hands before setting it down. Dragging his fingertips along his jeans, he paid attention to the grain of the denim while he pulled in more air — air that smelled like the old coffee his team had been using to stay alert all evening. Finally, he crossed his arms, feeling the waffle-weave of his shirt and digging his nails into his biceps, letting the pain of Dave's scratches flare. Another breath later and Rick felt as together as he had when Melissa was first grabbed — so, not great, but better than a minute ago. Despite his internal battle, he knew his outward demeanor had relaxed to a more ac-ceptable level because his team's body postures had softened from *about-to-snap-him-in-half-if-needed* to *ready-to-move-with-no-notice*.

"I'm okay," he said on a measured breath.

"Can see that, man," Dave said, standing beside Shawn and Susan at the secondary computer desk. Rick mentally noted that he wasn't okay enough to tell if Dave was being sarcastic or not. He continued to focus on his breathing as much as he could.

"Jeremy," Jade said, not taking her eyes off Rick. "What locations have you identified as possibilities?" Rick made sure not to look at his boss as she watched him; he was certain his eyes were not remotely calm.

A feeling of despair hit Rick as Jeremy ran down the list of locations at an impressive speed; Rick knew they couldn't check them all. Barres™ had a surplus of shady holdings and those were just the ones that were above board. There were other addresses held by Theo and various Wrappers where Melissa could potentially be. There were so many locations they didn't have any hope of satellite images helping if they got their hands on them.

That the Wrappers and Hughie had evaded all attempts to track them said a lot about their preparation despite their small size. Not a single dealer of theirs could be found at the moment — Neil's employee Conner had looked all over for a good two hours without finding a single person selling "candy." The Mavens had no way to test Rick's theory about the corded jewelry the Wrappers wore.

Jeremy flung his arms out to express how spread out the Wrapper-adjacent shady holdings were. His movement was so emphatic a few feathers flew off him into the air. Then, the desk phone rang. Jeremy scooped it up as if he'd reached out in preparation for just that phone call.

"That's unusual," he said into the phone.

Rick forced himself to turn toward Jeremy at a normal speed rather than an *I'm-going-to-rip-your-throat-out* speed. "Unusual" could mean anything, but when things were happening, it normally meant a lead.

"You tagged *all* the cars in the lot?" Jeremy chuckled as he tapped away at his keyboard and a cluster of tracking devices came alive. His lighthearted laugh was at odds with the atmosphere of the room.

None of the dots on the map were moving.

"There must be a jammer built into the car," Jeremy said. "Can you maintain a line of sight?"

Rick wracked his brain for who might be in a car they'd tagged. It had to be one of the Wrapper's cars, but whose? It couldn't be a dealer since they hadn't been able to locate a single one.

"You can't be spotted following the car," Jeremy said. "Try to stay with it and figure out which direction it's headed. If we have even a general direction, we can send people to possible destinations."

Rick consciously ordered himself to breathe. His team was on it. Team Kappa and Toby from Team Delta were on it. He had to let them do their jobs.

Jeremy made little "mmhmm" noises every minute or so, indicating he was getting steady updates from whoever had called in. Five minutes later, he said, "Good work, Toby," and hung up. Rick suppressed the urge to ask for clarification. Jeremy would say as soon as he had something useful.

Jade was leaning over Jeremy's desk with him as he moved around the puzzle pieces on the screens. Jade pointed to a number of locations, and Rick held himself still. He had to stay back. He couldn't crowd them. Jeremy was good. Jeremy was the best. There was a reason he was the co-leader of the team. Rick had to trust his team.

"Send Toby and Kappa to check them," Jade said.

"We should head out," Rick said. He was relieved his voice came out level rather than frantic.

"We can't waste your team by sending you all on a wild goose chase. Once we confirm they are at one of these locations, we'll make a plan and then send you." She raised her feathery brow at him in a silent threat — *if you can keep it together.*

Rick jerked his chin down once to say he could do that.

"Who was in the car?" he asked.

"Matt Helms," Jeremy said without turning to look at him.

From the data they had, neither Matt Helms nor Allison Barre ever did anything remotely sketchy. Their lack of nighttime activity was so noteworthy it was in every surveillance report Jeremy had dug up on Allison and the Wrappers. Going out after eleven was not their norm. This could be the mistake that cost the Wrappers everything.

Thirty minutes later, Toby and each member of Team Kappa had called in a negative report. No one was at any of the locations Jeremy had identified in the direction Matt had headed. And it wasn't like they just didn't see any signs of life, but rather that *no one* was there, inside or outside. They had checked every room of all seven places.

"That screen just flickered," Shawn said, pointing at a monitor with a small square of light on it.

Jeremy leaned back and looked at it.

"Is that one of ours?" Carl asked from where he lounged in the doorway to block any attempt Rick made to exit. His was a fair question. Rick didn't know what the other teams were working on besides helping his team (Rick's team was supposed to be on vacation after all). Team Delta was probably working a job since only Toby had been around lately. It could easily be a security feed from that job or it could be something Jeremy had hacked into since Melissa was kidnapped.

"Yes," Jeremy said. "It's Barres™. That's Allison's office light." Rick nodded at the information. He had helped Shawn set up the camera, not that it had any kind of decent angle into the room. People had to walk right in front of the window to be seen at all and not in great detail. The camera was too far away for anything more than circumstantial IDs.

"That was in the direction he went," Jade muttered.

"They wouldn't actually hold her at the factory, would they?" Susan asked, shocked at the audacity of the move.

"Bold," Dave said. "Bet that wasn't on your list of shitholes."

"It was not," Jeremy said. "It's at the top of my *too-legit-to-consider* list."

They all stared at the monitor. Nothing changed. No movement. No shadow. Nothing. Then, a wisp. Someone thinned by the shining light. And then, another skinny shadow.

"One of those shadows has to be Allison," Jeremy said. "It's unlikely she lets anyone in her office unsupervised, and without her, no one would turn on the lights to search the place."

Finally, a third shadow, a little wider. Then, "A fourth shadow," Rick breathed.

"A fat shadow," Carl added.

"Hughie?" Shawn asked what they were all thinking.

Jade shook her head. "Pull up the building schematics. Now, we have something to work with."

Chapter 41

Melissa

Melissa sat in silence while the cat hybrid secured her to the chair again. He'd just recuffed her legs after letting her use the bathroom for the second time. Apologetically, he'd told her to call him Sammy while helping her with her jeans and not looking at her. Of everyone she'd encountered during this nightmare, he was by far the nicest, but that didn't do much for her. He was still keeping her there for Theo to torture. If she didn't die under Theo's ministrations, Sammy was probably the one who'd clean her up and keep her alive for the next round. She didn't bother trying to say anything back to him. She just focused on trying not to give them any reason to inflict more pain than moving already did. When the voices outside her room took a decidedly weird turn, Sammy hurried out and locked her in again.

She didn't understand what the people outside her room were talking about. They thought she was controlling people with her voice? If she could do that, she'd have said, "Don't kidnap me," "Release me," "Don't torture me," or something else to get her out of her current situation. She was still their captive. How could they think she was controlling them?

Her wrists were still cuffed behind her back. Her legs were re-cuffed together. The rope made sure she didn't fall out of her chair. She couldn't do more than breathe. She was definitely not in control of anything and definitely not them. If Sammy, if that was even his real name, hadn't helped her to the bathroom and back, she'd now be soaking in her own bodily fluids. So, she had that to be thankful for. Yay her. But that didn't give her control over any of them.

Sitting in the dark, in silence, alone, her stress and exhaustion finally took their due and tried pulling her under. After jerking awake several times when the rope bit into her and stopped her from falling out of her chair, Melissa eventually found a position stable enough that she fell asleep.

Through her terror-soaked dreams, she felt a brush of cool fingers on her arms. She knew her mind was playing tricks on her when her arms tingled and swung to her sides, making her injured shoulder ache. The pressure on her calves lessened and then disappeared. Out of orneriness, her mind decided her legs were, in fact, free and tried to reposition them.

They moved.

Melissa's eyes shot open, and she saw a pair of jean-clad legs standing to the right of her chair. She wasn't wearing any leg cuffs. Wondering what she was being woken up for this time since it was too soon to be another bathroom break, she leaned her head to the side to work out the kinks from where it had hung toward her chest. Automatically, she moved her good arm and lifted a hand to rub the crick in her neck. She didn't realize her arms were actually free until her hand encountered her hair. Her heart raced. Slowly, she looked up to see whose legs were beside her.

It was the orange cat hybrid. Sammy. It was Sammy with a knife. Her eyes widened and whatever pace her heart had reached at finding her arms free was nothing to the speed it attained at that moment.

"Shh," he said as he knelt down beside her.

She already knew no one who could hear her would help. She'd cry-scream-yelled the first time they'd left her alone in the room for a while. No one had come then. No one would come now. But she wasn't going to go down easy.

"Akdwen, you slid down and got these tighter. There isn't time to work the knots," Sammy muttered. "Can you try sucking in your stomach? I don't want to catch you with the knife."

Melissa's intention to fight to her last breath wavered. She saw the cuffs lying by Sammy's feet while he brushed a finger over the rope at her waist that was tighter than she remembered him tying it after her bathroom visit. Hoping for the best, Melissa pulled her stomach in as if trying to make herself paper thin. Sammy slipped the knife between her and the rope and began sawing through the layers. When she couldn't hold it anymore, he withdrew the knife to let her breathe. She pulled her stomach in again, ignoring the pain it caused, and he went back to work. The ropes fell away.

"We don't have much time," he said. He flicked the knife closed and slid it into his pocket. "Theo'll be back in twenty minutes to guard the door during your cuff change."

"Okay," Melissa said, standing up slowly. Her limbs weren't working great even without the cuffs.

"Don't make a sound," he directed, padding silently to the door.

Melissa nodded and followed. Her body protested each step, and she did her best to move her middle and shoulder the least amount possible. She knew she would make more noise than he did; few people could match a cat in stealth. Still, she'd try.

The only sounds were their own breathing, and Melissa wondered where the voices she'd heard had gone. Sammy popped his head out the door to check if all was clear. He turned to the right and Melissa followed. The hall looked a lot like they were in a concrete basement. There were pipes running along the ceiling, but everything was a uniform gray in the dim light Sammy was carrying. Every step Melissa took sounded like a gunshot to her ears; especially because Sammy was just a rustle of fabric as he padded along in front of her.

When Sammy stopped and whirled around toward her, she froze. He pushed her against the wall with a hand over her mouth, muffling her whimper of pain, and then he flicked off his light, leaving them in complete darkness. Melissa could barely breathe with his hand over her mouth. Her mind argued that this was a lie.

He wasn't helping her. He had other plans for her.

When she heard footsteps echo faintly in the direction they had been going, reason pushed to the forefront. He was hiding them. That made a lot more sense. Forcing her panic down, she took slower breaths, and he adjusted his hand slightly, allowing her more air. The silhouette of a door in front of them appeared as a beam of light passed on the far side. Then, the footsteps faded. Sammy removed his hand while they waited for the other person to disappear. They stood there, pressed against the wall together, for a full minute before moving again.

They passed through two more hallways in a seemingly endless underground maze before Sammy pushed her into a sunken doorway and did his best to squeeze in with her. He was careful not to push her against the wall as suddenly as before and draw sounds of pain from her, which she appreciated. He turned out his light again, and they waited. She tried to breathe quietly and imagined Sammy's ears flicking their fluffy tufts around as they twitched at sounds she couldn't hear.

Her body refused to relax as they waited. Ever since Theo threw her in the van, nothing felt right. She was doing her best to trust Sammy, which normally wouldn't be hard, but now she wasn't sure about him. That she didn't trust someone who clearly seemed to be helping her was terrifying. Why couldn't she trust him? She trusted everybody....

After a minute of waiting and nothing happening, Sammy pulled her out of the small space, and they continued. Melissa focused on putting one foot in front of the other as quietly as possible while not aggravating her injuries. Every step hurt, but none more than the others, so maybe it was working.

She guessed they had been on the move for ten minutes, half the time until Theo returned. Assuming he didn't come back early. She didn't want to be here when he came back. Forcing that possibility out of her mind, she followed Sammy around another corner.

Melissa stumbled on something, and Sammy reached back and caught her before she hit the floor, pulling an agonized squeak of pain from her. By the time Sammy had her back on her own two feet, breathing hard, two shuffles of movement that even she could hear were making their way toward them from different directions. There was no time to hide.

Sammy pulled a baton off his belt as two dark figures came into view on either side of them. The one on the left made the one on the right look small, but Melissa knew they were both much larger than her. Sammy stepped in front of her, putting himself between her and the two newcomers. His hiss filled the air.

No one moved for a second.

"I'm already inclined to kill you," Rick's voice grated out from the figure on the right in a tone that made Melissa break out in a cold sweat. He didn't sound anything like the man she knew. "So just give me another reason."

Another, slightly smaller, silhouette came into view behind Rick when he finished speaking. Unlike Rick and the larger man, the third person was completely silent when he moved — like Sammy was.

Swallowing against the chill she felt coming from Rick, Melissa tried again to find the unshakeable belief that none of these people meant anyone, least of all her, harm. She didn't find that place inside her. She just felt scared.

"Just to be clear," she whispered. Her voice was so drenched in fear that she wouldn't have recognized it if it hadn't come out of her own mouth. "All four of you are trying to get me out of here, right?"

"Rizzo is getting you out of here?" Dave's voice came from behind Rick.

"Sammy?" Melissa said uncertainly.

"Same person," Carl's voice said off to the left.

"Do you know these guys?" Sammy asked, lowering his baton a little.

"Yes," Melissa said.

"She needs out of here fast." Sammy informed all three silhouettes as he clipped the baton back to his belt and pulled Melissa forward.

Melissa saw Rick lunge toward them and then jerk backwards as Dave jumped on his back.

"Damn it," Carl snapped. "Don't touch her, Rizzo."

Rizzo dropped her hand like she'd burned him. Before her eyes, Rick and Dave toppled backward. The grunt Dave made as Rick's weight smashed him to the ground echoed off the concrete and mixed with the noises of their continued scuffle on the ground.

"Melissa, try to calm him the fuck down before he hurts D more than he did earlier," Carl directed.

Not sure approaching Rick was the smartest thing to do, Melissa moved toward the two men rolling on the ground anyway. Either Carl or Sammy shined a light on the pair, and Melissa saw Dave had a choke hold around Rick's neck. Rick looked like he was going to tear someone to shreds, but his movements were fading.

Fighting through the pain, Melissa bent down and put her hand over one of Rick's where it dug into Dave's arm. Entwining her fingers with Rick's, she pulled his hand away, and it came without resistance. His warm fingers calmed Melissa a little. Dave's grip on Rick lessened, but Melissa could tell he was ready to reengage if Rick proved to be a liability.

"I want to get out of here," Melissa told Rick. "Theo will be back any second and know I'm gone."

"Shit," Sammy muttered behind her. "Shouldn't have left the cuffs behind."

"Fingerprint locks?" Carl asked.

"I'd say come with us," Dave said from beneath Rick, "but we can't guarantee he won't kill you for touching her."

"I don't want you to kill someone who's saving me," Melissa said in shock. "Please, just get me out of here."

"Let's move out," Rick rasped.

Carl led the way. Rick followed, never letting go of her hand. Behind her was Sammy, closely followed by Dave. It took another five minutes, but then they were outside in an alley. There was a van there that looked a whole lot like the one she'd been kidnapped in earlier.

Melissa froze at the sight of it.

"Come on, Mel," Rick said, pulling her a step closer.

"I'm not getting in that," she said, trying to tug her hand from Rick's, but the motion shot pain into her core.

"We need to get out of here. Couldn't bring my bike for this."

"I'm not being thrown in a van again." Bile choked her as she flashed back to the van from earlier.

"No one is throwing you. Come on," he coaxed.

Melissa was shaking by the time they reached the side of the van. The sliding door was open, and she could see the interior included seats and looked nice. She focused on the differences and tried to wrap her head around getting inside. It wasn't stripped bare like the last van. There was a leather bench with excessive amounts of legroom that looked like it belonged in a luxury car. Against her instincts, she climbed into the car with Rick. He pulled her onto his lap and held her. In the front seat was a fluffy white dog hybrid she'd never seen before.

"She needs someone to look at her shoulder," Sammy whispered from the back of the van where Melissa could see him crouched with Carl.

Dave made an unhappy noise from the front passenger seat, and Rick's hold on her loosened a little to make sure he wasn't hurting her. As if synchronized in advance, the fluffy dog hybrid climbed out of the driver's seat and into the back with them, kneeling in the extra legroom near her and Rick while Dave moved over to the driver's seat and started driving them away. No one said anything to coordinate the change of drivers, which reminded Melissa they had been doing this type of stuff since before her brother died.

"M knows what he's doing," Rick said. Melissa wasn't reassured that "M" knew what he was doing since Rick's statement sounded more like he was trying to convince himself than her.

Chapter 42

Rick

It took everything in Rick's power to let Shawn check Melissa over. She needed to be looked at. He needed to know if they should be driving straight to a hospital or not.

Shawn was a trained field medic. He'd learned all the necessary skills to give Melissa a decent once-over when he was in the navy. Rick just needed to let Shawn do what he'd been trained to do. At least, that's what he kept telling himself over and over.

He watched Shawn pull a pair of latex gloves over his fur, which he knew Shawn hated doing. Normally, if Shawn needed to do a med check on a team member while in his hybrid form, he skipped the gloves. Unless it was Rick. And now, Melissa. He didn't want to actually touch either of their skin if he could help it. But with Rizzo in the back, he couldn't give the maybe-ok guard another face to remember.

Shawn started with asking Melissa if she'd hit her head on anything. When she answered that she had hit it a few times on the floor of the van when she was first kidnapped, the desire to make sure that no one had to experience that again pulsed through Rick. Shawn checked her eyes but announced her concussion-free. When his hands probed Melissa's neck, Rick inhaled sharply and forced himself to stay still since she didn't seem to be in pain from that. His teammate's hands on her neck was even more upsetting than on her face.

"Now, I'm going to have to move your arm to see how bad your shoulder is," Shawn said to Melissa, but did it while staring Rick in the eye.

Rick nodded and repeated the reminder over and over in his head that Shawn was helping. That this was what Melissa needed. Her agonized whimpers as Shawn moved her arm were almost too much to bear.

"Deep breaths," Carl said from behind him. "In. Out."

Following Carl's rhythmic in and outs, Rick listened closely to Melissa explain how her shoulder had been hurt. It was just from being thrown in the van and held immobile in handcuffs, rather than something done specifically to inflict pain. Rick could tell that Shawn was taking the utmost care with her. He was doing his best to be precise in his questioning, trying to invite Melissa to say the least amount possible in her answers. Rick knew he shouldn't be touching her since she couldn't choose what to say because of their contact, but he couldn't release her to even let her sit in her own seat. Not that she seemed like she wanted to, which was its own form of relief.

"I'm going to lift up your shirt and check your stomach and ribs," Shawn informed Melissa, again making sure to wait till Rick nodded. When he got a good look at Melissa's bruised midsection, Shawn's face scrunched up, and Rick wanted to kill someone. He just didn't know if it was Dave, Theo, Hughie, or the cat hybrid in back with Carl.

It took several minutes of conversation and gentle prodding, for Shawn to get a full picture of Melissa's rib injuries. Without being able to stop herself, Melissa went into significant detail about what pain she'd experienced from Dave saving her — during which Dave shot Rick several apprehensive looks in the rearview mirror — and what they felt like now after having Theo's shoulder rammed into them and being thrown in the van. By the time Shawn felt comfortable saying a few ribs were cracked but that they weren't life-threatening, Rick knew he hadn't punched Dave nearly as hard as he should have earlier and that he would kill Theo on sight if the opportunity arose.

He had been so close to losing Melissa. Rick squeezed his eyes shut and buried his face in her neck, focusing on breathing her in. She was safe now. She was in his arms again. It was going to be alright. He stayed like that until Shawn finished the rest of the checkup, only loosening his grip on her to let his friend — he had to remind himself several times that Shawn was his friend and was helping — set Melissa up with a sling to immobilize her shoulder.

When Dave stopped the van, Rick saw that they weren't back at Trigg's Triad where they had planned on taking Melissa. They were in a suburban neighborhood in front of a house with a for sale sign.

Then, Rick remembered Rizzo in back.

They couldn't take him any place that made a clear link between them and the Mavens' Motorcycle Club. Using an empty house for a quick meeting was something they tried not to do, but sometimes it was unavoidable. Especially when they weren't on a government sponsored job with all sorts of resources at hand.

They all got out of the van, and Dave drove off to park it elsewhere for the moment — a mysterious van parked outside an empty house could easily draw attention at 1:30 a.m.. Carl and Shawn glanced at Rick and back at the front door. He shook his head. He couldn't let go of Melissa yet. While she'd answered all of Shawn's questions, she hadn't once looked out the window. Even outside of the van, she wasn't taking in her surroundings. Not paying attention was a quick way to die in Rick's book. He needed to stay with her and keep her safe. Carl knelt down, and after several long minutes, he managed to pick the lock and let them all in.

The house was beautifully staged for its upcoming open house, but Rick couldn't have cared less as he led Melissa into the living room near the back of the house. He pulled her down onto the gray couch while Shawn drew the curtains shut and Carl ordered Rizzo to sit on a stool he'd grabbed from the bar behind the couch. Then they waited.

Twenty minutes later, Jade arrived.

She took in the scene of Rick and Melissa cuddled together on the couch. Rick didn't know what she thought, but he was mostly just appreciating the fact that Melissa's breathing was normal and she'd started looking around. He was sure that Jade noted that Shawn and Carl stood on either side of the couch, guarding against him rather than worrying about Rizzo. Dave was all that stood between Rizzo and the sliding glass door that could be his escape. Rick was self-aware enough to acknowledge that it was a good strategic choice on their parts. He was much more volatile right then than Rizzo.

When Dave had taken him down back at the factory, Melissa had made it clear that killing people for touching her was unacceptable. Rick wasn't certain, but he might have gained some control since then. He hadn't liked Shawn touching her, but he'd let it happen. So, either Melissa telling him she didn't want him to act that way or her being within arm's reach was helping. He suspected it was the latter, but hoped the former might have a more long-term effect. He needed it to have a long-term effect. Rick squeezed his eyes shut to stop from wondering what it would mean if he kept trending downward.

"R," Jade said, not turning to look at him. In mixed company, the rule was that they all defaulted to their first initial, except for Shawn because Susan had been on the team longer. Shawn was M for his last name, Muller. While Jade and Jeremy could have been an issue, Jade just went by B for Boss or Boss Bitch if people were annoyed with her.

"Yeah?"

Jade twisted her head all the way around to look at him in the unsettling way some bird hybrids could. Her feathery brow scrunched together, and she widened her eyes as if to say, "heelllo." She jerked the back of her head at Sammy on the stool, and Rick realized what she wanted. She wanted him to do his job. Without Melissa there, he would have been ready to go. Knowing Melissa was not back to herself yet, he didn't want to leave her side. And he really didn't want to show her what his touch did without having talked to her about it first.

"Not sure that's a good idea," Rick mumbled.

"Why is that?"

"I had to put R in a choke hold to stop him from killing Rizzo," Dave said from his position behind the cat hybrid in question. Jumping on him from behind had been to Dave's advantage; Rick had been so focused on getting his hands on Rizzo that he hadn't been prepared to fend off his own teammate.

"For touching Melissa," Carl clarified.

Jade didn't say anything, and Shawn just shook his head at the news from where he stood to the right of the couch.

"My chances of survival are better here," Rizzo said quietly. "I'm not sure Theo would have done me in, but I wouldn't put it past Allison or Hughie. I crept back into the hall after they questioned me about their 'guest,'" he nodded toward Melissa, "in order to listen to what they were talking about doing to her." He shifted on the stool like the idea of what they had said rubbed his fur the wrong way. Rick's entire body tensed at the images his imagination conjured up. Melissa shook at his side.

"Maybe we could skip the details… for the moment," Rick suggested.

Jade twisted her head around again and looked at Melissa, who had started to visibly shake, before giving a permissive nod to Rizzo that he could omit the nitty-gritty details while Melissa was there.

"Can you control yourself, R?" Jade asked.

There was no way out of it. They needed to know that what Rizzo told them was the absolute truth, or the absolute truth as he saw it. And Melissa would be safer if they knew everything Rizzo knew.

"Yeah, B," Rick muttered. He stood up, and Melissa's hand convulsed tighter around his for a second. He squeezed back, before leaning down to brush a kiss on the back of her hand. "I'll be right back," he promised, sliding his hand out of hers for the first time since she grabbed it on the dirty basement floor. Rizzo looked at him with apprehension, which Rick didn't blame him for. Rizzo was as big as he was, but Rick was the one who had been willing to kill him not an hour earlier.

Stopping in front of Rizzo, Rick held out his hand as if to shake. Tentatively, Rizzo put his hand in Rick's. Rick gave him a slow handshake that puzzled the cat hybrid. Making sure to stay in solid contact with the pads of Rizzo's hand, Rick made a show of frowning and turning Rizzo's hand over like something had caught his attention. After a few minutes of focused "analysis," Rick held his hands out for Rizzo's other hand and looked it over just as carefully. Rick let out a beleaguered sigh and shook his head.

"I'm sorry I went berserk," Rick said. "Your hands are perfectly normal, and there's no reason I should have reacted like that to you touching Melissa." He looked Rizzo in the eyes and waited, still holding onto his hand.

"Thanks for the apology?" Rizzo said.

Rick nodded, released Rizzo's hand, and walked back over to a perplexed Melissa on the couch. Jade had twenty minutes to pull the truth out of Rizzo before they'd have to connive another reason for Rick to touch him for an extended period of time without hinting at what was really happening.

Jade proceeded to ask Rizzo question after question after confirming he had no idea who they were.

As his story unrolled, it turned out he was just a guard. He'd started out guarding Barres™ as any security guard might, but after a while he was put in charge of guarding certain parts of the factory that looked like any other except for the fact that they had guards 24/7.

When he overheard certain conversations that weren't on the up and up, he didn't react and didn't talk. Eventually, he knew what he was guarding — drugs. Drugs that looked like candy down to the literal wrappers. Barres™ had always paid well, but that was when he knew why.

He also started getting a few hours that were off the books. Those were normally making sure nothing happened to someone testing a drug for Theo.

"I worked as a guard," Rizzo said firmly. "Not a kidnapper. Never have I kept anyone anywhere against their will. I'm not that kind of person."

Melissa squeezed Rick's hand at that comment and nodded. Rizzo was apparently in her good graces. Rick took that in and immediately noticed he wasn't as angry at Rizzo as he was before.

"Once you found out Melissa wasn't there of her own free will, what did you learn?" Jade continued.

"At first, they wanted some sort of information from her," he said.

Melissa grimaced beside Rick at the reference, and he transferred her hand to his left so he could wrap his right arm around her.

"But I don't know what," Rizzo admitted.

"Melissa?" Jade asked, speaking to Melissa for the first time.

Instantly, Rick's gut clenched. He had not thought this through. After touching Rizzo, he'd gone back to Melissa's side and continued holding her hand. Skin to skin. Jade could ask Melissa anything she wanted, and Melissa would answer. At this point, if he stopped touching her, she'd speak truthfully for the next two hours easy.

"They wanted to know who I worked for," Melissa said, shaking her head. "It didn't matter that I own a coffee shop and work for myself. Th-Theo didn't believe me. He kept saying it was my cover. But pretty quickly, he switched to asking about," Melissa licked her lips as she darted her eyes at Rick, "R."

Jade nodded encouragingly. That nod told Rick that Jade was impressed by Melissa's quick thinking under his influence. The whole team was. She had accepted the initialized names as a truth, and it wouldn't cause her issues in discreetly answering questions.

"He wanted me to help lure him into a trap, which would have been significantly easier if he hadn't destroyed my phone with a hammer to disable whatever extra tracking device you put in my phone."

"I didn't put a tracking device in your phone," Rick said. He looked at the others. "Did J?"

"Not from our supplies," Jade answered, which wasn't a yes or a no. She turned back to Rizzo. "What changed to make them want something else from her?"

"Theo was convinced that torturing her wasn't a good idea. He apparently enjoys it a lot and is quite good at it." Melissa shuddered next to Rick, and he knew that whatever she had experienced, while not necessarily physical torture, had been torture all the same; though she'd clearly managed to touch Theo and save herself from worse. "But with his sudden change of heart, they decided she was magic or something."

"They? Be specific."

"Hughie Minfried, Allison Barre, and Matt Helms all believed she was magic. Theo didn't participate in what I overheard, other to say something about their suggestions not being good."

"What 'magic' did they think she could do?" Jade used air quotes to make the idea sound absurd.

"Convince people not to do things. They wanted to find a way to control her and make her do that for them. That was when the conversations went sideways. There was a lot of discussion about how Allison *tamed* Matt. It sounded a lot more like she broke him and rebuilt him how she wanted—" Rizzo said.

"That's all for now," Jade cut him off before he could say what was done to Matt or what they were discussing doing to Melissa.

Dave and Shawn immediately left with Rizzo since he wasn't exactly able to stop himself from continuing to answer Jade's last question; he clearly felt that what "taming" entailed was part of the response. Given how on edge the mere thought of any torture of Melissa made Rick, he felt a smidgen of relief that he wouldn't have to suffer right then through the descriptions of what they wanted to do to Melissa. The fact that the Maine coon hybrid was disturbed by the images was enough of an indication of how badly things could have gone for Melissa.

Rick knew they would stash the cat in a safe house and discreetly record anything else he said. Rick would likely be called in during the next few weeks to help get each excruciating detail Rizzo had, but there was a chance he wouldn't have to listen. When the time came, Rizzo would be pressured to officially testify against the Wrappers.

With Rizzo gone, it was time to head out. Carl put the stool back by the bar and fluffed the couch a little after Rick and Melissa stood up. Jade flicked the lights out, and Carl reopened the curtains. It was as if they hadn't ever been there.

Rick, Melissa, and Carl climbed into Jade's SUV to relocate to Trigg's Triad and debrief Melissa in the bar, as per the original plan. They drove in silence, and while Rick didn't reach for Melissa's hand in order to give her a chance of controlling what she said coming up, she reached for his and interlaced their fingers. Without having a moment alone with Melissa, Rick couldn't explain why she shouldn't do that when he liked that she *did* do it. That needed to be a private conversation.

Jade parked in the back garage next to Rick's motorcycle. Melissa might have known Trigg's Triad was the Mavens' hangout, but he'd honestly never talked about it with her, and he doubted Bobby had either. Bobby wouldn't have wanted his little sister in a bar. Period. That said, a quick Internet search would bring up the public faces of the Mavens and the garage and bar, so she had to know about it.

Despite what had to have been beyond an exhausting day, Melissa looked around the garage with tired interest, which soothed Rick to no end. He tried to see the garage through Melissa's eyes.

Given that it was between three and four in the morning, it was dark except for the single light overhead that guided them to the bar. Melissa would be able to see shadows of tools along the wall and of the miscellaneous motorcycle parts that littered the work-table below. A little easier to see were the four bikes in front of that which stood in various stages of dissection. Six motorcycles that were available to any Maven without an assigned bike hid the trapdoor on the other side of the garage that opened to a ramp to the lower-level where they kept cars and bikes of all types for different jobs.

Rick tugged on Melissa's hand when she would have lingered to take in the garage. They followed Jade into the bar proper, which had already been closed and wiped down for an hour or more. Jade flicked the lights on as she walked in.

The mirrored walls made the bar look three times its size. The black octagon tables around the edges sat partially encased in rounded, tufted red vinyl booths. Seemingly at the center of the room, but really along a wall of mirrors, was the black wooden bar counter that looked like an octagon when you included its reflection. Any wall that wasn't made of mirrors was white diamond tile with metallic gold and silver grout. What should have been jarring but fit when you filled the bar with hybrids were the plants; they emerged from every nook and cranny, making the whole place look like a modernized retro jungle bar.

Jade strolled behind the counter looking just as at home in her bar as in any of the ops centers upstairs. Without asking orders, she poured Rick a nice scotch, Carl a seal whiskey, and a green grasshopper martini for herself. She gave Melissa a glass of water. They all took a sip, and Rick waited to see what Jade would do.

When one of the TVs hidden among the plants flashed on, Melissa spilled half of her water on herself.

"Sorry, Melissa," Jeremy's over-sized face said.

"Update," Jade said.

"Shawn's staying with Rizzo until someone from Team Kappa can relieve him, but Dave headed to give Susan backup. There's been a lot of movement along the perimeter of the factory since we left. They figured out Melissa and Rizzo were gone two minutes after I restored their security cameras to live feeds." Jeremy's eyes flicked back to Melissa. "Nice to have you back."

"Anything to add to what we know so far?" Jade asked Melissa.

Melissa stopped wiping at her wet shirt and rubbed her forehead. For comfort, Rick gave her leg a squeeze, and she leaned her good shoulder against him.

"Mostly the details about what Theo was promising to do to make me cooperate." Melissa's head pivoted toward Rick when all his muscles locked.

"Perhaps we should do this without Rick here," Jade said in a quiet tone that made it clear she was ready to have Carl remove him. That was why Carl had stayed, which Rick had already subconsciously realized.

"I'm fine." Rick drank the rest of his scotch in one gulp and stared at his empty cup. "I'm fine," he repeated. He wasn't, but there was no way he was leaving Melissa alone again. And Jade wasn't known for her empathy, so he needed to be there. He wouldn't leave her at Jade's mercy. His boss always focused on the big picture, and he didn't like the idea of Melissa being part of her big picture.

"It wasn't anything you don't hear about or see in movies," Melissa said, shaking her head and looking back at Jade. Rick's cup filled in front of him; clearly Jade thought it better he drink more. He took another sip. "It's just different when it's on screen. It's removed, you know? Having him describe it in... in detail was different."

Beside him, Melissa shuddered, and Rick squeezed his cup as hard as he could.

"But he didn't do anything to you?" Jade asked.

"I started crying when he said he was going to start. I'd tried so hard not to, but I couldn't help it. Instead of following through with his threats, he wiped away my tears and then left."

"Was that his first time touching you?"

Rick's breath froze in his chest at Jade's question. He couldn't remember if he told her Melissa didn't know what she could do.

"No." Melissa shook her head. "He's the one who originally grabbed and cuffed me in the van. He's possibly the one who carried me to the room I was locked in, but I was wearing a hood before the person picked me up, so I'm not sure."

"Skin," Jade said. "I'm asking if that was the first time you made skin contact with him. Beside when he first tried to grab the Nolan girl."

Rick forced himself to breathe in. He had to remind himself that it was a reasonable question and one they needed the answer to.

"It might have been," Melissa said, trying to remember. "I wasn't conscious the whole time, but I think it was. What's that have to do with anything?"

"Maybe we should finish this another time?" Rick asked as the mere thought of Melissa hooded or unconscious with Theo and Hughie made him feel ill. When Jade and Melissa looked at him — impatience and confusion on their faces, respectively — he knew his voice had been too hopeful and pleading rather than concerned.

"Rick?" Melissa asked in the lingering silence.

He knew he should tell her. It was the right thing to do. His tongue flicked out and wet his lips, and he rubbed his clammy hands on his jeans. He searched for the words.

"Jade?" Melissa asked when Rick didn't speak.

Rick knew his eyes showed pure panic. It wasn't a feeling he'd experienced often in his life, at least not before the last two weeks with Melissa. Apprehension-filled panic, that was becoming a little more normal. He felt it every time he put himself out there and let himself be closer to Melissa than Bobby would have liked. Being with Melissa felt right, but being close to another person was so far outside of his comfort zone. Despite that, he just really wanted to be a good match for her. He didn't want this to end.

"Hughie and Allison were wrong about you," Jade said, tearing her eyes away from Rick's meltdown to look at Melissa. "Your voice had nothing to do with Theo deciding not to torture you. Touching your skin, on the other hand, did."

"My skin?"

"It's a *touch talent*." The words fell from Rick's lips in such a rush that he wasn't sure anyone had understood them. "It's a *touch talent*," he repeated more slowly. "Or an ability you exert on others when you touch them."

Melissa's breathing stopped completely.

"We both have it," Rick said.

"This is something you knew about?" Melissa asked. Disbelief rang through her voice, and she sucked in air.

"I found out when I was eleven."

"That's when you all started eschewing contact." Melissa's eyes widened, and then she winced, but Rick hadn't seen what caused her pain. Given her injuries, simply breathing sharply probably hurt. "That's when you found out about me? When I was eight?"

"No Mel, just me," Rick said quickly.

"When did you find out about me?"

Rick swallowed. "Your senior year."

"Of college?"

"Of high school."

"That's almost a decade ago." Melissa's voice came out in a calm, detached tone that alarmed Rick. He'd never heard her speak like that. There was a finality in her tone that churned his gut. "What do we do?" Her question rang hollow in the air.

"We don't do the same things," he said, searching her face and only finding blankness. "When you touch people, you make them want to be the best they can be, to do the right thing, to be good."

Jade spoke in a carefully measured tone he'd heard her use a few times in the field when someone they rescued was in acute medical shock: "We need to do tests to know exactly how your ability works because it isn't a switch you flip in people, and there might not be a time limit to the effects like Rick's." Jade paused when Melissa didn't say anything.

Rick reached out and grabbed Melissa's hand. Her hand didn't grab him back. This was too much too fast, but Rick didn't know how to stop this from happening.

Slowly, Melissa pulled her hand back into her lap, and her shoulders hunched forward like she was trying to make herself smaller.

"Do you want to know what Rick's touch does?" Jade asked.

Rick didn't bother looking at Jade to see what she was playing at; he'd been careful not to ask Melissa anything to force the direction of what she shared. He was too concerned about Melissa to think about Jade making him face this right now.

"Yes," Melissa whispered.

He didn't know if she'd wanted to answer or not, but since she had, he'd tell her.

"My touch makes people tell the truth if they speak," he said before the opportunity could slip away. He watched Melissa's eyes narrow and then widen into rapid blinks as what he said sunk in. Then, her eyes flit back and forth as if remembering something. Many somethings. He wondered again what she might have said without realizing she had no control over what she shared.

"It lasts for twice as long as I touched the person, unless my blood touches their skin, then it's four times as long. We don't know how the time limit changes if I touch people for an extended period of time or if it changes during, um," Rick looked at the ground and then back up at Melissa, "during intimate contact like yours does. We think that's what made some of your boyfriends... protective." Rick muttered the last word.

Melissa didn't say anything.

Rick reached out to rub her arm, but she jerked away from him so hard that she fell off the stool. A pained noise burst from her lips upon her impact with the ground. Tears were streaming down her face as she looked at him.

He reached to help her up, and she scooted away with her lips pressed tightly together. Rick yanked his hand back. He thought he might be sick. Melissa had learned the truth about what he could do, and she was rejecting him because of it. She sat on the ground sobbing and moving away from anyone who came near her until she was scrunched up under one of the octagonal tables.

Chapter 43

Melissa

"Hey," Susan said.

Looking up at her, Melissa vaguely noted that Susan looked different with her golden horse ears poking up through her platinum blond braids. Melissa, however, didn't move from her spot on the tiled floor. Her entire body ached; moving would make it worse. Her face felt stiff from the tears that had dried before she'd fallen asleep.

Someone, she didn't remember who, had slid her a pillow and a blanket when she'd refused to come out from under the table. Finding out that not only had Rick been keeping secrets from her but also that she was the reason his team had become skittish around him had shaken her. *She* was changing Rick just by touching him. She had to make sure he didn't keep touching her or her him. Melissa felt like a husk, lying on the floor. Empty and forlorn.

"A spare jacket and the gloves Rick had made for you." Susan held out the skin covering items as if they were a peace offering. Melissa slowly pushed herself up with her uninjured right arm. Careful not to touch Susan, she reached out and took the gloves.

Moving to put them on, Melissa rotated her slinged arm out from her body despite the pain. She couldn't let anyone help her and risk physical contact. The gloves were soft, supple leather biker gloves that fit like a second skin. They matched the exact shade of her jacket that was hanging in her coffee shop, which made the gloves look like she'd had them for years rather than a few seconds. She wondered when Rick had them made for her; it had to be before they'd slept together, or they wouldn't be ready so soon.

"Fur, feathers, and hair help mitigate the effect," Susan said. She looked concerned but didn't offer to help, which Melissa was both relieved and hurt by. "Whiskers are particularly susceptible, so keep that in mind."

Still hunched under the table, Melissa took the jacket from Susan and swung it over her shoulders in a movement that caused stabbing pain in her chest. Fighting to breathe, she remembered M — the fluffy white dog hybrid — had said she had some cracked ribs, but those took time to heal; there wasn't anything they could do for them. Melissa didn't bother trying to maneuver her injured shoulder into the jacket after that. Luckily, the jacket was larger than her normal one. She didn't know which Maven it belonged to, but she'd get it back to them somehow.

"Look at the bright side," Susan said when Melissa stayed silent, "your touch has mostly good effects on people. You turned an entire neighborhood around."

Jaw hanging open, Melissa stared at Susan.

"From what we've dug up, your regulars should have knifed you in the alley your first month open. Instead, they stopped all their criminal activities, fixed up the area, and now volunteer around the city."

"You think that was all because of me?" Melissa's throat was raw from everything that had happened in the past twenty-four hours.

"There isn't any other explanation," Jade's voice said.

Melissa scooted forward enough to stick her head out from underneath the table and saw Jade wiping down a glass that already shined. Much like the night before, Jade was wearing a dark, plunging vest that showed off her short, white plumage.

Melissa couldn't make out her expression, which probably meant she had it purposefully blank. Last night, Jade's face had been significantly more expressive than Melissa was used to encountering in a bird hybrid. Melissa guessed the dark, wide eyes that watched her didn't miss much. It was odd that her hands on the glass were scaled and had sharp talons; Melissa couldn't remember meeting a bird hybrid whose hands were scaled like their feet instead of feathered like their arm-wings.

"I made a few discreet inquiries," Jade continued. "City planners are fascinated with how the area turned around with no city support. No one has tied it to the exact time of your coffee shop opening, and it's better if they don't, but given how tactile you are, it's the only explanation."

Shuffling the rest of the way out from under the table, Melissa slowly stood up. She looked around and saw it was just the three of them. Susan walked over to the bar and returned with a glass of water and two pills. Melissa let Susan drop the painkillers into her hand before carefully taking the glass without making physical contact, even though she had the new gloves on. She didn't know exactly how careful she needed to be.

"Carl helped Rick upstairs to rest," Susan replied to Melissa's unasked question. "Do you want me to go get him?"

Melissa shook her head no, saying quietly, "I don't think that's a good idea." She downed the pills with a muffled groan of pain. Holding her breath before swallowing had been a bad idea.

Susan and Jade exchanged a look. It was clear they'd just had a conversation through a glance, possibly confirming something they'd discussed. Something that involved her. Melissa pushed down her growing unease.

"I know he'd like to see you," Susan said.

Melissa didn't doubt it. Rick had become incredibly protective as soon as they'd determined they were going to explore a relationship and slept together.

She knew she hadn't touched Rick over the years more than say Kate, but he had said intimacy affected her touch. He had been scaring his friends after one night. That was a lot more protective aggression than any of her ex-boyfriends had shown as far as she knew. Maybe the guys she'd broken up with had said things to her friends she didn't know about. She didn't think the girls would hide that from her, but Greg and Ted might have if she'd already sent the guy packing.

Melissa wrapped her good arm around her middle and slinged arm.

"Can I just go home?"

"Rick can take you." Susan's voice sounded hopeful, but Melissa couldn't do it. She shook her head.

"I'll take you," Jade said. Susan's head whipped around, her eyes bugging out as she looked at her boss, which told Melissa it wasn't a normal offer. "I remember the way. Maybe Jessy will be home." Amusement filled her voice with the last comment.

"Jessy?" Susan asked.

"Rick's mom?" Melissa said, just as puzzled.

"Wait, how do you know Rick's mom?" Susan asked. Melissa couldn't tell if she was just confused, alarmed, or deeply curious.

"She came over when Melissa's parents became overwrought at the news of Bobby." To Melissa, she added, "I doubt your parents noticed I stuck around for a while and chatted with Jessy in the kitchen. I've given bad news to families before, but none took it as badly as your folks."

Melissa tilted her head to the side in acknowledgment. Her parents still couldn't handle the news. They'd gotten new jobs and left more or less permanently without telling her.

She glanced at the clock on the wall. Assuming it was Saturday now and the afternoon, she'd missed her rescheduled call with her parents. She hadn't been ready to talk to them on Wednesday after what Rick had shared about them leaving and lying to her. She was even less ready now after being kidnapped and learning she and Rick had *touch talents*.

"I think you're supposed to follow her," Susan whispered.

Melissa looked up from her thoughts and saw Jade was halfway down the hall they had passed through that morning; though, it felt like several days ago. Susan stepped toward Melissa for a hug, but Melissa flinched away. Susan's eyebrows drew together and raised in concern, but Melissa just moved around her.

Her own actions made her remember all the times she had seen Rick give people more room than necessary when moving past them — herself included. Was that how she needed to live now? Shunning touch? She couldn't remember a day that she hadn't at least given a friend a hand squeeze.

Jade was waiting for her at the end of the hall in front of the door to the garage with one brow raised in what Melissa guessed was a mischievous look. It was hard to tell with the feathers on an unfamiliar face, even if her face was expressive. Instead of going out the door that led to the garage, Jade pulled a key from her elegant trouser pocket and unlocked a door to the left. A dark staircase opened up like a black hole into the bowels of oblivion. Jade started down it.

After glancing back down the hall and seeing Susan in the bar looking mildly panicked, Melissa wrapped her borrowed jacket tighter around herself and followed Jade.

The door slammed shut behind them, and the locks ground back into place. Melissa could only go down into the darkness now. With her free hand on the wall, she dropped her foot down one step and then another. Repeating the process in the pitch black. The wall curved after a few steps. Around the curve, light filtered up enough for Melissa to see where to place her feet.

Before her, an underground garage opened up. There were rows of vehicles. A few looked normal, like the van she'd been rescued with and Jade's SUV from earlier, but most weren't things you saw every day on the road. There was literally a tank the size of a normal car. Next to the mini-tank, everything paled in comparison, except for the car Jade was climbing into. The sleek black oval looked like a drop of ink. Melissa had only seen the Inkscape in a few ads. She didn't know if it slid, hovered, or rolled, but she did know it was the newest thing.

Afraid to touch it, Melissa walked around to the passenger side and barely managed to stifle a gasp that would have hurt her ribs when the door dissolved into the body of the car to let her climb in. The interior had that new car smell.

After she buckled her ink black seatbelt, which thankfully went over her good shoulder, the velvety seat shifted to better fit her body in an unsettling, fluid motion. Jade directed the car forward with her hand on what looked like a joystick. The Inkscape emitted a faint hum as it moved. A ramp ahead of them opened and whatever Jade did made the Inkscape shoot up it and out of the garage at a heart stopping speed.

"You've held up through this better than most," Jade said after several minutes of silent driving. "Therefore, I've decided to like you."

"Thanks," Melissa said. Her voice wobbled. She had the distinct impression Jade liking her was either really good or really bad.

"That means I'm trusting you."

Melissa didn't know what to say, but Jade didn't need a response.

"Everything you just saw isn't to be repeated. Someone from Team Gamma will talk with you before the police come and interview you so you know what you can share and what you can't."

"Team Gamma?" Melissa asked.

"That's Rick's team. Team Delta is all dog hybrids — you know, D for dog and all; Team Kappa has the cat hybrids; and Gamma is the mixed group. There's also Team Pi Rho who is more or less the public face of the Mavens."

"Pi Rho, like PR? Public Relations?" She'd caught on to the simplistic naming system.

"Yup."

"Then shouldn't someone from the public relations team come talk to me instead?" Melissa didn't know if she wanted someone she didn't know to come instead of one of Rick's friends. But for all she knew, they were all Rick's friends.

"They're the fake public relations — the motorcycle club face," Jade shrugged, dismissing the misnomer, and moved on. "Now, you shouldn't say anything about what your touch does to anyone, and it goes without saying that you can't share what Rick's does. You can talk about any or all of these things with anyone on Team Gamma, but no one else."

"What about my friends?" Melissa asked while she wondered why she couldn't talk to the other "teams." Did they not know about Rick?

"I recommend waiting to tell them until you know how your touch works, and then you'll know what you're comfortable sharing about yourself."

Melissa nodded and looked out the window. She should be uncomfortable with how Jade was weaving in and out of slower vehicles, but she was too numb from everything to worry about her driving. The hum of the vehicle hadn't increased as they'd picked up speed but was just loud enough to not make it feel silent as they drove. Jade let her stare off into space without talking until the edges of Granberg rose around them.

"Do you have any questions before I drop you off?" Jade asked.

"This is rude," Melissa said while thinking about the house she was going back to, "but how did my parents not notice you? I assume you know they both get rather giddy about unusual hybrids, and you are clearly unusual. The only thing they've been able to handle since Bobby died has been work, and you would've overlapped nicely into that distraction area when they needed it."

"Ah, I'm glad you brought that up. What's going to happen, you aren't even going to mention to Rick. I like to keep my aura of mystery strong."

"But if he asks me...?" She couldn't lie to him. Maybe she should be more bothered by that, but she was used to telling Rick the truth. She couldn't remember a time when she'd wanted to lie to him.

"One, I doubt he'd think to ask, but two, if he asks after touching you, just don't speak like you did earlier today."

"Okay...." Melissa said slowly. She hadn't realized that was what Rick had meant when he said "if they speak," but it made sense. He couldn't make her tell the truth if she didn't voluntarily try to say something. She could just keep her mouth shut. That was good to know, especially if Jade was about to tell her something she couldn't tell Rick.

"First off, you don't recognize me." Jade said, turning her head fully toward Melissa without moving her body an inch. Jade continued to weave them through traffic while facing Melissa, so she likely had one eye on the road or the Inkscape had an autopilot function specifically designed to break traffic laws.

"Second, you will call me Teresa when I'm not feathered." She took a taloned hand off the wheel and made a general motion at herself. "Third, you won't tell anyone about this."

"Why?"

"Like I said, I like my mystery."

Jade turned her head back to the traffic, but Melissa was still looking at her like she had lost it. What mystery was she going on about?

With a slight tilt of her beak, Jade shifted. Her feathers zipped into her skin like retracting spines and the wonder of the Inkscape seat flexed with her body to keep her in place as her tail feathers disappeared. Eyes wide, Melissa stared at the *very* familiar looking black woman with a mini afro next to her. She had chiseled cheek bones and an elegance that could not be forgotten. Melissa wracked her brain trying to think of why she knew her.

Had Jade never shifted in front of any of the Mavens? Was that what she was saying? Why couldn't Melissa remember who she was?

The Inkscape stopped, and Melissa realized they were at her parents' house.

She bit her lip and asked, "Is it safe for me to be here?"

"As safe as anywhere else." Teresa flipped her manicured hand to dismiss Melissa's worries. "Rizzo gave us so much information that even without you or your testimony, the Wrappers will be shut down. And there's enough to pull the head of the Minfrieds in for questioning too, which is all we need as long as we stick Rick in the room. Once they confess to the things we already know they did and who knows what else, they won't be offered bail. As of right now, the

head honchos — basically anyone you had the misfortune to meet —
are on the run.

"You have the security Jeremy installed, so the house is safe. Rick's
tracker on your bike will keep us informed about your general movements. But I'll help you put this on." Theresa held out a short necklace
with a black pendant no bigger than a pencil eraser that was hanging
from a Celtic knot. She had a similar one with possibly a sapphire
in the center hanging around her neck, nestled into an abundance
of cleavage; both the necklace and her exposed cleavage had been
hidden by her feathers before. Melissa remembered that Susan and
Felicia — the only female Mavens she'd met so far — had similar
necklaces.

"There's an undetectable tracking device embedded in this; it's
waterproof, so you don't ever need to take it off. On the off-chance
they come looking for you, which I don't think they will, we'll be able
to find you much faster."

Melissa nodded, even though she didn't like that she might be
grabbed again or that Rick had put his own tracker on her bike after
he'd removed the one Theo had installed. He hadn't told her about
that. She didn't love the idea of being tracked at all, but it was better
than falling back into Theo's hands. She also didn't know who the
"Wrappers" were or the "Minfrieds" for that matter, but she was too
overwhelmed to ask.

They both got out of the car, and Teresa came around and put the
necklace on Melissa so that she didn't need to move her arm more
than absolutely necessary. She managed to do it without making
skin contact, which was a relief. They walked to the front door of
the house, and Melissa realized she didn't have her key. It was in the
pocket of her jacket back at the coffee shop.

"We'll have to go get my spare from Jessy," Melissa said. She looked
down at herself and realized she didn't want to go in and see Jessy

right then. She was dirty, exhausted, and overall not okay. Jessy would fuss over her and try to hug her, and Melissa couldn't handle it right then.

"Here." Teresa extended two metal toothpicks with different shapes at the end that looked a lot like the bobby pins Rick had given to her to pick Tommy's lock.

"I don't know how."

"Just try. You picked the other just fine."

"I got lucky," she mumbled, not even questioning why Teresa knew she'd picked a lock before.

Melissa took the picks anyway and did an awkward half squat in front of the door to minimize her left shoulder movement. She slid the picks in and gave them a little wiggle and twist. After a few movements, she heard a click. Looking over at Teresa in surprise, she saw Teresa nodding like she'd expected that.

Melissa straightened a little and moved to the deadbolt. It took a little longer, but it slid open when she put a little muscle into her fingers. Teresa held her hand out for the picks and Melissa returned them to her, dumbstruck.

"Here's a tip to help you figure things out. Rick is good at picking locks because he knows how and because the locks tell him the truth about the best way to open them. You want the door to open, and you try to unlock it. The lock wants to be *good* for you. It unlocks. Think about how that could extend to objects in addition to people." Teresa tapped her temple and winked before heading across the lawn to see Jessy. Melissa stayed on the porch long enough to watch with complete bafflement as Jessy let Teresa into the house as if she were an old friend.

Inside, Melissa forced herself to have something to eat while she tried to remember where she'd seen Teresa before. But no luck there. Then, she took a hot shower, trying not to think about anything at all. Finally, she slid into bed with no intention of emerging any time soon. Maybe she'd stay there until her body stopped hurting.

Chapter 44

Rick

Rick couldn't believe Melissa had left without talking to him. He'd let Carl and Jeremy talk him into taking something to help him sleep after he watched Melissa curl up under the table. She'd scrunched herself up under there in a way that couldn't be good for her new injuries. All because she was trying to get away from him. When he'd awakened, it was dark and Melissa was gone. Gone without a word.

That was five days ago.

He'd sent her a message asking if she was alright, but she hadn't answered. He'd sent another to see if he could come over. Radio silence. He'd gone so far as to consult Dave before sending a third saying he'd like to see her. Still, nothing.

He was seriously thinking of going to see her anyway when all the guys showed up at his door — Dave dressed like he was going out on the town in a nice button up and jeans, Jeremy in his typical polo but missing his feathers, Shawn wearing a newsboy hat for some reason, and Carl in a tee-shirt that was bursting at the seams and looked painted onto his body as per usual. Dave pushed his way past Rick and inside. The others gave him a nod hello and walked in as if invited.

"Your place is a mess," Dave announced.

Rick looked around his apartment and saw it was, in fact, a mess. He had old dishes on most surfaces. Unfolded laundry had taken up residence on half of his couch. He had a stack of mail shoved against the wall by the door. If the puff of fresh air that came in with the guys was any indication, his place likely smelled too. He should have taken the trash out two days ago. It wasn't an inviting environment. He'd been too distraught to notice, much less do anything about it.

"Why are you *all* here?" Rick asked, shutting the door behind them. He might have expected any one of them individually, but not the full quartet. And if they were all there together, why wasn't Susan with them?

"We're here to help," Jeremy said. Rick didn't miss the questioning once-over Jeremy gave him. A glance down reminded him he was in pajama pants despite it being four in the afternoon.

"We know you don't have a lot of experience with women," Shawn added while making himself comfortable on the non-laundry end of Rick's black couch and reminding him why he had such great vacuum attachments. Shawn's white fur left a trail.

"And we all like Melissa," Carl said as he opened a window, confirming Rick's suspicion about the smell. Carl stayed by the window, too.

"Susan thinks Jade approves since she took Melissa home herself," Dave said. He sat down in the empty armchair Rick had spent most of the last few days in.

Time slowed as Rick and everyone else turned their heads to look at Dave, who had pulled out his phone and started typing away on it.

"She did what?" Jeremy blinked rapidly at the news. He grabbed a chair from the dining table and spun it around to sit next to Dave.

"Out of pure curiosity," Dave added, "Susan watched to see what vehicle Jade used because she took Melissa into the bowels rather than out into the garage."

"Melissa saw all the vehicles?" Rick asked, wondering if that factored into her lack of response. He figured most women avoided men who might drive small tanks around. Walking forward, Rick stood by his TV so he could see everyone's faces as they talked.

"So, which one did they take?" Shawn asked.

"The Inkscape."

"Seriously?" Carl asked, shaking his head and leaning against the wall.

They'd all given that vehicle a wide berth. None of them knew if it scratched easily or sucked unwanted advancers into the void it was. What they did know was the vehicle cost twice their annual salaries and required a pilot's license to drive.

"Yup," Dave said. He was acting like the news wasn't noteworthy. It was definitely noteworthy, but Rick had more important things on his mind than his boss's newest ride.

"What do you think Jade said to her?" Rick asked.

"I can't begin to even guess," Jeremy muttered with a deep frown creasing his forehead. His expression didn't reassure Rick.

"I will say," Carl offered, "she must have warned Melissa we'd debrief her before she spoke with the pretty police officer we worked with when she disappeared."

"One of you debriefed her?" Rick's voice sounded incredulous to his own ears.

It wasn't that the debriefing should have caught him off guard; it was standard procedure to make sure people they helped knew what they could or could not share with others. But he didn't know why he wasn't included in any debriefs — either as support for Melissa or as part of the Mavens' own standard mission debrief to make sure they didn't miss anything.

Now that he thought about it, not only hadn't he been debriefed, he hadn't been reprimanded for giving Dave a reason to choke him out while they were rescuing Melissa. Or about any of his other aggressive actions over the last two weeks. Why hadn't Jade already talked with him about that?

"Susan and I went over what she could share and what she couldn't," Carl said.

"How was she?" Rick asked immediately instead of worrying about a snag in post-job protocol. Even if she refused to talk to him, he needed to know how she was doing. He didn't even care if it made him look desperate. He *was* desperate. Maybe she'd said something about him.

"So, she hasn't answered your messages," Shawn observed. He turned a bit and kicked his legs up onto the couch, letting his shoes hang off the side when they reached the pile of laundry.

Rick dragged a hand down his face. On a job, they shared all details in case something was relevant and they hadn't picked up on it; they trusted each other to pick up the slack. Melissa wasn't a job though. But somehow, they all knew she'd ghosted him. Rick didn't even bother glaring at Dave for letting that tidbit out.

"How was she?" he repeated, stressing each word.

"Not great, but it was only Monday. She stayed a body length away from both Susan and me at all times — not an arm's length away like you do, a body length — and she barely spoke. When the officer came by to talk to her, Melissa said only what was necessary. The officer didn't look pleased with the limited information she got."

"So, no one has seen her since?" Rick didn't even care that he sounded plaintive.

"Oh, we've seen her," Jeremy said.

Instantly, Rick knew whatever they had seen wasn't good. He narrowed his eyes at his friend, silently demanding an explanation.

"She went into work yesterday and today," Jeremy said. "The temporary cameras I slapped up in her coffee shop haven't run out of juice yet. So, we've seen her."

"Meaning?"

"I've never met her," Shawn said. "Not officially. I don't count giving her a medical checkup in a moving van or standing guard between you and Rizzo with her there as meeting her. However, if her employees' and friends' reactions are anything to go by, she isn't okay. Also, she's out of her sling, which I'm not sure is the best idea, but I didn't want to ambush her at work to hassle her about keeping her shoulder immobilized if it's feeling okay, particularly given how poorly she's adjusting."

"Adjusting?" Rick pushed. What was there to adjust to after a kidnapping? Process? Sure. But adjust to? He'd follow up on her sling in a minute.

"She's standoffish and jumpy with everyone," Dave said.

"If you contrast how she didn't even blink when meeting me in your mother's kitchen and how she's acting with every single person now, you'd assume she'd been through some serious shit," Carl said.

Rick's chest tried to collapse into itself despite his ribcage's rigidity.

"And so, we're here to help," Jeremy said again.

"Susan is also helping," Dave said, looking up from his phone for the first time. "Her powwow with Melissa's friends is extremely fruitful, by the way."

"What?" Rick looked at him in confusion that wasn't shared by anyone else in his living room. "Powwow? Melissa's friends?"

"Yes, they are divided between thinking the kidnapping caused Melissa's trauma and that you tore out her heart." Dave looked back at his phone and read, "'Kate and Bethany are leaning more toward the kidnapping, saying you wouldn't hurt her. Greg and Ted are laying the blame solely at your feet. Danny thinks it's a combination.'"

Looking up again, Dave said, "At least that's what Susan's message says. Melissa has told them next to nothing about being kidnapped and hasn't mention learning about what she can do with a single touch."

"Maybe Jade ordered her to keep it to herself," Shawn mused.

"Melissa isn't a Maven," Jeremy pointed out. "Jade isn't her boss. She can't give her orders."

"So, what, exactly, are you all helping me with?" Rick asked. "We need to find a way to help Melissa, not me. How can we help her?"

"*We* are helping," Carl said. "Now, *you* need to."

"Me?"

"You're the only one of us who has a clue what she's going through," Jeremy said. He leaned forward and put his elbows on his knees.

"You've had to stop touching people," Dave said. "You got over the fear of influencing people. The guilt."

Rick just stared at Dave and Jeremy. Slowly, he looked over at Carl and Shawn, too. They were all looking at him with complete belief in their eyes. Melissa was struggling with her touch, and they thought *he* could help her.

They had no idea.

He'd never gotten over what his touch did. He might have accepted it. But he felt bad about it every time he touched someone who wasn't a criminal. He was terrified of people touching him without it being his choice. Terrified of everyone except Melissa.

"So, we are taking you to her," Shawn said.

"Communication is key, like I told you," Dave coached.

"You might not get back together," Carl warned, "but the point is getting her back on her feet."

"I'm voting for back together," Jeremy muttered more to himself than to the group while he frowned down at the coffee table in front of him. The tone of the comment was off enough to catch Rick's attention. Beside Jeremy, Dave was trying to hide a smirk which was suspicious.

"Into the car we go," Shawn said, jumping to his feet.

"After you shower and change, obviously," Carl said, nodding at Rick's pajama pants. Shawn dropped himself back onto the couch with a conceding grunt, and Rick headed into his bedroom to get ready as fast as physically possible.

An agonizing two-hour drive later, Shawn pulled in front of Melissa's house. The entire drive had been full of tips from each of the guys, none of which Rick could remember despite trying to listen carefully.

"Here," Dave said. "They're Melissa's." He dropped a set of keys into Rick's hand.

Rick stared at them. They were definitely the keys to Melissa's house. The set of keys with Bobby's red lanyard. The set that sat in the bowl of change in the kitchen. His mother's kitchen.

"Why do you have these?" Rick asked, fearing the answer.

"They were at my computer desk with a sticky note that said, 'Melissa's' in Jade's handwriting. I assumed Jade got them when she drove her home."

"You assumed Jade got my mother's copy of Melissa's keys when she brought Melissa home?" Rick repeated for clarification.

"How do you know it's—" Carl started to say.

"Bobby's lanyard," Rick said.

Everyone looked at the keys with more interest as they wondered what Jade had done to get them from Rick's mother — or maybe they just wondered what had ever compelled Bobby to braid a lanyard.

Suddenly, Melissa's front door opened, and their heads swung in unison to the figure in the doorway. A figure that hurried to the car and wrenched the door open.

"Don't just sit in the car."

Rick stared agape at his mother, shocked she'd just run out of Melissa's house. Somehow, Rick found himself outside the car. He wasn't sure if he got out or if he was thrown out by everyone else, but the car burnt rubber as it left him there. His mother didn't let it faze her. She just widened her eyes and flicked them toward Melissa's house with a great deal of meaning, then waved him forward with a small motion that was also somewhat frantic.

"What are you doing?" Rick asked her.

She latched onto his forearm with sufficient force for amputation.

"I ambushed her. Lindsay called me this afternoon and said Melissa had missed *two* weeks of phone calls and was not responding to any messages. So, I surprised her with dinner. I came over to cook it and chat, but she is *not* okay. I didn't get a hug. I barely made it in the door. She's staying away from me like I have the plague. And I think she's hurt; she's moving very carefully."

By the time she'd finished whisper-hissing in his ear, Rick was inside, and his coat was gone. Sparing a glance at his mother, he pulled his gloves off and set them on the cabinet under the jackets. His mother then whisked herself into the kitchen without a word. In the living room, he saw Melissa curled up on the couch, not even looking over the back toward the entry. He wasn't even sure she knew he was there.

After taking a deep breath, he walked over, rounding the couch, and saw she was wearing a long sleeve shirt with thumb holes in the cuffs so that the shirt covered most of her hands too. Given that it was warm enough for short sleeves, Rick knew the weather hadn't influenced her shirt choice. Melissa wore short sleeves and tanks as long as it didn't put her at risk of freezing in her leather jacket on her bike. It physically hurt to think that she was trying to shield herself from being touched.

When she saw him out of the corner of her eye, she pulled her legs in tighter to her chest as if to make herself smaller. Rick decided to ignore the action and sit beside her, in the middle of the couch.

"Hey," he said, not knowing what he was supposed to do. He couldn't remember if his friends had counseled him on how to start or not.

She looked at him but didn't say anything.

"I imagine you don't want me here," he muttered, looking at his hands instead of at her. "But I can help. I want to help. So, even if you never want to talk to me after this, let me help."

Her silence was agony.

"Please say something, Mel," he pleaded. He was sure if she didn't say something soon, his heart, which had slowed to a dangerous level if the beat in his ears was any indication, would stop.

She nibbled on her lower lip, which told him she was thinking. He just didn't know if she was thinking about doing something or saying something.

Rick's eyes shot open. "You can say anything you'd like. I haven't touched you."

"Why do you think I don't want you here?" she asked quietly, studying him more intensely than he could ever remember.

"Because of what I can do and what I didn't tell you."

Melissa licked her lips and glanced toward the floor. Rick's eyes darted down to her lips as her tongue slid over them, and he remembered the last time they'd been on this couch. Dave had said she'd picked *Opposites Collide* on purpose because she wanted to end up kissing him for the duration. His lips had trailed down, and she'd made the sweetest sound when he'd kissed her neck.

Rick gave himself a shake at what he was seeing.

At the base of her neck, Melissa was wearing a Maven Team tracking device. Had Jade given it to her? No one had mentioned it, but it was a relief to know she had another layer of safety. If any Maven she hadn't met yet saw her, they'd know she was one of them. Rick liked that.

"Also," he said, "you didn't answer any of my messages. Not one of them."

Her eyebrows drew together, forming a confused valley in her forehead that he wanted to smooth flat.

"Rick," she looked at him like he was crazy. "He smashed my phone with a hammer."

"Huh?"

"Theo smashed my phone with a hammer."

Rick slumped back on the couch. He was an idiot.

"You're not ignoring me, your friends, or your parents." He shook his head in disbelief.

"Not by phone."

"You know that's why my mother is here. Your mother is in a panic because you've missed two weeks of phone calls."

"I might be avoiding my parents," Melissa admitted with a frown.

"Did you know that, according to Susan, your friends think either I did something horrible to you or the kidnappers did? There's basically a fifty-fifty split. Your friends are *alarmed* by your change in behavior."

"You know I can't touch them." Melissa's whisper was full of anguish. "I'll hurt them."

"What?" Rick sat up at that. "You won't hurt them at all, Mel. It's fine. Your touch is a good thing."

"If it was a good thing, you wouldn't be scaring your friends so badly they're skittish of me."

"Ah, that. If it helps, I haven't had any homicidal thoughts about my friends or your exes this past week." Rick tried to make his comment sound like a joke by adding a half-hearted smile.

"Rick!" Melissa said loud enough his mother popped her head out of the kitchen to peek at them. Rick looked at the ceiling, and Melissa hid her face in her knees.

"Okay," Rick said when his mother started purposefully banging pots in the kitchen a few moments later. She had no chill. "Dave says the key to a successful relationship is communication."

Melissa pulled her head up from her knees and looked at him like he had officially lost it.

"You said he was a player."

"He is, but I had to start somewhere. So," Rick took a deep breath and braced himself, basing his next move on the fact that she hadn't ignored his messages. "I like you a lot, Mel. Do you like me?" He held his breath.

"Yes, but we have a slight problem. We can't have me touching you." She sounded tortured, but Rick couldn't help himself. He grinned. She liked him. Then, he frowned.

"Wait, you're worried about your touch. Not mine?" He was stunned. His touch had always been the problem. That she might not have a problem with what his touch did had literally never crossed his mind.

"I've never considered lying to you, so I don't know why I'd start now. But I'll mess you up. Make you more protective. In a bad way."

Feeling his world turn upside-down, he said, "We can figure that out." They could find a solution. She wasn't rejecting him for something he couldn't control.

"How'd you figure out your half of the touch issue with your previous girlfriends? Were they all just okay with it?" she asked.

He blinked at her, his mouth desert-dry. With effort, he swallowed.

"I... I—" He couldn't believe he was trusting Dave's communication advice. "I've never dated anyone before," he said in a rush.

Melissa's head pulled back a little, and she frowned at him.

"Okay, then. So, you never mentioned it to your one-night stands?" The last three words clearly tasted sour. He just looked at her in surprise. "One-week stands?"

He dragged a hand down his face, then looked at her, knowing he should just get it out there.

"In Dave's words, my first kiss that wasn't by assault was last week." Silence. "With you." Her shock was so loudly silent it was like a neon sign.

"Whenever I was with anyone, I'd have to touch them, you know, before kissing them," he explained as quickly as he could. "And there are a lot of people out there who saw a soldier or a biker and wanted a certain thing that wasn't actually me. They always said something that had me walking away before we'd ever kissed. You just wanted me. And... and I knew that because—"

"Because I told you," Melissa whispered.

"I always figured it was wrong to like you as much as I did, but when we're together, everything feels right. It feels like it's a good decision."

"So, you want to figure it out as we go?"

"If you're interested, that is."

"You know I'm very interested in not seeing other people," she said with a half-smile. His heart raced just like it had the first time she'd said it.

Rick reached out and tugged her against his side. He tried to be careful about skin contact since his mother was there, making an inordinate amount of noise in the kitchen. Melissa snuggled into him with a small whimper of discomfort at her own movements, but she didn't move away. If anything, she pressed herself closer.

"Let's start with trying the date that we were going to do last week," Rick suggested, thinking they could tack on getting her a new phone and talk about getting her back in the sling.

"Without the kidnapping?" Melissa's comment was meant to be joking, but sounded forced.

"Kidnapping?" Rick's mother choked on the word from behind them.

Rick and Melissa both peered over the back of the couch at his mother, standing there with a saucepan in her hand.

"Melissa had a rough week," Rick muttered.

Melissa snorted at his understatement and then pressed a fleeting kiss to his cheek that made him grin at her. They both ignored his mother's squeal of delight.

Epilogue

Melissa

6 months later

"I think it's too soon," Greg said again. "It's only been a few months." He was sitting at the table closest to the counter with Melissa. His healthy green smoothie looked highly questionable to her.

"I'm fine with it," Kate offered from the cash register. "If you ask Jessy, you two were destined to be together."

Melissa rolled her eyes at the comment before saying, "It makes sense to move in together. We'll be the same distance from each of our workplaces. Neither of us will take the brunt of the commute."

"Sixteen!" Tiffany called out when a guinea pig hybrid sneezed across the room.

"It's too soon." Greg repeated, ignoring the ASS game, and taking another sip of his drink.

Melissa just shrugged and focused on watching one of her many new hires go through their paces. Greg was unsure of Rick, and it didn't matter what Melissa said. The changes in her behavior had been too big to ignore. The truth would sway him, but she wasn't at liberty to say that Rick worked for an elite private operations team that contracted with agencies who used acronyms instead of names.

"How'd your parents take the news?" Tiffany asked after she gave a customer a grasshopper bagel.

"Mixed," Melissa said. "My mom is thrilled, like Jessy. You'd think they'd planned this from the moment they found out I'd be a girl the way they go on about it. They're already planning our wedding." When Greg opened his mouth to undoubtedly argue that it was too early, Melissa cut him off: "I said *they* were, not that Rick or I am. We're taking things slowly."

"Moving in together after a few months doesn't sound slow," Aaron, one of her immediate, post-kidnapping hires, said as he handed a customer their drink.

"Thank you!" Greg said, slamming his hand down on the table for emphasis.

Melissa had been pleased with hiring Aaron. He *had* just dressed up for his interview. On his first training day, he'd worn jeans, a tee-shirt from the rival university over in Nurlind, and a blue cargo jacket. Since it was his first opportunity in the service industry (it was hard to find a position as a rat hybrid), it had taken a little time to find his groove. He fit in, even if he did enjoy spirited debate more than anyone else. Having finished his training four months ago, he was currently helping with the newest hire.

"But," Kate said, "you have to take into account that they've known each other forever. It isn't like they just met."

Aaron tipped his head back and forth at her point. Then he yelled, "Seventeen!" and left the trainee at the espresso machine so he could head over and talk to a customer about moving their bag more under their table; number seventeen was the second person to trip on it and shift accidentally.

Melissa rolled the black pendant she still wore between her fingers. None of her friends or employees knew that what she meant when she said they were moving slowly was that the Mavens were monitoring her and Rick closely. They had to document all of their skin to skin contact by both time and type of intimacy, ranging from green or "toddler friendly" to red or "behind the paywall." Even though they were moving in together, they limited their physical contact based on Melissa's schedule at the coffee shop and with friends. Because her touch didn't have a time duration or effects they could anticipate, they were letting Rick's touch guide them.

Susan was in charge of monitoring Melissa for changes, which they hadn't seen any evidence of yet. The rest of Rick's team jointly monitored Rick for changes and documented them — so far, there hadn't been anything serious beyond Rick having issues with a job or two that had been a little too gray for his "good zone" measure. His over-protective and aggressive tendencies had diminished rapidly after the two of them had discussed what was good for him to do and what was over the top and bad.

Only Jade read the documentation of their skin-to-skin contact, which was the reason Melissa had agreed to it. Anyone else would have felt too invasive. Jade wasn't on the team or in their tight-knit friend group, so Melissa didn't see her regularly outside of meetings about her and Rick's *talents*.

"What about your dad?" Tiffany prompted when Melissa didn't return to the question at hand.

"He's not against our 'coupledom' as my mom and Jessy have been calling it, but he hasn't given Rick his approval. Granted, he hasn't seen him in person in five years now."

Melissa's phone chimed, and she slid her thumb across the screen. It was from Dave: "*Five years is a long time. People can change.*"

She held her sigh in and didn't flick her eyes to one of the fully installed security cameras. She had approved the new cameras to appease Rick and to make sure there wasn't another incident related to the Mavens that trickled over to her coffee shop.

"*Especially around me,*" she answered Dave.

She hadn't come to terms with how she influenced people, but she didn't feel as horrible about it as when she first found out. She took measures to limit unintentional contact, like wearing long sleeves instead of tee-shirts and tank tops.

Her close friends had all noticed that she'd changed her style. Once she found out that the way she was dressing was connected to the growing hostility among her friends toward Rick, she had grabbed all the girls, dragged them into a room with her, and took her shirt off, doing a spin. Telling them it was just a change in style. She was *not* covering up bruises or the like, and they were more than welcome to ask her any day to prove it until they were satisfied. That had taken a month, and she wasn't sure her "spot checks" were done yet. After that, everyone settled down and went back to tentatively liking Rick. Susan and Jade had deemed their behavior to be just looking out for her best interests and not as being *overly* influenced into protective behaviors by her touch. It was possible that being protective only happened if she was intimate with someone or they were a very young child that she interacted with a lot.

Because Greg wasn't in on the spot checks, he was a bit more hesitant to accept Rick again than her other friends. While Melissa tried to touch people less, she'd made it a point to touch Greg as little as was reasonable without making him feel like she was avoiding him; she remembered him commenting about looking into sketchy boyfriends she or the others had, and she didn't know if that was something she'd caused or not.

The biggest change Melissa had made, which hadn't been questioned at all when she made it directly after the kidnapping, was working fewer hours. She'd hired four new employees and was looking for a fifth. Danny had found a bartender position that "wasn't half-bad" and had stopped working at the coffee shop altogether. Then, between Melissa taking fewer shifts and most of the new hires' availability, four just wasn't enough. To top that off, in a couple months, Kate was going to be taking several weekends off to work the summer art festival circuit and try to grow her jewelry business in earnest.

Less time at the coffee shop reduced the amount of contact Melissa had with people that could result in inadvertent brushes. It also allowed her and Rick to continue their relationship without Rick's touch making her tell everyone at work her deepest and darkest secrets or just overshare in response to their questions.

After a while, she'd had to come up with a new explanation for her continued absence at her own business. Luckily, Jade had one ready. Melissa told her friends and employees she was getting involved in volunteering. And she was, sort of. It had been a team effort to convince Rick it was a good idea, but over the last two months, she'd volunteered with several different organizations to "test out" if they were a good match for her, but really it was just to cover her tracks with her friends.

The next week would be Melissa's first time going in to "volunteer" for Jade. Technically, she was getting paid, but it made her feel like she was doing something with her ability. She'd be going to a prison a few towns over, with a false name and a disguise, to do rehabilitation therapy with convicted criminals under the guise of being a meditation specialist. She would sit across from them, holding their hands, and together they'd meditate on what the criminals had done. The working theory was that if they thought about their actions while touching her, they'd see that what they'd done wasn't *good*, and hence never be a repeat offender.

She had to plan her visits to prisons around time with Rick because she couldn't do that work while influenced by his touch. Unsurprisingly, Jade had thought of that and planned extra sessions for her when Rick was off doing good deeds — rescuing damsels and children in war-torn countries or whatever nonsense Danny had concocted all those months ago.

"I'm here," Ilona shouted as she slid across the room, trying to slow herself down by raking her talons against the floor, and just managing to not knock a customer in line over (who didn't shift into their hybrid form if they had one). Aaron looked like his own life flashed before his eyes, and Tiffany laughed. The new hire looked at the recently promoted coffee shop manager with skepticism.

"Let's go," Kate said loudly. She dashed into the back to the staff area and grabbed both her and Melissa's purses before running back out. Melissa looked at Greg and then her employees to see if they knew what was going on. They didn't seem to. "If you're moving in with him, I want to see the place," Kate announced. "Now."

"I'm coming too," Greg said.

"Alright," Melissa laughed, shaking her head. If that made them feel at ease about Rick, she wasn't going to object.

Thirty minutes later, the three of them walked inside Melissa's new building. The concierge, who Melissa knew was an armed guard with a cleared dishonorably discharged mark on his record, called out a hello to Melissa and commented that he didn't know she was stopping by that afternoon. With a smile, she said her friends wanted to see the place and made sure she didn't say the emergency safe word Rick insisted be arranged. Then, up the elevator they went.

Melissa slipped her key into the lock and pushed the door open. As she flicked on the light, she just stared at the living room. Her things were there. Furniture that she and Rick had picked out, but wasn't supposed to arrive for several more days, was there. Their new dining table, that was not supposed to arrive until the next day, was covered in finger food and sweets.

"Nice place," Kate said, walking in and looking around.

"Very," Greg said *really* loudly.

Melissa looked at them, then back at the room.

"Were there supposed to be people here?" she asked.

Greg scowled, and Kate frowned.

"Careful! Careful!" Rick's voice came from outside the apartment.

"Hide!" Kate whispered, making shooing motions at Melissa.

They all darted behind furniture, and the door creaked open.

"You can't leave your door unlocked, man," Shawn grumbled.

"Bad form, Rick. Bad form," Dave mocked.

"I locked it," Rick said, mystified.

"Where can I set this?" Carl huffed.

"Over here," Danny said, walking by Melissa's hiding place and guiding Carl over to the bar area set up the keg in the corner.

"Hurry," Rick said. "I want this to be perfect."

Melissa couldn't help but smile as she locked eyes with Kate who winked at her. They planned a surprise apartment-warming party for her, and Rick had *lied* about the furniture delivery dates. My, my, my, wasn't that unfair!

"Do we have time for the streamers?" Susan asked urgently.

"Hand them to me," Bethany said. Her shadow darted around the high ceilings as she flew the streamers back and forth.

"Come on," Rick said. The front door's lock clicked back into place. "Now, when she turns on the light, what are you going to yell?"

Melissa could have sworn Rick sounded nervous. Really nervous.

"WELCOME HOME!" everyone practice-shouted with laughter.

Without hesitation, Melissa sprung out of her hiding place.

"I love it!" she yelled as she jumped into a shocked Rick's arms and destroyed the bouquet of flowers he'd been holding. Around them, everyone was silent for a second before breaking into cheers.

Yeah, they weren't planning their wedding. Not actively. But Melissa didn't think her friends were ready to know they were talking about it. For one day. In the future. When they were ready.

Thank you for reading *Touchy Talents*! If you haven't already, check out my other romances in this world, described below, or sign up for my newsletter to learn about my latest books before anyone else! When you sign up, you can grab a free short story from when the Crisis hit! Here's the link: https://daysgrant.com/contact-2/

Remember that movie Melissa and Rick made out during? Go back in time to when the movie first came out and join Kate's parents on their first date in *Opposites Collide*. This novella takes place 30 years before *Touchy Talents* and is the first in a mini-series of novellas that follow the movie releases. Grab your copy direct from the author or from your preferred retailer here: https://books.daysgrant.com/d4i ndrpovf

Shell Shocked is book 2 of the Mavens and follows Neil's romance with a certain pretty police officer. The start of the book overlaps with Melissa's kidnapping. Release updates will be in my newsletter and posted on social media.

Acknowledgements

First, I'd like to thank my family for their unwavering support as I explored my identity as an author and discovered where my writing journey would take me.

I'd like to thank Belinda, Darren, and Laural for finding the holes in my story. Without their help, this book wouldn't be what it is today. Would you believe that, originally, I didn't tell you, the reader, any details about Rick's job, even in his POV? Also, I'd like to thank Sarah, Angel, Jen, and Heather for beta reading the book to make sure it was ready to go out in the world.

This story would have taken much longer to get out if I didn't have the Author Ever After community behind me as I moved from the writing journey to publishing. Those are definitely two very different things, but a book doesn't get completed without both parts. I'm immensely grateful for their tips and quick answers to all my publishing questions.

I'd also like to thank my editor Kelly for taking a close look at my writing and making it the best it can be. Her work let me take a step away from my story and see the words that built it.

About the author

Day S. Grant's debut series is *The Mavens*, but she has other series that are fighting to be written next. Her story ideas all start from a single scene she saw in a dream, and they grow and evolve from there.

Her fascination with *the other* has grown throughout her life. She believes that things aren't as different as they seem. Her books consistently introduce opposites, others, and new perspectives that shift how people see the world.

A traveler at heart, when Day S. isn't traveling through the pages of a book with a steaming cup of tea, she is exploring new places. She loves nature and likes finding interesting trees to photograph. When she can, she takes her cats with her on her adventures.

Her passion for creating isn't contained to the blank page, but also manifests in doodles and in a life-long sewing hobby. She enjoys making clothes for herself and, on occasion, for her very patient cats.

Learn more about Day S. Grant and her upcoming releases by going to her website and signing up for her newsletter: Day S. Grant Gossips.

Also by Day S. Grant

The Mavens

Touchy Talents

Shell Shocked (coming 2026)

In the Mavens' World

Opposites Collide